The gre...
a n...

Mothering
Sunday

Two talented authors, two special historical
tales of family and romance!

Sarah Mallory was born in the West Country and now lives in an old farmhouse on the edge of the Pennines with her husband and family. Born in Bristol, Sarah left grammar school at sixteen to work in companies as varied as stockbrokers, marine engineers, insurance brokers, biscuit manufacturers and even a quarrying company. Her first book was published shortly after the birth of her daughter. She has published more than a dozen books under the pen name of Melinda Hammond, winning the Reviewers' Choice Award in 2005 from Singletitles.com for *Dance for a Diamond* and the Historical Novel Society's Editors' Choice in November 2006 for *Gentlemen in Question*.

Kathryn Leigh Albright, the daughter of a naval officer and a doll doctor, grew up in San Diego. Her journey to publication has included graduating from college, writing magazine articles, and reading voraciously. She currently resides in the Midwest with her husband and three sons.

Don't miss Kathryn Albright's beautiful romance, *The Rebel and the Lady*, available June 2009 from Mills & Boon® Historical romance.

On
Mothering
Sunday

SARAH MALLORY
KATHRYN ALBRIGHT

*M&B™ and M&B™ with the Rose Device
are trademarks of the publisher.
Harlequin Mills & Boon Limited, Eton House,
18-24 Paradise Road, Richmond, Surrey TW9 1SR*

ON MOTHERING SUNDAY
© by Harlequin Books S.A. 2009

More Than a Governess © Sarah Mallory 2008
The Angel and the Outlaw © Kathryn Albright 2007

ISBN: 978 0 263 86897 5

024-0309

*Printed and bound in Spain
by Litografia Rosés S.A., Barcelona*

More Than
a Governess

SARAH MALLORY

To Terry,
my rock and inspiration

Chapter One

Juliana Wrenn thought she had rarely entered a more uninviting chamber than cousin Pettigrew's drawing room in Bouverie Street. Unpolished panelling, dark hangings and dull green paint on the ceiling seemed to swallow up the sunlight that was valiantly fighting its way through the dirty windows. She felt a little hand gripping her fingers and looked down, summoning up a smile.

'Are you cold, Amy? I am sure Cousin Pettigrew will not keep us waiting much longer.'

Her little sister hugged her rag doll closer.

'I want to go home!' she whimpered.

Juliana sat down on a worn sofa and pulled the little girl on to her lap.

'You know we can't do that, love. We must see if Cousin Alfred can help us.' She smiled up at her younger brother, a stout twelve-year-old who was hovering beside them.

'Come and sit down, Tom.'

'I would rather go back to the kitchen,' said Thomas, thinking of the fruitcake he had left behind when they had been summoned upstairs.

At that moment the door opened, and the three of them jumped to their feet, their eyes fixed on the florid-faced, bewhiskered gentleman who came in.

Juliana gave him her best curtsy.

'Good afternoon, Cousin. Thank you for seeing us.'

Alfred Pettigrew advanced into the room, stripping off his gloves and dropping them, together with his silver-topped malacca cane, on to a side table.

'Yes, well, I have just got in—had to carry out the reading of a will in Mount Street. I gather you have been here all morning?'

'Yes, sir. We asked if we might wait for you and your housekeeper, Mrs Churwell, kindly looked after us.'

'She gave us cake, and a glass of milk,' added Amy and was nudged by Thomas, who hissed at her to be quiet. Juliana ignored the interruption.

'I wrote to you, Cousin.'

'Aye, you did, and I responded, did I not? Even more, I paid for your father's funeral, and saw to the settlement of his affairs for you.'

'Yes, sir, and we are very grateful. But that was three weeks ago, and circumstances have changed.' She hesitated, for the first time losing some of her self-assurance. 'The bailiffs called yesterday and removed everything, and Mr Crewe, the landlord, said he had already let the rooms, so we had to leave this morning.'

Mr Pettigrew looked at her.

'And what am I supposed to do with you?'

'We were hoping—that is…' Juliana took a deep breath. 'We need somewhere to stay. It need only be for a short time, until I can find employment—'

He gave an impatient snort.

'And what sort of employment could you find, miss, that would allow you to support the three of you?'

She drew herself up, her hands clasped in front of her rather shabby pelisse.

'Well, Cousin, I was thinking that if you could advance me a small sum, I could find a house for us and earn a living as a tutor. I am very good at French and Italian, and could possibly do a little translation, too…'

'Out of the question!' He waved a hand impatiently. 'Why, I would not see my money again for many a year, if ever.'

Juliana closed her lips firmly, quelling her retort. It was common knowledge that Alfred Pettigrew was a rich man, but it was equally well known that he was not a generous one. She had seen enough of the house to convince her that he was indeed what her father would have called a nip-farthing. She sighed. It was not a charge that could be laid at Papa's door.

'Well, then, what are we to do, Cousin Alfred?' asked Thomas. 'You are the only relative we have.'

'You have no need to remind me of that.' Mr Pettigrew scowled and his heavy jowls shook with disapproval. 'That my cousin Wrenn should leave his affairs in such disorder, with no means of support for the three of you—unforgivable.'

He paced the room while three pairs of eyes watched anxiously. At length he stopped.

'Very well. I'll tell you what I will do. I will send you all to Hinton Slade, my house in Devon. My mother lives there; she is not in the best of health and would welcome a companion, I am sure. That way, Miss Juliana, you can earn your keep. Thomas can help out in the stables and young Amy there can train as a lady's maid.'

Juliana looked at him in horror.

'But what about their schooling?'

'Tush, a boy of twelve doesn't need schooling. He is better

earning his living. And as for the young 'un, well, you can teach her all she needs in your spare time.'

Juliana looked down at her siblings, fighting the urge to take their hands and walk out of Cousin Alfred's house. Instead she said calmly, 'That is very kind of you, Cousin. Perhaps you would allow me a few days to consider the matter?'

'Don't see there's anything to consider.' His lip curled. 'Unless you have had any better offers?'

'No, but I would like to make a few enquiries.' She tried a winning smile. 'Please, Cousin, may we impose upon your generosity for a few days? I promise you we will be in no one's way.'

'Of course you will be in the way! This is a bachelor establishment—it would be most improper for you to be here.'

'Not if we kept to the servants' rooms, sir. Mrs Churwell told me that she was obliged to dismiss one of the kitchen-maids, so the three of us could sleep in her room for a few nights. We would be most discreet.' Remembering the house-keeper's advice on dealing with the master, she added, 'I'm sure Mrs Churwell would be grateful for a little help now she's one girl short in the kitchen.'

She held her breath. Mr Pettigrew frowned at the carpet, puffing out his cheeks. Amy moved restlessly from one foot to the other and Juliana put a reassuring hand on her shoulder.

'Very well, you can stay, but only for a few days. I can't have the three of you eating me out of house and home. If you've found nothing in a se'ennight, then it's off to Devon with you.'

'Oh, thank you, sir!' Juliana beamed at him. 'We will be no trouble, I promise you. You will not even know we are in the house.'

Juliana hurried Amy and Thomas back to the kitchens where the housekeeper was waiting for them.

'Well, miss?' she asked. 'It must be good news or you would be out the door by now.'

Juliana smiled. 'We can stay, and I can help you with the maid's work until you find a replacement.'

'Aye, I guessed that would sway him,' Mrs Churwell tutted. 'Miserable old skinflint, and him with more money than he knows what to do with.'

'He did say we could go and live with Aunt Pettigrew,' said Thomas, brightening when he found his half-eaten cake was still on the table.

The footman, sitting in one corner blacking his shoes, gave a derisive snort.

'Ha! She's worse than the master. You'd work your fingers to the bone for that one and not a penny would you get for it. I had a cousin as was groom there for a while, until he joined the army to fight the French. Said he preferred to face Boney himself than old Mrs P.'

'Aye, Lawrence is right,' agreed Mrs Churwell, shaking her head. 'The Pettigrews is a miserly family and no mistake.'

'And that makes it all the more imperative that I find employment,' said Juliana, sinking down into a chair by the table.

'Well, that's a problem for the morrow,' replied Mrs Churwell comfortably. 'Poor dear, I dare swear you have had no end of worry these past few weeks. Now you sit and rest, dearie, and these two youngsters can make themselves useful by shelling peas for dinner.'

Juliana rose early the next morning to find that Mrs Churwell had brought a pile of the master's newspapers to the kitchen, smiling as she put them down on the table.

'I thought you might find a suitable post advertised in

here, miss. Sit yourself down and study these news-sheets while I take up the master's breakfast. And don't you worry about Thomas and little Amy, I've set them to folding sheets upstairs, so you can have a bit o' peace.'

When the housekeeper returned to the kitchen some time later, Juliana was still sitting at the table with the news-papers spread out before her.

'Well, dearie?'

Juliana sighed.

'It seems there are far more advertisements for those seeking employment than requiring someone. Listen— "Governess seeks position, no salary required." What straits must that poor creature be in?'

'The same as you, Miss Juliana,' responded Mrs Churwell. 'You are not to be letting that kind heart o' yours worry about everyone else's problems. You have your family to consider, and if you let the master send you all off to Hinton Slade you'll be stuck in the middle of nowhere, and don't think old Mrs Pettigrew will help you to better yourself, because she won't, not when she sees she can have the three of you doing her bidding for a pittance!'

'I suppose you are right. Oh, Mrs Churwell, it seems a hopeless case.'

'Not a bit of it,' came the robust reply. 'Now, miss, what you must do is to place your own advertisement in the news-paper. And you must write down all the things you can do, just like you told them to me, so that everyone will know what an accomplished young lady you are and they will come begging you to teach their children.'

'That would certainly be very welcome!' laughed Juliana. 'I suppose I *could* advertise.'

'Of course you could! Mr P. will be in his office by now,

so there will be no one in the morning room, and you'll find paper, pens and ink there. You go and write it now, my dear. Strike while the iron's hot, as they say.'

'I will, Mrs Churwell.' Juliana rose. 'I will go and write the best advertisement you have ever read!'

She ran up the stairs, but checked as she reached the top. She could hear voices in the hallway and guessed that Mr Pettigrew was meeting a client. Peeping around the door, Juliana saw her cousin making a deep bow to a tall gentleman. The visitor had his back to her, so that all she could see of the man himself was his black hair and his many-caped driving coat which added even more width to his already large frame.

'Major Collingham—' Cousin Alfred's nose was almost touching his knee '—I am most honoured by this visit, sir, following on from our conversation yesterday. But you should not have come out in this rain, sir—I should have been quite happy to bring the papers to you.'

'No need, Pettigrew. I had to come this way this morning. I needed to place an advertisement and thought I could do it myself and call upon you on my way. I want to get everything signed and sorted before I leave town next week; thought I was doing well, too, until the children arrived yesterday evening, with the news that their governess had given notice!'

'How unfortunate for you, sir. Come into my office and I will find those papers for you.'

Juliana drew back behind the door as her cousin led the gentleman on, but before the door closed on them she heard the stranger say bitterly,

'Unfortunate? It's damned annoying, man! Particularly now, when I need to take the children into Lancashire with me. That's the third damned woman I've hired in as many months! What can be so difficult about looking after a couple of brats? I tell you, Pettigrew, I'd give a king's ransom to find a governess who could stay the course…'

The door closed upon the two men and Juliana stepped slowly into the hall, nibbling the tip of her finger. She looked at the footman, who was shaking out the man's greatcoat.

'Lawrence, that man—do you know him?'

'Major Collingham, miss?'

'Yes. Is he…is he one of Mr Pettigrew's clients?'

The footman shook his head as he laid the greatcoat gently over a large chest.

'No, miss. But he is trustee for one of 'em.' He added knowledgeably, 'He is the sort of well-set-up gentlemen that people like to appoint as executor to manage their affairs when they turn up their toes.'

Juliana smoothed her hands over her gown and said as casually as she could, 'And, do you perhaps know where he lives?'

'Oh, aye, miss. I've taken papers to his house in Burlington Street many a time.'

Juliana nodded, then turned and made her way back to the kitchen, where Mrs Churwell was busy making pastry.

'Well, now, that was quick!' exclaimed the housekeeper, up to her elbows in flour. 'Have you written your notice already?'

Juliana shook her head, and sat down at the table.

'No, but I think I have found a solution to my problems!'

Chapter Two

Later that afternoon Juliana put on her best walking dress of holly green with its matching bonnet and set off for Burlington Street. She was fortunate that the rain had stopped, but it remained overcast, and a chill wind stung her cheeks. Following Lawrence's directions, she found herself staring up at an imposing double-fronted façade. For a moment her courage failed her. Then, squaring her shoulders, she marched up to the front door and knocked loudly.

'Oh, come along, Juliana Wrenn,' she muttered to herself. 'He can't eat you, after all.'

A liveried footman admitted her to the house and showed her into a small study on the ground floor while he went off to carry her message to his master.

Too nervous to sit down, she stood in the middle of the room and looked about her. The walls were lined with oak panels from floor to ceiling in the same manner as her cousin's drawing room, but there all similarity between the two houses ended. The panelling in Major Collingham's study gleamed and several lively hunting scenes hung on the walls. She was just wondering if any of the figures depicted could be the master of the house when a deep voice sounded behind her, making her jump.

'You wished to see me, madam?'

'Oh—I did not hear you come in!'

'I am sorry if I startled you,' responded the Major, sounding not a whit remorseful.

Juliana looked at him. In her cousin's hallway she had only seen the back of his head. Now, staring up into the harsh, unsmiling face, her spirits began to fade. He was very tall, and dressed with military precision—there was nothing of the dandy about him, she noted with approval; the long limbs encased in buff-coloured pantaloons and black boots hinted rather at the athlete. His blue coat fitted perfectly about his broad shoulders and the crisp whiteness of his shirt and cravat enhanced his dark complexion, tanned by years in the sun—she knew he had been a soldier, and guessed he had seen action in the Peninsula. His bearing was upright and looked as solid and unyielding as his countenance. His voice, when he spoke again, was tinged with impatience.

'Well, madam, what can I do for you?'

'I—I came because—because you require a governess.'

Her words came out in a rush.

'Then it is my secretary, Brasher, you should see. I made it quite clear in the advertisement.'

He turned to go.

'Oh, I have not seen the advertisement—and it is *you* I wish to see, Major Collingham.'

He stopped and turned to face her.

'Not seen the—then how the devil…?'

His frown was not encouraging, but she screwed up her courage—she must do this for Thomas and Amy's sake.

'I am a cousin of Mr Pettigrew, the lawyer. I overheard your conversation with him this morning, about requiring a governess urgently. It—it is a fortunate circumstance for you, sir, that I am looking for just such a post.'

'I see. Well, if that is the case, I am of course delighted that you have come, but my secretary can handle the details—'

'But I do not wish to talk to your secretary, Major.' She swallowed. 'I—I want to talk to you about my terms.'

The Major raised his black brows.

'Terms?'

'Yes.' She drew a breath and put up her chin. 'I believe you require a governess to take up the post immediately, sir. Well, I am free to do that, upon condition.'

The Major stared at her. Juliana returned his gaze steadily, praying that he could not hear the rapid thudding of her heart. His countenance relaxed a little.

'I see this is not going to be the work of a moment.' He moved to his desk. 'Pray will you not be seated, miss…?'

'Miss Wrenn, Major.' She sat down on the edge of the chair, facing him.

'Well, Miss Wrenn, it is true that I am in need of a governess, but, as the employer, I was of the opinion that it was my place to set the conditions.'

She did not flinch from his hard gaze. Mrs Churwell had told her to have faith in herself, and she must do just that.

'In the normal course of events, yes, but you do not appear to be having much success; you told my cousin you would pay a king's ransom for a governess who could—ah—*stay the course* was your term, I think?'

He laughed suddenly, and the rather harsh lines of his face softened into something much more attractive.

'Quite right, Miss Wrenn, I did. Very well, why do you think you would suit my requirements?'

'Because I have had an excellent education, I am used to

dealing with children and can teach them all the usual accomplishments of reading, writing, a little arithmetic and geography, the use of globes; my French and Italian are very good, I play the pianoforte and the harp, I paint and draw, I am a skilled needlewoman and—'

'And you are desperate for employment.'

She blinked.

'You do not deny it, Miss Wrenn.'

'No, sir.' She looked him in the eye and said with more confidence that she was feeling, 'But I have imp—impeccable credentials.'

He sat back, folding his arms across his chest and fixing her with a hard stare.

'You are very young for such a post.'

'I am one-and-twenty, sir.'

'What is your experience?'

She clasped her hands in her lap.

'I was educated in a select seminary in Clapham until I was seventeen years old, and had some teaching of the younger girls while I was there. I learned all the usual accomplishments, and was especially good at languages—a gift from my father, I think. My mother's demise made it necessary for me to come home and for the past four years I have had the care of my brother and sister.'

'And what has changed, that you must now seek employment?'

She looked down at her hands. It was not easy to admit her straitened circumstances to a stranger, but it must be done. 'My father died a month since and all his effects were seized to pay his debts. That is why we are staying with my cousin, until I can find a way to support us all.'

'And how old are your brother and sister?'

'My brother is twelve years old, sir. My sister just nine.'

She looked up at the Major, but his face was impassive. She said, with a touch of defiance, 'I am not looking for sympathy, sir.'

'I have offered you none. You have been very frank, Miss Wrenn, so let me be equally open with you. I am a widower and have been so for the past eight years. My three children have been in the care of my mother—their grandmother—in Hampshire. Unfortunately, my mother died twelve months ago. Bonaparte had just escaped from Elba and it was impossible for me to leave my regiment at that time, so my sister took the children in; she lives nearby with her own young family. After Waterloo I was eager to settle my affairs and return to England, but it took me until a few months ago to complete my duties and get away.' He paused and sat forward, resting his arms on the desk. 'While in the care of my sister, my daughters were taught in the schoolroom with their young cousins, but I was naturally desirous to have the children with me, so I moved them back into Kewhurst, their old home, with a governess to look after them while I completed my business prior to taking them all to Lancashire. To date, as you pointed out to me, Miss Wrenn, I have been singularly unsuccessful in my choice of staff. The first governess lasted less than a week and left the house claiming that the place was haunted. The second I turned off when I discovered her addiction to strong liquor. The third, well, I thought she was settled, so I came on to London to put my affairs in order. I sent for the children to join me, and instead of the governess, they came with their aunt and their old nurse, and the information that the governess had discharged herself.'

'Oh…dear.'

'As you say, Miss Wrenn, oh dear.'

'How old are your daughters, Major?'

'Gwendoline is twelve years old, and Wilhelmina is eight. They are quite normal, Miss Wrenn—high spirited, perhaps, but not demons.'

'I do not doubt it. But you said you have three children, sir?'

'Yes. My son, Giles, is fifteen years old and for the past few years has been under the tutelage of a learned reverend. When I arrived in Hampshire I discovered that this gentleman has accepted a much more attractive position as bearleader to a young gentleman embarking upon the Grand Tour. However, Giles need not concern you; once we are settled in the north, I will engage another tutor for him.'

'You said you are leaving town at the end of next week?'

'Yes, on Friday. I have property in Lancashire that requires my attention. I want the governess to travel with us, and to take charge of the children on the journey.' Again Juliana found that harsh stare fixed upon her. 'After what you have heard, are you still eager for this position, Miss Wrenn?'

She sat up and adopted her most businesslike tone.

'I think it would suit very well, sir, if we can agree terms.'

'Miss Wrenn, I hardly think you are in a position to make demands....'

'Then we need discuss this no further.' She rose. 'Let me see, today is Saturday, your advertisement should be published on Monday, at the earliest. No doubt your secretary is very efficient; if he interviews the candidates quickly, I *suppose* it might be possible to engage a suitable person in time to travel on Friday, assuming he has received suitable references, of course...'

He held up his hand.

'Very well, Miss Wrenn, you have made your point. Can *you* supply me with suitable references?'

'I am sure Mr Pettigrew will vouch for my character, and

you may apply to Miss Shaftesbury at the Academy in Clapham. As to my education, you can test me, if you so wish.'

'No, I do not so wish!' he growled at her. 'Pray sit down again, madam, and tell me these terms of yours.'

Resuming her seat, she gave him a beaming smile.

'They are not really so outrageous. I will engage to look after the children, Major Collingham, and educate them for the next four months, that is, to the end of September. I would like you to pay me a lump sum at the end of that time.'

'How much?'

Juliana took a deep breath and named her price.

'What?'

She winced, but held her ground.

'You said you were willing to pay a king's ransom for this service, sir; I think you will agree that it is hardly that, but it would be sufficient for me to rent a little house in, say, Harrogate or Bath, and support my family by teaching. That is all I ask, Major.'

There was no more she could say. Juliana forced herself to sit still while the Major stared at her, his fingers drumming on the desk top. The remuneration she was asking was high, but discreet enquiries of her cousin had convinced her that the Major could afford twice that sum. Now she only needed to hold her nerve. She smiled to herself; perhaps she had something of her father's gambling spirit after all. At last he spoke.

'Very well. I will have Brasher draw up an agreement today.'

She found she had been holding her breath, for it now came out in a long sigh.

'Thank you, sir. I will not disappoint you.'

'I trust you will not. I shall make sure you do not get a

penny if you do not keep your side of this bargain. One more thing. What do you propose to do with your siblings for the next four months?'

She hesitated.

'I am hoping to persuade my cousin—'

He shook his head.

'Pettigrew is a lawyer and a bachelor. I'd wager he knows less than I do about children. You had best bring them with you. They will be companions for Gwen and Minna on the journey, and there will be plenty of room for them at Blackthorpe.'

'Th-thank you.'

He stood up and came round the desk towards her.

'Then let us shake hands upon it, and I will send for the children.'

Juliana rose and put out her hand. As he took her fingers in his strong grip she looked up into his face and wondered how she had ever managed to bargain with such a man. At close range he was even more intimidating. His eyes were as hard as granite; his countenance bleak and unforgiving. Dangerous. But even as she began to wonder if perhaps she had made a mistake, she saw a gleam of amusement in his grey eyes.

He said, 'Now what are you thinking, Miss Wrenn?'

She did not even consider prevaricating.

'That you would make an implacable enemy, sir.'

His grip on her hand tightened.

'True. But I am also a very good friend. Which would you have, Miss Wrenn?'

Juliana could not break away from his gaze. A small voice in her head was warning that he should not be asking her such a question. She swallowed and tried to answer calmly.

'Neither. I look only for a fair employer.'

He stared at her, a faint crease in his brows. Juliana looked down at his hand, still holding her own. Abruptly he released her and walked towards the window saying,

'I—um—I plan to marry—when we arrive in Lancashire: a neighbour's daughter, widow. There is an arrangement between the families. It has long been agreed. My wife will, of course, take over arrangements for the girls' education.'

'Then why not wait until you get to Lancashire to employ a governess?'

Even as the words tumbled out, Juliana wished them unsaid; she had signed no contract yet, and she did not want him to change his mind. The Major did not hesitate over his reply.

'I had considered that, but their nurse is far too old to have sole control of the children on such a long journey.'

Juliana's evil genius prompted her to play devil's advocate once more.

'But—forgive me—did you not say you will be travelling together, as a party?'

He turned to look at her, his brows raised in surprise, and just for a moment she thought there was a shade of unease upon those harsh features.

'I know nothing of the needs of young girls,' he said shortly. 'If it was only Giles, I should not hesitate. As it is—' He broke off. 'I shall summon the girls to meet you.'

He strode over to the door, barking his orders to a lackey.

Moments later, two little figures trooped into the room.

'Goodness, that was very prompt!' exclaimed Juliana, smiling at the Misses Collingham.

They were dressed in identical redingotes of claret-coloured wool with matching bonnets. The eldest girl raised her eyes, so like her father's, and looked directly at Juliana.

'We were waiting in the hall for Aunt Louisa, Papa.' She

addressed the Major, although she kept her eyes upon Juliana. 'She is taking us for a drive in the park.'

'Well, I shall not keep you long.' Major Collingham beckoned them to come forward. 'I want to make you known to your new governess. Gwendoline…' He paused as the older of the two children bobbed a curtsy.

Juliana curtsied back.

'How do you do, Miss Collingham?'

'Gwendoline was twelve years old last month,' said the Major. 'And this is Wilhelmina.' He nodded at the smaller child, who stepped forward and bobbed, saying as she did so,

'And I'm eight.'

'Indeed?' marvelled Juliana. 'You are very grown up for eight, I think. I am very pleased to meet you both.'

'Miss Wrenn will be joining us next week,' said the Major. 'You will have your first lesson with her at two o'clock on Monday—yes, Miss Wrenn, did you say something?'

'So—so soon,' stammered Juliana. 'I thought we should get to know one another first.'

'If that is what you wish to do, Miss Wrenn, I have no objection, as long as you do it in the schoolroom.'

'And out of the way, Major?' she murmured, bringing that frowning stare upon her again.

Whatever retort the Major was about to make was interrupted as the door opened and a tall woman in a rose-pink pelisse erupted into the room.

'Damon, do you have the girls here? I was about to take them out.'

'The children are here, Louisa, dressed and ready for you. I was introducing them to their new governess. This is Miss Wrenn—my sister, Lady Varley.'

Juliana found herself subjected to a head-to-toe scrutiny

and forced herself not to fidget. Her walking dress might not be as stylish as Lady Varley's fine wool pelisse, and one small ostrich feather could not compete with the three nodding plumes that adorned Lady Varley's high-crowned bonnet, but she knew her simple attire was perfectly suited to a young lady of modest means, and more than adequate for a governess. Lady Varley seemed to agree, for she gave a nod of approval.

'So, Damon, you have found someone already. How clever of you.'

The Major's lips curved up slightly.

'It would be more accurate to say that Miss Wrenn found *me*.'

Lady Varley waved one pink-gloved hand.

'Whatever the case, it would seem that I need not take the children out with me after all.' She paused, glancing down at the two little faces looking up at her. 'But they are dressed now, so I suppose I must. Come along, then. The carriage is at the door and you know your father does not like to keep his horses standing!'

She hurried the children out of the room, turning at the door to say, 'We shall not be too long, Damon. I have to stop off at Madame Fleurie's to look at the new muslin she had brought in for me and then I shall take the girls for a quick turn around the park, to give them an airing before dinner.'

'You must not mind my sister, Miss Wrenn,' remarked the Major as the door closed upon the little party. 'She felt obliged to come to London with the children when their governess walked out. She has not yet forgiven me.'

'That was very good of her; some aunts might have considered it sufficient to send the children with a servant.'

'Ah, but then I would not have felt obliged to pay for the gowns she has ordered from Madame Fleurie.'

Juliana was surprised into a laugh, which she quickly stifled—levity was not becoming in a governess. She should take her leave. As if reading her mind, Major Collingham walked to the door.

'Very well, Miss Wrenn. I will send my carriage to Bouverie Street on Monday morning at, say, eleven o'clock. You will bring your brother and sister with you. I shall have rooms prepared for your arrival.'

'Thank you, sir. You are very good.'

'No, it is a business arrangement. My man will have the contract ready for you to sign when you arrive.' He bent that hard gaze upon her again. 'I shall expect you to earn your money, Miss Wrenn.'

She met his gaze squarely.

'I expect nothing less of you, Major Collingham.'

She hurried back to Bouverie Street and made her way directly to the kitchens, where Mrs Churwell was waiting to hear her news. Juliana could not suppress her elation.

'He's hired me,' she cried. 'Major Collingham is sending the carriage here for me on Monday, and he says Thomas and Amy can come too. I was most surprised at that, I can tell you, but it is ideal for us all.'

'Oh, well done, dearie! I'm that pleased for you, I really am.' The housekeeper turned to the footman, who was relaxing in a chair with his feet up on the fender. 'You hear that, Lawrence? Miss Wrenn is to be a governess to the Major, and him a hero of Waterloo, no less!'

'Is he? I never knew that.' Juliana smiled, taking off her bonnet and placing it on a side table.

'Aye.' Lawrence poured himself another mug of ale. 'My brother was in his regiment, the 30th Foot. They fought off the French at Quatre Bras. Praised by Lord Wellington hisself, they was. But that's not all.' He grinned. 'Devil Collingham, they call him. Heard it from the man's groom hisself, I did, last time I delivered some papers to the house and stopped off for a glass of daffy on the way back. Devil Collingham—devil on the battlefield, and devil in the bedroom. They say in Brussels it was nothing for him to pleasure three women in one night.'

With a shriek Mrs Churwell cuffed him round the ear.

'I'll have none of that talk in my kitchen, my lad! You had best get back upstairs, now, before the master starts shouting for you. Go on, now! Don't you be taking any notice of what Lawrence says,' she added, when the footman had lounged away. 'I don't hold with servants' tittle-tattle.'

'No more do I,' agreed Juliana. She looked up at the housekeeper, a mischievous twinkle in her green eyes. 'However, it seems I have just made a pact with the devil!'

Chapter Three

'Well, what do you think of her?' Wilhelmina whispered to her sister as Lady Varley gave her instructions to the driver. Gwendoline wrinkled her nose.

'Miss Sevenoaks was much prettier, except when she had been drinking too much, then her face became very red.'

'Well, I think she's pretty,' replied Wilhelmina. 'And she had kind eyes.'

Gwendoline gave her a nudge as their aunt climbed into the carriage.

'Whispering again?' Lady Varley shook her head. 'I hope this new woman Damon has hired will teach you both some manners.'

They travelled in silence to New Bond Street; when they reached the fashionable dressmaker's establishment, Lady Varley took the children into the shop, declaring she would prefer to keep them under her eye. The girls gazed around them in wide-eyed wonder. At first glance the walls seemed to be decorated in rainbow colours, but closer inspection revealed shelves from floor to ceiling, packed with rolls of fabric, shiny silks and satin, soft muslins and cottons of every shade. There seemed to be half a dozen ladies in the room, but the girls soon realised that these were life-size dummies displaying the very latest fashions. Madame Fleurie herself appeared from the back of the shop flanked by two simpering assistants, each carrying rolls of creamy-coloured muslin for Lady Varley's inspection. The modiste curtsied, bowed, flattered and fawned over her patroness, uttering so many compliments in her lilting French accent that Gwendoline turned away, her lip curling. She led her sister to a satin-covered couch, half-hidden between rolls of fabric and piles of hatboxes.

'What are we going to do about the new governess, Gwen?' Wilhelmina climbed on to the couch.

'Well, I think we should try to send her away. We certainly don't want to have her with us all the way to Lancashire. It will be much more fun with just Nurse, because she always lets us have our own way.'

'We could play ghosts again,' suggested Wilhelmina. 'It worked very well with Miss Gillimore.'

'But she was very stupid.' Gwendoline's tone was dismissive. 'This one does not look stupid.'

Wilhelmina regarded her silently. It was clear that Gwendoline was thinking hard. Wilhelmina bore it patiently for a few moments, but soon wriggled off the couch and went in search of something more interesting to look at than Gwendoline's pensive face. Aunt Louisa was engrossed in discussing fabrics and patterns with the modiste, while the assistants hurried back and forth with bolts of cloth and pieces of lace for her inspection. Wilhelmina walked around the shop; it seemed a nonsense for Aunt Louisa to be taking so long to choose a gown—the dummies were all so elegant she could surely want nothing better. The one nearest the door was dressed in a beautiful gown of apricot silk with a demi-train of shiny beads. Rows of beads also decorated the sleeves and hem, glistening in the light. Wilhelmina went closer, then closer still. It was all a cheat! It was not a dress at all—the silk had been cunningly draped around the dummy with lengths of beaded ribbon pinned into place. In fact, Wilhelmina could see where one of the pins on the sleeve had worked itself loose—perhaps if she just pushed it back in....

'Wilhelmina, what are you doing?'

Aunt Louisa's voice cut across the room and Wilhelmina jumped back. Unfortunately, as she did so, a loose thread on one finger of her glove caught around some of the beads, dragging them off the dummy and pulling the apricot silk with them. With a little cry Wilhelmina shook her hand, the beads fell away, but it was too late; before her horrified gaze the beautiful creation was falling apart, the silk dropping into a blushing cloud around the base of the cloth dummy.

'You tiresome child, how many times have I told you not to touch?' Lady Varley's chilling accents brought a hot flush of guilt and embarrassment to Wilhelmina's cheeks. She ran back to the couch and scrambled up beside Gwendoline.

'Really, I do not know why I brought you. Just look at what you have done!'

'No, no, *madame*, it ees nothing, nothing,' cried Madame Fleurie, hands fluttering as she sought to placate her wealthy client. 'It ees the work of a moment to put it right.' She signalled to her assistants to attend to the disorder while she gently escorted Lady Varley back to the counter to finish making her selection.

Wilhelmina looked up at Gwendoline, who frowned and turned away, hunching a shoulder as if to disown her troublesome little sister. Wilhelmina felt the tears gathering in her eyes. Her bottom lip began to tremble.

'There, there, missy, don't cry.' The younger of the two assistants came past, winding up the beaded ribbon into her arms. 'There's no 'arm done, my pet. We was about to re-dress that model anyway.'

Wilhelmina gave a shuddering sigh.

The assistant dropped the bundled ribbon on to the counter and came back to kneel in front of Wilhelmina, her round face creased into a kindly smile.

'Ah, now, dearie, there's no need for tears.' She drew out her own handkerchief and mopped Wilhelmina's cheeks. 'All this fuss over a bit o' cloth, well, I never.' She sat back on her heels, then suddenly dived down beside the couch.

'Here.' She held up a small wooden doll, beautifully dressed in a brocaded gown with a silk apron and a mass of grey curls. 'Take it, my pet, and you dry your eyes. *Madame* gets them sent to her from France all the time, dressed in the latest fashions, to show to her lady clients, but heaven knows where this one came from—why, look at those panniers! We haven't made gowns like this for the past ten years at least!'

Wilhelmina gulped and stared at the doll.

'Oh, but—I shouldn't take her.'

'Oh, yes, you should, my lovely. She will only be thrown away, so you might as well have her, if you like.'

'Like? Oh, I should love her.' Wilhelmina's small hands closed round the doll. 'If you really think…'

Madame Fleurie called, and after a final nod at Wilhel-mina, the assistant rose quickly and trotted off.

'Gwen,' breathed Wilhelmina, 'Gwen, what do you think?'

'Keep her, if you wish,' muttered Gwendoline. 'Although it does seem odd to be rewarded when you have caused so much trouble.' Seeing her little sister's lip begin to tremble again, she gave her a quick hug. 'Goose. I know you didn't

mean to do it. Come on, Aunt Louisa has finished; we must
go.'

With regal grace, Lady Varley shepherded her two charges
back to the coach, while Madame Fleurie bowed and scraped
at her heels.

The children scrambled into the carriage and Lady Varley
climbed in after them, dropping back with a sigh on to the
well-padded seat.

'Well, thank heaven that is done. I shall not need to come
back now. Madame Fleurie can call at Burlington Street next
week for a fitting. Now…' she smiled brightly at her nieces
'…let us take that turn around the park. It is a pity the weather
is too inclement to put down the hood, but you will get an
airing, none the less.' Her glance fell to the doll Wilhelmina
was holding and she tutted. 'Oh, Minna, surely you are too
old to be bringing dolls for a ride with you?'

'No, Aunt, you see—'

'Next time you must leave her at home.' Lady Varley
carried on as if Wilhelmina had not spoken. 'Dolls should
be kept in the nursery. Dear me, your new governess will
have some work to do with you!'

Chapter Four

Juliana had wondered how Cousin Pettigrew would take the news that she had obtained a post and was relieved that he appeared quite sanguine. Once she had explained that she had overheard the Major's comments in the hallway of Bouverie Street, Mr Pettigrew seemed to believe that he had somehow engineered the whole thing himself, and had solved the problem of providing for his cousins at very little expense. He was therefore able to wave them off with perfect good humour. Mrs Churwell shed a tear at the thought of them all going so far away, and even pressed one last slice of fruitcake upon Thomas. He devoured it on the short journey to Burlington Street, explaining to his sisters that he would not wish to carry it with him into the Major's house, in case his staff thought it a slight upon their hospitality.

There was no sign of the Major when they arrived and they were greeted by the housekeeper who led them upstairs. She introduced herself as Mrs Hartley.

'The master sends his apologies that business takes him

out this morning, but he has asked me to ensure you have everything you need, miss.' She opened the door of a large apartment on the second floor. 'The master thought this might suit you, Miss Wrenn—there's a bed made up in the corner for your sister, and another in the adjoining dressing room for the young gentleman. It is for less than a week, but the Major thought you might prefer to be together, being in a strange house.'

'Yes, thank you.' Juliana looked around her in surprise. She had expected to be tucked away in an attic room, yet this apartment bore all the trappings of a guest chamber. 'The Major is most kind.'

'That he is, miss. Now, your trunks are on their way up, so I shall leave you to unpack.' She gestured towards the round table by the window. 'I shall send up a light luncheon for you shortly, and Nurse will bring the Misses Collingham to the schoolroom for you at two o'clock.'

When the housekeeper had gone, Thomas let out a low whistle.

'Lord, sis, this is much grander than I thought it would be.' He opened the door to the dressing room and peered in. 'My own room, too!'

'Yes, well, enjoy it while it lasts,' said Juliana, taking off her bonnet. 'I expect there was no room for us with the servants and he was obliged to put us in this guest room. But do not expect such luxury when we are travelling, or when we reach the Major's Lancashire estate—remember I am a paid employee.'

'And what are we?' piped up Amy, bouncing on the edge of her bed.

'You are to be travelling companions for his nieces.' She sat down beside Amy and pulled the little girl on to her lap.

'He has two little girls: one is twelve years old, the other eight, just a little younger than you, Amy.'

'Huh, I hope you don't expect me to play with girls!' declared Thomas, pulling a face.

'I expect you to behave like a gentleman, sir. The Major also has a son, some years older than the girls. I haven't met him yet, and he is not one of the schoolroom party, so perhaps we will not see much of him.'

Thomas shrugged. 'I don't see how we can avoid it, if we are all travelling together—'

He broke off as a large corded travelling trunk was brought in by two liveried footmen and, under Juliana's instruction, the two children spent the remaining time until luncheon unpacking their clothes and putting them into the chests of drawers and the big linen press that Mrs Hartley had told them they could use.

At two o'clock Juliana made her way to the schoolroom, Thomas and Amy hard on her heels. As she reached the door, Gwendoline's voice could be heard quite clearly coming from the other side.

'But we do not want her, Nurse! Why should we have a governess now, what can she teach us while we are travelling? Why, if she tries to make me read in the carriage, I shall be *sick*! It would be much better to wait until we get to Lancashire—Papa can hire a proper governess for us there.'

Juliana grasped the door handle and rattled it before opening the door. She moved into the room, smiling as if she had heard nothing of Gwendoline's tirade.

The young Misses Collingham were standing on each side of their nurse, an elderly, rosy-cheeked woman with curly wisps of snow-white hair peeping out around the edges

of her cap. Juliana thought she looked a good-humoured
creature, but just now her face displayed a mixture of mor-
tification and embarrassment as she realised her charge's
outburst must have been overheard.

Juliana gave her a brief smile and turned her attention
to the children. They, meanwhile, had realised that Juliana
had not come alone, and were staring open-mouthed at
Thomas and Amy.

'I dare say your papa forgot to tell you that I would be
bringing two travelling companions for our journey.' She led
her siblings forward and performed the introductions. Gwendoline and Thomas greeted each other with frosty politeness,
while the two younger children merely stared solemnly at
one another. An awkward silence ensued and Juliana was
about to break it when Amy spoke up.

'I have a doll, too,' she said, staring at the handsomely
dressed little lady that Wilhelmina was clutching before her.
'She's sitting on my bed at the moment. She is called Sarah.
What do you call yours?'

Wilhelmina hugged her doll even closer. 'Her name is
Lady Arabella,' she said.

Amy stared at the wooden figure in its brocade gown.
'She's very beautiful.'

Wilhelmina held it out. 'Would you like to hold her?'

Amy glanced at Juliana, who nodded, then stepped
forward to take the doll and the two girls moved off together,
talking in low tones.

'Well now,' murmured Nurse with a smile.

'A good start,' agreed Juliana. 'Thomas, perhaps you
would help me by making a list of the books on the shelf over
there. I am sure Nurse will help you to find a pen and paper.
Miss Gwendoline, shall we sit down, and you can tell me just
what you have learned with your last governess.'

* * *

Shortly before the dinner hour, Juliana was summoned to Major Collingham's study. At the door she paused to shake out the skirts of her grey silk gown, the only mourning gown she owned, then she knocked and went in. Major Collingham was seated at his desk, but he rose as she entered. He did not smile as she approached, confirming her belief that his request had not been one of courtesy, more a command. He was dressed for dinner in a plain dark coat and biscuit-coloured knee-breeches, the snowy whiteness of his shirt and necktie contrasting sharply with the black cloth of his coat and his equally black hair. He motioned her to a chair.

'I am sorry I was not here to receive you. I trust you have everything you need?'

'Yes, Major, thank you. Our rooms are very comfortable, and more luxurious than I had expected.'

'It was more convenient to put you and your family together. After all, it is only for a few days.'

'Have no fear, Major, I shall not forget my position here.'

'Is that comment designed to put me in my place?'

Her eyes flew to his face.

'Not at all, sir, I—'

'If I sounded impolite, I apologise,' he said bluntly. 'I am not in the habit of making pretty speeches. I understand that you have made your brother and sister known to my girls.'

'Yes. The older ones are still painfully polite, but Miss Wilhelmina and Amy are already firm friends.'

'Good. You may, of course, include your brother and sister in your lessons, if you wish.'

'Thank you, Major. I would rather they were occupied and under my eye.'

He nodded. 'Brasher tells me you signed the contract. Did you read it first?'

'Of course.'

'And?'

'The terms are very generous. It is good of you to allow either party to terminate the agreement upon two weeks notice, should it prove necessary.'

'That was Brasher's doing. I never contemplate failure, Miss Wrenn.'

Her chin went up.

'No more do I, sir.' She hesitated, recalling Gwendoline's hostility towards her. 'However, if it should prove impossible for me to win the children's regard, I should not wish to inflict myself upon them for the full four months.'

'Then you may be sure that you would not be paid for the full four months.'

A scorching glance accompanied these words, and Juliana had no doubt the Major had used such a look to make young soldiers quail. She had to remind herself that she was no raw recruit to be intimidated.

'I would expect to be paid for work carried out, Major. Mr Brasher assures me that you treat your employees fairly, and I am told you are an honest man.'

'Oh, so you have been making enquiries about me?'

'Of course, since I am entrusting the care of myself and my family to you.'

A faint gleam of approval lit his eyes.

'Then welcome to my household, Miss Wrenn.' He got up and went to a side-table where a selection of decanters and glasses rested on a silver tray. 'Will you take a little wine with me, madam, to seal our bargain?'

'Yes sir, thank you, for there is something that I wish to discuss with you.'

He threw her a frowning glance, but said nothing until he had given her a full glass.

She sipped her wine. It was smooth and fruity, nothing like the weak potions served in Mr Pettigrew's house. It confirmed her opinion that Cousin Alfred watered down his wines to make them go further.

'What is it you wanted to discuss with me, Miss Wrenn?'

He had returned to the side-table to fill a glass for himself.

'Oh, I beg your pardon. Yes, I know I said I wanted to be paid with a lump sum at the end of our agreement, but my visit to the schoolroom today has revealed a sad lack of books and games for the children. Oh, there are plenty of religious and educational tracts, but I need to make a few purchases if I am to keep the children amused, especially on a long journey.'

'Very well, madam. See Brasher tomorrow morning and tell him how much you need. You may also have my carriage for your shopping expedition. Brasher will arrange it, if you tell him what time you wish to go out.'

'Thank you.' Her eyes were straying around the room, and they alighted upon a small painting on the wall: three children at play in a garden. 'Oh, is that your family, sir?'

'Yes. My mother had it done for me, when I was in the army. I think it was to remind me that I had a family.'

She rose and went over to the picture. It hung on the wall above a console table, upon which rested a glass case of miniatures. She leaned forward to study the figures more closely.

'They were much younger, then, of course,' said the Major, 'but I think it is a good likeness.'

'Yes, indeed. They are all handsome children, sir.'

He came to stand behind her.

'Giles takes after his mother. As does Wilhelmina.'

'They are fairer, certainly, while Gwendoline has your own dark colouring—oh!' She turned back, but he was so close that she found herself trapped between his body and the table. She stared at his neckcloth, at the cleft in his strong chin, then raised her eyes to his mouth and found herself wondering what it would be like to be kissed by him. Her heart leapt to her throat as the Major reached out and took her arms. What was it Lawrence had said about him, a devil in the bedroom? She felt scandalised, elated and frightened all in a moment.

He said quietly, 'You are almost sitting on the glass case, Miss Wrenn.'

He gently moved her aside, then let her go and returned to the desk. She could feel her cheeks burning. How had she been so foolish. Had he noticed? Did he think she was trying to…it was too embarrassing even to think of it!

'Now,' he said. 'Is there anything else?'

'No, sir, I believe—'

She broke off as the door opened and she heard a deep, cheerful voice saying,

'No need to announce me, Fraser, I'll find him—and lay another cover for dinner, there's a good fellow!'

Unable to curb her curiosity, Juliana turned to see who dared to walk in upon Major Collingham with such insouciance. She saw a gentleman dressed in the first style of elegance, his short fair hair brushed forward to frame a handsome, good-humoured countenance supported—or more properly confined—by a collar whose points came up to his cheeks. A tight-fitting blue coat and white embroidered waistcoat encased his body, while inexpressibles of the palest cream and gleaming Hessians completed the picture of a top-of-the-trees man-about-town. If the gentleman heard the Major's curt demand to know what the devil was going on he gave no sign, but stopped just inside the door and made an elegant bow.

'Well, now, Fraser did not tell me you had company, Damon. How very remiss of him.'

The Major was regarding the newcomer with a mixture of amusement and exasperation. 'Would it have stopped you charging in, had you known?'

The gentleman gave a grin. 'I dare say I'd have allowed him to announce me.'

Major Collingham sighed. 'Your manners really are appalling, Richard. Miss Wrenn, may I present to you Sir Richard Mondwyck?'

Juliana stepped forward, her cheeks still warm from her recent embarrassment.

'Yes. That is, we—we have met.'

'By Jove, yes, I thought you looked familiar! I knew her father,' he explained to the Major. 'Clever fellow, Jonas Wrenn. Could always rely on him to decipher the more difficult codes I put to him.' Sir Richard took her hand. 'I was very sorry to hear of his death, Miss Wrenn. I was in France at the time or I should have attended his funeral. He was a very good man.'

'Thank you, sir.' She gently withdrew her fingers from his grip and Sir Richard moved across to the side-table to pour himself a glass of wine.

'Well, now, Miss Wrenn—what are you doing here with this reprobate?'

'Miss Wrenn is in my employ,' the Major responded curtly. 'She has agreed to act as governess for a few months, until I have settled the girls into Blackthorpe.'

'My father was not a rich man, sir,' she answered the question in Sir Richard's look. 'So now I must earn my living.'

She ended brightly, smiling, and Sir Richard merely nodded, understanding in his eyes.

'As must I, Miss Wrenn,' he replied in the same light vein.

'Fortunately, there are wealthy men such as Damon here who have need of our services occasionally.'

Major Collingham's lip curled. 'Thank you, Richard. Now, before my patience is quite worn out, perhaps you will tell me what you are doing here?'

'I wanted a little company, so I invited myself to dinner, Damon.'

'Really? Louisa will be overjoyed.'

Sir Richard almost choked on his wine. 'No! Is your sister in town? Well, I didn't know, but no matter. I shall be delighted to see her again. This really is a superb burgundy, Damon—shall I refill your glass? And we are all standing around like perfect strangers! Miss Wrenn, will you not be seated, ma'am?'

'Thank you, but I think Major Collingham and I have finished our business, and I must get back to my charges. If that is all, Major?'

'It is for now. You will oblige me by bringing the girls to the drawing room after dinner, Miss Wrenn.'

'As you wish, sir.'

Sir Richard opened the door for her and Juliana gave him a fleeting smile as she went out. She was feeling a little light-headed as she made her way back to the schoolroom. She attributed this to the wine, but could not deny her pleasure at seeing Sir Richard again. He had been an infrequent visitor to her father's house, always on business, but on the rare occasions they had met he had treated her with respect and she felt now that his acknowledgement of her had added to her standing with her new employer. All at once she found herself looking forward to going downstairs after dinner.

Chapter Five

'So you are taking the children back to Lancashire,' said Sir Richard.

'Blackthorpe Hall is their home, and mine, too.' Major Collingham tossed off his wine and walked to the side-table. 'I have hardly been there since their mother died. There is much to be done.' He held up the decanter and Sir Richard came over with his empty glass.

'And you plan to marry that neighbour of yours—the widow?'

'Lady Frances. Yes. She was in town with her father a few weeks ago. Nothing was said, of course, but much was hinted at.'

Sir Richard grimaced.

'Too cold for my taste, old friend. I cannot ever recall seeing a spark of warmth in her.'

Damon shrugged. 'She will make the girls a good mother. That is all I want.'

Sir Richard sipped his wine, saying nothing. The Major eyed him for a moment, then set down his glass with a snap.

'Damnation, man, say what is on your mind.'

'If I did that, my friend, you would call me out.'

'You think I am making a mistake?'

Sir Richard looked down at the toe of one gleaming Hessian as he traced the pattern on the carpet. 'I do not think Lady Frances will make you happy.'

'I am five-and-thirty, Richard, past the age of romantic notions. So, too, is Frances. I want a mother for my children, nothing more.' He paused, then said with some difficulty, 'I loved Harriet. To lose her was—agony. I have no wish to go through such pain again. Frances and I understand each other—we have been neighbours for many years. She will bring up the girls and look after my house, leaving me free to get on with the business of running the estate. We shall be very comfortable.'

'Then I wish you happy. And you have found a governess to look after the children. How did you manage that so quickly?'

'Miss Wrenn is related to Pettigrew, the lawyer dealing with my cousin Willoughby's affairs—you will remember he made me trustee before he died. Miss Wrenn and I struck a bargain—she is contracted to me until September, which will give me time to arrange matters in Lancashire.'

'There were other children in the Wrenn family, as I recall.'

'Aye. Two. They are travelling with us.'

'The devil they are!' Sir Richard laughed. 'What has come over you, Damon? I thought you didn't like children above half!'

'Nor do I.' He scowled. 'You may take that look out of your eye, Rick, I'm not going soft in the head, if that's what you are thinking. They would have to follow their sister at some stage, so it seemed expedient to take them with us. They will be company for my own girls.'

'True, and Miss Wrenn will be looking after them, will she not? I doubt they will bother you.'

'That is my hope. You knew her father, you said?'

'Aye. He spent some years in France as a young man and his knowledge of the country and language was quite exceptional. In my work for the government, I often have need for someone to decipher the notes we intercept from French spies. Wrenn was one of the best.'

The Major studied his wine glass. 'And how well do you know his daughter?'

'We met once or twice, when I called on her father. That is all.' Sir Richard laughed. 'You need not worry, Damon. She was never one of my intrigues. Her reputation was—and is, I am sure—spotless.' He bent his shrewd gaze upon his host. 'Perhaps you have an interest there yourself?'

Damon thought of the little governess in her dull clothes with her soft brown hair braided so modestly around her head. 'Not my line at all, my friend. She might be quite pretty, if she were dressed up.' He sipped his wine, imagining the girl in an evening gown. Silk, he thought. It would cling to her slender body. And emerald green, to match her eyes, eyes that could suddenly gleam with mischief. He gave himself a little mental shake. 'No, I've no interest there, Rick. It has never been my way to tamper with innocents, or raise false hopes.'

'No, your taste has always been for more dashing beauties, eh, *Devil* Collingham?'

Damon laughed. 'Will I never live down that damned Brussels party?'

'It would appear not, my friend. The stories grow more outrageous every time they are retold.'

Damon shook his head. 'We were at war and a little reckless. Who wants such stories now? The war ended over a year ago.'

'But it pleases the ladies to remember. And it seems you *did* please 'em, Damon, the married ones, at least.'

'Safer that way.' The Major raised his glass. 'They know I don't offer 'em marriage. A flirtation, a little pleasure on both sides, then we go our separate ways.'

'Like Lady Ormiston? You were very close when you came home for the Peace Celebrations in 'fourteen.'

'That affair lasted only as long as the peace,' said Damon, his lip curling. 'Veronique is indeed a beauty, but she has a heart of stone.'

'You make a fine pair, then,' retorted Sir Richard, smiling faintly. 'Ormiston is still playing least in sight. It seems he prefers his Scottish acres to living with his wife. I believe she has young Leeson paying court to her now; they say he's besotted.'

'Silly young fool.' The Major lifted the decanter again. 'We might as well finish this off before we go into dinner. For God's sake, sit down, man, and you can tell me the real reason you are here.'

Sir Richard lowered himself into an armchair on one side of the empty fireplace. 'I am chasing diamonds, dear boy.'

'The devil you are! Is that what brings you back to England?'

'Yes. Bonaparte's followers have been trying to raise a force to free him from St Helena. From the letters we have intercepted we know that the Princess Borghese donated a pair of diamond earrings to the cause.'

The Major raised his black brows. 'Bonaparte's sister? How was she persuaded to part with them?'

'No idea, my friend. Her passion for jewels is legendary— the Emperor himself acquired these stones in Egypt and had them made up into ear-drops for the princess. Perhaps she wanted to make a gesture of sisterly devotion.'

'Then it would be her first! More likely one of her other—ah—admirers persuaded her to be generous.'

'One of her lovers, you mean? Possibly. In any event, the diamonds were sent from Italy to Paris. We arrested a number of conspirators, but the gems had already been moved on.'

'Did you identify the courier?'

'No. We caught one or two suspects at the coast, but it seems the diamonds were hidden in rolls of cloth bound for London. We have traced the consignment and are going through all the delivery papers and bills of exchange, but that is slow work. I am investigating other possibilities.' He crossed one elegantly shod foot over the other. 'One thing is certain: the diamonds have not been sold. I have my contacts in the markets and there is not a whisper of such fine stones being available.'

'What is their value?'

'Enough to buy and fit out a ship to take Bonaparte off St Helena.' He studied his wine glass. 'I was going to ask you to help me track them down.'

'Alas, Rick, I am leaving town on Friday. Besides, I am no longer in the army.'

'True, but you do have an uncanny ability to ferret out information. Oh, never fear, I have some very clever fellows looking for these gems, so I shall find 'em.' He finished his wine. 'Now, you had best take me to meet the lovely Louisa, since I am joining you for my dinner.'

Nurse and the children were gathered in the schoolroom when Juliana went in, and she found herself facing a row of expectant faces.

'Tomorrow,' she announced, 'we are going shopping. We shall make a list of everything we need for the schoolroom; we seem to be especially deficient of books.' She saw their horrified looks and burst out laughing. 'Do not look so shocked, it will not be so bad, I promise you.' She swept Amy up into her arms. 'There will be plenty of time for playing games, too.'

'Miss Sevenoaks said games were for babies,' scoffed Gwendoline.

'Then I pity her pupils,' chuckled Juliana. She looked around as the door opened.

A young man walked in. Despite his light brown hair he was so much a younger version of her employer that Juliana guessed immediately his identity. His first words confirmed it.

'My father said I should come up and make myself known to you. I am Giles Collingham.'

Juliana immediately brought her brother and sister forward to be introduced.

'You have been with your friends today, I understand?'

'Yes, which is why Papa has said I should join you for dinner, and get to know you, since we will be travelling together.'

'Oh, poor you.' Juliana gave him a sympathetic smile. 'How dull for you to be consigned to the schoolroom.'

Giles coloured a little. 'Yes, well, it is not so bad, you know.'

'I am sure you would prefer to be dining with Papa when you know who is with him,' put in Gwendoline as they took their places for dinner. She cast a quick, triumphant look around the table. 'Sir Richard Mondwyck! Nelly told me he walked in, bold as brass, and directed Fraser to set another place for him.'

Nurse tutted. 'Now, Miss Gwendoline, you should not be listening to servants' gossip, nor repeating it, neither.'

'I'll wager Aunt Louisa will be in high dudgeon,' grinned Giles, ignoring Nurse's mild strictures.

'Oh, he will turn her up sweet,' returned his sister, giggling. 'She thinks he is a charmer.'

'Enough, if you please,' said Juliana firmly. 'Such talk shows little respect for your aunt or your father's guest.'

Giles flushed and Gwendoline scowled across the table at her governess.

Wilhelmina looked up. 'Sir Richard was in the Peninsula with Papa, was he not, Giles? But he was only a mister then.'

'He was knighted last year, for services to the country,' said Giles. 'Father says he is an intelligence officer, collecting information against our enemies.'

'A spy!' Gwendoline's eyes grew round.

'If he is, then it is perhaps best we do not talk of it,' responded Juliana. 'Wilhelmina, shall I help you with your napkin?'

Juliana thought back to Sir Richard's visits to her father, the bound notebooks and closeted meetings. Suddenly, it all seemed to make sense.

While the soup was being served there was a sudden clatter to Juliana's right, where Wilhelmina was sitting.

'Oh, dear, Minna,' said Nurse. 'You have dropped your spoon.'

'I'll get it!' Gwendoline was out of her seat and racing around the table.

'Gwendoline, there is no need,' Nurse expostulated mildly. 'Really, dear, do stop waving your arms, your napkin is almost in Miss Wrenn's face.'

With mumbled apologies Gwendoline returned to her place. Juliana picked up her spoon, but as she was about to dip it into her soup she stopped. There, in the middle of her bowl, was a small, black beetle.

She heard Wilhelmina stifle a giggle. Across the table, Gwendoline was addressing herself to her food, a picture of

innocence. Juliana put down her spoon and began to talk to
Nurse on some unexceptional topic until the soup bowls
were removed and she could help herself to one of the other
dishes on the table.

As soon as the meal was over, Giles excused himself and
went downstairs, but Juliana waited until she received word
that the gentlemen had joined Lady Varley in the drawing
room. Nurse promised to take care of Thomas and Amy, and
Juliana glanced at her two charges to make sure they were
looking neat and tidy.

'Very well, shall we go?'

As they went down the stairs, Juliana let Wilhelmina run
on ahead while she moved a little closer to Gwendoline.

'That was a very neat trick you played at dinner—no,
please do not deny it. Where did you find the beetle, in the
schoolroom?'

Gwendoline tossed her head. 'Yes, if you must know.'

'Well, let me warn you, Gwendoline, that I will not be
put off by your tricks or stratagems. Your papa has engaged
me until the end of September and I do not intend to give
up this position, however unpleasant you try to make it.'
She glanced down at the mutinous little face beside her.
'Please try to make the best of it, Gwendoline—the time
will pass much quicker if we work together. And remember
that I have a younger brother and sister, so I have a few
tricks of my own.' She lowered her voice, 'Beware how
you get into bed tonight!' She laughed at Gwendoline's
quick, alarmed glance and patted the girl's arm. 'Come,
Gwendoline, cry friends with me; I am not an ogre, I
promise you.'

They had reached the drawing room and Juliana took Wilhelmina's hand. The footman threw open the door and, with

a bright smile pinned in place, Juliana escorted her charges into the room.

Lady Varley greeted the schoolroom party with regal graciousness and called the children to her. Juliana would have taken a seat in one corner of the room, but Major Collingham beckoned her forward.

'So you have spent your first day with my girls, Miss Wrenn.' He led her to a chair next to Sir Richard. 'I hope they have been no trouble?'

She saw Gwendoline look up quickly, and gave her a reassuring smile. 'I think we are in a great way to understanding each other, Major.'

Even if she had not made peace with Gwendoline, it was, she hoped, a truce.

'And you are to accompany the family to Blackthorpe Hall, Miss Wrenn,' said Sir Richard. 'I hope you have a strong constitution. Collingham here likes to travel at a fearsome pace.'

'The children's needs will dictate our progress,' returned Juliana calmly.

'I have already allowed for it,' nodded the Major. 'Brasher has written to the hotels where we shall stay. He will go on ahead with Benns to check the accommodation personally, and they will then travel on to Blackthorpe.'

Lady Varley looked up. 'You are sending your valet on ahead, Damon? Is that wise?'

'My dear Louisa, I am quite capable of dressing and shaving myself, you know,' retorted the Major. 'Besides, we shall only be on the road for three nights.'

Sir Richard grinned. 'Everything organised with the efficiency of a military operation,' he said. 'I hope you are impressed, Miss Wrenn?'

'I shall be impressed if we carry it off.'

Juliana found herself subjected to the Major's steely gaze.

'Do you doubt my planning, then?'

'No, sir. I am sure your planning is impeccable, but it is not wise to rely too heavily upon plans and timetables where children are involved.'

'Very true,' put in Lady Varley. 'I know from my own little ones that they are the most delightfully unpredictable creatures.'

'Good Gad, Miss Wrenn, do you follow Rousseau's philosophy for the education of children?' cried Sir Richard gaily.

'Certainly, I believe they should be allowed to express themselves, and have room to play.' She felt a flush stealing into her cheeks and she added quickly, 'Not that I expect such considerations to affect our journey.'

'I am very glad to hear it,' growled her employer.

'However,' she continued, 'the children are very young, and if they need to stop a little more frequently I shall not hesitate to bring it to your attention, Major. But it is by no means certain; they may prove themselves to be excellent travellers.'

Major Collingham stepped closer, frowning down at her. 'Let me make myself plain, Miss Wrenn. The journey is set. It is up to you to ensure my girls are looked after at each stage. Keep them amused, by all means, but you will not bother me with trifling concerns.'

She gave him back look for look, refusing to be intimidated by his menacing tone. 'Of course not, sir. I should not dream of troubling you with trifles.'

His eyes narrowed. 'But?' he said. 'I feel sure you are about to add a rider to that last remark.'

Juliana regarded him with an innocent stare. 'We are both concerned with the children's welfare, Major. If that is in question, then of course I will bring it to your attention.'

'By Gad, Damon, she's got you there,' murmured Sir Richard. 'But you have the right of it, Miss Wrenn. Damon will like nothing better than to know his children are being cared for.'

One glance at the Major's tight-lipped face convinced Juliana that at that moment he would like nothing better than to strangle her. With a curt nod he moved away and began to converse with his sister.

Juliana turned to Sir Richard. 'Oh dear,' she said ruefully. 'Do you think I shall be turned off before we even leave London?'

'Not a bit of it!' he reassured her. 'Damon would be the first to tell you he knows nothing about children. He will welcome your advice, despite his frowns. He is not nearly so harsh as he would have us believe.'

As there was no one to overhear them, she murmured, 'Not really the devil he is named, perhaps?'

'Oh, so you've heard that tale, have you? Well, you may rest easy, Miss Wrenn. Collingham is a true gentleman. As a member of his household you fall under his protection, and he'll take dashed good care of you, take my word for it.'

Chapter Six

The following morning Juliana sallied forth upon her shopping expedition, accompanied by the four children. No sooner had the Collingham carriage departed than another, much less elegant equipage pulled up and the occupants were shown to Lady Varley's sitting room.

'Madame Fleurie!' Lady Varley came out of her bedchamber, her eyebrows raised in surprise. 'I had not expected to see you so soon. You have made up the gowns already?'

'We 'ave been working through ze night, *madame*, but ze primrose muslin is of such a complexity that I need *madame* to try it on, if *madame* would be so kind?'

'Oh, very well, but you must be quick, for I am very busy today.'

Lady Varley called for her maid and allowed herself to be draped in the soft fabric, which had been cut and partially sewn. Madame Fleurie set her minion to pin up the hem of the gown.

'It ees a very becoming colour for you, *madame*,' she said. 'If I may mention it, my lady, when you did me the honour to visit me earlier this week, one of my assistants made a mistake: she gave one of your leetle girls a fashion doll. It was an error, *madame*, and I have reprimanded her, *naturellement*, for you see this was a special doll, dressed expressly for another of my clients. *Madame*, I am *desolée*, but I must have thees doll. Do you think—would it be possible for me to take it with me today?'

Lady Varley looked blank for a moment, then she nodded and instructed her maid to go to the schoolroom. 'You are to find a doll.'

'A leetle wooden lady, dressed in cherry brocade, *à la Pompadour*,' added Madame Fleurie.

'Yes, well, go and find it, and bring it here directly.'

'*Madame*, you find me very grateful. If eet was for myself I would give your little children all my dolls, but this one is for a very special client, a very exacting lady…' She let the words trail away, giving the impression that not all her clients were as accommodating as Lady Varley.

'If you please, ma'am,' said the maid, coming back into the room, 'there is no doll in the schoolroom, nor in the children's bedrooms either. And Miss Wilhelmina and Miss Gwendoline have gone out with the new governess.'

Lady Varley shrugged. 'No matter, I will ask the children about it when they come back. Now, can we get on?'

The fitting had just finished and the gown was being packed away when a footman entered with a letter for Lady Varley. She snatched it from the tray, her brow clearing as she recognised her husband's distinctive scrawl.

'It is from Sir James. At last. I have been waiting to hear how the family goes on without me.' She looked at Madame Fleurie. 'I take it we have done, now?'

'Indeed, *madame*, thank you for your time.' She ushered her assistant out of the room, stopping at the door to turn back. 'And if I may remind my lady, you will not forget the doll?'

'Yes, yes, I will see to it,' responded Lady Varley, impatiently waving her away.

She barely waited for the door to close before she tore open the letter and immersed herself in news from her home.

Juliana returned from her shopping trip feeling that she had achieved a great deal. She had made her purchases and placed orders for several books at Hatchards in Piccadilly, but, more than that, she thought that her charges had begun to accept her. Wilhelmina was no trouble at all; she and Amy had become firm friends. By the time they returned to Burlington Street, Wilhelmina was chattering away to Juliana as though she had known her all her life. Gwendoline was more reserved, but she had been perfectly well mannered during their excursion and Juliana was encouraged to think that the child was unbending a little towards her.

With the move to the north so imminent, Juliana did not attempt to establish a routine to the afternoon lesson, but chose instead to show the children maps and pictures of the north country, well aware that such a long journey to a place they had not seen for many years must be exciting and somewhat unnerving for her charges. She asked Mr Brasher for details of their route, and used the guidebook she had bought to describe the various towns they would pass through.

Juliana dined in the schoolroom again with the children, although Giles did not join them. He dined instead with his father and aunt, and Juliana found him in boisterous good spirits when she brought the girls to the drawing room later.

He teased Wilhelmina about her freckles and then drew Gwendoline to one side, whispering to her to make her giggle. Juliana was aware of Lady Varley's frowning looks and knew she would be expected to act. She waited until she was sure the Major was engrossed in conversation with his sister, then walked over to the youngsters. Giles rose as she approached.

'Gwendoline, you know how impolite it is to be whispering thus. If it is such a good joke, then let us all share it.' She spoke quietly, but her words made the girl scowl.

'It is no crime to talk to my brother!'

'No, indeed.' Juliana's smile embraced them both. 'But when you are in company, you are insulting those around you by such secretive behaviour. Master Giles must know that, even if you are not quite old enough to appreciate it.'

Her mild rebuke hit its target. Gwendoline flushed and her brother muttered an apology.

The entrance of the tea tray caused a distraction. Lady Varley called Gwendoline over to help her prepare the tea. Juliana watched her go and turned back to Giles.

'If your sister resents me, I am sorry for it,' she said gently. 'However, your father hired me as her governess and I am obliged to correct her when it is necessary. It will help me greatly if you do not encourage her to flout my authority.'

'I—I don't, I wouldn't!'

She smiled at him. 'Then I am relieved, and very grateful to you.'

Flushing, Giles bowed, muttered his excuses, and lounged away. With a sigh, she went back to sit beside Wilhelmina.

'So, Gwendoline, what have you been doing today?' Lady Varley posed the question while she prepared the tea. 'What have you learned with Miss Wrenn?'

'In truth, Aunt, nothing.' Gwendoline put her chin in the air and cast a defiant look at Juliana.

The room was suddenly very still. Wilhelmina wriggled uncomfortably on her chair. The Major had been talking to Giles on the far side of the room, but now he looked up.

'What do you mean by that, Gwen?'

'That Miss Wrenn is a fraud, Papa,' declared Gwendoline with awful clarity. 'This morning we did nothing but shop— a frivolous exercise—and this afternoon…'

'This afternoon we studied England,' said Juliana calmly. 'With the use of maps Mr Brasher looked out for us, we plotted our journey, once we had calculated how far we might travel in one day. That, of course, meant we had to decide how fast the carriage could go. What did we decide was our likely speed, Wilhelmina?'

'Eight miles in an hour.'

'Yes, very good. Then we had to work out the distance between towns.'

'And stops for changing horses,' put in Wilhelmina, glad to be able to contribute again. 'Thomas thought of that!'

'Yes, he did.' Juliana nodded at her. 'So you see how we practised our powers of calculation and arithmetic. Then, of course, we looked up in the guidebook the towns we are likely to pass through. Barnet, of course, where we shall look out for the Barnet Pillar, put up to mark the famous battle.'

'That was where Edward IV beat Henry VI to become king,' said Wilhelmina.

'Yes, in 1471. And St Albans—what can you remember of St Albans, Wilhelmina?'

The little girl wrinkled her nose. 'There was a battle when Queen Margaret brought her army and rescued King Henry, but he could not have been a very good king, because Edward beat him at the Battle of Barnet.'

'Yes, and where else might we be travelling?'

'Derby,' said Wilhelmina, swinging her legs. 'Where the rebels turned back in the 'Forty-five and they were followed back into Scotland, where the King's brother followed them and killed them all!'

The Major raised his brows. 'A very bloodthirsty summary.'

Juliana chuckled. 'More interesting than mere dates and places, Major.'

'Undoubtedly. And from there, Minna?'

'Macclesfield,' cried the little girl. 'Where there are mills that weave fine silks for Aunt Louisa's shawls!'

Major Collingham laughed and patted her head. 'Very good.' He looked hard at Juliana. 'Perhaps Gwendoline was not paying attention today.'

'No, Major, I cannot blame her—for she was sewing a fine lawn handkerchief for Lady Varley as I talked. After all, it was never intended to be a serious lesson.'

Wilhelmina tugged at her father's sleeve. 'When we were out this morning, Miss Wrenn gave us a whole sixpence each to spend, as long as we could reckon up the pennies we had in change. And I did, Papa.'

He lifted her into his arms. 'How clever of you. Now, ten more minutes while we drink a dish of tea, then bed for you, children.' He set her on her feet and smiled over her head at Juliana. 'Congratulations, Miss Wrenn. You make the journey sound exciting, even to me. I have no doubt Gwendoline will take more interest in future.'

'I have always maintained that girls should be taught to know their way about,' declared Lady Varley, pouring tea into the delicate porcelain cups. 'Gwendoline, my dear, please take this cup to your father. Thank you. Yes, girls need to be able to read and write, and to reckon a column of figures, but beyond that there is little value in book learning for them.'

'But, ma'am, how are they to stand their ground with their brothers, or their husbands, without a matching education?' objected Juliana.

Lady Varley shook her head. 'A man doesn't want a clever wife, Miss Wrenn. He wants a dutiful one. Gwendoline, this cup to Miss Wrenn, if you please.'

'An educated woman may still be dutiful,' put in the Major.

'Unless her husband is particularly dull-witted,' murmured Juliana.

Major Collingham laughed.

'A clever woman will learn to have her own way,' replied Lady Varley, 'but she does not need an education for that.'

Juliana looked up. The Major was watching her, and she found herself responding to the smile in his eyes. Gwendoline approached with a cup of tea, but as she reached out for it, the girl stumbled and the contents of the cup were thrown over Juliana's best grey gown.

There was an immediate commotion. The Major berated Gwendoline on her clumsiness and she burst into tears. Giles came forward to defend his sister, while Lady Varley bewailed the broken cup.

Juliana stooped to collect up the pieces.

'Pray, Major, do not scold her. I am sure it was an accident. Master Giles, ring the bell and fetch a servant to clear up this mess, if you please.' She rose, looking down at her wet gown and trying to hide her dismay. 'Let me take the children upstairs, sir. It is their bedtime.'

He was still looking thunderous.

'Very well. Leave them with Nurse and give your dress to Mrs Hartley. She will know what to do to clean it. You will then put on a fresh gown and come back here.'

Lady Varley stared at him. 'Damon!'

'Really, sir,' stammered Juliana, 'I should retire—'

'You will come back, Miss Wrenn.'

His tone was implacable and she knew it was useless to argue. Closing her lips firmly, she nodded, took Wilhelmina by the hand and led the two girls out of the room.

Her silence as they went up to the schoolroom seemed to unnerve Gwendoline. She said, 'It was an accident, you know.'

'If you say so.'

'Will the stain come out?'

What do you care? thought Juliana, and immediately scolded herself for being as childish as her charges. She said, 'I hope so. I do not have the luxury of another silk gown.'

'We could buy you one in Macclesfield,' suggested Wilhelmina.

Juliana squeezed her hand and forced a smile. 'Yes, we could. In the meantime, let us hope the housekeeper is as good as your papa says.'

She handed the children over to Nurse and went off to change into her only other evening gown, a cream robe with long sleeves caught up with lime-green ribbons. It was the last gown her father had bought for her, and she had been saving it for a special occasion. It occurred to her that there would not now be any special occasions, for a while at least. She threw a black silk shawl about her shoulders and looked at herself in the mirror.

'Far too bright for mourning.' She sighed. 'However, he insists I return, so it will have to do.'

Pausing only to say goodnight to Amy and Thomas, who were already in their beds, she ran lightly down the stairs and back to the drawing room. There was a martial light in her eyes as she walked in, but the Major merely nodded at her and Lady Varley addressed her with unusual graciousness. 'I have made more tea so that you may join us, Miss Wrenn. I was mortified at my niece's clumsiness.'

'No matter, ma'am. Mrs Hartley has taken the gown to clean it.'

'You shall have a new one, I will buy it for you,' announced the Major abruptly.

Lady Varley cast a sympathetic look at Juliana as she handed her a cup.

'It is so simple for my brother, Miss Wrenn. He says he will buy you a new gown, as if there were any number made up, just waiting for you to choose one. You forget, Damon, that you leave town on Friday. Why, even Madame Fleurie could not turn out a decent gown in such a short time. Although I have been most surprised at her endeavours on my behalf this week—she called here today for a fitting and I had only chosen the muslin yesterday! And that reminds me, dear brother. I must crave your indulgence and ask you to let me stay on here for a few more days after you leave for the north, because my gowns are not complete, and although I have had word from Sir James, begging me to return as soon as ever I can, I really must stay in town until all my gowns are ready.'

'Yes, yes, Louisa, but you are straying from the point. Surely you know where to buy a new gown for Miss Wrenn that she can take with her?'

'Sir, I pray you, it is no matter,' put in Juliana, distressed by so much attention. 'I am sure there will be no lasting damage; besides, I will not be requiring such a gown again for some months.'

'Well, you may leave one of your old dresses with me, Miss Wrenn,' pronounced Lady Varley. 'I will have my modiste make up another to fit and it shall be sent on after you. Not another word, Miss Wrenn, my mind is made up. Now, let us talk of something else—Damon, did you go to White's today? I hear Meyler was there, telling everyone that Mr Brummell is quite done up.'

The Major frowned. 'Aye, I saw him.'

'I have never liked Meyler. Bad *ton*, I always thought.' She refilled her brother's teacup. 'How has Mr Brummell taken it?'

'I have no idea. He was not there.'

'But this is not good enough, brother. I made sure you would know.'

The Major shook his head. 'I admire Brummell's style of dress, Louisa, not his way of living.'

Giles had been sitting quietly in the corner all this time, but now he came forward. 'I thought you were one of his friends, Papa.'

'Sufficiently so that I would not listen to Meyler's accusations. However, it is for the Beau to refute them.'

'And will he do so, do you think?' asked Lady Varley.

'With Brummell one never knows. He has come about in the past: we shall see what he does over the next few days.'

However, Thursday morning brought even more exciting news for Lady Varley. Juliana had already joined the Major and his daughters in the breakfast room when she came in, saying as she took her place at the table, 'Damon, you will never guess! I have had word that Lady Maltby is in town. I must call upon her this morning.'

'Must you, Louisa?' asked the Major, helping himself to a cup of coffee.

Lady Varley gave a little sigh. 'Of course I must. She is James's cousin, you know, and I would not want to be thought backward in paying her any attention.'

'Especially since she is a viscountess,' he murmured.

'And what if she is?' retorted Lady Varley. 'Family connections are important. I shall take Gwendoline and Wilhelmina with me, if Miss Wrenn will give them leave—Lady

Maltby was very taken with the girls when she came to stay with us last year.'

'Ooh, yes, please. May we go, Miss Wrenn?' asked Wilhelmina.

Gwendoline said nothing, but Juliana saw her hopeful glance.

'Of course,' she said, 'if Major Collingham agrees.'

He shrugged. 'If that is what you wish, Louisa...'

'Damon, how can you be so tiresome! A connection with the viscountess could be very useful for the girls when it comes to finding them husbands.'

Major Collingham gave a bark of laughter. 'Good God, I trust I have several years before I need to address that issue!'

'One should always be prepared,' replied his sister. 'Now, come along, girls, finish your breakfast, for we must make you ready. Miss Wrenn, I do hope I am not interfering with your plans?'

'Not at all. I have to collect some last-minute purchases, which I can do this morning while you are out.'

'I will send one of the maids with you—'

'Oh, there will be no need for that, Major,' Juliana interrupted him quickly. 'I shall have Thomas and Amy with me—there is no need for any other companion.'

The Major would not countenance Miss Wrenn and her family taking a hackney carriage and, as Lady Varley would be using the landau, he ordered his own travelling carriage to be made ready. This was a large, impressive vehicle complete with liveried servants hanging on the back, and Juliana was not surprised to see a group of ragged boys standing on the opposite side of the road, watching with interest as the carriage rolled away.

'This is the carriage we shall be using for our journey,'

she told Amy and Thomas. 'Miss Gwendoline and Wilhelmina will be travelling with us, while Nurse and the Major's man will follow in the baggage coach.'

'And Major Collingham will be leading the way in his curricle, with Mr Giles beside him,' added Thomas. 'We shall create quite a stir when we drive through the town.'

'And there will be plenty of room for the five of us in here,' Juliana observed, leaning back with an appreciative sigh against the padded seat.

'Then we will be able to bring Sarah and Lady Arabella?' asked Amy, holding her doll on her lap.

Juliana smiled at her. 'Yes. They shall have a seat to themselves.'

Due to the press of traffic in New Bond Street, Juliana had decided it would be quicker to walk between the shops and she ordered the coachman to pull up and wait for her. The errands were soon accomplished, ending with a visit to Hatchards the booksellers, and with the children beside her she began to retrace her steps. They had not gone far when she saw Major Collingham walking towards them. He stopped, looking a little surprised.

'Miss Wrenn. I had thought you would be in New Bond Street, buying bonnets and gloves.'

'I would not bring Tom and Amy along for *that*, they would find it very tedious work. No, you will see that our parcels are quite small—paper and pens for drawing, and I have purchased more reading books. I ordered them Tuesday and they promised to have them ready for me today. We are on our way back to the carriage now.'

'I, too, have concluded my business, so I will walk with you, if I may?'

He turned to accompany her. Juliana took his proffered

arm, glancing back to make sure the two children were close behind.

'And have you ordered another gown, Miss Wrenn, as I instructed?'

'No. Mrs Hartley has worked miracles with my grey silk and it will be ready to take with me tomorrow.' She saw he was looking severe and added, 'Lady Varley has already wrested an old gown from me, and will use it as a pattern for the new one that is being made up for me. She has promised to send it on as soon as it is ready.'

'Quite right. I am very sorry for what happened last night.'

'It was an accident.'

'We both know it was nothing of the kind,' he retorted. 'Gwendoline does not want you to come with us. I shall talk to her today, and make sure she understands I will not tolerate her disobedience.'

She stopped. 'Oh, pray do not be harsh on her, sir. It—it might make her resent me even more.'

Major Collingham turned to look at her. 'Then what would you have me say, Miss Wrenn?'

Juliana hesitated. She said slowly, 'I think we should agree that if Gwendoline is of the same mind when we reach Lancashire, we will terminate the contract. She will learn little from me if we are constantly at loggerheads.'

'Rousseau's teachings, Miss Wrenn?'

'Common sense, Major. I will do my best to make her like me, but you know that we cannot always order our affections.'

'And you would have me tell her that she may decide once we get to Blackthorpe?'

'Why, yes. I would like Gwendoline to know that I have no wish to inflict myself upon her against her will.'

'But to leave then—you would be miles from your home, Miss Wrenn.'

'I have no home now, sir,' she said quietly. 'There are no relatives to make it desirable for me to remain here. I can as easily find employment in the big towns of the north, and—'

A scream and commotion behind them made her break off. Turning, Juliana saw that Tom and Amy had fallen some way behind, and Thomas was fighting with two larger boys while Amy stood behind him, screaming for help. Passersby hesitated, but the Major was there before any of them could act. Grabbing Thomas's assailants by their ragged collars he pulled them away and banged their heads together. The two boys staggered back and, as the Major turned his attention to Thomas, they tore themselves free and took to their heels.

Juliana had snatched Amy into her arms, but now she turned to her little brother. He was panting heavily and holding a handkerchief to his bloody nose.

'In heaven's name, what happened?' she asked as Amy sobbed against her shoulder.

'They—they pounced on Amy,' Thomas said thickly.

'Aye, I saw it.' An old gentleman stopped beside them. 'Dashed footpads, to attack a child, and in daylight too. Scoundrels!'

Juliana nodded, unable to speak. Silently she hugged Amy and watched while the Major took out his own handkerchief and began to wipe the blood from a cut over Thomas's eye.

'Don't worry, this looks worse than it is. There, that's better. Well done, my boy. You gave a good account of yourself there. But you are sadly lacking in science.' He straightened and patted Thomas on the shoulder. 'Remind me to give you a few lessons.'

'I will not have you teaching Thomas such a rough sport,' objected Juliana.

'I would teach him to defend himself better, Miss Wrenn,' retorted the Major.

'Coo, sis, this is nothing,' said Thomas. He looked up at Major Collingham and added shyly, 'I should very much like to learn to box, sir. To learn properly, that is.'

'Well, we can discuss that later,' said Juliana. 'For now we should take you both back to the carriage. If I stand you down, Amy, do you think you could walk a little? There's a good girl.'

She gathered up her packages and the parcel of books that Thomas had dropped when he had rushed to defend his sister, then, with the children walking safely between herself and Major Collingham, they set off towards New Bond Street.

It was not to be expected that such exciting news could be kept secret. As soon as they were back at the house, Juliana took the children upstairs, where it was necessary to explain their dishevelled appearance to Nurse. Thomas and Amy lost no time in giving the kindly old retainer the full story, while she and Nelly, the chambermaid, did their best to repair the damage to clothes and persons.

Nurse confided only in Mrs Hartley, the housekeeper, but Nelly thought it a fine tale with which to regale her colleagues in the servants' hall, and although Lady Varley's superior dresser did not consort with the lower servants, she overheard enough to pass on the story to her mistress.

Thus it was that when Juliana brought Gwendoline and Wilhelmina to the drawing room that evening, the subject under discussion was not the visit to viscountess Maltby, but the attack upon Miss Amy Wrenn.

'My dear, I have made Damon tell me the whole.' Lady

Varley addressed Juliana as soon as she entered the room. 'How is little Amy, and Thomas, the brave boy?'

'They are fully recovered, ma'am, thank you. Thomas has an interesting black eye and a few cuts, but that is all, and he has enjoyed himself thoroughly over dinner, telling the Misses Collingham how he acquired his wounds.'

Lady Varley shook her head. 'You see, brother, why I insist on taking a footman about with me when I am in town? The streets are no longer safe.'

'You refine too much upon it, Louisa. Such attacks are not common.'

'I should not have let the children fall behind,' admitted Juliana. 'I can only think they believed Amy to be alone and unprotected.' She shuddered, then said in an attempt to throw off the gloom, 'At least the ruffians did not get away without some punishment; they will have very sore heads now, I think.'

She smiled gratefully at the Major.

'I hope so, Miss Wrenn, although I wish I had held on to them, and handed them over to the magistrate.'

'Well, 'tis too late for that now,' said Lady Varley. 'Tomorrow you leave for the north. What are your plans, Damon?'

'I have arranged three nights on the road, at Northampton, Derby and Macclesfield. We leave early tomorrow morning.'

'I am to ride in the curricle,' said Giles with a grin. 'I hope you will let me handle the ribbons, Papa.'

'Aye, for part of the journey.'

'But what of Fewell?' asked Lady Varley. 'You told me Benns is to go on ahead, but surely you will not travel without your groom as well as your valet.'

'By no means. He can sit up behind us or on one of the

coaches, if he would prefer it. Giles will act as my groom, when necessary.'

'Oh, by Jove, yes!' cried Giles. 'I can handle the yard of tin, and make sure we are not delayed at the turnpikes—'

'We will not be racing, Giles. I intend to keep in sight of the carriages.' The Major saw the disappointment in his son's face and his lips twitched. 'Well, most of the time.'

Lady Varley shuddered. 'Well, I wish you luck, brother. I brought the children with me from Kewhurst. Less than half a day's travel and that was enough for me.'

The Major's good humour was not diminished. He turned his sardonic glance upon Juliana. 'I think it is Miss Wrenn who needs your good wishes, Louisa. She will have charge of the children, not I!'

Chapter Seven

Inside the Major's elegant travelling carriage an air of excitement prevailed, even though the rain beat steadily against the roof and the windows were already misted.

Juliana smiled at her companions.

'I have bought a scrapbook,' she said. 'It is to be a record of our journey. We will all add notes and drawings of everything we see and do on our travels.'

Gwendoline looked at the rain-streaked window and pulled a face. 'There will be precious little to put in it.'

Juliana laughed. 'But we have not yet been travelling an hour. There will be plenty to add during our journey, never fear. But I agree that for the present there is very little to see, so we shall entertain ourselves instead with making up a story.'

Thomas looked up. 'Juliana is very good at make-believe.'

'Thank you, Thomas, but I want everyone to join in. We shall make up a story of great adventures and when we stop in the evenings you can write it down, if you wish, and draw pictures to illustrate it.'

'Well, I cannot think of anything.' Gwendoline pouted and turned to the window.

'No matter,' said Juliana. 'I am sure that Minna and Amy will start us off. First of all we need our characters.'

Amy held up her doll. 'One can be called Sarah.'

Wilhelmina leaned forward. 'And can we have Lady Arabella, too?'

'Of course.' Juliana smiled. 'But we must also have some male characters. Thomas?'

'Leo,' said Wilhelmina. 'And he can be a farmer.'

'That's too dull,' said Amy. 'He should be a…a doctor!'

'No, a sailor,' cried Thomas. 'And he can have a wooden leg, and just one eye!'

Gwendoline looked round. 'That's silly,' she said. 'He would not be a hero.'

'Oh, yes, he would,' retorted Thomas. 'Lord Nelson had only one eye, and one arm.' He saw Juliana frowning at him and added pacifically, 'We could have another hero, if you want.'

'Very well.' Gwendoline thought for a moment. 'He will be called Roland, and he will be a soldier.'

Juliana sat back while the children continued to create their make-believe world. Even Gwendoline was drawn in, and the morning was spent discussing the lives of their favourite characters, until they made their first stop at a wayside inn and the children tumbled out of the carriage and into the inn, still chattering.

The Major raised his brows as he helped Juliana to alight.

'Congratulations, Miss Wrenn. I thought you would have been at cap-pulling by now.'

He took her arm and hurried her through the rain to the inn.

'Not yet, Major. They have decided to write a novel, where the hero and heroine will undergo the most appalling hardships.' She laughed as she preceded him indoors. 'You would be amazed to know the gruesome fate they have in store for the poor villain.' She stopped and put a hand to her mouth. 'Oh—that is, pray do not think that I allow them to run too wild in their imaginings, sir. I—'

'You do not need to explain to me,' he said, stripping off his gloves. 'I trust you.'

He reached out and brushed a curl of wet hair off her face. She flushed, partly at his words, and partly at his touch. She had to steel herself not to rub her cheek against his hand.

'You t-trust me? Oh, but…'

He looked amused.

'Come, Miss Wrenn. You told me yourself that you have impeccable credentials.' He took pity on her confusion and explained. 'I drove to Clapham on the day you moved into Burlington Street, to follow up your references with your old schoolmistress. She gave a glowing account of you. You look surprised—do you really think I would entrust my children to the care of a stranger?'

'Many fathers do so.'

'I am not one of them.' He guided her through the passage, where the landlord was holding open the door to a private parlour. 'So, Miss Wrenn, I have every confidence in you.'

It was not to be expected that the good mood of the party would last for ever. As soon as they had eaten, Juliana shepherded her charges back to their coach, but the novelty of travelling had worn off and the two younger girls were tired and fractious. The older children took two of the corner seats, where Thomas proceeded to fall asleep and Gwendoline stared out of the window at the rain, yawning openly and declaring that she was bored. Sitting between Wilhelmina and Amy on the other bench seat, Juliana settled the children against her and began to tell fairy stories.

Another hour passed. There was no easing of the rain, and as they travelled farther from London the state of the roads became worse until they were little more than rutted tracks that slowed their progress at times to walking pace. Juliana soon realised that the Major's first easy stage would not be accomplished until well into the evening.

Chapter Eight

The Northampton hotel that the Major's secretary had arranged for them could not be faulted, but by the time the travelling carriage drew up at its welcoming portal, the children were too tired to do more than pick at the choice dinner set out for them in the private parlour that had been reserved for the sole use of the schoolroom party. As soon as the children were settled in their beds, Juliana went in search of Major Collingham, who had been allocated private rooms on the first floor away from the bustling main street. She found the Major and his son sitting over the remains of their dinner.

'Oh, I am sorry. I will come back....'

They rose.

'No, come in, Miss Wrenn. We have finished now, and Giles was about to go out and check the horses for me.'

Giles laughed.

'As any good groom should,' he said, and with a bow to Juliana he went off.

Juliana waited until the door had closed behind the young man, then looked at the Major, clasping her hands before her.

'I wanted to speak to you, sir.'

'I realise that. Have you eaten?'

'Yes. I dined with the children.'

He took her elbow and led her to the table. 'With four tired children to look after, I doubt you had time for more than a mouthful. Sit down. There is plenty of food here.'

'Oh, but I had Nurse to help me. I—I couldn't—'

He ignored her protests and she found herself sitting at the dining table, a clean plate set before her and instructions to help herself from the assortment of cold meat on the platter. The Major poured her a glass of wine, topped up his own glass, then pulled up a chair and sat down, watching her.

'I was right, you are hungry. Did you eat *anything* of your own dinner?'

'At the time it seemed more important to feed the children,' she admitted. 'That is why I wanted to talk to you....'

'Later, Miss Wrenn. Let me recommend you to take a peach—they are excellent.'

'Peaches, so early?'

'I had them sent up to town from my own succession houses and brought some with me.'

She watched him select a ripe fruit from the dish and carefully cut it into pieces for her.

'You are very kind.'

'Nonsense. I am merely looking after my investment. If you do not eat, you will not be fit to take care of the girls.' He pushed the plate of prepared fruit towards her, his eyes narrowing as he saw her hesitate. 'Eat it, Miss Wrenn. Or would you like me to feed you?'

He had turned to face her, one arm resting along the back of her chair. He was too close, too intimate, the gleam in his eye definitely dangerous. Suddenly it was easy to imagine him as Devil Collingham, choosing a slice of peach to offer her, those strong fingers picking up the delicate fruit in a gentle clasp that did not bruise it and holding it to her lips…

Juliana felt herself blushing. Heavens, what had come over her? She sought to cover her confusion by saying crossly, 'Do you always impose your will on people, sir?'

'Only when it is necessary. You eat barely enough to sustain a bird. A wren, perhaps.'

She ignored him and popped a slice of peach into her mouth. It was sweet and succulent, made all the sweeter because he had prepared it for her. As she raised her napkin to her lips, her hand trembled. Sweet heaven, such idle thoughts must be suppressed. She had heard of many poor women who had developed a slavish adoration for men with power over them. Indeed, in her own home some of the female servants had become infatuated with her father and she knew of more than one family where the governess was blatantly besotted with the master of the house. She had thought them all poor creatures, objects of ridicule. It would not happen to her, she would not allow it.

'Miss Wrenn?'

'I—oh—my apologies, Major. Wh-what did you say?'

'I merely asked if you would like more wine.'

'No. No, thank you.' She pushed her chair back and rose. 'Your kindness has almost made me forget my reason for being here.'

He sat back in his chair and watched her. 'And what was that?'

She began to pace the room, frowning over her words. 'To ask if you could send a message to Mr Brasher, to make new arrangements for the morrow. This wet weather has turned the roads to a quagmire and I fear it will disrupt your—our plans. It was full eight o'clock before we reached Northampton, sir. Far too late for the children.'

'Impossible.'

She stopped before him. 'For myself, sir, I do not object to the long hours in the coach, but the children—'

'Madam, I have no wish to make the children suffer, but Brasher is even now at Derby. How do you expect me to contact him?'

'You could send a messenger.'

He got up and strode to the window. 'No, Miss Wrenn. I am sorry, but the arrangements must stand. We travelled greater distances in the Peninsula, you know, and over rougher ground.'

'But you are not eight years old,' she persisted. 'And then there is Nurse. She says nothing, but I know her hip is paining her from sitting for such long periods.'

She waited anxiously for his reply. He did not speak, but looked out at the leaden sky and the steady rain puddling in the lane below.

'Tomorrow may be better. If that is the case, we shall reach Derby and the hotel Brasher has secured for us with time to spare.'

'But—'

'No more, Miss Wrenn.' He turned to face her. 'It has been an exceptionally wet spring, but the rain cannot go on for ever, you know.'

Juliana knew it would be useless to argue further. She returned to her rooms, where she found Nurse waiting for her, sitting in a chair with one foot upon a gout stool, her hands busy with her knitting.

'Well, miss, what did he say?' She lowered her knitting to her lap.

'The Major thinks we shall do better tomorrow, if the rain stops.'

'There you are, then,' said Nurse, picking up her needles

again. 'If the master sees no difficulties, then we shall do. He is a seasoned traveller, after all.'

'But even he cannot control the weather,' Juliana pointed out.

Nurse gave a comfortable smile.

'When you've known the master a little longer, miss, you will learn to trust him, as I do.'

Closing her lips against an unwise retort, Juliana retired to her bed, aware that Nurse was exhibiting the trait she most despised in a female, slavish devotion to the master.

Chapter Nine

Juliana made sure her charges were ready to travel at the appointed time the following morning and greeted the Major with determined cheerfulness. It was a dry morning, but from the lowering clouds Juliana thought the respite would be brief, and by the time they had reached Market Harborough a steady rain was falling. The muddy road was stony and uneven and the coachman was obliged to slow down to walking pace, for the large puddles gave no sign of how deep the ruts might be. At last they pulled into the stable yard to change horses at Oadby, and even before they had come to a halt Giles was at the door.

'It was not planned, but Father says we will stop here for a short while, so that the children may have luncheon,' he announced, preparing to hand Juliana out of the carriage. She threw up her hood over her bonnet and descended to the yard, where she was glad to hang on to Giles's arm as they crossed the slippery cobbles. Giles left her at the door, saying he would go back and help Nurse. Juliana gathered the children together and they followed the landlord to a large parlour, where they found the Major standing before a cheerful fire.

'Now that is a welcome sight,' she exclaimed, untying the strings of her cloak. 'There is nothing like a good blaze to make one feel more the thing on a wet day.'

The Major took her cloak from her. 'We have not made the progress I intended. No doubt you would like to say I told you so?'

She twinkled up at him. 'No, sir. That would be very ignoble of me.'

His lips twitched. 'It would indeed, Miss Wrenn, and you are too magnanimous for that, are you not?'

'Of course. Now, if you have bespoken a bedroom from our host, I will take the children upstairs to tidy themselves.' She glanced at the large table set with eight chairs. 'Are we to eat together?'

'You will hardly expect an inn of this size to have more than one private parlour.'

The Major's retort made her smile. She shepherded the children towards the door, saying over her shoulder, 'Then we shall be delighted to have you join us, Major Collingham.'

Juliana had to admit that the party gathered for luncheon was a large one. She had suggested that she and Nurse could dine with Thomas and Amy in an upstairs chamber, but the Major would have none of it.

'Good heavens,' said Nurse as she came in, 'this is a real family party and no mistake.'

Following Nurse into the room, Juliana bit her lip hard to prevent herself from laughing aloud at the look of unease on the Major's face.

'You need not fear, sir. The children's table manners are excellent.' She smiled at him. 'They will not disturb you with their chatter.'

'No, but we have not started our meal yet, so I can ask

Papa how he likes my hair,' said Wilhelmina. 'Miss Wrenn braided it specially, so that I would look well for you.'

'Very smart,' he replied gravely. 'And did Miss Wrenn help you with your hair, Gwen?'

'Miss Gwendoline did not need assistance,' said Juliana. 'She is very able.'

'But you showed me how to make the ends curl,' admitted Gwendoline, determined to be fair.

'Does this betoken a truce?' murmured the Major to Juliana as he held her chair for her.

'I hope so,' she replied quietly.

'Well, well, so like old times!' Nurse beamed around the table. 'It quite takes me back to when I had Master Damon and your aunt Louisa in my nursery.'

'And were they troublesome?' asked Giles, grinning at his father.

'Not a bit of it. Good as gold, they were, although it did help that I could get about better in those days, and did not need a stick. Such a lot of travelling as we did then. The family would spend the spring and summer at Kewhurst or London, then off to Blackthorpe Hall for the autumn and winter, when the old master wasn't away visiting his friends.'

'Did the children go too?' asked Gwendoline.

'Of course, my dear. The mistress, your grandmother, God rest her soul, liked to have Master Damon and his sister with her whenever she could, so we travelled with them to each one of their houses. Of course, I was younger then, and the journeys didn't affect my bones so much.'

'You have only to travel a little farther today,' said the Major, helping himself to a slice of the huge pie in the centre of the table. 'I have spoken to the landlord, and there is a very decent inn, the Queen's Head, at Loughborough. Less than twenty miles from here.'

Giles looked up.

'I thought we were stopping at Derby tonight, Papa.'

'It would take too long to reach Derby.' His glance flickered to Juliana. 'I have sent Fewell ahead to reserve rooms at the Queen's Head.'

'Will Lady Frances be waiting for us at Blackthorpe, Papa?' asked Wilhelmina.

'No, silly, she has her own house,' said Gwendoline. She turned her dark eyes towards her father. 'Is she already in Lancashire, sir?'

'I have no idea,' returned the Major. 'I expect so; she knows I am coming north.'

'Then we will meet her before the wedding.' Wilhelmina nodded. 'I am glad of that.'

Major Collingham looked amused. 'Of course you will meet her. I would not foist a new mother on you without giving you time to get to know her.'

'You foisted Miss Wrenn upon us,' said Gwendoline.

A nervous silence fell over the table. Outside the rain pattered against the window, the sky as dark as the scowl on Major Collingham's face. Juliana caught his eye and gave a tiny shake of her head, silently begging him not to reprimand his daughter. He seemed to understand her. Instead he growled, 'It would not have been necessary, had you not driven away your old governess.'

'Well, I am *glad* Miss Wrenn is with us,' declared Wilhelmina, 'because now I have Amy to play with.'

'Perhaps, sir, you would tell the children a little something about Lady Frances,' said Nurse, anxious to turn the conversation.

'Yes, Papa, please do,' Giles urged him.

The Major shrugged. 'What would you have me say? I have known Frances since she was a girl. She married Rid-

lington, my neighbour, but since his death she has spent
much of the time with her parents.'

Gwendoline looked up. 'She is the daughter of an earl, is
she not, Papa?' she asked.

'Yes, Lord and Lady Mattishall.'

'And is she very beautiful?'

'I believe she is considered so.'

'And accomplished?' persisted Gwendoline. 'Can she
sing, and play the piano, and speak many languages?'

'Of course. She has had the benefit of an excellent education.'

A veritable paragon, thought Juliana, her spirits sinking.

The road into Loughborough was in a particularly poor
state of repair and the constant rain had turned much of it into
a running stream. The carriages bumped and jolted along at
a snail's pace. Juliana amused the children with songs and
stories until they reached the edge of the town, when they all
gave their attention to looking out for their destination. The
Queen's Head turned out to be a good-size coaching inn
with an impressive frontage, two bay windows flanking a
wide doorway. Juliana climbed down thankfully from the
carriage and took the children inside, where Major Collingham was already in discussion with the landlord, who was
explaining regretfully that he did not have sufficient rooms
to meet the Major's requirements. Juliana listened for a
moment, then she went over, put a hand on the Major's arm
and drew him aside.

'I believe we could manage, sir. From what I overheard, the
landlord has four bedrooms free for tonight: Nurse and the two
younger girls could share one room, Gwendoline and I another.
That would leave a room for Giles and Thomas, and one for
yourself. I am sure he could find somewhere for your groom.'

The children had gathered round, and Amy now tugged at her sister's sleeve.

'Yes, please, I want to share with Minna.'

Juliana smiled down at her. 'I know, my love,' she said gently, 'but it is for Miss Gwendoline and Wilhelmina to decide. Well, girls?' She looked at Gwendoline, well aware that she was torn between choosing to sleep with her little sister or sharing with a governess she was determined to dislike.

'Let Minna and Amy sleep together. I will share with Miss Wrenn.'

Juliana tried not to allow too much of her relief to show. She looked an enquiry at the Major.

'That still leaves the problem of one parlour.'

'I am sure you endured much worse hardships in the army, Major.'

'Of course, but that was with…'

'That was with your comrades?' she finished for him. 'Then surely to share a parlour with your family will be a pleasure.'

His eyes narrowed. 'I can hardly contradict you, madam, when they are listening to every word.'

She laughed. 'No, so pray tell the good man that we will take it, and we can order dinner.'

Juliana approached the dinner table that evening with some trepidation. In Burlington Street it had been the custom for the Major to see the children at breakfast and for only an hour after dinner. Now, not only had they all taken luncheon together, but would be confined to one room for the whole of the evening. Nurse had elected to take her dinner in her room and Juliana had at first suggested that Thomas and Amy should join her, but Major Collingham had overruled her, saying that if he was obliged to dine with his own young-sters he did not see that another two would make much dif-ference. His tone was not encouraging, but Juliana was becoming used to his brusque manner and she hoped he would not find himself out of patience with such childish company. In the event she found the Major perfectly affable, the children were all on their best behaviour and since the dinner was good, if plain, fare, the meal passed off much better than she had expected. However, the long day's travel had taken its toll, and by the time the covers were removed both Amy and Wilhelmina were almost asleep at the table. Juliana rose to take the girls to their rooms, but the Major waved to her to sit down again.

'You have not finished your wine. Giles will take them all upstairs and deliver them to Nurse.'

'Of course, Father.' Giles rose. 'With your permission, sir, I was going to check the horses. Fewell thought one of the carriage horses was blowing too much, and feared a touch of colic.' He hesitated. 'Perhaps Tom would like to come out with me?'

'Ooh, yes, please!'

Juliana nodded.

'What a kind young man he is,' she said, as the young people left the room. 'Thomas is very impressed with your horses, Major, and will welcome the chance to see more of them.'

He refilled her glass from the decanter on the table. 'I will ask Dawlish to let him sit up on the box for a spell tomorrow.'

'Tomorrow? Surely you will not travel on a Sunday, sir.'

'We are already behind on our journey, Miss Wrenn.' She did not reply, and after a brooding glance at her face he set down his glass with a snap. 'Hell and damnation, we will never get to Lancashire if we do not press on.'

'It is only one more day, Major.'

He scowled, but she was not to be intimidated.

'Naturally if you were travelling alone the case might be different, but you would not wish to subject your children to censorious gossip.'

'And who the devil is there to see them?' he demanded.

Juliana did not reply, and feigned deafness as he cursed quietly beneath his breath.

'Oh, very well,' he said at last. 'We will remain here for another night. I shall send a man ahead to Blackthorpe to advise Brasher that we will be delayed.' He bent a frowning look at her. 'I hope you don't object to a *servant* riding on a Sunday?'

'I believe that will be unavoidable, Major.'

The scowl disappeared and he laughed suddenly.

'By God, you are a cool one.'

'You employed me to do a job, sir, and I take my responsibilities very seriously.'

'I'm glad to hear it. So what do you plan to do with yourself tomorrow?'

'Perhaps you would like the children to go to church. Then, if it is dry, I shall take them for a walk.'

He glanced out of the window. 'The sky is certainly clearing, but even if it does not rain again tonight, the road will be muddy.'

'The girls all have pattens to put over their shoes. I am a great believer in exercise.'

The rain held off that night, and the following morning, after a visit to the local church, Juliana took the girls out for the promised walk. Thomas had made good use of his introduction to the stables and there was more than a touch of pride in his voice when he told his sisters that he would not

be able to walk with them because he was going to help
Fewell in the stables. The walk was a pleasant one, keeping
to the main streets of the town. Amy and Wilhelmina skipped
ahead and Juliana used the time to talk to Gwendoline, asking
questions and gradually drawing the girl out. They returned
to the inn to find a fashionable cabriolet stopped at the front
door. The driver of this handsome black equipage was
leaning down to converse with the landlord, who was scratching his head. Seeing Miss Wrenn approach with the children,
the landlord nodded towards her.

'Perhaps you should address yourself to the lady, sir. She
is with Major Collingham's party.'

The gentleman looked up and seemed a little discom-
posed.

'Oh—oh, yes. Well, my good man, if you will have one
of your boys drive this rig to the stables, you can take my
bag up to my room.'

'Well, if you'd said in the first place that you was wishing
to stay…' the landlord grumbled as he took the gentleman's
bag; calling to one of his lads to take the gentleman's carriage
round to the back, he disappeared inside.

Juliana was at the door by this time. The gentleman
jumped down and swept off his curly-brimmed beaver hat
as he made her an elegant bow. He was a pleasant looking
young man, with sandy hair brushed back from a pale brow
and light brown eyes that held a hint of diffidence as he
smiled at her.

'Your pardon, madam, you must be wondering who I am.'
His smile encompassed them all, and the three girls looked up
at him with undisguised curiosity. 'My name is Leeson, Charles
Leeson. I believe Major Collingham is putting up here?'

Juliana nodded. 'I am merely governess to the children,
sir. If you have business with the Major—'

He disclaimed quickly, 'No, no, I am travelling north to visit relatives and have to break my journey, and if this is good enough for Collingham...'

'But is it just gone noon, you could travel for hours yet,' observed Gwendoline.

Mr Leeson looked a little taken aback, but after a slight hesitation he laughed. 'I could, indeed, Miss Collingham, but my horse has been on the go since dawn and I need to keep him fresh for the long haul tomorrow.'

'Papa would not let us travel on a Sunday,' remarked Wilhelmina.

Mr Leeson nodded. 'Yes, well, there you have it. I should not carry on today, should I? But you will not want to be standing out here with me, you will have a private sitting room, I suppose? Allow me to escort you to it.'

Juliana was surprised at this excess of gallantry, but gathered the girls together and ushered them into the wide passage. They had just finished removing their muddy pattens when the door of their parlour opened and Major Collingham came out, only to pull up short in the doorway when he saw them.

'Ah, Collingham, well met!' Mr Leeson stepped forward, nodding genially. 'Taking the family to Blackthorpe, I suppose?'

'Yes.'

Juliana was stooping to help Wilhelmina remove her gloves, but she looked up at the Major, surprised how discouraging he made the one word sound. However, Mr Leeson pressed on.

'Strange that we should both choose this inn to stop. Of course, the landlord was telling me that you have the only parlour, but I have a very pleasant room, he assures me, so I shall manage.'

Juliana wondered if he was expecting the Major to invite him to join them but if so, he was to be disappointed. Major Collingham merely looked at him until the gentleman gave another bow and moved off into the taproom in search of refreshment.

'What a strange man,' said Gwendoline, leading the way into the parlour. 'Is he a friend of yours, Papa?'

'An acquaintance, merely,' said the Major, shutting the door behind them.

'I think he wanted to share our parlour,' observed Wilhelmina.

The Major grunted. 'Enough that I must have the whole family plus their attendants in here!'

Juliana looked up. 'You have had the room to yourself all morning, sir, have you not?'

'Well, yes. Nurse has kept to her chamber and Giles and your brother have not yet come in from the stables.'

Juliana removed her bonnet. 'Then you will not object to a little company this afternoon,' she told him serenely. 'The children will be making a start on our journal, and then we shall be reading *Gulliver's Travels*. You are very welcome to join us.'

'Thank you, but I have letters to write.'

The entrance of Giles and Thomas at that moment caused a diversion, and as the talk turned towards horses, Juliana took the girls upstairs to change out of their muddy dresses.

The day passed quietly enough and when they sat down to a family dinner, Juliana was relieved to find that the Major was in a particularly mellow mood. He was persuaded to tell them a little of his life as a soldier. His stories were told with humour, and tailored to his young audience, but Juliana guessed from the tightening of his jaw when he spoke of the heavy casualties suffered in the Peninsula, and then at Waterloo, that he had suffered deeply from the loss of his comrades. She was pleased to think he was not one to glory in the violence of war.

She did not linger after the meal, but took the four younger ones upstairs to their rooms, leaving the Major to discuss with Giles the revised plans for their journey north. The rain had kept off all day, and the Major had ordered an early start the following morning, so Juliana and Nurse were agreed that they should all go to bed at a reasonable hour. Juliana had never travelled so far before and she found the long hours in the coach exhausting, even though the Major's travelling carriage was very luxurious. She was glad to climb into her own bed as soon as she had settled her charges. She bade Gwendoline goodnight, snuffed out the candle and was soon fast asleep.

Chapter Ten

The Queen's Head was a busy posting inn with coaches arriving and departing throughout the night. The rooms allocated to Major Collingham's party stretched across the front of the inn and although there was some inevitable traffic driving past their windows, the noisy business of changing horses was carried out at the back. Thus when Juliana was awoken in the early hours of the morning she lay for a moment, wondering what had disturbed her. Then she heard it: the scraping of the door handle being turned. She lay in her bed, her heart thumping wildly. The door was bolted, and she thought that if the person outside should attempt to force an entry her screams would soon bring help. She opened her eyes, wondering what time it could be; it was very dark, a low cloud blotting out any light from the moon and stars. The handle turned again and Juliana sat up, fumbling for the tinder box. It was the work of a moment to light her candle and scramble out of bed. At the door she paused, straining her ears, but she could hear nothing. Finally she unbolted the door and stepped out in to the passage, holding her candle aloft.

'Where the devil do you think you are going?'

Juliana jumped and almost dropped her candlestick. She looked round to see Major Collingham standing outside his room. From the dim glow of her light she could see he was dressed only in his shirt and breeches.

'Someone tried the door of my room,' she said in a low voice. 'Was it you?'

He came towards her, his bare feet making no noise on the boards.

'At this ungodly hour? Of course not. Someone tried my door, too.'

A sudden shriek interrupted them. The Major pushed past her and dashed to the next room along, where Nurse was screaming and shouting while another, deeper voice struggled to make itself heard.

'Madam, my apologies—ouch! Madam, please—aah!'

As the Major reached the door a man appeared, followed closely by Nurse, who was setting about him with her stick. The Major grabbed his arm.

'Got you! Bring that candle closer, Miss Wrenn. Now then, let's have a look at you. Leeson! What in hell's name—?'

'Thief!' cried Nurse, still brandishing her stick. 'Breaking in, creeping about the room…'

'No, no, you mistake me!' cried Mr Leeson, cowering away from her. 'Damme, Collingham, tell her I ain't a thief! Merely mistook the room, that's all.' He was slurring his words, and even in the gleam of the single candle Juliana could see he was looking sheepish.

Major Collingham nodded to Nurse. 'The children are stirring, go and reassure them, if you please.'

'All a misunderstandin',' muttered Leeson as Nurse went back into the room. 'B-been imbibing a little too freely with our host, so I went out for a walk to clear my head—damned bad brandy he serves here, Collingham. Be advised by me, don't touch it.'

'The landlord shut up some hours ago,' said the Major, still holding his arm.

Mr Leeson swayed slightly.

'I know, but there was that p-pretty little chambermaid out in the yard, just waiting to—ah—entertain me.' He dug the Major in the ribs. 'You understand me, eh, Collingham? I know your reputation, devil in battle, devil in—'

'Yes, yes, enough.' Major Collingham pushed him away, his mouth twisting. Leeson did not appear to notice his disgust.

'Anyway,' he slurred on, 'came back in, couldn't remember my room. Simple mistake.'

'Then why did you not withdraw immediately, when you saw the room was occupied?' demanded Nurse, coming back out of her room.

'Too dark to see anything at first. I had just turned to leave again when the lady woke up.' He gave a shaky bow. 'My profound apologies for frightening you, madam.'

They heard footsteps on the stairs, and the landlord appeared, carrying a lantern in his hand, his nightcap askew on his head.

'What is it? What's amiss?' he hissed.

'Ah, our host.' Mr Leeson staggered towards him and clasped his shoulder. 'Can't for the life o' me remember where I'm sleepin'. Can you help, my good fellow?'

The landlord raised his brows as he looked at the little group.

'He went into one of our rooms,' explained the Major. 'Disturbed us all.'

'Then I am very sorry for it, sir.' The landlord took

Leeson's arm. 'Your chamber is this way, sir, on the next floor. Come along, I'll show you the way.'

'Well, what a to-do!' exclaimed Nurse as the landlord led his guest to the stairs.

'I will check on Giles and Thomas,' muttered the Major, disappearing into the darkness. Finding that Gwendoline had not stirred, Juliana slipped next door and went over to where Amy and Wilhelmina were tucked up in their beds.

'They are not harmed, miss,' Nurse whispered, standing beside her. 'They went back to sleep as soon as I told them all was well. In fact, I doubt if they will remember any of this in the morning. But it fair shook me up, it did, to wake up and find a man in the room, standing over the children's cots, he was! I feared for their lives, I did, so I set up such a scream and he turned and would have run out the door, but I got to him, and laid about him with my stick.'

'Well, no harm done,' said Juliana. 'Go back to bed, now, and let us hope the rest of the night passes more peacefully for you. There is a bolt on your door, Nurse—be sure you use it.'

'Yes, and so I will, miss. Goodness knows why I didn't do it first thing, then we would not have had all this commotion.'

'No, well, goodnight now.' Juliana left the room and was surprised to find the Major waiting for her outside. She said, 'The little ones are both asleep, and no sign of the room being disturbed. Gwendoline slept through the whole.'

'So did the boys.' Major Collingham nodded.

'They will be sorry to have missed so much excitement.' He did not smile, and she continued, 'It would appear the gentleman really did lose his way. He certainly smelled strongly of spirits.'

'Yes.' He frowned at her. 'But what were you thinking of, to come out here dressed like that?'

For the first time Juliana realised that she was wearing only her nightgown. She flushed.

'I might ask you the same question!' she retorted.

'I was prepared to apprehend a villain—what did you plan to do, swoon at his feet?'

'I never faint. Of course I was not going to accost him, but—'

'Well, thank God for that!' he interrupted her. 'He would have ravished you as soon as he saw you.'

Juliana gasped. She glanced down at herself: the ribbons at the neck of her nightgown had come loose and one white shoulder was exposed. The Major reached out and gently pulled the thin muslin back up over her arm. Juliana froze. She found she was unable to move as he calmly re-tied the ribbons at her neck. She noted how his white shirt seemed to glow in the candlelight. His fingers brushed her skin, setting up a tingle that raced through her veins and down into her very core.

'Th-thank you.'

Embarrassment seared through her; what a silly thing to say. She wished she could think of something witty, but her mind was as stodgy as the porridge slowly cooking in the kitchens for their breakfast. Suddenly he laughed.

'Jenny.'

'My name is Juliana, sir.'

'Jenny Wrenn,' he said firmly. 'You look up at me like a fragile little bird, entrusted to my care.'

She swallowed hard. It was very tempting to think that there was someone to care for her. She dare not raise her eyes, and found herself staring instead at the opening of his shirt, where a few crisp dark hairs were visible on his chest. Juliana felt a strong desire to step forward into his arms, to feel them close around her, protecting her from the world. Her heart began to race, as if she had suddenly become aware of some danger. Her hand holding the candlestick trembled so much that the hot wax dripped on to her fingers, recalling her to her senses. She moved back, putting more space between herself and the powerful figure who threatened her peace.

'I am a governess, Major Collingham.'

She could see the flame of the solitary candle reflected in his eyes as he looked at her. In the sudden silence the shadows danced eerily around them.

'Then you had best go to bed, Miss Wrenn, lest we forget that.' He turned and strode back to his own room, saying over his shoulder, 'And bolt your door!'

Despite the excitement of the night, Nurse brought the children to the breakfast table in good time the next morning. There was no sign of Mr Leeson, and upon enquiry the landlord shrugged and said the gentleman had not yet left his room. None of the girls had any recollection of the night's events, and after a warning glance from Juliana, Nurse merely said that a gentleman had been a little the worse for drink and caused a disturbance. As they settled down for another long day's journey, Juliana was left with an uneasy conviction that the greatest disturbance of the previous night had been to her own composure.

Chapter Eleven

Monday had dawned cloudy but dry, and the party set out in high spirits, to arrive in good time at Derby, where they stopped to take luncheon. The inn was large and commodious and when Juliana remarked upon it, Major Collingham informed her that he had originally planned to stop there overnight.

He was escorting her back to the carriage to resume their journey and she glanced around her. The inn was built up on three sides, with several floors of rooms reached by open galleries that overlooked the bustling courtyard.

'It is an excellent hostelry, I am sure, Major, but I have no doubt that the children's rest would have been disturbed by the constant noise of the coaches coming and going through the night.'

'If I know my man, Brasher would have booked rooms for us on the quiet side of the inn, with the two parlours as I ordered.'

Juliana paused at the coach steps. 'Then the children would not have had the pleasure of your company at dinner for the past two nights, sir.'

'A pleasure for them, perhaps, but I did not expect to spend my evenings with a schoolroom party.'

'No, of course not,' she said soothingly. 'And I admire the way you moderated your behaviour to suit the company.'

His black brows drew together. 'Just what are you implying, madam?'

She met his darkling look with her own innocent gaze. 'I know very little of the ways of gentlemen when they are on their own, Major, but is it not the fashion to drink to excess and to—er—swear like a trooper?'

'Not amongst my particular friends!'

'Oh. I thought that was why you needed a separate parlour for yourself, sir.'

He gave a crack of laughter. 'Baggage! Up into the carriage with you, Miss Wrenn, and after another full day with your charges, you tell me whether you, too, would not like a separate parlour!'

Their next overnight stop was to be at Leek; without the constant rain, Major Collingham was able to make much better progress in his curricle. Juliana soon lost sight of it and when at last the travelling carriage pulled up at the Greyhound Hotel, Giles was waiting to hand them down.

'Did you have any trouble at the turnpike?' he asked, assisting Nurse to alight. 'I am getting quite handy with the yard of tin now, and blew up in good time, but the old fellow moved at a snail's pace. We have been here for an age, and I have had time to see Father's cattle safely stabled and the curricle too, is under cover, which is a good thing, for it is threatening to rain again and it does it no good to be stood in the wet overnight, as it was at Loughborough. Here at least Fewell will be able to get the hood waxed to make it watertight again.'

Juliana looked up at their accommodation. The Greyhound was a large new building, erected to meet the needs of a prosperous, growing mill town.

'This looks big enough to afford the Major his separate room,' she murmured as Giles turned to help her down.

'Very likely, but Papa has reserved only the one parlour. I hope you do not dislike it, Miss Wrenn, but I told him that by some chance I had never read *Gulliver's Travels*, which you have been reading to the children, and I thought I might sit in again this evening, if you was to read some more, so Papa said that if we were all intent on being together, he would not sit in majestic isolation.'

Thus it was that once dinner was over and the dishes cleared away, Juliana found herself in a particularly domestic scene. The large room set aside for them faced full east and therefore did not benefit from the evening sun, but it glowed with the light of a dozen candles. Thomas and Gwendoline were playing backgammon on a small table while Minna and Amy worked on their samplers. Giles had taken a chair close to the empty fireplace where he was whittling a piece of wood into shape to replace a missing knight from his chess set. Juliana sat at the table with a pair of branched candles at her elbow as she read from Mr Swift's entertaining book. Nurse was dozing in her chair, her knitting lying abandoned in her lap, and only the Major had no secondary occupation. He had taken a chair in the far corner of the room, where he sat at his ease, his long legs stretched out before him and crossed at the ankles. Juliana was aware that he was watching her as she read aloud, but she did not allow it to affect her. Major Collingham had been driving all day, and it was quite reasonable to suppose that he was tired, and wanted only to relax.

At the end of a chapter she put down the book. Immediately Gwendoline looked up.

'Oh, can you not read a little more?'

'I am sorry, it is time for you to go to bed.'

Roused from her slumbers, Nurse tutted. 'I should think so, indeed. Why it is quite dark now.'

Gwendoline looked ready to argue and Juliana said cheerfully, 'An early start in the morning and we shall be at Blackthorpe Hall by tomorrow night, is that not so, Major?'

'Aye. It is little more than fifty miles from here.' He rose. 'Come, Gwen. Kiss me goodnight and go to bed—tomorrow you shall be in your own room.'

'I will, Papa!' Wilhelmina ran forward to be swung up into the Major's arms.

'Goodnight, sweeting.' He kissed her and set her back on her feet. 'Off you go now, and be a good girl. Gwen…' He bent to kiss her cheek, '…goodnight, my dear.'

'What a tiring thing it is to travel,' sighed Nurse when they had finished putting the children to bed. 'I declare I am ready to drop, and it is not yet ten o'clock. And I have the children's samplers to pack away, yet.'

'I will go down and take care of that,' said Juliana.

'Would you, dearie? I would take it as a kindness, for my old knees object to going up and down these stairs more than once, I can tell you.'

Juliana patted her arm. 'Then stay here and rest. I will make sure the children's sewing and games are all packed away in readiness for the morning.'

She went back to the parlour, where only the candles on the table were still burning. She jumped as a figure detached itself from a shadowed corner.

'Oh, Major Collingham. I thought everyone had retired…'

'Not yet. I did not expect you to come back.'

'The girls' sewing things.' She waved towards the litter of silks and fabric on the table. 'It will be in the way when the maid comes to set the table for breakfast in the morning.'

'Well, then, when you have packed that away, if you are not too tired, perhaps you would indulge me in a game of backgammon?'

'Oh. Well, yes, of course, if you wish. But—could not Master Giles…?'

'My son has gone to bed, taking with him your book. I hope you do not mind that he has borrowed it?'

'Not at all. I am pleased that he has taken an interest.'

'It is an entertaining tale, and a good choice for a journey, Miss Wrenn.'

She gathered up the silks and put them into the workbasket, but as she did so she watched him setting out the backgammon counters.

'The table is cleared now—perhaps you would like to move the board here?'

'Why? This little table was sufficient for Gwen and Thomas.' He came to pick up the branched candlestick. 'This should be sufficient light for us. When you are ready, Miss Wrenn.'

She quickly finished packing away the children's samplers and threads and placed the basket in the windowsill. Then she took her seat at one side of the low table. The Major had placed the candlestick on the mantelshelf, from where it cast a flickering yellow light over the board.

'I should tell you that I am considered something of an expert at this game,' she warned him.

'Then at least you should be good enough to give me some sport.'

She put up her chin. 'I do not think you will find me deficient, Major.'

He glanced up at her, a smile glinting in his eyes. 'That's put you on your mettle.'

She scowled. 'Oh, be quiet and play, sir!'

The first two games went to Juliana, and earned her a word of praise from her opponent. The Major narrowly won the third game, and Juliana did not object when he suggested they should play again. She was enjoying herself, and in concentrating on the game she forgot that they were master and employee.

'Our landlord has left a bottle of burgundy—would you care for a glass, ma'am, or would you prefer brandy?'

'Is it usual for ladies to drink brandy, Major?'

'No, but you are an unusual lady, Miss Wrenn.'

She laughed at the unexpected compliment. 'A glass of wine would be very welcome, sir.'

She set out the counters again while he poured the wine and brought it back to the table, with a glass of brandy for himself. The fourth game was closely fought, but an error by Juliana gave her opponent an advantage, and she shook her head as she watched him bearing off his counters to win.

'I allowed you too many hits,' she remarked. 'Should I plead fatigue, Major, or accuse you of trying to befuddle my brain with the wine?'

'Neither. Merely admit I am the better player.'

'Such arrogance! We have won two games each, sir. The honours so far are even.'

He sat back, sipping at his brandy. 'So they are. Shall we play a deciding game?'

She nodded eagerly.

'Do you wish to change colours, ma'am?'

'I am happy to let you have the black.'

He gave her one of his rare smiles. 'The devil's colour, is that it?'

She chuckled. 'Precisely.'

* * *

From the first throw of the dice Juliana was determined to win. The wine had warmed her, but she did not believe it had lessened her ability to think clearly. The Major grunted as she moved her pieces into blocks, leaving no counter exposed.

'Defensive play, Miss Wrenn.'

'Necessary play, Major, when I know you are ready to pounce upon my slightest error.'

They were sitting forward, leaning over the board, intent on the play. A false move by her opponent allowed Juliana to make some gains, but the Major countered immediately and the advantage was lost. Vexed, Juliana rattled the dice-box and cast a little wildly. One die bounced over the edge of the board and on to the floor.

'Oh, how careless of me!' She slipped off her chair, searching the shadows under the table. 'Ah, there it is. A six! Will you allow that, Major, or will I have to throw again? It would be very ungentlemanly of you to deny me!'

She was on her knees beside him, laughing up into his face, quite forgetting any restraint. The Major sat motionless. The light from the candles was behind him and she could not see him clearly, but she caught his sudden stillness. Silence settled over the room. Juliana's laughter died away, but she remained at his feet, transfixed. He reached out and cupped her face in his hands. He was going to kiss her, she knew it, and with a sudden, blazing certainty she realised there was nothing she wanted more. He leaned forward, his black shadow enveloping her as his lips touched her own. It was a gentle kiss that sent icy threads of fear and excitement through her body. It was everything she had expected, but nothing as she had imagined it. Instinctively she reached up her hand to touch his face, and the whole world exploded.

He dropped down beside her, his chair scraping back and

catching the edge of the little table, sending the backgammon board and pieces flying. The table toppled over, counters skittered in all directions across the floor, adding a brighter tapping to the drumming of blood that already filled Juliana's head. His mouth was hard on hers now, demanding. His hands moved down to grip her shoulders. She was aware of no pain, only an urgent desire. She clung to him as he lowered her unresisting to the floor. He pulled the muslin fichu from her neck and his lips left her mouth to trail lightly down across her throat. Pushing her gown from her shoulders, he pressed his kisses on the exposed skin while his fingers moved on, slipping inside her bodice to cup one breast. Juliana gasped, feeling the nipple grow hard and erect under his circling thumb. She threw her arms about his neck, excited by the feel of his taut body pressing against her. There was a tingling ache between her thighs, an urgency that she did not understand. When his lips returned to her mouth, she kissed him ardently, her body pressing against his, inviting his caresses. He raised his head and the next moment his mouth closed over the breast where his hand had been so effective in rousing her. Juliana closed her eyes, giddy with new sensations. Her fingers slid up from his neck to bury themselves in his sleek black hair; the pleasure was exquisite, almost unbearable. Juliana arched against him, her body aching for more, and she gave a little whimper, murmuring his name. The Major grew still. He lifted his head to stare at her, his breath ragged and warm upon her face. He stared at her for a long moment, as if trying to bring her into focus. With a groan he turned away.

'I—am—sorry,' he said curtly, his back to her. Juliana's hand crept to her cheek. She was stunned, unable to think clearly. She became aware of the hard wooden floor beneath her and slowly she sat up, readjusting her gown with trembling fingers. She did not understand the tumult of emotion he had aroused. Her reaction to his touch had overwhelmed her, and she was frightened at her loss of control. She wanted to cry, and in defence tried to be flippant.

'Is—is that why they call you a devil in the bedroom?'

He jerked to his feet and crossed to the window. 'So you have heard that. A stupid jest, born of the, ah, the wild parties we held before Waterloo.' He turned and came back to her. 'One thing you will *not* hear is that I tamper with innocent young women. What has just happened—I apologise for my lack of control, Miss Wrenn.' She was on her feet now, and he bent to scoop up the fichu and hand it to her, a strange smile twisting his mouth. 'I must blame it on being cooped up in this damned inn. It will not happen again.'

'It was indeed foolish beyond permission,' she muttered, shaking out her gown. The excitement had drained away, leaving her exhausted and depressed.

He raked one hand through his hair.

'What can I say? Miss Wrenn, I am more sorry than I can tell you. Please forgive me.'

Juliana moved towards the window, away from the candle-light. She had been about to say that she was equally to blame. True, he had kissed her first, but she had made no attempt to repulse him. Indeed, she was well aware that she had encouraged him. The thought of what might have occurred had he not broken away made her shudder. She had the instincts of a harlot. It was a lowering thought. Juliana drew a steadying breath. She was at an inn, miles from anyone that she knew, without money, without power. She must tread carefully.

'I am contracted to you as a governess, Major.'

He sighed. 'Of course. No doubt you wish to have nothing further to do with me or my family.'

His tone was harsh, but Juliana knew his anger was directed at himself. She wanted to run to him, to take at least some of the blame for what had happened, but then what would he think of her? Why, to admit her desire would show herself to be no better than a strumpet.

But she did not want to leave him.

'I have grown very fond of your children, Major Collingham, and my financial position has not changed in any way. I am contracted to you until September and I would like to fulfil my obligations.'

He was watching her closely. 'And this?' he said. 'Would you have us pretend this did not happen?'

She swallowed. 'I believe you are right, sir. It was the consequence of being too much thrown together. And the wine, Major. I shall be at pains to ensure that there is no opportunity for such a thing to happen again.'

She walked towards the door, but his voice stayed her.

'But you will stay? For the children?'

She looked back. 'Yes,' she said quietly. 'I will stay for the children.'

Chapter Twelve

Juliana dreaded meeting the Major at breakfast the following day and her cheeks grew warm when he greeted her, but his manner was curt, and his subsequent behaviour so politely indifferent that she began to wonder if she had dreamed the previous night's encounter. He did not escort her to their carriage, but stood talking to his groom while Giles performed the service. That he was trying to spare her embarrassment Juliana was sure, but still she found his coldness depressing.

With the prospect of reaching Blackthorpe that evening the children were happy to be on their way. Gwendoline and Thomas had discovered a travel chess set Juliana had purchased for them and were soon engaged in a deep combat while the younger girls were busy making up stories. With no need to entertain the children, and Nurse settling down to sleep in her corner, Juliana had nothing to do but look out at the undulating hills and pleasant scenery. Unfortunately, this gave her far too much time to think, and her mind kept returning to the Major's caresses and the way she had abandoned herself to him.

The Major's kiss had surprised, but not outraged her. Men, she knew, were prone to such lusts. A lady would have pushed him away, not encouraged him to continue with his gallantry. Juliana reflected sadly that her reactions had been most unladylike. She cast a quick look around the carriage, half-expecting to see the children regarding her with disapproval. If they knew the wanton way she had behaved, they would look upon her with horror. The fact that the Major had not turned her off instantly was a relief. With no money, if he had abandoned her then she, Thomas and Amy would have become beggars. They had seen many such pathetic figures during their journey from London. Some were ex-soldiers, discharged from the army now the war was over and left to fend for themselves. At one farm they passed, she had seen a ragged woman taking food from the pig trough to feed her child. It was a frightening prospect, and one Juliana would do anything to avoid.

She closed her eyes, but the memory of the Major's kiss would not go away. She had wanted him to kiss her! Juliana remembered reading of monks who flayed themselves with birch sticks to rid themselves of lustful thoughts. If such good men had problems, why should not she? A small, treacherous voice whispered that she should be making efforts to attach the Major, not keep him at a distance. As an impecunious teacher with two children to support, she was unlikely to attract a husband—would it really be so bad to enjoy the Major's attentions for a while? Marriage was out of the question, she was well aware of that, for he was promised to his paragon of a neighbour with all her fortune, and Juliana was not fool enough to think her charms sufficient to make him give up his plans. Indeed, the idea of Damon falling at her feet in blind adoration was laughable—so why did it make her want to cry?

Her little demon whispered that it was not too late, that with a few smiles and compliments he would again take her in his arms, but she resolutely crushed such thoughts. Damon had hired her as a governess for his children and that is what she would be. Last night's encounter was a salutary lesson to her: she would be on her guard in future. She would earn her money, then walk away from Major Collingham and his family with her pride and her virtue intact.

Such a resolution should have brought contentment, but it did not, and Juliana was settling down to enjoy a prolonged spell of self-pity when the carriage lurched to one side and she was thrown off her seat and on top of Nurse, who awoke with a shriek.

For a few moments all was confusion. The carriage body was resting at a drunken angle and there were shouts and cries from inside the coach and out. Juliana pushed herself away from Nurse and tried to comfort the children, who were tangled in a heap in the far corner.

'I think we have broken a wheel,' said Thomas, clambering towards one door, which now hung down over the bank. He managed to open it, and jumped down, calling cheerfully, 'Come on, it is quite easy to get out.'

Within a few minutes the children had all climbed down and Juliana helped Nurse to alight before nimbly jumping out and scrambling up the bank on to the road. It was easy to see the cause of their accident. The road at this point was built around the contours of the hill, with dense woodland rising up to the east and on the west the ground falling steeply away to the valley bottom. A sudden dip in the road surface had been filled with loose rubble, which had given way under the weight of the coach and the subsequent jolt had shattered the front wheel.

The coachman was calming his frightened team, and as

soon as Juliana assured him they were all safely out of the coach he coaxed the horses forward, dragging the carriage back on to the road, until it was in no immediate danger of slipping farther down the hillside.

'I was right, Mr Dawlish,' declared Thomas, surveying the damage. 'It is the wheel.'

The driver climbed down and walked round the carriage, shaking his head.

'Aye,' he muttered. 'Smashed beyond repair, she is.' He kicked at the road with his boot. 'Just look how this crumbles away. It's all the rain we've had this spring, it's breaking up the surface, and doubtless it has washed away the foundations, too. We was lucky the whole carriage didn't go a-tumbling down the bank.'

As they all surveyed the wreckage, Major Collingham came bowling back along the road in his curricle.

'Fortunately we were not too far ahead and Giles saw you stop.' He jumped down. 'Is anyone hurt?'

'No, sir, everyone is well,' replied John Dawlish, tugging his forelock. 'It's just a broken wheel, but she's smashed, and we'll need to find a wheelwright to repair her.'

Juliana looked up and down the road; the fields and woods stretched away in every direction.

'Where are we, do you think?'

'We have gone no more than five miles from Leek,' said the Major.

'Heavens, don't say we have to walk all that way back,' cried Nurse in alarm.

'No, no, Rushton Spencer is no more than a mile farther on, and it's downhill into the village,' responded the Major. 'There might be a wheelwright there, I think. What say you, John?'

The coachman rubbed his nose.

'I disremember, sir. There will be a forge, of course, but we might have to go back to Leek to fetch a new wheel. However, if I remember rightly, there's a respectable inn at Rushton Spencer where the ladies can rest.'

'Then that is the way we shall go.'

By this time the baggage coach had lumbered up and the situation had to be explained to the driver and to Fewell, the Major's groom, who was sitting up on the box. A quick discussion, a few instructions and Major Collingham had everything arranged.

'Giles will drive Nurse in my curricle to Rushton Spencer, and find the inn John mentioned. Is it on this road, John?'

'Aye, Major. On the crossroads, you can't miss it.'

'Good, then you go there, Giles. We shall follow on foot. Fewell and the coachmen will send on the baggage wagon and arrange for a new wheel.'

Gwendoline pouted. 'I do not want to walk.'

The Major shrugged. 'Then you had best see if Fewell will let you sit up on the roof with the trunks—there is no room inside.'

Juliana looked at the two coachmen who were moving the small trunks from the broken vehicle into the already laden carriage. It was clear that there would be very little room for a passenger. She smiled and held out her hand.

'Come, Gwendoline. I need you to help me show the little ones the way. Perhaps the Major will tell us how he used to march when he was in the Peninsula.'

Major Collingham had been giving final instructions to Giles in the curricle; as that vehicle set off, he turned back, his harsh features softening as he regarded the little party looking up at him so expectantly.

'Well, let me see. First we need a drummer. Thomas, you shall lead the way, and the others shall follow two by two.'

'And you, Papa, shall be the Duke of Wellington,' declared Wilhelmina. 'Keeping us all in order.'

They set off, the two younger girls marching along quite happily beside the Major, swinging their arms in time to the beat of Thomas's imaginary drum. The day was dry and warm, and the Major was persuaded to recall from his army days some of the more acceptable marching songs to help them on their way.

Juliana walked behind them with Gwendoline at her side. Major Collingham turned occasionally to speak to Gwendoline, but not once during their walk to the village did he address Juliana, and in the face of his seeming indifference it cost her an effort to remain cheerful.

Fortunately the section of road leading down to Rushton Spencer was smooth and well drained and they soon covered the mile down the hill, where Juliana was heartened by sight of the freshly painted inn at the crossroads.

'That looks pleasant enough,' she said. 'I have no doubt we shall comfortable here.'

Thomas looked up at the inn sign. 'The George. And look, sir, there is your curricle standing in the yard.'

At that moment Giles appeared in the doorway and hailed them. 'I have been looking out for you,' he said, grinning. 'They have a parlour, sir, and sufficient bedrooms for us all, so I have told them we will take them, because I cannot see the wheel being mended for us to travel on today.' He led them into the inn, throwing open the door to a large comfortable room where Nurse was sitting in a chair in the deep bay window.

'No, don't get up,' said the Major as she went to rise. 'We shall stand on no ceremony here. Have you ordered food? Good. Perhaps by the time we have eaten, Fewell will be here to tell us how long a delay we may expect.'

Juliana untied the strings of her bonnet. 'I am sure Nurse and I can look after the children, sir, if you wish to go on: you could still reach Blackthorpe Hall before dark.'

'Thank you, ma'am, but we have travelled thus far together. I can wait a little longer to reach Lancashire. I have no intention of abandoning my family.'

He looked towards her as he spoke, but his gaze was somewhere over her head and a bolt of remorse shot through Juliana. It could not be more clear that he was keeping his distance. She turned away, tears starting to her eyes at his brusque tone. Biting her lip, she walked to a far corner to divest herself of her bonnet and cloak, keeping her back to the room while she tried to regain her composure. She jumped when the Major spoke again, close to her shoulder.

'I have upset you,' he murmured. 'I am sorry, I did not mean to imply I do not trust you.'

She muttered a quiet thank you, blinking away her tears. Two strong hands caught her shoulders, obliging her to turn and face him. She could hear the children chattering away to Nurse, describing their march down the hill, and she was thankful that she was shielded from view by the Major's body, made even broader by his many-caped driving coat.

'Come, what is this?' He placed two fingers under her chin and forced her to look at him. 'You have never minded my rough tongue until now.'

She turned her head away. 'I am tired, that is all.'

'I would that it were all. Ju, I—'

'Papa, did you see the bills posted on the wall when you came in?' Giles came up, excitement bubbling in his voice. 'There is a mill hereabouts tomorrow—well, at Congleton, which is very close! If we are to stay here, sir, can we go?'

The Major's hands dropped to his sides. Juliana turned away quickly and busied herself with her cloak, taking some comfort in his use of her name. She heard him speaking to his son.

'A mill, you say?'

'Aye, sir. I do not know who is fighting, but the landlord tells me there should be some good sport. I know Thomas would like to go too, wouldn't you, Tom?'

Juliana moved around the Major and saw that her brother was standing hopefully beside Giles.

'I would,' he said shyly. 'And you did say you would teach me to box, sir, so would it not be a good idea for me to see a real sparring match?'

Major Collingham reached out to ruffle his hair. 'I did promise, you are right, and I have been sadly behindhand with you, have I not?'

'So can we go, sir, please?' said Giles.

'Well, let us wait for Fewell to tell us the state of the carriage. Then, if we are to remain here, and Miss Wrenn has no objections, we shall go.'

Juliana found two pairs of eyes fixed upon her.

'I do not like the sport, I admit, but if the Major sees no harm…'

His unfathomable gaze rested on her again. 'You may be sure I will take good care of your brother, Miss Wrenn.'

'Ah, refreshments,' exclaimed Giles as the landlady came in with a tray. 'I ordered wine, cakes and lemonade to be brought in…oh, and ale for ourselves, sir—I hope you do not object?'

'Not at all, my son. I admire your foresight.'

'Well, I only thought of the wine and the ale,' Giles admitted. 'It was Nurse who said that the young 'uns would like lemonade.' Giles beamed at them all. 'So we have something for everyone to enjoy. All we have to do now is wait for Fewell to turn up.'

* * *

It was mid-afternoon before Fewell arrived at the George. Juliana had collected the children at the table with pencils and paper from her sketching block and they were engaged in drawing pictures for their journal. Major Collingham and Giles had gone out to the stables and Juliana looked up as she heard their voices outside the door. The Major entered with Giles and the groom behind him.

'And he cannot be persuaded to have the carriage ready for the morning?' demanded the Major as he came in.

Fewell touched his forelock towards Juliana before answering.

'No, sir. The wheelwright says he cannot have the wheel ready before noon at the earliest, then there's the fitting.'

'And by the time the carriage is ready to travel it will be too late to set out,' growled the Major. 'We shall be here until Thursday.'

Juliana glanced from his dark frown to Giles's cheerful countenance and smiled inwardly. She had no doubt the young man was thinking of the boxing match at Congleton. Major Collingham exhaled.

'Well, if there's no help for it. Miss Wrenn, are you happy to stay here for two nights or would you like me to see if there is another, larger hotel in the vicinity? We could go back to Leek, if you wish…'

'This inn seems clean and comfortable enough, sir. I think we shall do very well here, thank you.'

He nodded. 'Then it is settled. Fewell, you had best find accommodation for yourself and the others, and see if you can arrange for the carriages to be under cover for our stay, in case it comes on to rain again.'

The groom went out and Giles looked hopefully at his father.

'So we are to stay, Papa. And shall we go to the mill?'

'Would you have me leave your sisters here for the whole day?'

Juliana looked up. 'Pray do not worry about the children, Major Collingham. Nurse and I will take care of them. It is, after all, what we are employed to do.'

His gazed scorched her. 'Thank you for reminding me of the fact, Miss Wrenn.' Looking at Thomas, he continued in a milder tone, 'Well, my boy, do you want to come with us tomorrow?'

'Would I? Oh, sir, yes, please!'

For the rest of the day the Major treated Juliana with a punctilious politeness that she found more daunting than his abrasive manner, so it was with relief that she saw the curricle drive away towards Congleton the following morning. The children were persuaded to spend the morning at their reading, but after so many days of rain, the blue skies and sunshine were too good to be wasted and when Gwendoline suggested they should play out of doors after luncheon, Juliana was happy to agree.

'The maid says the landlord owns the orchard at the back and would not object to our playing there, as long as we do not climb the trees or damage the fruit,' added Gwendoline.

'Bless your hearts,' Nurse beamed at them. 'A little fresh air will do us all good, for we shall be cooped up in that carriage again tomorrow. If we could have a chair moved outside for me, I would happily sit with the children, Miss Juliana. I could take my knitting and watch them play.'

'We shall all go outside,' declared Juliana. 'I will talk to our host about it now.'

Half an hour later they were established under the trees in the small orchard behind the inn, with two chairs for the ladies and a stool for Nurse's feet, plus a rug for the children. The orchard was bounded by trees on two sides and the inn buildings to the west, so they were sheltered from any breeze. A lane ran back behind the inn, but was separated from the orchard by a low wall that prevented the children from running out into the path of any farm wagons or animals that might be on the move. Juliana leaned back in her chair and closed her eyes, turning her face to the sun, enjoying its warmth on her skin. The children were playing tag around the trees, their happy laughter filling the air.

'Ah, 'tis wonderful to see the little ones so happy,' remarked Nurse, her fingers busy with her knitting. 'I am so glad the master let you bring young Amy and Thomas along with us. Amy and Minna play together so well, and even Gwendoline is settling down.' She chuckled. 'Lord, how she disliked the idea of having a governess with us, but now it is Miss Wrenn says this, and Miss Wrenn does that—you are a firm favourite with her.'

'I am glad. I had said I would leave you when we reached Blackthorpe Hall, if she was still set against me.'

'The child was against anyone, Miss Wrenn. Such a stubborn, headstrong girl she is, just like her father, but they are both of them good at heart.'

'Did they miss Major Collingham, while he was away with the army?'

'Dear me, miss, he was in the Peninsula for several years, so they hardly knew him. Indeed, I think they have seen more of him during this journey than ever before.'

Juliana gave a little laugh. 'Then perhaps it was a good thing Mr Brasher's plans were overturned.'

A sudden anguished cry made her open her eyes. Amy was running towards her.

'Gwen has fallen and cut her knee!'

Juliana hurried towards Gwendoline, who was sitting on the grass holding her leg. Her stocking was torn at the knee and a little blood was already oozing from a jagged gash.

'There was a stone in the ground,' she said, clenching her teeth.

Juliana took out her handkerchief and wiped carefully around the wound. 'It is nothing serious, but it will be sore for a few days. Oh, you have torn your hem, too. Come indoors with me and we shall bind you up and repair your skirts. Then you will be as good as new.'

She helped the girl to her feet and they made their way to the inn. As she held open the door for Gwendoline to go in, Juliana looked back towards the orchard. The younger girls had given up their game of tag and were playing with their dolls on the rug with Nurse sitting close by in her chair, her feet resting on the footstool. Her hands were no longer moving the knitting needles and Juliana thought it would not be long before the old lady was asleep.

'Look after each other,' she called to the girls. 'We will be back very soon.'

Juliana took Gwendoline up to her bedroom where the cut on the knee was soon washed and dressed, but the stitching up of her hem took a little longer.

'You are unlike any governess we have had before,' remarked Gwendoline, watching Juliana as she plied her needle.

'Because I mend your skirts? Surely anyone would do as much.'

'No, that's not it.' She stopped, then said slowly, 'I have been very unfair to you—I tried to make Papa think you were not a good teacher, and you have not said anything about it.'

'Well, there has been no need.'

'And I *did* spill the tea on you deliberately,' Gwendoline confessed.

Juliana's eyes twinkled. 'I know, and you may think yourself fortunate I could not find a toad to put in your bed that night!'

'I am very sorry.'

'If that is so, then we can forget all about the matter.'

'Yes, but—I don't want Papa to dismiss you now, and I am afraid that he will do so, because you have given us no lessons, no *real* lessons. You have given us nothing to learn by heart.'

'There will be plenty of time for that when you are settled in your new home. Until then we shall do what we can to improve your reading and writing while we are travelling, and perhaps do a little sketching.'

'I like drawing.'

'Yes, I thought as much—your drawings for our journal are very good.'

Gwendoline shook her head. 'Faces,' she said. 'I can never draw faces as I would wish.'

'Then we shall work on it. There, your hem is mended. Let me put away my scissors and needle and we will go back and join the others.'

'Papa says our new mama will want to choose a governess for us.'

'Well, that will suit me very well. I am only contracted to your father until September.'

'Do you not *want* to stay with us?'

'I thought you did not want a governess.'

'Well, if we must have someone, I would as soon it was you as anyone.'

'Thank you,' said Juliana, smiling. 'However, we agreed you should not make any decision until we reach Lancashire.'

'But if I decided I wanted you to remain, would you not stay longer?'

'I am afraid not, my dear. I have my own family to think of.'

'So what will you do?'

'I shall rent a little house where Thomas and Amy and I can live together.'

'But you could all live with us.'

'I do not think your new mama would want that, Gwendoline.'

'Well, I cannot see that she should object,' the girl replied, shaking out her skirts. 'Papa says Lady Frances is a great lady, and used to large households. And in all likelihood we shall see little of her—Papa will take her off on a long honeymoon and we shall be left at Blackthorpe, all alone, and when they come back they will have new babies that they will both love, and we shall be forgotten.'

'That is nonsense, Gwendoline. I am sure that your new mama will love you all very much indeed.'

'How can she do that when she does not know us?'

'She will come to know you, my dear, and to love you, just as I—' Juliana bit her lip and continued after a pause, 'Come along, let us go back outside and enjoy the sunshine while it lasts.'

Juliana ushered her charge before her, suddenly feeling very tired and dispirited. She should be glad that at last Gwendoline had given her approval, for she could now look forward to continuing her contract and earning enough to secure her independence. She told herself she should be happy, that there was no reason for these megrims; she could only think that the journey was proving more tiring than she had anticipated.

As they made their way to the back of the inn, Juliana noticed that the door to their private parlour stood open. She looked in to see her little sister sitting at the table, drawing on her slate.

'Amy? I thought you were playing with Wilhelmina.'

'She wanted to play tag again, but I was tired and wanted to sit down,' said Amy, not looking up. 'Minna called me a *baby*.'

'Well, we are going outside now,' said Juliana. 'Bring your slate and we will play some word games—would you like that?'

She waited for Amy to climb down from the chair and the three of them made their way through the narrow corridor and out of the door at the back of the inn. As they passed a window Juliana noticed that the clouds were growing thicker, and she was wondering if she should go back for her shawl when there was a cry from outside.

'That's Minna,' said Gwendoline, pushing open the door. 'I expect she's fallen out of a tree or some such thing.'

Juliana followed her outside and looked towards the orchard. The rug was empty and Nurse was sitting up in her chair, rubbing at her eyes as if she had just woken up. A feeling of foreboding crept over Juliana. She ran forward until she was clear of the inn buildings. A black cabriolet was drawn up in the lane, close to the orchard wall.

'Minna!' Even as she called, there was a crack of a whip and the carriage moved off. Juliana raced for the wall, and saw with chilling horror that the driver was holding on to a small, struggling figure on the seat beside him.

'Oh, heavens!'

Juliana scrambled over the wall, and followed the cabriolet towards the crossroads beside the inn, but even as she reached the corner, the vehicle picked up speed and drew away from her, heading up the hill and into the trees. Juliana watched, aghast, but just as she turned to head back to the inn and call for help, another vehicle swept into sight from the Congleton Road. She recognised Major Collingham's curricle and she ran towards it, waving frantically. The Major had already slowed to turn into the inn yard but now he pulled up beside her on the road.

'Good God, what is the matter?' he called.

'Minna—kidnapped!' she gasped, gripping the edge of the carriage for support. 'He—he has driven off with her, up that road. You must go after them, now!'

The Major turned to the two boys sitting beside him.

'Get down. You must look after the ladies.'

Giles hesitated. 'Should I not go with you?'

'No, Fewell can stay on the back. You will be needed here.'

'I am coming with you.' Juliana ran round and prepared to climb into the curricle.

'No. Stay with the others.'

She ignored him and climbed into the curricle. 'Minna may need me when we catch up with them.'

His mouth tightened. 'Very well.'

She hardly had time to sit down before he had turned the horses and set off up the hill at a canter.

'It was the man from the Queen's Head,' she said. 'The one who stole into the girls' bedroom.'

'Leeson?'

'Yes.'

'Tell me what happened.'

Briefly she told him all she knew.

'I am sorry,' she ended. 'I should not have left her alone.'

'She was not alone, Nurse was with her. You cannot blame yourself.'

'But why? What can he want with her?'

'That we shall find out when we catch up with him,' muttered the Major, whipping up his team.

Juliana clung to the side of the curricle as they bounced over the uneven surface.

'If my memory serves me, this is the old road back to Leek,' said the Major. 'They built the new section about ten years ago, to avoid the hill. I know this area quite well; we shall catch him, never fear.'

Charles Leeson set his horse to a gallop along the straight road that stretched ahead of him and glanced down at the sobbing child beside him. What a fix he was in now! He would not blame Lady Ormiston for this. How could he? He had sworn to help her, vowed that he would give his life for her if necessary. Veronique had explained it to him so carefully. It had all sounded so simple, but Charles had younger sisters of his own, and in his experience they were the very devil to deal with. He had nearly succeeded at the Queen's Head, when the children were asleep, but just as he had been about to lay his hands on the prize, the old biddy had set up such a screech! He flicked his whip across the horse's rump. He had carried it off rather well, he thought, convincing them all that he was in his cups. Since then he had kept his distance, waiting for another opportunity, and it was a stroke of luck that he had come upon them here and seen the girl playing with her doll, with no one near her save the old dame sleeping in her chair. The brat had remembered him from the Queen's Head, and she did not run away when he climbed over the wall to talk to her. But then she would do nothing more than sit on the rug, hugging her doll so there was nothing for it but to clap a hand over her mouth and bundle her into the carriage. He thought of Veronique. How grateful she would be; she would smile upon him again; he would be in favour once more. Not only that, she had promised to pay him handsomely if he succeeded, more than enough to settle his gambling debts. He did not know how he had managed to lose so much, but it would have to be paid: it was a matter of honour.

The road levelled out and he allowed the horse to slacken its pace and glanced idly over his shoulder.

'Damnation!'

Just coming into view behind him was a curricle, thundering along at breakneck speed.

Chapter Thirteen

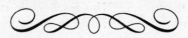

'There they are!'

Juliana's cry was unnecessary; she knew Major Collingham had seen the cabriolet as soon as they crested the rise on to a long straight. It was about half a mile ahead of them.

'He's stopping.'

'No,' said the Major, his eyes fixed on his quarry, 'he's picking up speed again. He has seen us.'

Juliana looked at her companion. His face was impassive, the hands on the reins were quite steady, his eyes fixed on the carriage ahead of them. It soothed her frayed nerves to see him so calm.

'How far will he go?' she asked.

'I have no idea, but he won't escape me now. I've a pair to his one horse, we shall soon catch him.'

The harsh note in his voice made her shiver.

The cabriolet turned off the road and was lost to sight. Juliana said nothing, but she held her breath as the Major raced to the turning, barely checking his horses as he swung into the lane. She saw the cabriolet briefly before it was hidden by a bend in the road. They were racing along through an avenue of trees, with hedges and fields on both sides, permitting them only occasional glimpses of their quarry. The distance was closing, but slowly. Juliana glanced at the Major.

'You have just driven back from Congleton,' she murmured. 'Your team must be tired.'

'They'll do,' he said shortly.

'Don't you worry, miss,' said Fewell from his perch on the back of the curricle, 'This team would run all day if you'd let 'em.'

The clouds that had been gathering during the afternoon had blotted out the sun, and beneath the canopy of the trees the lane was damp and rutted. The Major held his team together, setting a cracking pace. Juliana kept her eyes fixed on the vehicle in front, wanting only to reach Wilhelmina and find her safe. Occasionally she saw the child's head appear over the back of the chaise. Juliana closed her eyes and prayed that she would not panic and jump out.

'Now we've got him!'

Juliana opened her eyes. Ahead of them, a herd of milch cows were making their leisurely way in the same direction, and effectively blocking the lane. The carriage slowed and she saw the driver standing up, gesticulating towards the farmer's boy who was following the cows. She almost laughed to see the boy staring up at Leeson, and even from a distance his stance showed that he was not intimidated by the raging figure demanding that he move his animals to one side.

'He'll never get by!' she muttered, her voice breaking.

'No, he's going to try to cross the field,' muttered the Major. 'The fool, he's likely to be overturned, if he doesn't break the axle first.'

Juliana watched in horror as the carriage lurched on across

the field, coming to a halt by the wall on the far side. Leeson jumped down, pulled Wilhelmina from the chaise and set off across the fields.

'Now what is he doing?' she said, her throat tight with fear. 'Why is he taking Minna?'

The Major pulled a deadly-looking pistol from its holster.

'Because he knows I cannot shoot him while he has her so close. He must be heading for the moors. I'll follow him on foot, it will be as quick as trying to drive.'

The curricle came to a stand by the gap in the hedge. Juliana climbed down even as the horses were plunging in their harness.

'I'm coming with you. Fewell can stay with the horses.'

'Then you must keep up with me. I will not wait for you.'

Leeson was running up the hill towards the ridge, dragging Wilhelmina with him. Juliana followed Major Collingham into the field. The ground was wet and the mud clung to Juliana's soft kid boots. The crop, whatever it should have been, was stunted and sodden and she lifted her skirts to prevent them from getting too wet as she struggled to keep pace with the Major. He was striding across the ground, his eyes fixed upon his quarry. Juliana was out of breath by the time they reached the stile into the next field. Major Collingham helped her across and took her hand.

'Come on, we must hurry.'

He moved off and Juliana was forced to run to keep up with him, but she did not complain, her whole attention fixed on the fleeing man in front of them. Grey clouds moved across the sky, and a breeze had sprung up, cooling Juliana's hot cheeks. When Major Collingham slowed, she looked at him anxiously.

'I have no idea what's on the far side of the ridge,' he said, pulling the pistol from his pocket. 'I will not lose him.'

Juliana shivered.

'But what of Minna?'

His lips drew into a thin line.

'I will not hit her.'

He took careful aim. The shot rang out across the fields, sending the rooks flying from the trees behind them.

'He's hit!' cried Juliana. 'He stumbled. You have winged him.'

'Aye—if Minna had not been so close, I would have aimed to kill him.'

The Major dropped the pistol back into his pocket and began to run, leaving Juliana to follow. She caught up with him again on top of the ridge. A low wall separated the field from rough land that stretched away for miles in every direction.

'He's heading across the moors,' said Damon. 'There's no cover for him amongst the bracken—he will not get away. Come on.'

He helped her over the wall and they set off again. Leeson was following a sheep track through the bracken. He had thrown Wilhelmina over his shoulder and was running and stumbling along in the distance.

'I should have gone back for a horse,' muttered the Major. 'I could run him down.'

'But we are gaining on him,' panted Juliana.

They continued at a steady pace across the bleak landscape. The sun made an occasional appearance between the heavy clouds, each time a little lower in the western sky. The moors stretched out around them, not a sign of a building and only the mournful cry of birds to be heard on the wind. Juliana's world had become one vast, desolate expanse of heather and bracken, her only goal the figure of Charles Leeson trudging tirelessly onwards before them.

'There's a small copse down there,' said Damon at last. 'He is heading for cover, but we can catch him before he reaches it.'

He quickened his pace, dragging Juliana with him and gaining on Leeson with every step. They were heading towards the trees, which filled a small, sheltered hollow in the land. They were only yards from the edge of the woodland when the Major shouted out. 'You will not reach the trees, Leeson. Stop now, and let the child go.'

Leeson turned, lowering Wilhelmina from his shoulder and pinning her in front of him. He drew out a small silver-mounted pistol and held it to her head.

'If you come any closer, I'll shoot her!' he cried, his voice quivering with a mixture of fear, exhaustion and panic.

The Major stopped. 'Put that down, lad. You know you do not want to harm the child.'

'I—I will if you come nearer.'

Juliana put her fist to her mouth to prevent herself from crying out. She marvelled at the Major's control and his calm, reasonable tone.

'Then I will stay here,' he said. 'Will you tell me what this is about, Charles?'

'I c-can't.' Leeson's voice quivered.

'Let the child go, lad, and we can talk this out. Your arm is bleeding. Let me bind it up for you.'

'Too late!' Leeson shifted uneasily from one foot to the other, the pistol shaking dangerously. 'It's all up with me now.'

'If that's true, then what good would it do to harm Minna?' Damon took another step forward, holding out his hand. 'Give me the pistol. Let me help you.'

Leeson shook his head, looking down at Wilhelmina.

'No one can help me now. I'm ruined. I'm... Damn you all to hell!'

With an anguished cry he pushed Wilhelmina away from him, turned on his heel and dashed for the trees. Juliana rushed forward to Minna, who was shaking uncontrollably. She saw the Major running past her and reached out for him.

'Where are you going?'

He stopped. 'To kill him.'

'No! Damon—no, please. He is armed, he might kill *you*.'

'Let him try.'

Her fingers clawed at his sleeve. 'No, you must not—we need you here, Damon, *please*.' Her voice sank to a desperate whisper. 'Please don't leave us.'

She saw the tightening of his jaw. His eyes narrowed as he watched Leeson disappear into the woods.

'You are right, of course,' he muttered, 'But he won't get far, I promise you I'll find him one day.' He looked at Wilhelmina, who was clinging tightly to Juliana. 'How is she?'

'Very frightened, but unhurt, I think. As is Lady Arabella,' added Juliana, glancing at the doll that Minna was hugging to her. She knelt down and said quietly, 'Can you tell us what happened, dear?'

Wilhelmina laid her head on Juliana's shoulder.

'Lady Arabella and I were playing on the rug when the man stopped and said hello.'

'And Nurse was asleep?' put in the Major.

'Yes.' She hiccupped. 'He—he climbed over the wall and picked me up and threw me into his carriage.' She looked up. 'I banged my head.'

'Did you, my dear? Let me see.' Juliana gently kissed her forehead. 'You will have a bruise there, I think. Poor Minna.'

'What happened then?' asked Damon.

'He drove off and held me so that I couldn't get out. Lady Arabella was very frightened.'

'It was fortunate she had you to comfort her,' responded

Juliana. Wilhelmina's head dropped back on her shoulder. Juliana looked up. 'We must get back, Major. She is very tired.'

'We will have the doctor look at her as soon as we get back to the inn.' He reached out. 'Here, let me take her, she is too heavy for you.'

She looked anxiously over her shoulder.

'And Leeson? What—what if he should come back?'

'I don't think he will. Leeson is no killer, he panicked. But you must walk ahead of me, just in case. My body will shield you both.'

The walk away from the woods was an ordeal. Juliana looked repeatedly over her shoulder and wanted to run, afraid at any minute that a figure would break from the cover of the trees and take aim at them. The thought that any bullet was most likely to hit the Major did not comfort her at all.

'We are safe now, Ju,' Damon said at last. 'He could not hit us from this distance even if he wished to do so.'

She gave a long, ragged sigh.

'I hope you are not going to faint on me,' he remarked, striding on.

'Of course not,' she flashed.

'I'm glad to hear it. I should be obliged to leave you here if you did.'

She managed a shaky laugh and looked up to find him smiling at her.

'I'm glad you are here, Ju.'

She felt herself blushing, inordinately pleased.

'Yes, well,' she said gruffly, 'I shall be glad to get back to the inn and out of these muddy clothes.'

Major Collingham stopped. 'Unfortunately I am not sure when that will be.'

He nodded towards the west and Juliana's heart sank. On

the far hills was a wall of low cloud and it was rolling towards them, enveloping the moors in a thick, grey blanket.

'How far can we go before it reaches us?' she asked, trying to stay calm.

'Not far enough. Our route back is not a well-defined one, we could be stranded on the moors all night if it does not lift. You and Minna have no surcoats, and your gowns are too thin to offer much protection from the damp and cold.'

She looked around her desperately.

'Look,' she pointed. 'There is a cart track; hopefully it leads to a farm of some sort. If we can reach the track before we are caught in the mist, we should be able to follow it, don't you think?'

'It is certainly a possibility,' he said, shifting Minna more comfortably into his arms. 'Come along, and stay close to me.'

They set off down the hill and were only yards from the cart track when the grey mist rolled around them. The air was cold and damp; Damon pulled his coat around Minna to protect her, but the mist clung to them, leaving droplets like tiny diamonds on their hair and clothes. Juliana shivered in the unearthly light, and moved closer to the Major.

'Hold on to my coat,' he said to her. 'I do not want to lose you in this fog. And watch your footing, the stones are very uneven.'

'But at least the track looks well used, sir. Let us pray it leads to a house.'

They walked on, and Juliana uttered up a silent prayer of thanks when they reached a gate. The stony lane was replaced by a cobbled yard. The sounds and smells of a farm greeted them, and Damon walked forward, shouting for the farmer.

A tall, shambling figure in a ragged coat emerged from the mist, a pitchfork clutched in one large, bony hand.

'Good day to you,' said Damon. 'Is this your farm?'

'Aye.'

'Is there somewhere we can shelter until the mist clears?' Damon persisted. 'We have come from Rushton Spencer.'

The farmer turned his shaggy head and spat. 'No ways you're gettin' back there, then.'

'No, so we require somewhere to stay for the night. We would, of course, pay you for the inconvenience.'

A sly look came over the man's features. 'You'd pay?'

'Of course,' said Damon. 'Handsomely.'

'You'd best come in, then.'

They followed the figure across the yard until a large, stone farmhouse loomed out of the mist before them. He pushed open the door and led the way into a long, low room. A sullen fire smouldered in the hearth and beneath their feet the floor was little more than hard-packed earth. He picked up a lamp that was burning on a side table and held it aloft. Juliana took the opportunity to observe the man. She was not encouraged. He was as tall as the Major, but thin and stooping, with an unkempt appearance. His sandy hair hung in a shaggy bush about his head, while an equally unkempt beard covered most of his face. A pair of curiously light eyes peered at them from beneath thick brows. She thought he had a sly, calculating look about him.

'You'll pay, you say?'

Damon patted his pocket, and a faint jingle of coins could be heard. 'Aye, for a room, and a little food.'

The farmer nodded. 'Then I can let you have a room, and one for the woman—'

'My wife and I will share with the child, thank you,' cut in Damon. 'One room will suffice. We would not put you and your wife to too much trouble.'

The old man spat again. 'Ain't got no wife, see, but I can find you a bite to eat and a bed, like,' he added quickly. 'If you've the money to pay for it. Foller me.'

He led them through a maze of small rooms, up a creaky staircase and along a dark passage to a large chamber. Juliana guessed it was directly above the room she had seen below. It was of similar proportions, with a wide stone hearth at the far end. In the dim light of the lamp it could be seen that the room was sparsely furnished with an ancient tester bed, a wooden settle beside the fire and a small table under the window. The bed hangings were missing, and there were no curtains at the window, but a once-handsome rug was stretched out before the hearth.

'Ye can have this room, then, and welcome to it. There's the bench that will do for the bairn, and you and your missus can get cosy on the bed.' He leered at them. 'Payment in advance.'

Damon handed Minna to Juliana and reached into his pocket.

'Ten shillings on account,' he said, fixing the man with his hard stare. 'We will settle up the rest in the morning.'

The farmer squinted at the coins for a long moment, then nodded. 'Very well.' He pulled a taper from his pocket and lit it from the lamp, then he went around the room, lighting the tallow candles in their holders. 'I'll have to fetch you up sheets and blankets. You'll be wanting a fire as well, I suppose.'

'And a hot brick for Minna, if it is possible,' added Juliana.

The man dragged his sleeve across his nose. 'I'll see what I can do.'

'I'll come with you and help you,' said the Major. He shrugged off his jacket and placed it around Wilhelmina, murmuring to Juliana as he did so, 'Stay here; I will have a fire for you as soon as may be.'

The two men went out, and Juliana shivered in the gloomy chamber. The room smelled of old soot and dust and the dim light cast menacing shadows. Wilhelmina stirred and began to cry. Juliana sank down upon the settle and cuddled her, rocking her gently until she grew quiet again. She began to sing softly, as much to cheer herself as Wilhelmina. By the time she heard footsteps outside the door she had exhausted her store of nursery songs and her arms were aching from holding the child.

The farmer came in with an armful of wood, followed by Damon carrying a pile of sheets and blankets. Juliana noted idly that they looked as grey as everything else in the house. While their host proceeded to build a fire, the Major began to make up the bed. In a very short time there was a cheerful blaze in the hearth and the farmer withdrew, promising to bring up the hot brick as soon as it was ready. Juliana carried Wilhelmina to the rug in front of the fire.

'Come along, my dear, we had best get you out of your damp clothes.'

Wilhelmina blinked and said querulously, 'Where's my nightgown?'

'At the inn, Minna. Tonight you must sleep in your chemise.'

'Why must I?' Wilhelmina rubbed her eyes sleepily.

'Because we are on an adventure,' said Juliana as she stripped off Minna's gown. 'Good, the wet does not seem to have soaked through to your undergarments. Come along, Minna, up into the bed with you. You are very honoured,' she continued as she tucked the girl up between the sheets. 'I'd wager very few people have had your father make up a bed for them.'

'True,' agreed Damon, coming forward to lay a hand on his daughter's head.

Minna gave a sleepy chuckle. 'What a lot I shall have to tell Gwen and Amy tomorrow.'

'Indeed you will.'

'You will not leave me?' Wilhelmina reached out to cling to Juliana's hand.

'No, Minna.' Juliana squeezed her fingers. 'I promise I shall not leave you, my dear.'

Damon stooped to plant a kiss on the child's brow. 'I am with you too, Minna. You will be quite safe.'

Wilhelmina smiled. 'Yes,' she said sleepily. 'I shall be safe enough if you are both with me.'

Juliana sat on the edge of the bed, holding Minna's hand. She looked up to find the Major watching her. She gave a faint smile.

'She seems unharmed by her ordeal.'

'I pray you are right,' he murmured, walking over to stand before the hearth. 'Our host's name is Stopes, by the way. He has a farm lad who seems bright enough. I have sent him off to find Fewell and bring him back here in the morning. He seems to think he can find his way across to Rushton Spencer in any weather.'

'I hope so; I would like to get Minna back to Nurse's care as soon as possible.'

'As would I. In the meantime, let us think about your health, Miss Wrenn. Your clothes must be as damp as Minna's.'

She began to unbutton her short jacket. 'My spencer is a little damp.'

'But your muslin skirts are wet and muddy. Take off your gown and we will dry it before the fire.' He observed her hesitation and added roughly, 'Come now, Miss Wrenn, this is no time to be prudish. As you said to Minna, we are on an adventure.' He picked up one of the spare blankets and shook it out. 'You may wrap yourself in this, if you wish, but do not worry on my account—you will not shock me.'

'No,' she muttered, slipping out of her gown, 'I have no doubt you have seen many women in a state of undress.'

'Dozens,' came the cheerful reply. He lifted two corners of the blanket so that it formed a triangle and placed it about her shoulders. 'And you need not fear that I have any designs upon your virtue—tonight at least.'

They heard a shuffling step in the passage and the next moment the farmer came in. Juliana pulled her makeshift shawl about her.

'Here, for the bairn,' said Stopes, holding a hot brick wrapped in flannel cloth.

She thanked him and quickly pushed the brick into the bed, close to Wilhelmina's feet. Stopes watched her for a moment, then nodded and shuffled out of the room. Juliana tucked the covers around Wilhelmina again and held her hand until she was sleeping soundly. Major Collingham collected up the damp dresses and spread them out over the back of the settle together with his jacket.

'At least we have plenty of firewood; we shall keep the fire burning well tonight to dry out our clothes.'

Juliana smiled. 'I am impressed, Major. Tending fires, making beds—I had not thought you so accomplished.'

'Did you think me a gentleman of leisure, capable only of making pretty speeches?'

She laughed at that. 'I have never yet heard you making *pretty speeches*, Major.'

'No…' He gave her a wry smile. '…I am more likely to snap your head off, am I not?' She watched him piling more logs on the fire.

'Why did you say we were married?'

'At first glance I had little opinion of our host. If there was any other choice I would not stay here, but if we must do so I would rather we remain together overnight.'

She nodded. 'I admit I shall feel happier if you are close by, but where will you sleep? I had considered the settle, but it is far too narrow even for me.'

'You will share the bed with Wilhelmina,' he replied. 'I shall use the remaining blankets to make up a bed on the floor in front of the fire.'

'Will that not be uncomfortable?'

'Not half so uncomfortable as sleeping out on the moors.'

'No, of course not.'

There was a knock at the door and Stopes entered with a supper tray.

After he had left them, Damon inspected the contents by the light of two of the tallow candles. 'Hmm, rye bread, butter, cheese and meat—although I would not like to guess what sort—and small beer. A pity our host has no woman to keep house for him—there is no tea for you.'

'No matter,' said Juliana. 'I shall share the beer, if you do not object. Mr Stopes has sent up a pan of gruel to heat up for Minna when she wakes. That was kind of him. Perhaps he is not as bad as we first thought.'

'No? Did you not see the way he looked at you?'

'Thankfully, no. I avoided looking at *him*.' She shuddered. 'How fortunate that you are with me.' He looked at her, a faint smile lifting the corners of his mouth. She put her head on one side. 'What is it, Major?'

'You are a remarkable woman, Juliana Wrenn. You should be railing at me for embroiling you in this damned uncomfortable fix. Instead you make light of it.'

She shrugged.

'A fit of the vapours would help no one at the moment. Now, perhaps you will help me bring the table closer to the fire, then we can enjoy our supper in comfort, although I vow I am so tired I have little appetite.'

'That will never do.' He smiled at her. 'You cannot be a heroine on an empty stomach.'

'Is that what you think me?' she said, feeling her cheeks grow warm again. 'How very foolish of you, Major Collingham. Pray now, stop your teasing and pour me a little of that small beer.'

Once they had finished their supper, Major Collingham collected up the dishes and carried the tray downstairs, saying he did not wish their host to have to come to their room again. He returned a few moments later to find Juliana trying to peer out of the window.

'You will see nothing,' he said to her. 'The mist has not lifted, it is completely black outside.'

She came away from the window. 'I hope the farm boy managed to reach Fewell.'

'We shall not know that until the morning.'

'Then I suppose we should try to get some sleep.'

A rueful smile lit his eyes. 'I don't think I shall have any difficulty there. I shall put the table across the door, in case our host should try to come in during the night.'

'Do you think that is likely?' asked Juliana, looking anxious.

'No, but I would rather not be taken unawares. Come now, get you to bed.'

She watched him place the remaining bedding on the floor before the fire.

'Here.' She took the blanket from her shoulders and held it out to him. 'I shall not need this now.'

'Thank you.' He caught her hand and held it. 'Thank you for coming with me.'

* * *

Juliana awoke to find sunlight streaming in through the dusty windows. For a moment she lay still while she remembered the events of the previous day. Minna was sleeping peacefully beside her and Juliana raised her head to look about her. The logs had burned away to a pile of grey ash, leaving the air sweet with woodsmoke. Damon was still asleep on the floor, his breathing deep and regular. Juliana slipped out of bed and padded across to the settle. Her dress was clean, but sadly muddied. Shaking it out, she slipped it on and was tying the sash when the Major's deep voice made her jump.

'So you would deny me the pleasure of watching you dress.'

She did not look at him. 'I want to be ready when Fewell arrives.'

'How practical you are, Miss Wrenn. How eminently sensible.'

'Do not mock me, sir.'

'I do not mock you, Ju, I mock myself, for wanting to prolong this interlude. We are about to go back to our real world, where you are the governess and I am your employer. We must behave the way our world demands, and I will no longer be able to talk with you, to eat with you and to…sleep with you in the same easy manner that we have enjoyed here. And, apart from the danger to Minna, I *have* enjoyed it, Juliana. Although I have not laid a finger on you I have revelled in your company.'

Juliana blinked rapidly. Her fingers trembled as she finished tying the ribbons on her gown. 'You have said yourself sir, this is not real. We have to go back to our duties and responsibilities.'

'Juliana—'

A whimper from Wilhelmina made him break off and they both hurried to the bed.

'So you are awake now, Minna,' said the Major. 'How do you feel?'

'Hungry,' said Wilhelmina after a slight pause.

'And the bruise on your head, does it hurt?' he asked.

'Only if I touch it.'

Juliana put a gentle hand on her brow and nodded at Damon. 'She is quite cool. There is no fever.'

'Good. I shall go and see what Mr Stopes has to offer.'

'And while your papa is away we shall get you dressed,' said Juliana, pulling aside the bedclothes. 'Fewell should be here soon with the carriage to take us back to the George. What an adventure we shall have to tell the others!'

Damon looked at her, the ghost of a smile on his lips. 'Are you never out of spirits, Miss Wrenn?'

Her lips curved involuntarily. 'Never in front of the children, Major.'

Their arrival at the George brought the whole party out to meet them. Wilhelmina was handed down to Giles to be borne gently up to her room while the Major barked out his orders. A doctor and magistrate must be summoned, pens, paper and ink to be brought to his room immediately. Juliana climbed wearily down from the carriage and went indoors with Thomas and Amy, reassuring them that all was well. As she went upstairs to change out of her muddy gown, Gwendoline followed her.

'Miss Wrenn, is Minna injured? What can I do?'

'She was very frightened yesterday, Gwen, and was a little wet from the mist, but I think she has suffered no other hurt. Perhaps you should go and ask Nurse if you can help her, I am sure she would be glad of your assistance.'

'Yes, yes, I will.' Gwendoline brightened perceptibly and ran off to find Nurse.

* * *

The rest of the day passed in a bustle of activity. Once she had changed into a dry gown Juliana went to help Nurse. She was on hand to see the doctor and ordered lunch for the children, a meal which seemed to have been forgotten in all the excitement. The doctor was optimistic that, although distressed by her ordeal, Wilhelmina was suffering from nothing more than exhaustion, but upon hearing that she had banged her head he recommended that she should not be moved for a few days and that someone should sit with her throughout the night. Since Nurse was the obvious person to look after the invalid, it fell to Juliana to look after the other children until they went to bed.

At ten o'clock she relieved Nurse in the sickroom. Wilhelmina was sleeping soundly, and Juliana settled down in her chair to watch her. Half an hour into her vigil there was a light scratching on the door and the Major came in.

'Oh, Miss Wrenn. I thought Nurse would be here.'

'She has gone to lie down for a few hours. We are sharing the night watch.'

'Of course. How is Minna?'

'Peaceful, thank goodness. The doctor left a sleeping draught in case she grew restless, but I am hopeful that it will be a very tedious night, with little to do but watch her.'

'May I join you?'

He pulled up a chair and sat down on the other side of the empty fireplace. A lamp on a table in the corner cast a warm glow over them, but left the bed and its occupant in semi-darkness. In Farmer Stopes's dusty chamber Juliana had been comforted by the Major's presence—now it unsettled her. She sought for a topic of conversation.

'Thomas has told me something of the prize fight you attended—not everything, of course, for he is old enough to know that some things are best not shared with a sister. However, I am grateful that you allowed him to go with you.'

'It was no hardship. Thomas is a fine boy, and he and Giles get on very well, despite the difference in their ages. Giles has even started to give him sparring lessons, since I have not yet had the time to do so. I hope you do not object?'

'No, not at all. I am pleased that he has some male company and I do not believe you or Giles will lead him into bad ways.'

'Thank you, Miss Wrenn. Your confidence almost unmans me.'

'Nonsense,' she retorted, flushing. This was dangerous territory, she moved away from it. 'You—you have seen the magistrate, Major?'

'Yes. I have given him my statement, but do not expect much to come of it. I hope that my letter to Mondwyck will be more effective. If Leeson turns up in town, Richard will apprehend him.'

She shuddered. 'I dread to think what would have happened if you had not come back when you did.'

'Well, it is over and you need have no fear now. Fewell and my coachmen are on watch in case Leeson should come back, although I think that is unlikely.'

'So, too, do I. But I cannot understand why he should abduct Minna. You know Leeson, sir—could it be some sort of revenge against you?'

He shrugged. 'I wish I knew. I have seen Leeson in town, of course, but I know little of him, except that...' He paused. Juliana waited expectantly. He looked up at her, then continued gruffly, 'We have...we *had*, a mistress in common. There, I have said it. Are you shocked, Miss Wrenn?'

'I am too anxious to understand Mr Leeson's actions to

worry about social niceties, Major Collingham,' she responded coldly.

'I had a brief, ah, flirtation with a lady I believe is now Leeson's mistress. Or perhaps it would be more truthful to say that he is *one* of the lady's lovers.'

Juliana studied her hands.

'And your…connection with the lady?'

'Ended within weeks of its beginning. Satisfied, Miss Wrenn?'

'It is really of no interest to me, except where it concerns the children, of course.'

A chilly silence descended. The Major spoke again. 'Do you propose to sit here all night with nothing to do?'

'I have my book to read, and there is some mending…' She waved vaguely towards her workbox.

'Excuse me.'

Major Collingham rose and left the room. Juliana sighed; disturbing as she found his presence, it was preferable to sitting alone in the darkness. She went over to the bed to Wilhelmina, who was still sleeping soundly. The lack of light had robbed that part of the room of its colour, even the scarlet gown on Wilhelmina's precious doll was almost black. As Juliana straightened she heard the door click again and looked around to see that the Major had returned, carrying a bottle and two glasses.

He smiled, his teeth gleaming white in the low light. 'You are confined to this room, but there is no reason why you should not enjoy some pleasures.'

'I—I am not sure,' she stammered. 'Perhaps a little water for me—'

He put down the glasses and proceeded to fill them, ignoring her protests.

'Here.' He held one out and she looked at it doubtfully.

'Do you think I am trying to make you drunk?' he growled at her. 'To seduce you in my daughter's sickroom?'

'No, no—of course not! I—'

'You look with suspicion upon everything I do for you.'

'No!' She looked anxiously towards the bed, knowing her voice had risen, but Minna did not stir. 'No,' she said more quietly, hanging her head. 'It is my own weakness that frightens me.'

He put his fingers under her chin and forced her to look at him.

'I am an ogre to distress you so. If I give you my word to behave with the strictest propriety, to treat you with unimpeachable politeness, will you cry quits with me?' He dropped his hand. 'Now, what have I said to make you smile?'

'Propriety and politeness are not words I associate with you, Major Collingham.'

He laughed. 'That's better. Lord, how I like your frankness, Miss Wrenn. Are we friends again?'

'Yes, sir.'

'Good.' He raised his glass to her. 'I want to thank you for your help in rescuing Minna.'

'I did very little.'

'I was glad to have you with me.'

'Th-thank you.' She was unaccountably cheered by this, and managed to give him a small smile. It was reflected in his eyes.

'That's better. Now, we shall sit down and drink a glass of wine together while we keep watch over the patient.'

When a clock somewhere in the house chimed one, Juliana suggested he should retire.

'There is no need for you to give up all your sleep, sir. Besides, Nurse will be returning shortly to relieve me.'

'And you would not want her to find us together?'

'She might not understand the nature of our…friendship, sir.'

'I'd wager Nurse knows me as well as anyone, but I can see from your expression that you are adamant, so I will take my leave of you. Until the morning, Miss Wrenn.'

When Major Collingham had gone, Juliana sat for a long time, staring at the chair he had vacated. In the day there had been anxiety for Wilhelmina, but the doctor had put her worst fears to rest and she had been able to enjoy her glass of wine. The Major had been with her for more than two hours, yet she could not recall what they had talked about— everything and nothing. She thought she had never felt so content as in that quiet, dark room with the occasional hooting of an owl outside the window, and Minna as their chaperon. Juliana felt a sudden constriction in her throat. She took out her handkerchief and blew her nose defiantly. There was a saying that half a loaf was better than none. Well, she had only a few crumbs, and she feared that they were proving to be infinitely worse than no loaf at all.

Chapter Fourteen

The next morning Nurse came downstairs to report that Wilhelmina was recovering well. The rest of the party were gathered at the breakfast table, and the old lady beamed at them all.

'She is sitting up, and Gwen helped her to take a little gruel for her breakfast.'

'When may I see her?' asked Amy.

'The doctor is to call again at noon,' said Juliana. 'We had best wait for his opinion. To pass the morning we will take a walk across the fields to the tiny church on the far side of the valley. Look, you can see it from the window here.'

Gwendoline pouted. 'Will that not be muddy?'

'Perhaps a little, but there will be a path leading from the village, so we shall go and see. We can always come back if it is too bad.'

'You will not go unattended,' put in the Major. 'The landlord must send one of his servants with you.'

'It is already agreed,' she replied, meeting his harsh gaze with a bland smile. 'It will mean taking his man away from his duties, but I said you would not begrudge the extra charge.'

His frown deepened, but she observed the twinkle in his eyes and turned away to hide her smile.

'Do you mind if I do not go with you?' put in Thomas. 'Giles and I wanted to see the carriage.'

'Oh, is it mended?' said Juliana.

'The new wheel was fitted yesterday and the carriage is now safely under cover,' replied the Major. 'I would like the boys to look it over and make sure my driver is happy with it. And Giles, ask Fewell to make sure the leather hood of the curricle has been waxed again; it was leaking yesterday.'

'So may I go with Giles, Juliana?' Thomas turned his hopeful gaze upon his sister.

'Very well. I will take Gwendoline and Amy for a walk, and we will look for more wild flowers to press for our journal.'

The Major held the door as she ushered her young charges off to collect cloaks and bonnets.

'You are never at a loss for amusement, Miss Wrenn,' he muttered as she passed him.

'Activity prevents boredom, Major Collingham,' she told him. 'And boredom, as we know, leads to mischief, for adults as well as children.'

The doctor called again promptly at noon and declared himself satisfied with Wilhelmina's progress. He recommended another night of rest, but agreed that Major Collingham could resume his journey the following day, if Wilhelmina continued to improve. The children went to bed in good time that evening in readiness for their early start and, after wishing them all goodnight, Juliana returned to the private parlour where she found the Major and his son engaged in a game of chess.

'Are the children asleep already, Miss Wrenn?' asked the Major, not looking up.

'No, sir, but they have been persuaded to lie down on their beds—Gwendoline is reading to Amy and Nurse will look in upon them later to make sure they do not leave a candle burning all night. She tells me she will sleep on a truckle bed in Minna's room tonight, so I am relieved of my sickroom duties.'

'Careless, Giles.' Major Collingham's hand hovered over the chessboard. 'You allow me to take your bishop. So, you are at leisure to please yourself, Miss Wrenn. What do you propose to do? You never seem to be idle.'

'Well, tonight I shall be,' she declared, going to the window seat. 'Our host tells me there will be a fine moon rising tonight, and I intend to sit here and watch it. Pray do not let me disturb your game.'

Juliana made herself comfortable in the window, but instead of looking out for the moon she watched the game of chess and studied the two opponents. They were very alike, both tall, but Giles was fairer and still had the ranginess and exuberance of youth; by contrast, his father exuded an air of calm strength. Juliana watched the Major as he gave his attention to the chess pieces. The flickering candles highlighted the strong lines of his face, giving him a harsh, intractable look. Many called him a hard man, but she had seen the tender way he had carried Wilhelmina back across the fields, and she remembered the way they had talked, late into the night. There was kindness beneath his harsh exterior. She was glad he had not gone on to Blackthorpe and left the school party to follow. With an effort she tore her eyes way from the two men and looked out at the butter-yellow moon climbing over the valley. Really, she was becoming quite weak-willed, quite mawkish. It would not do. The sooner she set up her own establishment the better.

* * *

'Papa, you have me in checkmate! I made sure you could not do that.' Giles's laughing protests cut through her reverie.

'I told you that you were too careless with your smaller pieces,' said the Major. 'Next time take more care over your moves. Will you pack the set away, please?' He rose and came over to the window, bending a little to look out at the sky. 'If you wish to see the moon, Miss Wrenn, perhaps you would care to step outside. You will have a clearer view from the road.'

She hesitated, and he turned to his son.

'Giles, would you like a little fresh air before you retire?'

'Thank you, no. That replacement knight I made does not sit quite steady, so I am going to work on it again.'

Major Collingham looked back at Juliana. 'So it is just you and I, Miss Wrenn. It is a fine night; you will come to no harm.'

The temptation was too great to resist. She uncurled herself from the window seat. 'I will get my shawl.'

The heavy rain clouds of the day had broken up and a full moon was climbing high and bathing the village in a silver-blue light. The road outside the inn was in good repair and the few puddles were easy to negotiate. She walked beside the Major, making sure she kept a distance between them.

'So,' she said at last, ' tomorrow you will be at home.'

'Aye, if all goes well.'

'I have never been so far north—will you tell me about Blackthorpe?'

For a moment she thought he had not heard her but at length he began to speak.

'It lies amid the hills and high moors to the north of Manchester. At one time Blackthorpe was a hunting lodge, but the forests and woods have for the most part been cleared for farming, although there is still a fine park surrounding the house.'

'Has it been in your family for long?'

'Aye, generations. The Collinghams made their money as wool merchants, then my grandfather wanted to be done with trade and to live as a gentleman.'

'You do not sound as if you approve of his decision,' she observed.

'He sold off the best of the farming land on the northern estates. What was left was not sufficient to support the lifestyle my father adopted and the estate was reduced even further. I am not a pauper, far from it, but the income is dwindling and will continue to do so, unless I can turn around our fortunes.'

Juliana pulled her shawl more tightly about her. 'With an advantageous marriage, perhaps?'

'Yes,' he said curtly. 'Marriage to Lady Frances will combine our estates—indeed, a fair portion of her inheritance is land her husband's family bought from mine. The alliance will more than double the income and allow me to pass on a healthy inheritance to Giles as well as providing good dowries for the girls.'

A dull ache had settled inside Juliana. She raised her eyes to the moon, idly noting how it had turned from a large yellow ball to the cold silver disk now shining down upon them.

'My first marriage was a love match,' he continued. 'Harriet and I were both very young. My father tried to advise me against it but I would not listen. I did not then understand how matters stood, and even if I had done, it would not have made a difference: the estate would support us as it had always done. It was not until the children were born that I realised how little there would be to pass on to them.'

'Then your duty is clear.'

He stopped. She risked a look at his face, grey in the moonlight, with a muscle working in his jaw as if he were trying to control some inner turmoil. Suddenly he turned and dragged her into his arms, his fingers biting into her flesh.

'Duty be damned!' he muttered.

Even as she opened her mouth to protest he kissed her, so hard that her senses reeled under the assault. His arms came round her like steel bands, almost crushing the breath from her.

'No, Damon. Pray don't—stop!' Juliana tried to push him away.

He did not release her, but he raised his head, and with a sob she buried her face in his coat.

'You promised me!' she cried, her voice muffled against the cloth.

'I know, but talking of marriage to Frances, I—' his hold tightened. 'Juliana, I love you.'

She whimpered softly. 'Oh, Damon, no. You cannot love me.'

He gave a shaky laugh that Juliana, her cheek resting against his chest, heard as a deep rumble.

'But I do. God knows why, for you use no arts to attract me, and take delight in crossing me at every turn! But after these past few days, I cannot contemplate a life without you.'

She blinked away her tears and raised her head. His eyes burned down into her soul; it would do no good for her to deny she loved him, he would read the lie in her face. As he went to kiss her again, she reached up and put her fingers against his lips.

'No, Damon, we must not. You have told me now why you

must marry. There is no other way. You must provide for your children, as I must look after Thomas and Amy.' The thought of her family gave Juliana the strength to push herself out of his arms. 'When we get to Blackthorpe, I will look for another appointment. I—I do not think I could bear to stay now until September.'

He gripped her hand. 'You will—you must,' he said savagely. 'We have a contract.'

'You cannot hold me to it.'

'I can and I will. Leave me now and you will get not one penny.'

She looked up at him, anger sparking in her own eyes. 'I will serve my two weeks' notice.'

'And leave the children to wonder why you are deserting them?'

'That is too cruel, sir!'

'Perhaps, but it is the truth.'

She felt her resolve weakening. 'I will not stay in the house once you are married. Surely you would not ask that of me.'

He let her go. 'No. No, I would not ask that.' He looked up at the sky. 'But there are ways other than marriage—you do not have to leave the area…'

She gave an exasperated sigh. 'Would you make me your mistress? Would you take away the little dignity I have left?' She hunted for her handkerchief. 'I—I joked when I first embarked upon this venture that I had made a contract with the devil. How true that has turned out to be!'

'Ah, love, don't cry.' He pulled her into his arms again, his anger gone. 'We will find a way out of this coil.'

She allowed herself to lean against him, to breathe in the heady mixture of wool and skin and spices that she associated with him. She sighed. 'If I were to discover I was an heiress, perhaps there could be a solution. Until such a miracle, we must both do our duty.'

He buried his face in her hair. 'Even though it tears at my very soul?'

'To do otherwise would destroy us. You know it is so, Damon.'

With a growl of frustration he pulled her closer. 'I want you as I have never wanted anyone, Juliana. *Why* should I not have you?' he muttered savagely, driving the fingers of one hand into her hair and forcing her head back until she could not avoid his searing gaze. 'What is to stop me dragging you into that barn yonder and taking what I want? After all, it is not as if you are unwilling; I know you want me as much as I want you. And once I have taken you, I will set you up as my mistress—you will have nothing more to lose then.' His arms tightened. 'Why should I not do that?'

He held her so close she found it hard to breathe, and her blood ran cold at his words and the wild look in his face. Struggling to free one hand, she reached up and touched her fingers to his cheek.

'You will not do such a thing because you are an honourable man, Damon Collingham, and you know that such an action would kill my love for you.'

Juliana held her breath, watching his face. It was grey and hard as stone in the moonlight. His fingers curled in her hair, straining painfully against her scalp, but she did not regard it.

'I could break you,' he muttered. 'You are so small, so frail here in my arms. With one swift movement I could extinguish you. And yet you have such power over me.' With a long sigh he let her go and half-turned from her, staring up at the moon with his hands clenched at his sides. 'I would lie down and die for you, Juliana Wrenn, yet you want me to live—without you. You condemn me to purgatory.'

'I ask the same of myself.' She waited a moment, and when he did not reply she slipped her hand through his arm. 'We must go back, sir. To the inn.'

He looked down at the fingers lying against his sleeve, then covered them with his free hand.

'Yes, of course. You will not go without telling me?' he asked her as they turned their steps back towards the George. 'You will not take Thomas and Amy and disappear? When you leave me, I want to know that you are safe. Promise me.'

'I give you my word I shall not leave in such a way. Unless you give me cause.'

'Hah! I should have known you would put the responsibility on my shoulders.' They had reached the door of the inn and he stopped. 'I will bid you goodnight, Miss Wrenn. I will not wish you pleasant dreams. I am selfish enough to want you to suffer, as I do.'

She gave a sad little smile. 'Oh, you may be sure of that, sir. Are you not coming in?'

'No.' He kissed her fingers, gave them a squeeze and let them go. 'I shall walk on for a while. I have a sudden desire for some vigorous exercise.'

Juliana watched him stride away, then turned and slowly made her way up to her room. She felt desperately tired, but guessed that no amount of sleep would relieve the black depression that filled her heart. She did not believe Major Collingham would refuse to pay her something if she chose to leave, despite his harsh words. She would look for another post, but how long would that take? Weeks, at least, which would give her time to see Gwendoline and Wilhelmina settled into their new home. She realised that she was almost as fond of them as she was of her own family. She thought dismally that, if it were not for the children, she could end her own misery by drowning herself in the local horse pond. As it was, she would continue the journey to Blackthorpe and hide her despair as best she could.

Chapter Fifteen

'Here we are, dearies.' Nurse leaned forward to peer out of the coach window. 'You'll soon have your first view of Blackthorpe Hall.'

They had been climbing for some time, travelling across wild desolate moorland with only the occasional farmhouse and its stone-walled enclosures to relieve the emptiness. Now the road was curling about the side of a hill and as they swept around for their descent a wide, green valley came into view below them covered with a mix of woodland and pasture. Winding through the lowlands was the new canal, the ground around it brown and scarred by the recent construction. To the west and east the land rose up gently, but in the far north smoky grey peaks indicated a wilder landscape.

'Look!' cried Gwendoline, 'There's the Hall. You can just see the gables.'

'Bless you, dear, and you nought but a tot when you was last here,' exclaimed Nurse, admiring.

'There is a painting of the house in the drawing room at Kewhurst,' put in Wilhelmina, 'so I remember it too!'

Juliana followed Gwendoline's pointing finger. To the eastern side of the valley was a small park with a ribbon of white drive curving through it to a long, low house of creamy stone. There was an occasional glimpse of stone-mullioned windows but the gables and twisting chimneystacks were plainly visible above the trees.

'I love this part of the journey,' said Nurse, settling back into her seat. 'I am always reminded of the devil taking our Lord up on to a high mountain and showing him all the kingdoms of the world to tempt him.'

'Yes,' nodded Wilhelmina, remembering her lessons. 'And the Lord said, *"Get thee behind me, Satan."*'

Nurse chuckled. 'So he did, well done, Minna.'

'Yes, well done,' Juliana echoed, watching the tiny figures in the curricle ahead of them—Wilhelmina's words were a timely reminder of the task she had set herself. She said aloud, 'Blackthorpe is beautifully situated.'

'Aye, miss, 'twas always the master's favourite. In his grandfather's time, of course, the family owned nearly the whole valley, but it is all gone now.' Nurse shook her head, and mouthed the word 'gambling' over the children's heads to Juliana. 'But the Major still owns the land to the east of the house, as far as the eye can see.'

Juliana looked up at the hills, stark and bare against the rich farmland to the west. Her spirits sank; if this was the remains of the Major's estates, it was no wonder he needed to marry well.

'Of course,' Nurse continued, 'some days the cloud is so low there's nothing to see but a grey mist until you reach the valley bottom, but today we are fortunate—we can see clear up to the mountains of Westmorland, where the poet Mr Wordsworth lives, but Miss Wrenn can tell you all about that in your lessons.'

* * *

For the first few days at Blackthorpe Hall, Juliana was busy organising the schoolroom and settling the children into their new home. In such a large, rambling building it was not difficult for her to avoid seeing Major Collingham. The great hall was the oldest part of the house, containing the main entrance and an open gallery that linked the two main wings with the grand staircase that rose majestically from the centre of the hall. The nursery, schoolroom and the rooms set aside for herself, Thomas and Amy were all in the east wing above the library, while the family rooms and the estate offices occupied the ground floor of the west wing with the main bedchambers and guestrooms above. She wondered if some previous owner had planned it for just such an occasion, in order that the schoolroom party would cause as little inconvenience as possible to the lives of the parents. The two main corridors leading from the gallery were almost identical, each lined with carved oak panelling, the long stretches of polished wood broken by plinths bearing a series of marble and alabaster busts. The housekeeper, Mrs Plumstead, told Juliana that there were thirty-two of the busts around the house.

'The master's grandfather was a great collector, miss,' she said, when she was giving Juliana her first tour of the house. 'He had been to foreign parts, you see, and took a fancy to the old statues he saw there. There's everything from Greek gods and goddesses to the likeness of Milton outside the blue guestroom. You will find them all over the house, miss, but the finest examples are displayed in the main passage, which leads to the master's rooms and the guest rooms. Mostly marble they are.'

'But did I not see some examples outside the schoolroom?' enquired Juliana.

'Oh, yes, miss, although most of them are chipped or marked.' She lowered her voice. 'If it was up to me, I would throw out the damaged ones, but the master won't hear of it. Ancient, he says they are, to be preserved for the family. But I says Miss Gwen and Miss Minna would much prefer some nice new statues to look at, if they was given the choice.'

Juliana smiled to herself as she accompanied Mrs Plumstead on the rest of the tour. It was plain that despite her disapproval of the old relics with which Blackthorpe was filled, the housekeeper was proud of her domain and kept everything in gleaming good order. She was also proud of her master, and was willing to tell more anecdotes of the Major than Juliana could bear to hear.

Juliana took her dinner with the children in the schoolroom and sent them with Nurse to visit their father for an hour after dinner each evening. Thomas had been given permission to visit the stables, and on the second evening he came back with the news that the Major had instructed Fewell to find ponies to suit him and Amy, and that they were to be given riding lessons with his own girls. Juliana could not but be pleased at their inclusion and to feel gratitude for the Major's kindness, but there was no mention of her joining in this treat and she was obliged take herself to task for feeling disappointed; after all, the Major spent a great deal of time with his horses, so it would be much better if she avoided the stables altogether. No, she told herself, if she was careful, it was very possible that she could go for weeks without seeing Major Collingham.

The dry weather of their arrival was replaced by a lowering cloud and a fine, chilling rain that blew across the land in hazy drifts, as though Nature was regretting her earlier kindness. The schoolroom windows faced east and looked out across the high moors to the back of the house. The tops of the hills were shrouded in cloud, but there were plenty of tracks through the heather and gorse, and Juliana was eager to explore. A few days after her arrival she sought the secretary in his office to inform him of a crack in one of the schoolroom windows and was emboldened by his friendly attitude to ask him about the moors.

'Mr Brasher, I wonder, can you tell me—are the hills accessible from here? I would dearly love to walk out that way, once the weather improves.'

'Why, yes, miss, there's a track leads directly from the Hall up on to the moor, but you would be wise to keep to the wide tracks and within sight of the Hall. The land is very wild, and the weather can turn in the wink of an eye, and you would not want to be caught out overnight in these bitter winds. It is a dangerous place, Miss Wrenn.'

'You are not native to these parts, I think,' she ventured.

Mr Brasher gave her a rueful smile. 'No, miss, I'm a Hampshire man, born and bred, and more used to Kewhurst, where the soil favours crops and cattle. Farming at Blackthorpe is a perpetual struggle, given the house's situation. Still, with investment, the returns can be improved.'

'And that will happen when the Major marries Lady Frances?' she asked.

'Aye, miss,' beamed the secretary. 'A good day that will be, I am sure.'

On her fourth day at Blackthorpe Juliana was able to escape from the house and set out alone to explore. A stony track led away from the grounds and wound its way upwards. Green pastures soon gave way to gorse and heather and large tracts of rough grassland dotted with sheep. It was a bright, blustery day, with thick white clouds sailing high in a blue sky. Although it was the end of May, a chill wind was blowing and Juliana was glad of her thick pelisse, although the exertion of the ascent soon had her cheeks glowing. She stopped and turned to look back over the valley. The westerly wind whipped at her bonnet and she ripped it off, laughing as the breeze tugged at her hair, pulling strands free from the clips she had so carefully placed earlier in the day. She was breathing hard from her climb, but the exercise had refreshed her, and she felt happier than she had done for months. The sad death of her father and the worry over how she would support the children seemed to have lessened, and even her longing for the Major could be contained as a dull but constant ache. She could be happy here, she thought. If she could find a small house in one of the towns, she could survive in this rough land. Immediately below her she could see Blackthorpe Hall, its stone walls almost glowing in the sunlight. It resembled a large creamy letter E against the green of the lawns and gardens, with the gravel drive winding away through the small park. She would bring the children up here, she decided. On the next dry day they would bring their drawing materials and sketch the house.

'Beggin' yer pardon, miss, but ye should be headin' down now.'

Juliana jumped when the guttural voice spoke behind her. She looked round to find a small, weatherbeaten face peering up at her from under the brim of a battered hat. An old man in brown homespuns touched his forelock, then nodded towards the southern sky.

'Clouds rollin' in. You had best be getting 'ome.'

Juliana looked around and saw the heavy grey cloud massing on the horizon. 'Yes, I will, thank you.' She gave the old man her friendly smile. 'Do you work at Blackthorpe?'

He shrugged. 'Not at the Hall, no, but I does work for the family. Aye, man and boy, I bin tendin' sheep on the moors. Without me most of the families in yon valley would starve.'

'Oh, you provide their meat, then? Do the sheep not belong to the estate?'

The man gave a cackling laugh. 'You bain't from these parts, I can tell! Staples, miss.' Juliana looked blank. He said patiently, 'Wool. The womenfolk spins it, and the men sits up at their looms and weaves their pieces to take to the market.'

'Oh. And does that provide a good living?' she asked him.

The old man spat. 'It suits some. Me, I'd rather be out 'ere under the clouds than cooped up with a clacking loom all day.'

'You must love these moors.'

'Aye, miss, I do. And there's riches 'ere, for them as knows where to look. Gold,' he whispered.

She could not prevent her smile. 'I think not,' she said, putting on her bonnet. 'Because I am new here does not mean I am a simpleton.'

'No more than the rest,' he called after her. 'They can't see it, but it's here, right enough. Black gold.'

With a laugh and a wave of her hand Juliana set off down the hill. The clouds to the south were billowing over the sky, and by the time she reached the park the sun had disappeared and the fresh breeze had grown chilly. Juliana headed for the stable yard and the quickest way into the house. As she turned in through the gateway, she saw a diminutive groom leading a beautiful long-tailed grey to the mounting block. Almost immediately Major Collingham came out of the house, escorting a tall woman in a deep-blue riding habit.

Juliana hesitated, but only for a moment. They had seen her, and to turn back and scuttle away would only draw attention to herself. Squaring her shoulders, she walked quickly across the yard towards the side door, pausing only when the Major called her name.

'Lady Frances, let me present Miss Wrenn to you before you leave.'

'Ah, yes, the governess,' murmured Lady Frances, giving Juliana a faint, cold smile. 'I had expected her to be in the schoolroom.'

In that few moments Juliana learned everything she wanted to know of Lady Frances Ridlington. The lady was built on queenly lines, and the velvet riding suit had been tailored to accentuate her generous figure. An abundance of flaxen hair was swept up beneath a wide-brimmed beaver hat trimmed with ostrich feathers that curled around her face. Her features were regular, there was nothing to displease. Juliana had heard her described as serene, but thought she looked smug, and immediately castigated herself for this uncharitable opinion.

'Yes,' remarked Major Collingham, 'Why are you not in the schoolroom with your charges, Miss Wrenn?'

'We have finished our lessons for the day, sir, and I left them in the care of Nurse, sewing their samplers.' The wind tugged at the curls that were escaping from her bonnet and she became aware of her windswept appearance. 'I took the opportunity to walk up on to the moor.'

The Major's eyes narrowed. 'So I see.'

Lady Frances laughed gently. 'Do not be too angry with her, Damon; the wind here is enough to make any female look positively frightful. No doubt you will allow Miss Wrenn to bring the children to the drawing room after dinner tomorrow night, and she will be a little more prepared for a meeting with me.'

Juliana's cheeks flamed. She bobbed a curtsy and walked to the house, using all her will-power to prevent herself from breaking into a run—she would not scurry away like a frightened minion.

She spent some moments at the door, vigorously scuffing the mud from her boots while her anger cooled. Behind her she could hear the muted voices as Lady Frances took her leave, and the clatter of hooves on the cobbles, but Juliana went inside without a backward look. She had reached the main staircase when she heard the Major calling her. She stopped and looked back.

'What were you doing on the moors?'

'I told you, I went for a walk.'

'Alone? I gave orders to the contrary.'

She raised her brows. 'I thought that applied only to the children.'

As she put her foot on the first stair he reached out and caught her wrist.

'No, you foolish girl, you are as vulnerable as they…and as dear.' His thumb rubbed gently into the palm of her hand and a sudden sting like lightning shot down through her body. She tried to pull away, but he held her firm. 'Did you see anyone while you were out?'

'Only an old man—wizened and brown as a nut. He told me he looked after the sheep.'

'Old Caleb. He's harmless enough.'

'If a little confused; he said there was gold on the moors.'

He smiled faintly.

'If only that were true! Very well. Go and look to your charges.'

'I had best tidy myself first.'

'Aye.' He scowled at her. 'How dare you walk through my yard looking like a regular blowsabella and frightening my guest?' The scowl disappeared. He chuckled. 'Oho, that's made you show hackle, eh?'

'I have no idea what it means, but I infer that you are trying to insult me,' said Juliana furiously. 'Let me go!'

'It means a country wench,' he said, smiling.

With a little cry of frustration and anger Juliana swung her hand up to slap his face, but he was too quick for her, and in an instant she found herself pinned to his chest, both wrists held firmly behind her back. She glared up at him.

'How dare you!'

'I would dare a great deal more,' he growled, his hard eyes glinting down at her.

She felt the tears pricking her eyelids and suddenly the fight left her. She hung her head, whispering into his coat, 'Damon, you promised.'

He sighed. 'Aye, so I did.'

He released her and stepped away so quickly that she was obliged to reach for the baluster to steady herself.

'I have tried to keep out of your way,' she said. 'It would be best if I did not come down to the drawing room to-morrow night….'

'No, you must be there. Frances wants to talk to you about the children.' He raked his fingers through his hair. 'Promise me one thing: you will not leave the house again unaccompanied. Until I know why Minna was abducted, I would not put any of you at risk. My people will not take it amiss; I have told them something of the danger, and asked them to be on the watch for strangers.'

'Very well, sir. But may I take the children on to the moors? I would like them to sketch the house from the hills.'

He turned, saying over his shoulder, 'Yes, yes, as long as you take Fewell or one of the footmen with you.'

Juliana watched him walk away and felt her heart sinking. This was intolerable: she must find another post. How were they ever to bear this torture until September?

Chapter Sixteen

High winds and frequent heavy showers put an end to any hopes of going out of doors the following day and Juliana kept the children in the schoolroom for most of the morning. Thomas sulked at first, because Giles had asked him if he wanted to go out rabbiting, but Juliana was firm—Thomas was behind on his lessons and must stay indoors. A diversion was caused shortly after luncheon when a large parcel was brought up to the schoolroom.

'It is addressed to you, Juliana,' cried Gwendoline, taking the package from the footman and carrying it to the table. 'And there's one of Papa's visiting cards tucked under the string, look.' She lifted it out and turned it over to read the message scrawled on the back. *'Louisa has sent this for you,'* she read. *'You will oblige me by wearing it this evening.'*

'It is the new dress Aunt Louisa has had made up for you,' said Wilhelmina. 'To replace the one Gwen spoiled.'

'Yes, well, never mind that,' said Gwendoline hastily. 'Will you open it now?'

Juliana smiled. 'Why don't you open it for me?'

'I'll fetch a knife,' said Thomas, running to the desk.

With Amy and Minna looking on, Thomas cut through the string and Gwendoline carefully peeled away the paper to reveal a large printed box. She threw back the lid and pulled out a long, creamy dress packed in layers of tissue paper.

'Oh, it is lovely!' breathed Amy as Gwendoline shook out the material and held it up for inspection.

Juliana caught her breath. The gown was made of the finest muslin and seemed to float on the air. The frilled hem was decorated with pink ribbon and appliquéd acanthus leaves, with a matching decoration around the deep neckline and tiny puff sleeves.

'Oh, I cannot wear it!' she whispered, pressing her hands to her cheeks.

'Of course you can,' said Gwendoline, holding the gown against herself and taking a few skipping steps across the room. 'It is perfectly exquisite.'

'That is just it,' sighed Juliana. 'It is far too fine for me.'

'No, it isn't,' declared Amy, 'you will look beautiful.'

'But I am still in mourning for Papa.'

Wilhelmina spread her hands. 'Aunt Louisa did not know that,' she said.

'The Major insists that you wear it,' said Thomas, waving the visiting card. 'Besides, when Papa died and we had no money for mourning clothes, you said people in straitened circumstances should not worry about their dress, as long as their grief was sincere.'

Juliana frowned. 'Your memory is far too good, Thomas,' she said severely. She took the gown from Gwendoline and carefully folded it back into the box. 'No,' she said, trying not to sigh, 'my grey silk will be much more suitable for this evening.'

'Oh no, please, Juliana!' Gwendoline caught her hand

and gazed up at her imploringly. 'If you are taking us down
to meet Lady Frances, please wear your new dress. Lady
Frances is always so...so *bang-up prime* that you will want
to look your best!'

'Gwendoline, where in heaven's name did you pick up
that phrase?' demanded Juliana, trying to sound severe. 'If
Thomas taught you that—'

'No, no, it was Giles,' said Gwendoline quickly. 'But
that's not the point—Nurse is always telling us that Lady
Frances is terribly modish.'

'And she is an earl's daughter,' put in Wilhelmina.

'Yes,' nodded Gwendoline. 'So *surely* you would not wish
to look like a dowd tonight?'

Remembering her encounter with Lady Frances, Juliana
was aware that she desperately wanted to look her best that
evening. She tried one last argument. 'But I have no gloves
or slippers to match.'

'Yes, you have!' cried Amy, diving into the box. 'Lady
Varley has sent you some.' She held up a pair of shell-pink
slippers and matching long gloves.

'And a fan, too,' added Wilhelmina, who had been rum-
maging through the packaging.

'How—how kind of Lady Varley,' uttered Juliana in
failing accents.

'So you see, you have no excuse not to wear it,' concluded Gwendoline.

Juliana looked at the happy, expectant faces around her
and capitulated.

Juliana stared at her reflection.

'I suppose it will do,' she sighed.

'Do?' cried Nurse, bustling around the room behind her.
'You look as fine as fivepence, and no denying it!'

'The children are behaving as if this is some sort of special treat for me.'

'And so it is: you have the perfect opportunity to wear your new gown. They are very much looking forward to going downstairs; they have heard so much about Lady Frances and at last they are going to meet her.' She sighed. 'It was said she would have married the Major first time round, if he had not set his heart on Harriet Blakeney. Now, well…he's a widower and she's a handsome widow; 'tis only natural they should think of marriage.'

'Yes.' Juliana felt as if a lump of lead was lodged in her chest. She squared her shoulders. 'Are the children ready, Nurse? It is time to take them downstairs.'

'Aye, Miss Juliana, they have been ready and waiting these ten minutes past.'

Juliana cast another look in the mirror. 'The neck is so low; if only I had a shawl to put about me…'

'Nonsense, you look positively lovely.' Nurse came over and kissed her cheek. 'Now off you go, dearie. Keep your head up, and smile; you look as fine as any lady, I promise you.'

With these words of support ringing in her ears, Juliana called to Gwendoline and Wilhelmina to join her, adjured Thomas and Amy to be good and set off for the drawing room. Plumstead, the Major's butler, was waiting to open the door for them.

After the gloom of the main staircase and hall, the drawing room was glaringly bright. The rain clouds had given way at last to a blue sky and the evening sun blazed in through the long windows, filling the room with a dazzling, golden light. Juliana stopped in the doorway, blinking. When her vision cleared, she observed that the dinner party had been a small one. There were only two ladies present: Lady Frances Ridlington and an older lady whom she guessed was Countess Mattishall, Lady Frances's mother. Besides the Major and his son, the only other gentleman was a cheerful-looking man in a green frock-coat. Earl Mattishall, she concluded.

Major Collingham came forward to greet her. 'So you came.' He added in a low voice, 'I wondered if you would heed my request.'

'Request, sir?' Juliana murmured, bringing the children into the room. 'I thought it more in the nature of an order.'

'And you are wearing your new gown.' The Major continued as if he had not heard her. 'I knew it would suit you; Louisa has such excellent taste.'

She blushed, and could not think of a reply, but none was necessary for he was already taking his daughters forward to introduce them to Lady Frances. She immediately embraced them and presented each of the girls with a small, elegantly wrapped package. She smiled down at them.

'Now you must open them immediately, and tell me if you like your gifts.'

The bows were untied and the wrapping speedily torn away.

'Ooh, a stocking purse!' cried Wilhelmina, holding up a long knitted tube ornamented at each end with coloured beads. 'Thank you, ma'am.'

'My cousin-companion Beatrice made it,' explained Lady Frances. 'She is for ever knitting, so I thought she might produce something useful for me.'

'And I have a brooch,' said Gwendoline, holding the ornament on her hand. 'Look, Papa, emeralds, fashioned like a bow of ribbon. How pretty, thank you.'

'They are only paste, so you may be easy, Damon,' said Lady Frances. 'I know how careless children can be. If it is broken or lost, it is of no great moment.'

Gwendoline opened her mouth to protest, but Juliana caught her eye and urged her to silence with the tiniest shake of her head.

Major Collingham took Lady Frances by the hand. 'You are very kind to think of them,' he said, raising her fingers to his lips.

Lady Frances inclined her head, and gave a little smile. 'I am glad they like them. I trust Giles is as happy with his sketch block and pastels.' She raised her voice as she spoke, and directed a look of enquiry towards the young man, who was sitting in one corner.

'Oh, yes,' he said, flushing slightly. 'Thank you, ma'am, very useful. Although it is Gwen who is the artist.'

But Lady Frances was not listening. She was giving the Major an arch smile.

'Having no brothers of my own, I have no knowledge of just what a young boy would like.'

'It was very good of you to think of the children at all,' he replied.

'Yes, thank you,' Giles said again. He rose. 'Papa, if you will excuse me, one of the pointers picked up a thorn while we were out this afternoon, and, although I pulled it out, I want to make sure there is no infection.'

With a bow to the company Giles strode to the door, but the glance he gave Juliana as he passed was eloquent of the relief he felt to be escaping from the drawing room. Juliana was moving away to a quiet corner when she was called back by Lady Frances.

'Miss Wrenn, I shall not allow you to hide yourself away. You must come and sit over here, where I can talk to you without having to shout across the room. Mama, this is Miss Wrenn, the children's governess. You will recall I mentioned her.'

Juliana made her curtsy towards the large, iron-haired lady sitting in majestic state in a winged chair and the man in the green frock-coat, standing behind her.

'My parents are paying me a short visit before they go off to the Continent,' continued Lady Frances. 'It was so fortunate that they arrived in time to accompany me here, Damon, for it means that I could give Beatrice the night off.' She gave a tinkling little laugh. 'So tiresome she must find it to follow me everywhere.'

'Nonsense, my love, I am sure she is very glad to repay you for taking her in.' Lady Mattishall returned her attention to Juliana, looking her up and down in a considering way. 'So, Major, Frances tells me you had three governesses before Miss Wrenn.'

The children had come to sit beside Juliana on a sofa, and she was aware of Gwendoline's anxious glance at her father.

'Yes,' he said shortly. 'They did not suit.'

'I have always considered it most important that children are taught correctly,' declared Lady Mattishall. 'A really good governess is a very rare thing. Miss Wrenn, you do not look to be long out of the schoolroom yourself—I suppose you must have sufficient experience for your position?'

'I like to think so, ma'am,' Juliana replied coolly.

'The children like her, at all events,' added the Major.

'The children's wishes in this matter are of little importance,' stated Lady Mattishall with majestic finality.

Juliana closed her lips firmly to suppress her retort, reminding herself that it was not her place to express an opinion.

'Oh, fie on you, Mama,' cried Lady Frances playfully, 'I vow you would have us think you an ogre, but I know you would not wish any child to be miserable. I remember I was very happy when I was at school.' She turned to Juliana.

'Major Collingham tells me that your younger brother and sister participate in the lessons, Miss Wrenn. Do you not find that difficult? I mean…' she gave another little laugh '…do you insist they call you *Miss Wrenn* when you are teaching them?'

'They call her Juliana, as do we,' put in Wilhelmina, who was playing with the shells on her new purse.

Lady Frances raised her finely arched brows. 'Indeed? Is that not a little…irregular? Does not the lack of respect engender a lack of discipline?'

'Not at all,' returned Juliana. 'I find they all mind me very well.'

'Perhaps they do, for now, but you have been with them for, what, a couple of weeks.' She raised her eyes to Major Collingham. 'I am surprised at you, sir, allowing such laxity. I cannot think that you, as an army man, approve.'

The Major shrugged. 'I leave the running of the schoolroom to Miss Wrenn. It is, after all, why I employ her. Lord Mattishall, I have ordered coffee to be brought in, but there is a very fine cognac here that I think you will like…'

Lady Frances accepted the Major's rebuff without demur and began to talk with her parents about their plans to tour the continent.

'Think of it, Damon,' she said. 'Paris, then Switzerland in the summer months, and for the winter, Naples and Rome! How I would love to see Rome.'

Lord Mattishall chuckled as he accepted his glass of brandy from Major Collingham. 'Aye, my little puss likes to be on the move—London, Brighton, wherever society is at its liveliest.'

'And what of the country?' asked the Major.

'Oh, one tires of the country quicker than anything,' said Lady Frances, rising. 'Unless, of course, one is kept well entertained.'

She smiled at the Major, who raised his glass to her.

'Then we must do our best to amuse you.'

Lady Mattishall questioned Juliana about her family, and although she thought some of the lady's questions impertinent, she answered truthfully, glad that she need not give her attention to the little group in the corner, where Lady Frances was conducting a lively conversation with the two gentlemen. Once the coffee was finished Juliana sought leave to take the children away. The Major gave his permission and she prompted the children to bid the guests goodnight.

'Lady Frances really is beautiful,' said Wilhelmina as they trooped up the stairs.

'Yes,' agreed Gwendoline. 'Just as Papa told us she would be. Did you notice her gown? The bodice studded with pearls and little embroidered roses all round the hem and sleeves.'

'Just like a fairy princess,' breathed Wilhelmina. 'And she gave me a purse, even if I have no pennies to put in it at the moment.'

'That was very kind of her,' said Juliana.

Wilhelmina turned to her sister. 'Do you like your brooch, Gwen? It looks very well against your gown.'

Gwendoline looked down at the bow-shaped ornament pinned to her bodice. 'Yes, it is very pretty.'

'Tomorrow you shall both write a thank-you note to Lady Frances; then she will see how neat is your handwriting.' *And she will know that I am teaching them something*, she added silently.

Chapter Seventeen

The following week dragged by. The rigours of the journey north paled for Juliana as she struggled to maintain a cheerful demeanour while an aching unhappiness grew within her. She took her meals in the schoolroom, sending the children down to the drawing room each evening with Nurse. Her only glimpse of Major Collingham was from the schoolroom windows. In fair weather or foul the Major rode out every day, and every day Juliana stood by the cracked window pane and watched him trotting out of the yard and cantering through the park on his powerful black hunter. She tried to tell herself that he was merely riding over his own lands, but it was difficult to continue with this comforting thought when Nurse made constant allusions to the changes soon to come to Blackthorpe.

'It is a match, you mark my words,' she said to Juliana. 'He will soon propose to Lady Frances, I am sure.'

The children had gone to bed and they were alone in the schoolroom. Juliana did not reply, but continued to tidy the room, putting away the books and returning the globe to its place on the top of a large cupboard. Nurse lowered herself into the rocking chair by the hearth and gave a contented sigh.

'I have always said it's time the master married again. It's not natural for a man to live alone, and the children need a mother. I don't deny that he was head over heels in love with Miss Harriet, but it is eight years now since the poor lamb died.'

'Lady Frances is a very suitable match,' remarked Juliana, feeling that some response was required.

'Aye, that she is, and it's not as if the master will be marrying her for her wealth alone, for Lady Frances is an accredited beauty, and that's enough to gladden any man's heart—oh, Miss Wrenn, now you've dropped the chalks on the floor. Dear me, let me help you…'

'No, no, it will not take me a moment.' Juliana dropped to her knees and began to gather up handfuls of chalks. 'So careless, I do not know what came over me.'

'Why, my dear, you are tired, and no wonder, when you have been obliged to keep those children occupied indoors these past few days. Take yourself off to bed now, Miss Wrenn; there's nothing here that won't wait for the morning.'

Juliana took Nurse's advice, but it was long before she slept that night. It was not enough to hide herself away from Major Collingham; she was living in his house, there were reminders of him everywhere, his whip and gloves discarded in the hall, his portrait in the gallery—she could even sense his personality in the fabric of the house, with its dark panelled corridors and the rooms full of vibrant colour, as bold and energetic as the man himself. And then there were the girls. She had been told that both girls had inherited their mother's beauty, but Juliana could see the Major in the tilt of a head, a sudden, fleeting expression, or in Gwendoline's granite-grey eyes, so like her father's that Juliana's heart would clench in despair and longing for what she could never have. Then there was Thomas; her little brother slipped away from the schoolroom as often as he could to help out in the stables or to join Giles for his sparring lessons with the Major. He returned from these forays in high spirits and eager to talk. Thomas declared that Major Collingham was true as a gun, never talking down to one and a good teacher. His conversation became littered with things the Major had said. Juliana endured it all with a calm smile, but each mention of the Major stung her like salt on an open cut. She would not for the world dissuade Thomas from confiding in her, and she was wise enough to realise that if he was looking to Major Collingham for his model, she could not wish for a better example for him to follow. Juliana therefore struggled to overcome her own unhappiness, comforting herself with the thought that she need only endure life at Blackthorpe until September, or the Major's marriage, whichever came the sooner.

The next day brought a welcome break in the weather with a dry, bright morning that gave Juliana her chance to take her pupils to the moors with their paints and sketchbooks. Thomas excused himself, saying that Giles had invited him to ride out with him and visit a new mill that was being built, so it was only Juliana and the three girls who toiled up the hill, accompanied by one of the under-footmen, Juliana having requested Plumstead to provide her with an escort, in accordance with the Major's wishes. She had also asked Mrs Plumstead to pack up a picnic for them; with such a treat, it was no wonder that they all enjoyed the break from routine, and came back down the hill late in the afternoon in the highest of spirits.

The sunshine and fresh air had acted as a tonic for Juliana and she returned to the house much refreshed. She brought the children into the great hall just as the Major was coming down the stairs with a gentleman at his side. Juliana smiled in delight as she recognised Sir Richard Mondwyck.

'Miss Wrenn, I was just asking Collingham about you. How are you?'

'Very well, sir, thank you. How good it is to see you again.'

He took her hand and raised her fingers to his lips. 'Damon was telling me that you have been sketching from the hills—did you not see my coach arrive?'

'I did indeed see a carriage, but I thought it was Lady—' She broke off, smiling. 'Do you mean to make a long stay?'

'Oh, well now, that depends upon how long Damon can put up with me.'

Major Collingham had been talking to the children, but now he came up to stand beside his friend. 'As long as you like, Rick, you know that.' His eyes, dark and hard as the rocky outcrops on the moors, rested on Juliana. 'Perhaps your presence will persuade Miss Wrenn to come down to the drawing room after dinner.'

'Yes, pray do, Miss Wrenn.'

Juliana found herself responding to Sir Richard's friendly smile. 'I will,' she said, preparing to follow the children up the stairs. 'I will come down this evening, with pleasure!'

Chapter Eighteen

'You appear to be much more at ease with your children here,' remarked Sir Richard.

Damon watched the little party disappear from the upper landing.

'During our journey north I was in much closer proximity with them than I had ever before—enjoyed.'

'Good for you!' Sir Richard laughed as he followed his host to the library. 'And they like their new governess?'

'I think so. Yes. Very much.'

'And yet it is not usual for Miss Wrenn to accompany them downstairs of an evening?'

'No. She has the care of them all day. Their nurse is quite happy to be with them for that short time.' Damon saw the knowing look in his friend's eyes and felt the colour mounting to his cheeks. 'God damn you, Richard, let it be! I am as good as married.'

'You have offered for Lady Frances, then.'

'No. It is implied, but not yet agreed.' He gave an exasperated sigh. 'You did not come all this way to discuss such matters. Out with it, Rick.'

'Very well. It was your letter that brought me here.' Sir Richard accepted a glass of wine and settled himself into one of the armchairs.

The Major filled his own glass. 'Any word of Leeson?'

'Not yet. My men are looking out for him, but we fear he may have escaped abroad.'

'Damnation, I was afraid of that. I wish I could have caught him, I would have found out what his game is.' He thought back to that day, the hectic chase across the fields, Juliana clutching his arm, fearing for his safety. He remembered it so clearly: her green eyes dark with alarm, her voice begging with him not to leave them. His instinct had been to go after Leeson, to beat him senseless, but Juliana's pleas had cut through his white-hot anger. Dear heaven, how she had got under his skin! Sir Richard's voice brought him back to the present.

'Your letter said this was not the first incident.'

'No. Just before we left town, Miss Wrenn's little sister was attacked.'

'She is of an age with Wilhelmina, I think,' mused Sir Richard. 'Child abductors?'

The Major frowned. 'I wondered about that, but Amy was attacked on a busy street by two young ruffians. God knows what they thought they were about, for I was only a few paces away. And Leeson, well, he made off with Minna, but... Rick, he did not seem like a man acting for himself. I would swear he never meant to harm her; why, he was shaking so much he could not even hold the pistol. Yet I cannot believe these were random attacks.'

'Do you have any enemies?'

'No more than any other man, I dare say. But until I know the reason for these attacks I am taking no risks. I have warned my people to be on their guard, and Ju—Miss Wrenn has instructions that none of the children are to go out of the house without a manservant to attend them.'

'And I am here now, so I will help you to watch over them,' said Sir Richard.

'Thank you, Rick, but can you be spared? I thought you were busy searching for the Borghese diamonds.'

'Alas, that trail has grown cold. My men will keep looking, of course. They know what they are about, and if they need me they will send word. I can be in London in a couple of days.' He grinned. '*I* am travelling light, old friend.'

Damon gave a crack of laughter. 'You are fortunate. You do not have to transport a parcel of brats with you.'

'You could have gone on ahead.'

'Aye, but heaven knows what might have happened to Minna if I had not been there.' He paused. 'The children are all I have now, Rick. What I do is for them, to provide for their future.'

'And the little governess, Juliana Wrenn?'

Damon rose abruptly. He went to the sideboard and refilled his glass. 'We have a contract. She stays until September, or until the wedding.'

Sir Richard tossed back his wine. 'If that's the case, you'll marry as soon as possible and let the girl leave here. It will not do to let the children grow too fond of her.' He stood up. 'Now, we had best change for dinner. Did you tell me that Lady Frances will be joining us tonight?'

'Yes, with her parents. They are visiting the north before going off to the Continent.'

'No doubt they want to see the banns posted before they leave the country.' The Major's growled reply was inaudible, but Sir Richard merely laughed and clapped his host on the shoulder. 'Come on, you old bear, if we delay much longer you will not be ready to greet your future bride.'

* * *

Dinner in the schoolroom was a noisy affair. Thomas had returned from his visit to the new mill with Giles and was full of the wonders of water, steam and power looms.

'They are building such big mills, now,' he told them, in between mouthfuls of food. 'Whole families work there, day and night, and they use the power of the local water supply to spin the cotton and work the looms, too.'

'How did you learn so much?' asked Juliana. 'I hope you did not get in the way.'

'Not a bit of it,' returned Thomas, helping himself to more potatoes. 'Fewell's brother is the engineer there, and we had a letter of introduction to him. Of course he would have received Giles in any event, as Major Collingham's son, but when he found we were *truly* interested in the machinery, he showed us all over, including the new steam engine.'

'Lady Frances is coming to dinner tonight,' said Wilhelmina, bored with the subject. 'We have not seen her since the night she gave us our presents. Nurse says you are to take us down, Miss Wrenn.'

'That is so.' Juliana nodded.

'Is that why you are wearing your new gown?' asked Gwendoline

'That's to impress Sir Richard,' giggled Amy.

Juliana frowned at her. 'It is not to impress anyone. I merely want to look my best for the Major's guests.'

'I wish I could come down,' sighed Thomas. 'I would dearly love to meet Sir Richard. Giles says he is a real topper.'

'Does that mean he is interested in machinery?' asked Juliana, her eyes twinkling.

'Yes, but not merely for the mills. Giles says he invests in foundries—iron and steel—and he knows a great deal about the new steam engines.'

'I have no doubt you will meet him tomorrow, Master Thomas,' said Nurse, giving him her kindly smile. 'But you know it wouldn't be right for you to go to the drawing room.'

'But Juliana is going,' argued Amy, waving her knife.

Juliana gently pushed her arm down. 'That is because someone must be there to look after Gwen and Minna,' she said.

'Well, I wish Amy could come down as well,' said Wilhelmina. 'It would be much nicer if I had someone to play with.'

'Heavens, you mustn't play in the drawing room!' exclaimed Nurse, half-shocked, half-laughing. 'You are there for your father to show you off to his guests.'

Juliana shook her head. 'You make them sound like trophies, Nurse, not children.' She rose. 'Now, if you have finished your meal, girls, I think we should make you as neat as pins before we join your father.'

Gwendoline and her sister ran ahead of Juliana to the drawing room, eager to meet Lady Frances once more. Juliana was forced to hurry to catch up with them, afraid they might burst into the drawing room without her. As the footman opened the door she entered, flushed and a little out of breath, not at all as composed as she would have liked. She was relieved to see the gentlemen had already come in from the dining room. Sir Richard was talking to Giles, who was looking very smart, if a little uncomfortable, in his dark coat and knee breeches; Lord Mattishall was standing beside his wife's chair, smiling benignly at no one in particular; and Lady Frances had taken up her position on a sofa in the centre of the room and appeared to be holding court. Juliana could not deny that she looked magnificent in a high-waisted gown of bronze lustring with diamonds adorning the slender

column of her neck and winking from her ears. The thought
that she was a trifle overdressed for a country dinner Juliana
quickly dismissed as springing from jealousy. She sighed,
and began to wish she had not come. Gwendoline and her
sister immediately went forward to make their curtsies.

'Ah, look, Mama, the little Misses Collingham,' cooed
Lady Frances. She patted the sofa beside her. 'Come and sit
by me, my dears.'

'You see, I have my purse with me,' said Wilhelmina,
climbing up on the sofa. 'And Gwen is wearing her brooch.'

'Lovely, but you must hush now, my dear, because young
ladies must learn to sit quietly until they are addressed. Now,
Sir Richard, what were we saying? Ah, yes, poor Mr
Brummell. It is true, then—he has fled the country?'

'Yes, ma'am. It would appear he quit London a few hours
earlier than Damon.'

'Then I hope he enjoyed a better journey,' returned the
Major, smiling at his friend. 'I heard nothing of it on
Thursday.'

'No, it was very quietly done,' explained Sir Richard. 'He
was seen at the opera on the Thursday night, but it seems he
had a chaise waiting for him, for he did not go to his rooms
again.'

'No doubt the creditors were waiting there,' remarked
Lord Mattishall, shaking his head. 'Dashed wolves, waiting
to pounce as soon as they hear a man's pockets are to let.'

'They have their own families to feed,' remarked Major
Collingham. 'Brummell has existed for years on credit.'

'As do many in town,' put in Sir Richard.

'Aye, and pass their debts on to their children,' growled
the Major, a frown in his dark eyes.

'Well, I for one will miss Brummell's wit,' announced
Lady Frances. 'But such dismal news is all of a piece with

this dreadful weather. We have had such a wet spring here. My steward was telling me this cold wet weather has rotted the seed in the ground. And it is the same everywhere, is it not, Papa?'

Lord Mattishall nodded. 'Aye, my love. I fear we are in for a poor summer.'

Juliana had chosen a seat in one corner of the room, well away from the main party, but where she could watch the girls and be ready to step in should they forget their manners or grow too noisy. She was grateful for the opportunity to regain her composure after her hasty entrance, but scarcely had the flush died from her cheeks than Sir Richard approached.

'I will not ask how you go on, Miss Wrenn, for I can see that you are in high bloom.'

'Thank you, sir. To be out of doors today has been of benefit to us all.'

He sat down beside her. 'You know Damon wrote to me about your journey and what happened at Rushton Spencer?'

'Minna's abduction? Yes. It was truly terrifying.'

'He has had nothing but praise for your cool actions.'

'Me?' Her cheeks grew warm again. 'I did very little, Sir Richard.'

'But you saw as much as anyone, and you went with Collingham to chase Leeson. If it would not upset you, I would like you to tell me everything—and also I would like to hear about the attack on your sister.'

She looked up. 'You think there is a connection?'

'I hardly know. Damon has already told me about it, but I am hoping that there may be some clue to help us unravel this mystery. Until we know why these attacks occurred, we cannot be sure that the danger is over.'

'Of course I will help, if I can.' She frowned a little and

after a slight hesitation began to recount everything she could remember until the moment they had Wilhelmina safe. The night spent in the farmhouse she skipped over, and was thankful that Sir Richard did not question her too closely.

'Thank you, Miss Wrenn,' said Sir Richard, when she had finished. 'I know it must be painful for you to relive these events.'

Juliana nodded, aware that the pain of recollection was not wholly connected with Wilhelmina's adventure. There was a general bustle as Plumstead entered with the tea tray and Sir Richard rose and held out his hand to her.

'I think it is time we were a little more sociable. We should join the others.'

'Oh—no, sir. Pray, go and take your place, but I am merely the governess, I should remain here.'

He took her hand and pulled her to her feet. 'I insist, Miss Wrenn. Damon does not wish you to be so excluded, I am sure.'

'Goodness, Sir Richard, you and the little governess have had your heads together for a full half-hour,' exclaimed Lady Mattishall as he escorted Juliana to a sofa nearer the centre of the room. Gwendoline and Wilhelmina immediately ran across to join her.

'Hush, Mama.' Lady Frances gave a soft laugh. 'Can you not see that you are putting Miss Wrenn to the blush?'

Juliana felt a spurt of anger at the insinuation. Her indignation grew when she saw the Major frowning at her, for surely he must know why Sir Richard wanted to talk to her. She allowed Sir Richard to bring her a cup of tea, his easy manner doing much to calm her agitation as he gently teased the children and included them in his conversation. At first Juliana struggled to respond, but soon she relaxed and even laughed aloud at some of his more amusing anecdotes. Giles, she noticed, was talking in an animated fashion to his father, and she realised that he was holding forth very much as Thomas had done earlier, although with slightly more clarity, on the wonders of the new mill being constructed at Burnley. Even while she listened to Sir Richard, she was aware of the mention of spinning mules, water frames and jennies. It was impossible to ignore his enthusiasm, and even Sir Richard cast an amused glance at him.

'Young Mr Collingham has a great interest in machinery,' he murmured to Juliana. 'I took him to see the new mint building at Tower Hill when he was in London. He was enthralled by the coining presses, worked by steam power, of course. I begin to think he has the makings of an engineer—what do you say, Miss Wrenn?'

Before she could respond she heard Lady Frances say in a bored, carrying voice, 'Really, Giles, your papa cannot be interested in all this talk of mills.'

Giles flushed a little. 'I think we should consider building some ourselves. We have the land and sufficient water, and there is the new canal almost running past our door—'

She threw up her hands in mock dismay. 'Really, Giles, that smacks of trade.'

Giles ignored her and turned back to his father, enthusiasm shining in his face. 'But we should consider it, sir.'

'I did consider it some years ago,' replied the Major. 'There is barely sufficient head of water in Blackthorpe Clough for one small engine.'

'But we have coal in the hills,' said Giles. 'Steam is the new way of powering the machines.'

Greatly daring, Juliana raised her voice to join in. 'When I was on the moors, the old man—Caleb—said something to me about black gold. Do you think he meant coal?'

The Major considered her words. 'Possibly. They used to

collect it from the tops, but it was close to the surface and easily dug out. However, that seam was worked out in my father's day.'

'There are new ways of mining now, sir,' put in Giles. 'When we were in Leek, the wheelwright there was talking to a man, an engineer—'

'My dear Giles, you must accept that your father knows best in these matters.' Lady Frances's voice cut across the room, carrying clearly to everyone present. 'Damon, Mama tells me they plan to be in Rome by the autumn. You have been there, have you not? Do come and tell us all about it…'

Giles, flushed with embarrassment at the snub, looked as if he wanted to stride out of the room, but Sir Richard beckoned to him.

'That new mill has fired your imagination,' he said, smiling.

'If there is coal in the moors, then we should mine it,' muttered Giles in a furious undervoice.

'It should certainly be investigated,' put in Juliana. 'I read that there is a way of finding out these things, of looking at the landscape.'

The boy nodded enthusiastically. 'It is in the layers of rock, the way they are laid down. The—the strata.'

'I, too, have heard that,' said Sir Richard, nodding. 'A man named Smith has produced a geological map of the country.' He looked up at Giles. 'You should find out a little more—I will help you if you like, then you can put the case to your father. But not,' he added with a twinkle, 'when you have company. Choose a time when he is not occupied with social niceties!'

Chapter Nineteen

For the first time since arriving at Blackthorpe, Juliana awoke from her night's sleep refreshed and eager for the day. Looking back at the evening, she thought it the most pleasant she had spent at the house. The conversation had been lively, and Sir Richard's kindness had ensured that she had not been excluded. She acknowledged that there was nothing of the lover in Damon's attentions to Lady Frances, and although it did not lessen the dull ache of longing inside her, she felt her emotions were under good regulation.

Juliana set the children to work on their lessons and ran down to the library in search of an atlas. The morning was well advanced, and she knew enough of the household's routine to be confident that Damon and his guest would be engaged in some outdoor pursuit. She skipped downstairs, humming and went into the library without knocking.

'Oh!' She stopped in the doorway. 'Oh, I am sorry—I thought you had gone out…'

Major Collingham was sitting at his desk, engaged in mending his pen. He looked up as she entered. 'As you see,

I am still here. Richard has gone out riding with Giles and left me to attend to my business—no, don't run away. Come in and close the door. I want to talk to you.' He said as she came towards him, 'You were singing when you came in, and you were in spirits last night.'

'Sir Richard is charming company. He went out of his way to entertain me.'

'As I do not.'

His voice was taut with anger. She forced herself to speak calmly.

'I do not expect it, sir.'

'You enjoy Mondwyck's company?'

'Why, yes.'

'No doubt that is why you were so delighted to see him yesterday afternoon.'

'Yes, I was pleased to see him,' she retorted, nettled. 'As I would be pleased to see any old friend.'

He walked to the window and stared out. 'Perhaps you would like him to be more than a friend.'

'No!'

'Why not? *I* cannot marry you, so why should you not set your cap at him?'

Her cheeks flamed. She replied furiously, 'I would never *set my cap* at anyone. That is a crude term and I find it offensive.'

'Oh, do you?' He flung himself across the room and stood before her, frowning down at her with such a dreadful scowl that she stepped back, only to find the unyielding edge of the desk behind her. 'Well, *I* find it offensive that you are flirting with him in my house!'

She gasped. 'How dare you accuse me of flirting. How dare you!' she railed at him, seething with anger. 'I see what it is— you are jealous. You think because you cannot have me—'

'Can I not?'

With something that sounded like a snarl he grabbed her. She looked up to protest and his mouth swooped on her. The force of his attack made her senses reel, and all the emotions she had held so rigidly under control were released. She was overwhelmed by him, by the familiar hint of spice on his skin, the strength of his arms around her—it was intoxicating. For a moment she clung to him, then reason reasserted itself and she pushed against him, tearing her mouth free.

'No, Damon, this is wrong.' She glanced up into his face and suffered a shock; there was a wild look in his eyes, no sign that he understood her. He cupped her face with one hand and kissed her again, even more savagely. When she pushed her hands against his chest, it was not the Major who gave way. With the desk behind her she felt herself bending backwards. Damon was pushing her down, using his arm to sweep everything out of the way as he lowered her on to the desktop. She heard the clatter as the inkwell and pens fell to the floor, followed by the heavy thud of the paperweight. She found herself looking up at the strapwork on the ceiling, noticing the carved cornices on the top of the tall bookshelves; her world was quite literally turned on its head. Then every thought was obliterated as he kissed her again. Inwardly she fought against her own desire while struggling against him, but her feet no longer reached the floor, and she had no strength to fight him off. She had no *will* to fight him off; her resolve was slipping away. *This must not happen*, she told herself, turning her head aside to avoid his mouth, knowing that if he continued to kiss her she would be unable to prevent her body giving in to his demands. Her heart was thudding so hard it made the blood sing in her ears. Denied her lips, his mouth moved over her cheek, gently now, the tip of his tongue tracing the line of her jaw up to the tender lobe of her ear. She bit her lip hard to stop herself from responding. Her panic grew as he began to trail kisses down her neck—she was losing control. He tore aside the muslin fichu and began to kiss the swell of her breasts. A groan was wrenched from her.

'Damon, we should not be doing this.'

He raised his head and stared at her, his eyes blazing. 'You want me,' he muttered, breathing heavily, 'You know you do.'

'Yes, yes, I do, but not like this!' Even as she spoke he lowered his head again, his body crushing her on to the desk. She gasped, for his touch had turned her insides to molten fire. She arched towards him, giving the lie to her whispered pleas for him to stop. She was losing control. Her hands beat a futile tattoo on his shoulders. Another minute and it would be too late, the hot liquid in her belly was spreading to her limbs, making them wayward, responding to his touch rather than her will. It would be so easy to give in to him, to abandon herself to the heat of the moment, but there was a part of her that told her she would regret it; even more painful, she was sure that Damon would hate himself when he realised what he had done to her. Unable to push him off, her hand groped around the desk, knocking a sheaf of papers to the floor, brushing against the feathers of a pen. Then her fingers touched metal. She stretched out and grasped the handle of the pen knife. Summoning up the last shreds of her resolve, she brought her arm round and drove the knife with as much force as she could muster into his arm. Restricted as she was, the blow had little force, but it was enough.

With an oath the Major pulled away from her. Juliana rolled off the desk and scrambled away from him, holding the knife before her.

'That may be the way you take your whores, but you shall not treat me thus!' she hissed at him.

She had moved out of reach, watching him, ready to fly if he should come towards her, but he remained by the desk, feeling his arm.

'You stabbed me, you little vixen.'

He was breathing heavily, but she noticed with relief that the mad light had gone from his eyes.

'Have—have I hurt you very much?' She could not resist the question.

'Not as much as I deserve,' he said ruefully. 'Ju, I am sorry.'

'I asked you to stop.' She blinked away the tears that were welling up. Silently she straightened her bodice. He sat down on the edge of the desk, clutching at his arm with his good hand.

'You did. I am sorry.' He looked chastened. 'I never expected you to defend your honour so fiercely. I thought you cared for me.'

'I do!' She dashed her hand across her eyes. 'I *do*. But you are engaged to marry another woman and I cannot—will not—come between you. Do you not see? You are an honourable man; I would not have you demean yourself—or me.'

'But we love each other, Ju. There can be no shame in that.'

She shook her head at him, raising her hands in frustration.

'What would you have me do—become your mistress? If I did that, I could no longer teach your children. And what of Thomas and Amy? Are they to grow up knowing that their sister is—is a—' She turned away, her voice suspended in tears.

'No, you are right.' He sighed. 'You see everything so clearly, and you are so much stronger than I. You must be my

example, Juliana. I will try to match your fortitude in future.'
He paused. 'Do you think you could help me out of my coat?
You need not look so suspicious, I give you my word I will
not touch you, but I would like to see how deep you have cut
me.'

Juliana went to him and eased the coat away from his
shoulder. The woollen sleeve had taken most of the force and
there was no more than a tiny tear in the shirt, but it was surrounded by a bright red stain.

'Oh, heavens, what have I done?' gasped Juliana, tears
coming to her eyes again.

'Well, let us see.'

He shrugged himself out of his flowered waistcoat, unbuttoned his shirt and pushed it off the shoulder to expose
the wound on the top of his arm. Juliana blinked and swallowed hard. Not at the sight of his injury, which was nothing
more than a small cut, but at the shadow of dark hair on his
chest, and the hard bare muscle of his shoulder.

'There is a clean handkerchief in the pocket of my coat,'
he said. 'Perhaps you can find it; we must bind up the arm
until it stops bleeding. I could call for Plumstead, of course,
but I would rather the servants did not know of this.'

Juliana found the handkerchief, shook it out and proceeded to fold it into a bandage. The Major watched her as
she bound up his arm, but she kept her eyes resolutely on her
task, aware that the emotion sizzling between them a few
moments ago was in abeyance, but it had not disappeared.

'There.' She stepped back. 'I think that will hold. I am
relieved it is nothing more serious. Truly.'

He grunted. 'It is merely a scratch, but you have ruined a
perfectly good coat.'

She did not smile. 'It will not work, sir. I cannot stay
here.'

There was a silence, broken only by the steady tick, tick of the clock.

'So you will leave me.'

'I think I must. I *know* I must.'

Silently he put on his waistcoat and walked over to the window. He sighed. 'Yes, you must. I cannot be trusted when you are near me. I shall buy you a house. Do not argue with me, Ju. I will not let you leave here unless I know that you are safe. If not for yourself, accept it for Thomas and Amy. It shall be wherever you please. Harrogate, or perhaps Manchester—that is a growing town, there will be many rich merchants who want a good education for their daughters. You may be sure that I shall give you a glowing reference.'

Juliana nodded. Her heart felt like lead and she did not care where she went since it meant she would not see him again.

'I will set Brasher on to it. You can tell him what it is you require; I shall not interfere.'

He began to collect up the pens that were scattered across the floor.

'I must be gone within the week, sir.'

He looked up at that. 'So soon? You would have me pay dearly for my loss of control.' He suddenly saw the tears rolling down her cheeks and jumped to his feet. He would have taken her in his arms, but Juliana put out her hand, mutely shaking her head at him.

'If you will not let me comfort you, then dry your tears,' he said roughly. 'To see you cry is more than mortal flesh can stand.'

'I must go. The children will wonder where I am.' She wiped her eyes, then turned to the mirror and arranged the muslin around her shoulders. Her hair had escaped from its pins and she did her best to scrape it back into some sort of order. In the mirror she watched the Major go back to his desk and sit down. The tears welled up again when she saw how tired he looked. It would be better for them both once she was gone away. Damon would busy himself with his estates and soon forget her: she would retire to a genteel little house in Harrogate and wait to die.

Juliana squared her shoulders. That was silly talk. She had Amy and Tom to look after. She could not afford to indulge in such maudlin behaviour, and neither could Damon.

'I shall see Brasher in the morning, and when I have decided upon where to live I shall ask him to find me lodgings until such time as we can find a house. If you have no objection, I would like to continue teaching the children— I would prefer not to tell them I am leaving until I have some idea of my direction.'

'They will miss you.'

She raised her chin. 'I shall miss them, but they have much to occupy them, a wedding and a new mama.'

'Yes, there will be a great deal to do in the next few weeks. Which reminds me…' He began sorting through the papers he had retrieved from the floor. '…Brasher informs me that the glass has arrived to replace the cracked window in the schoolroom. They plan to do the work tomorrow—would you be able to teach the children in the morning room?' He looked up, his mouth twisting into a humourless smile. 'It should only be for the day, and you have my word I will not disturb you.'

'Thank you, sir. I am sure we will manage very well.'

'Then it is settled. You had best go now. Have no fear, Miss Wrenn: your colour has returned to normal, and with that muslin wrapped around you so demurely no one would guess how near you have come to being ravished.'

A thread of laughter fluttered inside her; how like Damon to show humour when they were in the midst of a nightmare.

Chapter Twenty

Heavy, lashing rain delayed the replacing of the window and three days later Juliana was still using the morning room as a makeshift schoolroom. When the day dawned dry and bright, Juliana took the children out of doors for an early morning walk to collect leaves and flowers for a drawing lesson. They were all quietly employed at this task when the door of the morning room burst open and Lady Frances swept in, the velvet skirts of her riding dress caught up over one arm. She stopped in surprise when she saw them.

'We have been ejected temporarily from the east wing by the workmen,' Juliana explained. 'Did Brasher not say?'

'I did not see Brasher,' came the curt reply. 'I came in through the garden door. I expected to find Collingham here.'

Juliana blinked. 'Major Collingham went out early this morning, with his son and Sir Richard,' she said quietly. 'If he is expecting you…'

'No, no.' Lady Frances strode about the room, tapping her riding crop against her gloved palm. 'We made no plans, but he should have known I would ride over on the first fine day.'

Something very like a pout marred her serene features.

She walked around the room, looking at the children's work. She stopped beside Wilhelmina and picked up the sheet of paper at her elbow. It bore sketches of several different leaves.

'Ju—Miss Wrenn drew that,' offered Minna, holding up her own attempt. 'This is mine.'

Lady Frances put the paper back down. 'I wonder the Major does not hire a drawing master for you.'

'Perhaps he will,' murmured Juliana, 'if they show an aptitude for the art.'

Lady Frances raised her fine brows. 'And are you qualified to tell if they have a talent, Miss Wrenn? Really, I think they would do a great deal better at school.'

Thomas looked up from his sketchpad, quick to take offence at this insult to his sister. Juliana gave him a little smile and the tiniest shake of her head. She thought it best not to reply. After all, in a few days' time she would be gone, and the Major would be free to consult his future bride about his children's education. She withdrew to a sofa at the side of the room.

'And these…' Lady Frances pointed her riding crop at the dolls propped up on a chair. 'What place have such toys in a schoolroom?'

The two younger girls looked up anxiously and Juliana smiled to reassure them.

'It is usual for Wilhelmina and Amy to leave their dolls in their bedrooms, but with the workmen making such a noise upstairs, we decided to keep them with us today.'

'I do not hold with such indulgence,' announced Lady Frances, continuing her perambulation. As she moved away, her crop caught the hair of Wilhelmina's doll and it toppled off the chair. Wilhelmina gave a gasp. Lady Frances did not notice, and continued to walk up and down the room with quick, angry strides. Wilhelmina waited until she had turned away again, then scrambled down from her chair to retrieve her doll.

Unfortunately, Lady Frances had allowed her skirts to slip from her arm, and as Wilhelmina jumped down, her feet caught the edge of her train. There was a ripping sound, and Lady Frances jerked to a halt.

'Oh, oh.'

Wilhelmina stepped back quickly, whimpering. Lady Frances swung round.

'You clumsy child!' she cried, her cheeks scarlet with anger. 'Why can you not be more careful? It is no wonder you were the death of your mother.'

A sudden stillness fell over the room. Gwendoline gasped, Amy and Thomas looked anxiously at each other and Wilhelmina, white-faced, turned and ran to Juliana, who pulled the little girl on to her lap. Lady Frances noticed none of this; she was examining her skirts, and muttering to herself.

'No great damage done, thank heaven. The stitching is pulled, but with a little pressing it might not show.'

Juliana gave Wilhelmina a quick hug and set her down on the sofa. She rose and went across to Lady Frances.

'Ma'am, it was an accident. Wilhelmina is distraught— will you not find a kind word for her?'

'I will not,' retorted Lady Frances, shaking out her skirts. 'The child is wild to a fault. And I lay the blame firmly at your door, Miss Wrenn.'

Juliana fought down her indignation. She said quietly, 'But to imply that Minna was responsible for the death of her mother—'

'It is no more or less than the truth,' came the terse reply. 'Everyone knows that Harriet died giving birth to that child.'

'You cannot blame Wilhelmina for that.'

Lady Frances drew herself up. 'And why not? Would you tell me that Major Collingham would not rather have his wife than that…that brat?'

Juliana gasped. 'Madam,' she said, 'that is an unjust and heartless thing to say.'

'How dare you criticise me!' Lady Frances's face flushed with anger.

Juliana saw that Gwen had gone across to sit beside Wilhelmina, who was sobbing uncontrollably. She tried again.

'Pray consider, ma'am. Will you not tell Wilhelmina that you did not mean those words? Will you not retract?'

'I will not. Let me remind you that you are nothing more than a servant here.'

'I am governess to these children,' retorted Juliana. 'Their welfare is my first concern and I cannot allow you to upset them so.'

'You cannot allow—' Lady Frances stared at her. 'Why, you impertinent hussy. How dare you speak to me in that way!'

'I do dare, madam,' flashed Juliana, thoroughly roused, 'And I also dare to warn you that your callous words will not endear you to these children.'

Lady Frances went pale with fury. She lifted her riding crop. Juliana raised her chin, daring her to strike. After a long, tense silence, Lady Frances lowered her arm.

'Such behaviour is not to be tolerated,' she snapped. 'You and your family will leave Blackthorpe immediately. I—'

'What is going on here?'

They had not heard the Major come in. He strode into the room, still dressed for riding in his brown coat, buckskins and muddy top boots.

'What the devil is the meaning of this?' he demanded. 'I heard your voices from across the hall.'

'Damon, thank heaven! This—this *creature*—' Lady

Frances pointed to Juliana '—has had the effrontery to criticise me—*me*! You cannot allow such behaviour in a servant.'

'Certainly not, if it is true.'

Juliana had walked across to the table, but she turned her head now, her anger barely concealed.

'Oh, yes, it is true,' she said. She took Amy's hand. 'Come, you too, Thomas. We must pack.'

She did not look at the Major, but swept out of the room with her head held high.

'Are we really leaving?' asked Amy, running to keep up with her. 'Where will we go?'

'I neither know nor care.' Juliana strode up the stairs and into the bedroom where she dragged her trunk into the middle of the room.

'But we have no money,' said Thomas.

'Then we shall walk into Burnley and I will take a post as a chambermaid if I must!' She sighed, her shoulders sagging. 'No, no, that is anger speaking. I shall seek out Mr Brasher and ask him for the wages I am due.' She looked down at the two anxious faces. 'You must not worry, my loves. We are no worse off than when we applied to Cousin Pettigrew.'

'But we are hundreds of miles away from London.'

'So we are, Tom. We must make a new life for ourselves. Is that not exciting?'

The words sounded hollow, even to Juliana. She shrugged, and set her mind to packing. There was a knock at the door. The Major came in without ceremony.

'Miss Wrenn, I would like to speak to you. Privately.'

She continued to throw the children's clothes into the trunk. 'You can have nothing to say that the children should not hear.'

From the corner of her eye she observed the tightening of his jaw. He addressed Thomas.

'Will you take Amy outside for a while, if you please? You will find the girls having luncheon in the breakfast room.'

Juliana looked up. 'You will stay where you are, Thomas! We will take nothing further from this house.'

'Now you are being foolish in the extreme,' retorted the Major. 'Go along, Thomas; Giles is out with Sir Richard, so you will find only Gwen and Minna there, no one else,' he added with a meaningful glance.

He waited until Thomas had taken Amy out of the room and closed the door behind him. Even then he did not speak, but stood watching Juliana as she continued to pack.

'Gwen told me what happened.' He waited. 'Will you not talk to me?'

'There is nothing to say.'

'There is much to say! I understand Frances said Minna was to blame for her mother's death.'

'Yes.'

'It is not true and I said as much to Minna before I came upstairs.' He walked over to the window. 'I have also done my best to reassure her—and Gwen, too—that much as I loved their mother, I would not give them up now. They are my world.'

'That was kind.'

'It is the truth.' He cleared his throat. 'Frances has gone. I—we decided we should not suit.'

Juliana found her hands were shaking as she dropped another pile of clothes into the trunk. She said nothing, mechanically folding Tom's shirts and putting them away. After a short pause he continued.

'The—sacrifices I have been prepared to make have all been for the sake of my children. It has been forcibly borne in upon me that to marry Lady Frances might provide for their future security, but it would scarcely make them happy.'

She closed her eyes.

'Well? Have you nothing to say to that?'

She shook her head, her throat too tight with unshed, angry tears for her to speak. He turned towards her.

'Damnation, woman, will you not answer me?'

She continued to bundle her clothes into the trunk. 'It is not my place to offer an opinion.'

'Then it will be the first time since we met that you have not done so!'

'I am merely a governess—'

He swore roundly, making her wince. 'You have never been merely a governess and you know it! You are a most outspoken and opinionated young woman!'

She threw back her head at that, incensed. 'And if I am, it was because I found it necessary to combat your arrogance!'

He continued as if she had not spoken. 'You are headstrong, hot at hand, damnably independent and you have become quite indispensable to my family.'

She froze.

'Juliana, please don't go.'

She swung round, unwilling to face him. Her anger had carried her thus far; now the contrition in his voice confused her.

'You—you cannot want me to stay,' she murmured, her voice barely above a whisper. 'I—I stabbed you.'

'A scratch, and nothing more than I deserved.' She felt his hands on her shoulders, the heat of his body close behind her. She resisted the impulse to lean back against him. 'Ju—I have been such a fool. Can you forgive me for putting you through all this? Can you…love me?'

'I will always love you,' she whispered.

Damon gave a deep sigh. His breath was on her neck. He

turned her round and gathered her into his arms. She leaned against him, her cheek resting against the rough wool of his coat. For a long time they remained thus, standing in each other's arms, and Juliana thought she would ask for no greater happiness.

'So you will stay?' His words rumbled against her cheek and she smiled into his coat.

'Yes.'

He tilted up her face and kissed her. 'Unpack, then. This is your home now. For ever.' He threw up his head. 'Now what the devil is that racket?'

From the stairs came the sounds of running feet and loud voices. Damon opened the door and stepped out, almost colliding with a chambermaid.

'Beggin' your pardon, sir. There's a coach arrived.'

'A coach? What the devil is this now?' He strode away and Juliana followed, bemused.

The long passage to the gallery echoed faintly with the sounds of voices from the hall below. The sounds became louder as they approached the stairs.

'What the…?'

Coming to a halt behind Major Collingham, Juliana peeped around him. Below, the floor of the hall was littered with bandboxes and trunks, while a thin woman in a severe black redingote was directing the servants as they brought in even more bags. Standing quietly in the midst of this confusion was a lady in a pale-blue travelling gown. Hearing the Major's voice, she turned and looked up, and Juliana found herself looking at the most beautiful face she had ever seen.

Chapter Twenty-One

'Lady Ormiston, what a pleasant surprise.'

As Major Collingham descended the stairs to greet his visitor, Juliana drew back into the shadows of the gallery. The lady in the hall was a ravishing brunette with glossy ringlets peeping out from beneath her modish bonnet while the excellent cut of her travelling robe showed her figure to advantage. She had large black eyes fringed with long, curling lashes, smooth cheeks delicately flushed and a pair of red lips that had curved now into a dazzling smile.

'Damon, my dear! You are surprised, no? I am travelling to Scotland to join Ormiston, and when I realised how close we would be to you, I ordered my driver to divert.' The enchanting little face showed a moment's anxiety. 'You will not turn me away, *mon ami*? If it is inconvenient…'

'Not at all,' he said politely 'You are very welcome, Veronique, if unexpected.'

She gave a light, tinkling laugh and cast a roguish glance at her host.

'I was ever that, *non*?' A harsh, hacking cough made her look around at the woman in the black redingote. 'Ah, poor

Sophie. Major Collingham shall tell us which rooms we are to have and then, while you unpack, we shall have a tisane prepared for you, is that not so?' She directed a look of enquiry at Plumstead, who gave a stately bow.

'Of course, madam.'

'*Bon.*' She looked up at the gallery. 'But who is that little thing, hiding up there? Is it one of your children, Damon?'

He laughed.

'Hardly. Come down, Miss Wrenn, and let me present you to Lady Ormiston. This, Veronique, is my children's governess.'

'Ah, and do they make your life very difficult, *mademoiselle*?' asked Lady Ormiston as Juliana came down the stairs. 'My sister and I, we were very naughty for our tutors, but perhaps Damon has little angels?'

Juliana allowed herself a faint smile. 'They are children, *madam*, nothing more.' Now she was closer she could see that Lady Ormiston was older than she first appeared, with tiny lines around her mouth and at the corners of her eyes, but these merely added character to her beauty, as did the lilting French accent.

The Major turned to Juliana. 'It is time you went back to your charges, Miss Wrenn. They should have finished their luncheon by now.' He held her eyes for a moment. 'We will talk later.'

Juliana nodded and began to walk away. She did not look back, but as she heard Lady Ormiston's playful tone she imagined her taking the Major's arm and fluttering her absurdly long lashes at him.

'Now, Damon my dear, tell me truly if I am in the way. But this is such a big house, and you must have a *little* room somewhere that I can use for a night or two? I require very little luxury, after all; during the Terror in Paris, I slept in a hovel on straw, you know.'

'I am sure we can do better than that for you...'

Juliana heard the laugh in the Major's voice. She slipped into the morning room and closed the door firmly behind her. Instead of making her way to the breakfast room in search of the children, she sank down on to one of the cushioned window seats. Her head was spinning with the events of the past few hours. It could not be much past noon, yet already she felt she had not slept for several days. She had never known such anger as she had felt for Lady Frances that morning. Even now her hands clenched tightly at the memory of her callous words to little Minna. She had been prepared to take Thomas and Amy out of the house that very hour rather than make an apology. Then, when her temper was cooling and the first threads of anxiety had started to wrap themselves about her heart, Damon had come to her and told her what she had dreamed of hearing for weeks past; that he was not going to marry Lady Frances.

The sudden transition from despair to elation had shaken her, but Lady Ormiston's arrival had robbed her of the opportunity to talk to Damon about her situation, and her feelings were still in turmoil. She remembered Damon telling her that Lady Ormiston had been his mistress. It had been a brief affair, he had said, but he had not told her who had ended it. Now her own particular demons whispered that the lady was far too bewitching to be cast aside, that it must have been the lady who had ended the affair. Juliana had no illusions about Damon. He was too masculine not to be attracted by the lady's luscious beauty. Juliana sighed. There was nothing she could do to mend matters, she told herself; she had best put aside these melancholy thoughts. She rose and went briskly to the breakfast room, where the children were coming to the end of their luncheon.

* * *

'Ah, Miss Wrenn, such goings on as the children have been describing to me!' Nurse greeted her with a shake of her head as she came in. 'I was mortified when Gwen told me what that woman had said to Minna, and not a word of it true, as the master told her first and as I have been telling her since, for I was there when Mrs Collingham gave birth to my little poppet, and I know how happy she was about it. "Another girl," she says to me. "A beautiful healthy little sister for Gwendoline."' Nurse wiped her eyes. 'It was a few days later that my poor mistress caught the fever and died, and even then she bade me to take Minna away to the wet nurse rather than risk her becoming ill. "Nurse, you look after my little angels," she says, and so I have, all these years, bless her memory.'

The children looked at one another and fidgeted uncomfortably at this display of emotion.

'The Major is not going to marry Lady Frances,' announced Amy.

Juliana sat down at the table. 'So I understand,' she said cautiously.

'It is true.' Wilhelmina nodded. 'He sent us away, but Gwen and I listened at the door. He told her he was sorry, but it would not work, and it was fortunate there had been no announcement.'

'You should not be eavesdropping, and you certainly should not be repeating anything you overheard,' said Juliana, trying to look severe.

'Well, under normal circumstances we would not do so,' said Gwendoline. 'But this was too important to miss. And we shall only tell *you*. Well, then there was a pretty kick-up—'

'Gwendoline!' gasped Nurse.

'Thomas says it.'

'Then he should reserve it for when he is in the stables,' retorted Juliana, frowning at her little brother.

'Very well, then,' continued Gwen. 'Lady Frances railed at Papa, saying he should send us to school to learn some manners, and how everyone knew they were to be married, and they would all say he had lost his senses—'

'And Papa says, "No, madam, I have just found them,"' growled Wilhelmina, and went off into a fit of giggles.

'And then Lady Frances stormed out of the house.'

'And Papa saw us in the hall, and he must have known we heard everything, but he never said a word about it.' Wilhelmina's cheeks grew flushed. 'Instead he—he told us about Mama…'

'I am very glad he did so.' Juliana kissed her.

'Now,' said Nurse, rising from the table, 'Plumstead came in earlier to tell us that the workmen have finished in the east wing, and we can go back to the schoolroom. Miss Wrenn, would you like something to eat before we leave the table?'

'No, thank you. I am not hungry.'

'You are a little pale.' Nurse looked at her closely. 'Are you sure you're not sickening, miss?'

Juliana tried to smile. 'No, I am just—I feel a little faint. Perhaps I should take some air.'

'Bless you, dearie, why didn't you say so?' declared Nurse. 'You take a turn around the garden, miss; the children will come upstairs with me. Unless you would like me to come with you?'

'No, I shall be quite well again in a moment.'

Juliana slipped out through one of the long windows on to the terrace. It was but a step from there to the shrubbery, where the gravel path was sufficiently well drained for her to walk without ruining her thin slippers. A few deep breaths calmed her and she could appreciate the warm sun on her skin, the soft breeze rustling through the bushes. She was not given long to enjoy her solitude. She heard the scrunch of footsteps on the gravel and turned to find Major Collingham striding towards her.

'I saw you come out here. Are you unwell?'

'No, not now.'

He held out his arm and with only the tiniest hesitation she took it.

'An eventful day,' he said.

She smiled at his understatement.

'You are silent, Ju—do you not agree with me?'

'I am still trying to organise my thoughts on all that has happened. But—if you are not to marry Lady Frances, what of your plans to improve Blackthorpe and provide for the children?'

'Oh we shall come about.' He squeezed her arm. 'I am not exactly a pauper, you know.'

'Of course not, but…'

'But?'

'You wanted to rebuild your fortune.'

He stopped and pulled her into his arms.

'I already have my fortune here.'

He kissed her, and Juliana relaxed against him, admitting to herself for the first time how she had longed for this, to feel his arms about her, his mouth on hers, and to know that he was as free to give his love as she was to accept it. Her lips parted beneath his, and as his kiss became more urgent the liquid heat surged through her, pooling somewhere between her hips, which pressed against Damon of their own accord. All too soon the kiss ended. Damon threw up his head, listening.

'Someone is coming.' Disappointment washed through her as she heard the approaching footsteps. He kissed her again, quickly. 'I am thwarted at every turn.' He stepped away from her just as Sir Richard appeared from a side path. 'Rick, are you looking for me?'

'Aye. Plumstead tells me Lady Ormiston has arrived.'

'Yes, alone, too,' said the Major. 'It is too much of a co-incidence. Do you think Leeson has contacted her?' He observed Sir Richard's hesitation and continued bluntly, 'You need not mind Miss Wrenn, she knows as much of this affair as anyone, including the fact that Leeson and Lady Ormiston were lovers.'

'Very well, then. I believe she plans to succeed where Leeson failed.'

Juliana gasped. 'The children!'

'They have Nurse and Matthew, one of my footmen, looking after them at the moment,' said Damon. 'I made sure of it before I came out here.'

'Good, but I do not believe they are in any immediate danger,' mused Sir Richard. 'It is more likely that Leeson snatched the child as a way to manipulate Damon.' He looked at the Major. 'What could he hope to gain from that?'

Damon frowned. 'Do you think I haven't considered that, Rick? I have no influence at Court, no state secrets to hand over. Good God, I do not even have a fortune to tempt him.'

They began to stroll along the path, Sir Richard swinging his quizzing glass gently to and fro on its black ribbon.

'Then if you will let her remain here as your guest, Damon, we must watch and wait for Veronique to make her play. You look troubled, Miss Wrenn. What is on your mind?'

Juliana felt the colour rising to her cheeks.

'Come, Ju,' said the Major roughly. 'What is it?'

'You—you say you will wait for Lady Ormiston to

make her play, but what if it is for...for—' She broke off, blushing furiously.

'You think she might try to seduce me?' The Major laughed. 'I am not a man to be caught twice by that trick. However, you are very right to remind us of the proprieties, Miss Wrenn. You had best go off and change your dress, Giles has sent word that he is dining with Fewell's brother in Burnley—and will be talking of engines all night, I have no doubt! We need you to make a fourth at dinner.'

Chapter Twenty-Two

Juliana dressed with care, not with the intention of pleasing the gentlemen, but more in the spirit of going into battle. She rejected her new cream gown in favour of the grey silk, which showed no signs of the tea Gwendoline had spilled over it, and the rustle of the skirts gave her confidence as she made her way to the drawing room. She found Major Collingham there alone, and stood, hesitating, at the door.

'Come in, Miss Wrenn. Our guests have not yet left their rooms.' He came forward and said, as the butler closed the door and left them alone together, 'You look nervous. There is no need, I am sure you have not forgotten the social graces required at the dinner table.'

'No, sir, but—'

He continued as if she had not spoken.

'As my hostess, I expect you to take your place opposite me, at the foot of the table.'

'Oh no, surely—'

'It is essential.' He stood before her and ran one finger down her cheek. Even that light touch made the blood sizzle in her veins. 'If I have you any closer to me, I shall not be able to keep my hands off you.'

That treacherous finger moved past her chin and began to trail down her neck. She reached up to clasp his hand in both her own.

'Oh, please don't say such things to me. How can I remain calm when you treat me thus?'

His blazing look turned her insides to water and she closed her eyes, fighting to maintain her composure. How could she doubt that he loved her? She heard him laugh softly.

'You are quite right, Miss Wrenn. We must observe the proprieties this evening, must we not?' He gently withdrew his hand from her grasp and stepped away from her. It was not a moment too soon, for the door opened and Plumstead ushered Lady Ormiston into the room.

Juliana sank down on to one of the straw-coloured sofas and began to fan herself gently, as much to disguise her shaking fingers as to cool her cheeks.

Lady Ormiston immediately crossed the room to Major Collingham. 'Forgive me for keeping you waiting, Damon.'

He kissed her fingers. 'You did not, ma'am. We still await Sir Richard.'

She did not look too pleased with this answer, but her smile widened and she turned to look about the room.

'Well, this is to be a cosy little dinner, is it not?' She appeared to notice Juliana for the first time. 'Oh, is it the custom for the governess to dine with you, Damon?'

The Major replied easily, 'Miss Wrenn has agreed to act as my hostess while you are here, Veronique.'

Lady Ormiston's silvery laugh rang out. 'But, Damon, you and I do not need a chaperon, I am a married woman!'

'All the more reason not to give Ormiston cause for suspicion. And while I think of it, Veronique, how long are you planning to stay? Thursday is the day of the Burnley fair, you see. It is a tradition at Blackthorpe that the staff are given a half-day's holiday. That is the day after tomorrow. There will be nothing but a cold luncheon for us and we take pot luck with our dinner when Cook returns. For the afternoon we will be left to our own devices.'

She gave him a roguish look. 'Oh, I am sure we shall contrive to amuse ourselves, Damon.'

'I am sure we will.' Damon looked up as Sir Richard entered. 'Ah, in good time, Rick.' He held out his arm to Lady Ormiston. 'Madam, shall we go in to dinner?'

'Miss Wrenn?'

Juliana looked up at Sir Richard and relaxed a little when he winked at her.

'My knees are shaking,' she confessed in a whisper as he escorted her to the dining room. 'I depend upon you, Sir Richard, to help me through this.'

When Juliana had left the garden, she had taken a circuitous route through the back rooms to avoid a chance meeting with Lady Ormiston. She had seen the footmen storing the mahogany leaves from the table in their green baize-lined slots in the corridor behind the dining room, so she knew the table had been reduced for what Mrs Plumstead described as a snug little party, yet when she was seated at one end of the table with the Major facing her and their two guests on either side, Juliana was aware of a strong sense of isolation. A dazzling array of silver covered the space between her and the other diners, and the distances seemed vast. Her spirits drooped as she watched Veronique flirting with the gentlemen. She was recounting an amusing anecdote and flashing those huge black eyes towards each man in turn. As the meal progressed, Sir Richard left the Major to entertain the vivacious Frenchwoman and turned instead to talk to Juliana, who responded gratefully, while part of her attention remained fixed on Lady Ormiston. She wondered if she was being too sensitive, but the lady seemed intent on fixing her interest with her host. She was leaning forward, turned slightly towards Damon as he replied to a question, as if she was telling him he was the only man in the room.

Juliana glanced at Sir Richard, who was calmly eating the lamb fricassee. The occasional glances he cast at his guest were merely amused. Juliana wished she could be so complacent, or that she was close enough to deliver a well-aimed kick at Damon's shin, since he had designated her as a chaperon for the evening. As it was, she could only curb her frustration and wait for the Major's sign that the ladies should retire. When it came, she rose solemn-faced from the dining table and led Lady Ormiston from the room.

'Well,' said Sir Richard, once the ladies had gone, 'what do you think she wants?'

Damon watched as Plumstead filled their glasses with brandy, then dismissed him with a gesture.

'Veronique is too clever to let me know that yet,' he said when they were alone. 'I believe she is trying to set me at my ease.'

'Have a care, my friend,' said Sir Richard. 'She is a fascinating woman.'

Damon gave a crack of laughter. 'A lovely piece of work, ain't she?' He frowned at his glass, then tossed back the brandy, saying in a quite different tone, 'Miss Wrenn was very quiet at dinner—I depended upon you to look after her, Richard.'

'We talked a little, but in the main we were enjoying the performance you and Lady Ormiston were putting on for us.'

Damon frowned. Even while Veronique had been flirting so

outrageously, a blatant invitation in her eyes, he had been aware of the grave little figure sitting opposite him, picking at her food.

'You may have enjoyed it, my friend, but I am damned sure Miss Wrenn did not.'

'No, you are right.' Sir Richard reached for the decanter. He gave his host a speculative glance. 'Taking little thing,' he said. 'Of course, in looks she cannot hold a candle to the lovely Veronique.'

'But she has a heart, and I would not see it bruised,' retorted Damon. 'I must talk to her. I would to God I had refused to let Veronique stay. I should have sent her away and foiled her little scheme.'

'But then we would never learn what that scheme is, and I am very anxious to find it out.' He sat back, holding up his glass to study the contents through half-closed eyes. 'It will do no harm to let her think she is succeeding in charming you—she may let slip just what she wants.'

Damon frowned. 'But you think she is involved in something that could have national importance.'

'Yes, I do.'

'Out with it, Rick.' Damon refilled their glasses. 'What is in your mind? Come, my friend, we have known each other too long for secrets, even state ones.'

'Very well. I suspect the lady to be involved with the plot to rescue Bonaparte. You will recall I mentioned it to you in London. Somehow, you and your family have become embroiled in her scheme.'

'Then we must try to find out what it is.'

'Exactly, but I would not ask it if I thought there was any real risk of harm to your family. The fact that Veronique has come here so openly suggests that she means to take what she wants by stealth.'

'Don't worry, Rick, I will protect my own.'

* * *

Juliana glanced at the clock. The gentlemen had been sitting over their brandy for nearly an hour. She knew such rituals could go on for much longer, but surely if they suspected Veronique of planning mischief they would come in soon. The ladies had made themselves comfortable on the satin sofas that flanked the empty fireplace and engaged in desultory small talk that Juliana found extremely trying. Now a difficult silence had settled over the room.

'Will we see the Major's delightful children this evening, Miss Wrenn?' asked Lady Ormiston at last, when other subjects like the weather and the state of the roads had been exhausted.

'Yes, I believe Major Collingham has requested that they should come down.'

'And what are they like, these little girls—are they in awe of their papa?' She gave a soft laugh. 'No doubt he is very strict with them, is he not? He is an army man, after all, and used to order.'

'Naturally he likes the children to behave well.'

'But children like to play and run wild, do they not, Miss Wrenn? No doubt they have much more freedom here, to use up their energies. The moors must be an exciting place for them to roam free.'

'The children are never allowed out of doors unaccompanied,' said Juliana, choosing her words carefully. 'Major Collingham is very conscious of the children's safety.'

She looked round hopefully when the door opened, but it was not the gentlemen as she had hoped. Nurse stood on the threshold, asking diffidently if the children should come in.

'But of course!' cried Lady Ormiston, spreading her arms wide to welcome them. 'Bring them in—ah, little darlings, come here, that I may look at you.'

Gwendoline and Wilhelmina approached and made their

curtsies to their father's new guest, who gave them her dazzling smile, complimented them on their pretty gowns and asked them how they liked Blackthorpe. Gwendoline made some polite reply, but Minna merely stood beside her sister, staring wide-eyed at their beautiful visitor. Lady Ormiston put her head on one side and smiled at her.

'Little Wilhelmina, you have said nothing—you are not afraid of me, are you? Of course not. And you have your little doll with you—how charming. What is her name?'

Wilhelmina drew back a little, hugging the doll even closer.

'That's Sarah,' offered Gwendoline, adding with the superiority of her twelve years, 'It is Amy's doll. Minna couldn't bring her own doll downstairs because her arm came off and Thomas is mending her. She wouldn't come downstairs without a doll. She takes one everywhere.'

'Everywhere?' Lady Ormiston's amused glance turned to Juliana. 'Even into the schoolroom?'

The two children looked towards Juliana. She realised from their anxious faces that they were thinking of Lady Frances's visit that morning.

'Not generally, ma'am. We leave the dolls to Nurse's care while we take our lessons.'

'Papa!' Wilhelmina ran across the room as Major Collingham and Sir Richard came in. With a laugh, he swung her up into his arms.

'Well, Minna, have you been entertaining our guest?'

'She has not said a word,' scoffed Gwendoline.

'She is a little shy, but I think we will all be great friends.' Lady Ormiston waved her fan gently as she watched the Major set his daughter gently on her feet. 'This is a side of you I have not seen before, Damon.'

'I believe Collingham is becoming quite a family man,' observed Sir Richard, following his host into the room.

'I think you are right, Rick, and you may believe I will go to any lengths to protect them.'

The Major's implacable tone sent a shiver through Juliana—was he trying to warn Veronique off? If so, the lady did not appear to notice. She continued to talk to the children, but, despite her best efforts, Wilhelmina could not be induced to give her more than monosyllabic answers to her questions. The little girl stood beside Juliana, clutching her doll and watching Lady Ormiston with a direct, solemn gaze.

'Oh, dear me.' Veronique gave an uncertain little laugh. 'I fear I have frightened poor little Wilhelmina, she looks at me so sternly.'

Juliana put her hand on the child's shoulder. 'I think she is a little tired. We have had an eventful day.'

'Then what are you doing, allowing the children to stay up so late?' growled Major Collingham. Impatiently he waved her back into her seat as she made to rise. 'No, no, there is no need for you to go—Nurse will take them upstairs.'

He beckoned to the old woman, who left her chair in one shadowy corner and came forward.

'Goodnight, my dears.' Lady Ormiston smiled at them fondly as they left the room. 'What little dolls, I vow I am quite smitten. Perhaps I should find myself a pageboy.'

'Pageboys grow up,' replied Sir Richard. 'Perhaps you should buy a pug instead.'

'Yes, perhaps. Damon, do you remember that frightful Lady Corston and her three pugs? She insisted on taking them everywhere with her, even the Duchess of Almonham's rout.'

'Where they disgraced themselves on the Aubusson carpet.' The Major grinned.

* * *

Juliana sat back and listened as the conversation ranged around London society with anecdotes and gossip about people she did not know. She did not object, for she felt battered by the day's events and was glad to sit quietly and allow her thoughts to wander. However, by the time the party broke up it was nearly midnight and Juliana was fighting to stay awake. Lady Ormiston declared she must retire or fall asleep where she stood.

'Perhaps, Damon, you will escort me to my room? The corridors in this house are so very dark.'

'No need,' he replied easily. 'Miss Wrenn can do that.' Lady Ormiston pouted prettily, but he carried on inexorably. 'You will find Plumstead has put the bedroom candles ready at the bottom of the stairs. Our guest is in the blue room, Miss Wrenn, in the west wing, beyond the bust of Milton.'

'I know it, sir.'

Juliana watched from the door as Lady Ormiston said goodnight to the gentlemen. They both kissed her hand, but it seemed that Damon held on to those slim fingers a fraction longer, that his eyes followed her as she glided out of the room. Juliana led the way up the stairs and along the landing to the west wing.

'No doubt all the bedrooms are here,' remarked Veronique as they turned to walk along the main corridor, where their candles reflected dimly in the polished oak panelling. The tall plinths with their marble busts threw out long shadows as they approached them; the cold, impassive faces with their sightless eyes appeared ghoulish in the candlelight. Juliana thought of the less-than-perfect head of Prometheus on display outside the schoolroom. She had passed it many times in the dark and never found it as disturbing as these less familiar sculptures. They seemed to look upon her with disapproval.

'Which room does Major Collingham occupy?' asked Lady Ormiston.

Juliana blinked at the blunt question. 'I—I am not sure.'

It was a lie. Mrs Plumstead had pointed out the master's room to her during their tour of the house. It was the door nearest the gallery, but Juliana was not sharing that information with Lady Ormiston.

'No, this is not your side of the house, is it, Miss Wrenn?'

The contempt in the lady's voice was unmistakable. Juliana closed her lips firmly and walked on, offering no reply. The only sounds to break the silence were their slippered feet pattering on the boards and the whisper of silken skirts. As they reached the bust of Milton, Juliana stopped.

'Your room is here, ma'am. I am sure you will have all you need, but I understand this part of the house has a new bell system. You only have to ring if you require anything more.'

'So there are no lackeys on duty during the night?' she murmured. 'No footmen standing outside my door?'

'No, madam.'

With a nod of dismissal, Lady Ormiston disappeared into her chamber and Juliana made her way back through the corridor and across the gallery to the east wing. Upon her arrival at Blackthorpe Hall she had been allotted a suite of rooms for herself, Thomas and Amy, but Nurse had suggested it would be much more sensible for the children to sleep in the spare bedrooms in the nursery, where she and the Major's daughters had their own chambers. Thomas and Amy had not objected to this, but now as Juliana entered her apartment, she was aware of the emptiness, and for the first time wished that she had the children with her. The clock in the schoolroom began to chime: midnight. She decided it was too late to look in on the children. The nursery was situated under the eaves, reached from another flight of creaky stairs at the far end of the passage, and Juliana did not wish to disturb their slumbers. She must go to bed.

It took her some time to undress and slip into her thin cotton bedgown. With her father's diminishing income she had not had the luxury of a maid for many years and generally did not regret it, but tonight all she wanted to do was to lie down and sleep and she did not relish the thought of tidying away all her clothes. However, she knew that if she did not smooth her gloves flat and shake out her gown before folding it away carefully in the linen press, then they would be sadly creased when next required. Even when all her clothes were put away, Juliana had to unpin her hair and brush out the tangles. She snuffed the candles around the room and sat on her bed with only the bedroom candle still alight as she pulled the brush through her hair with long, even strokes, allowing her mind to wander. In the space of one day, she had known raging anger at Lady Frances, despair at the thought of leaving Blackthorpe, then elation when Damon had come to ask her to stay. But even her happiness had been short-lived. Now, with Lady Ormiston's appearance, there was a new fear gnawing at her. If Sir Richard's suspicions were correct, then Lady Ormiston was a dangerous enemy to be carefully watched. But even if she was not the enemy the gentlemen considered, she was very beautiful, and she had been Damon's lover once before. To Juliana's inexperienced eye, Lady Ormiston seemed intent upon reviving that relationship.

The brush snagged on a tangle of hair and Juliana gently teased the bristles through until the brush ran freely again, but the little doubt nagging in her head was not so easily smoothed away. Damon was a strong-willed, passionate man, and she had no doubt that he could withstand Veronique's blandishments, should he wish to do so.

'Aye, there's the problem,' she muttered to herself. 'What if he does not wish to resist her? Oh this is ridiculous!' Juliana tossed her hairbrush on to the dressing table and scrambled into bed. She blew out the candle and tried to make herself comfortable, but although she had entered the room feeling almost too tired to undress, now sleep eluded her. She longed for Damon, wanted to feel his arms around her, wanted him to kiss away all her doubts. If he had knocked on her door at that moment, she would have welcomed him into her arms and into her bed without a thought for the consequences. But he did not come, and she tossed and turned in the darkness. After an hour she gave up the struggle and felt around in the dark for her tinderbox.

Not only did the occupants of the east wing have to do without ladies' maids, she thought resentfully, they also had to manage without a personal closet. On her tour of the house, Mrs Plumstead had proudly shown Juliana the guest chambers, each with their own servant's room and a separate closet, but the schoolroom wing did not have such luxuries. The nursery rooms up under the eaves were equipped with a closet of their own, but Juliana's suite of rooms had not been similarly improved and her nearest privy was in a recess on the far side of the schoolroom. Preferable to a chamber pot under the bed, perhaps, but not ideal. With a sigh she slipped out of bed and picked up her lighted candle. At least it was warm enough for her to make the trip without her wrap.

Juliana opened her door and padded along the silent corridor to the little closet. A wind had sprung up, rattling the windows and whistling through the old house, but Juliana paid no heed. Old buildings were noisy places; she had even made it a game with the children to find all the creaking floorboards in the long corridors. Juliana reached the closet, taking care not to let the door bang and rouse the children sleeping above. She was just as careful when she left a few minutes later, quietly closing the door and retracing her steps. As she turned into the main corridor she gave a gasp and nearly dropped her candle when she saw a ghostly white figure hovering before her.

Chapter Twenty-Three

'L-Lady Ormiston!'

Holding up her candle and stepping closer, Juliana realised that the floating effect was caused by the diaphanous folds of the lady's fine muslin wrap swaying around her feet. Veronique's candle wavered.

'I could not sleep, and lost my way.' She stepped aside into the schoolroom and held her candle aloft. 'Is this where you hold your lessons for the little ones? How charming.'

'Yes, madam.' Juliana followed her into the room.

'Oh—so many toys.' Veronique moved closer to the shelves, casting the candle's feeble glow over each in turn. 'But some of the shelves are empty—why is this?'

'The carpenter has been fitting new windows to this room,' explained Juliana, watching her. 'Not everything has yet been put back.'

'It must be difficult, Miss Wrenn, to make sure all the children's playthings are suitable for them. I suppose you must know every toy that they own?'

'I had not considered it.'

Lady Ormiston's free hand crept inside her wrap.

'Well, consider it now, Miss Wrenn. I would like—' She stopped.

Above the keening wind was the sound of footsteps on the boards, a heavy-booted tread. Light flickered in the corridor and the next moment Major Collingham stood in the doorway, dressed only in his shirt, buckskins and top boots.

'Is anything wrong, ladies?' The light from the branched candlestick in his hand threw the angular planes of his face into strong relief, giving him a hawkish appearance. 'I was in the stables checking on my horse and saw the light up here.'

The white shirt billowed over his broad shoulders, unconfined by even a waistcoat, and his body seemed to fill the doorway.

'Lady Ormiston lost her way,' murmured Juliana. She had not realised how tense she was until she tried to speak, and the effort rasped her dry throat.

'So silly of me,' confessed Veronique with a little laugh. 'I could not sleep, and when I found myself up here, I was enchanted by all these reminders of childhood.' She moved towards Major Collingham. 'You will remember I told you, Damon, when I was a child in Paris during the Terror, we lost everything, my home, my nursemaid and my little friends.' She delicately wiped a tear from her cheek. '*Mon Dieu*, those were dark days.'

'Indeed they were, madam.' He held out his handkerchief to her.

'*Merci*. You are too kind.'

'Dry your eyes now,' said Damon. 'Miss Wrenn will take you back to your room.'

Juliana opened her mouth to protest, met his fierce stare and closed it again. She did not understand this game, she certainly did not like it, but if Damon did not wish to chal-

lenge the lady, she could hardly do so. She moved towards
the door.

'Ma'am, if you are ready?'

As the Major stepped aside to let them pass, he caught
Juliana's arm.

'Do not be alarmed if you meet one of the footmen on the
stairs, I have asked Matthew to sleep at the foot of the nursery
stairs tonight. Minna was looking a trifle feverish and I want
someone on hand, should Nurse call for assistance.'

His tone was light, but there was no mistaking the
message. Juliana nodded and went on her way, guiding Lady
Ormiston back through the darkened house. They did not
speak, and although Veronique dabbed at her eyes, she did
not seem overwrought. At the door of the blue bedroom
Juliana bade her goodnight, and when the door had closed
again she began to make her way back along the empty
corridor. She was about to step out onto the gallery when a
door opened behind her and she heard her name called in a
fierce whisper.

She turned to see Damon, his figure black against the
glow of candlelight from the room behind him.

'We cannot talk here. Step inside.'

Juliana hesitated.

'This is my dressing room, Ju. You need go no farther.'

He stepped back and, gripping the candlestick a little
tighter, she crossed the threshold into his apartment. As she
passed him she realised Damon was wearing a brightly
coloured dressing gown, the belt pulled tight and knotted at
the waist. It enveloped him from neck to toe, covering those
long limbs she found so unnerving.

The room was dark, the shutters had been closed across
the window and the only light came from the two candles in
a branched holder on a small side table. Outside their warm

glow everything was in shadow, the curtains, the panelling all robbed of their rich colours. Instinctively she moved towards the table, her own candle adding to the pool of light. The room smelled of brandy and spices. And man. It was a very masculine room. Damon's room.

'Veronique is safely back in her chamber?' he asked, closing the door.

'Yes. I saw her go inside. I doubt she will stir again tonight, knowing Matthew is on the stair.'

He grinned. 'Yes. Not at all subtle, but I hope she has taken the hint.'

'What does she want, Damon?'

'I don't know.'

'But you know something,' she persisted. 'I can see it in your face. Please tell me.'

'Very well.' He walked to a daybed and sat down. 'Come over here.'

The daybed was in a shadowy corner of the room, and Juliana took her candle with her, placing it on a nearby console table.

'Afraid of the dark, Ju?'

He sounded amused.

'No, sir,' she replied calmly as she sat down beside him. 'But I would like to see you.'

'So you like to look at me.'

She took her bottom lip between her teeth to prevent a smile escaping her. 'That is not what I meant.'

Damon put one arm around her shoulders and turned her towards him, tilting up her chin with his free hand. She put her hands against his chest, feeling the heavily embroidered silk beneath her fingers.

'Damon, let me go or I shall have to move away.'

'Don't you like being in my arms?'

His voice had deepened suddenly and she felt the now-familiar fever coming over her. A shiver tingled through her spine.

'No,' she lied, trying to sound severe. 'You were going to tell me what you suspect.'

With a sigh he let her go and threw himself back against the padded scroll of the daybed. One arm was lying along the backrest and Juliana sat up very straight, knowing that his fingers were only inches away from her.

'Tell me,' she repeated.

'Very well. Richard was investigating a plot to free Bonaparte from St Helena. He had discovered that supporters in France were sending diamonds here to pay for a ship and enough men to storm the island. He was hoping to intercept the diamonds and catch the plotters, but he did not succeed, and those involved went to ground.'

'But who would do such a thing? Surely no true Englishman—'

'Of course not, but there are many in London who owe no allegiance to our country. Richard has his suspicions, but without proof he can do nothing.'

Juliana was thinking, a tiny frown creasing her brow.

'Lady Ormiston,' she breathed. She looked up, her eyes wide and dark. 'Sir Richard suspects that she is involved, and that Leeson, as her lover, was drawn into her schemes.'

'Well done, my love. You have your wits about you tonight.'

She brushed aside his approval. 'From what you have told me, it was the obvious conclusion.'

'And you are happy to think Veronique a villain?'

She felt her cheeks growing warm.

'Well, yes,' she said, unable to meet his eyes. 'But you cannot let her stay here, Damon, it is not safe!'

He caught her hands.

'Richard thinks she intends no harm, and I agree with him.'

'No harm—but what of Mr Leeson—he ran off with Minna!'

'I think that was a mistake. He panicked.'

'But—'

'Hush.' He laid a finger on her lips. 'If we send Veronique away now, we will never know what she was planning, and Richard is very keen to find out. And, I admit it, so am I. Now, will you help me?'

Juliana looked up into his eyes. 'Of course,' she said simply.

'Good girl.'

She knew she should object to his calling her a girl, but his tone turned the words into a caress that tingled through her body. She could feel his fingers at her back, playing with her hair. She looked away quickly.

'I must go.'

'Must you?'

'Yes.' Her mind was telling her to get up, but her body refused to move. She sat very still, feeling as if she was a glass that might shatter at any minute. Damon leaned towards her. She could feel the heat of him through the silk. He was smiling at her. His fingers curled under her chin, forcing her head round until he could brush her lips with his own. The touch was featherlight, but the effect was to send the familiar liquid heat surging through her.

'You are cold,' he murmured, drawing back.

'No,' she followed his gaze and saw that her nipples were pushing against the thin cotton of her nightgown. 'Oh, heavens,' she gasped, horrified, 'I should have put on my wrap!'

'Indeed you should, but it is too late now.' He pulled her towards him and kissed her again, fiercely this time. Juliana did not resist him. Instead her body seemed to melt into his arms of its own accord. His mouth teased hers and she found her lips parting voluntarily. She began to kiss him back, the pleasurable excitement growing within her so that when he broke away she found herself almost moaning with disappointment. Suddenly she found herself being pushed backwards while with one hand he swung her legs up until she was lying fully on the daybed. Damon was kneeling beside her and even in the light of the single candle the glow in his eyes was unmistakable. Juliana felt her breath catch in her throat.

He lifted a hand to smooth a strand of hair from her cheek. Her eyes widened.

'You are trembling,' she whispered.

'I know.' He drew an audible, ragged breath. 'You had best tell me to stop now, Ju, or by God I swear it will be too late for you.'

'Oh, Damon, my love, it is already too late.'

With a groan she reached up her hands to cup his face and pull him down so that she could kiss him again. Her lips parted beneath his mouth, and his flickering tongue tantalised her senses. Without warning Damon broke away and she found herself being lifted into his arms.

'Not here,' he muttered, burying his face in her hair. 'I want to be able to enjoy you without fear of falling off that damned couch.'

Her hands crept around his neck and she rested her cheek against him, listening to the thud of his heart. He carried her into the bedroom, walking with an unerring step through the darkness to lay her tenderly on the bed. For a moment she panicked as he moved away from her, but it was only for a moment as he shed his dressing gown. She stretched out her hand and touched not cloth, but skin. Damon climbed up beside her, and she felt a jolt of excitement to know that only her thin nightgown lay between them. And then even that was gone. Damon gathered it up and began to pull it gently over her head. She lifted her arms to free herself of the garment and gasped as Damon used the opportunity to swoop down upon her breasts, catching one taut nipple between his teeth while his fingers circled its twin and her body writhed beneath his touch. Freeing her arms from the nightgown, Juliana drove her fingers into his thick hair as her body arched towards him. She was aching for him to do more, although she had no idea what it was her body wanted. She could feel his lean, hard limbs pressing against her own. She breathed deeply, inhaling the heady mix of soap and spices and skin. Her excitement grew. An unfamiliar sensation was building deep within her.

He trailed kisses up over her neck and captured her mouth again while one hand moved gently over her body. Tentatively she moved her own hands, exploring the unfamiliar curves of his shoulder. The firm skin beneath her fingers excited her. She drew her hand across his chest, threading her fingers through the fine covering of hair and all the time his hand was caressing her, tracing the curve of her waist and massaging the flat surface of her stomach. As her hand moved up to his face, his moved gradually downwards and she found her body moving instinctively beneath his fingers. She felt relaxed, fluid, all tension gone.

Juliana gave a little gasp as his fingers crept between her thighs and moved into her most private space. She felt herself opening for him, lifting her hips to offer herself up to him completely. With a groan he shifted on top of her, measuring the length of his body over hers while he kissed her cheeks and her eyelids, his lips gentle as a breeze on her skin. She became aware that Damon was tense above her, holding himself off as though afraid that his weight would crush her. Juliana shuddered and sighed, desperate for his embrace. She twined her arms around his neck and pulled him closer. He lowered himself on to her, gently easing himself into the space his fingers had prepared so well. She was surprised into a little cry and immediately Damon froze.

'Do I hurt you—do you want me to stop?' he muttered.

'No, no.' Her fingers dug into his shoulders. 'Go on, go on!'

She took her bottom lip firmly between her teeth as he moved within her, feeling pain, but even more aware of a savage satisfaction. She tried moving her hips and heard Damon groan. She moved again and he gasped, his body tensing over her. His rigidity frightened her, but the next moment he was relaxing, falling on to the bed beside her, breathing heavily as if he had been running hard.

'Darling Ju,' he murmured. 'Did I hurt you?'

'Not much,' she answered truthfully.

'I wanted to take longer, to please you, but you—moved.'

She frowned in the darkness. 'I don't understand.'

'No.' He pulled her into his arms, wrapping his body around her. 'No, but you will soon.'

Juliana lay very still, cocooned in the warmth of the very male body pressed against her own. She could tell by his steady, regular breathing that Damon was asleep. It was very pleasant, to be sure, but she was nagged by a vague sense of disappointment. On several occasions her feelings had threatened to overwhelm her, and when Damon had kissed her she had been obliged to fight to prevent herself from yielding to him, but now she had done so, and there had been a brief moment of pleasure, but surely it was a very small reward that hardly satisfied the terrible, aching love she felt for Damon. His breath tickled her cheek and she snuggled closer against him. She was very innocent, she knew that, and Damon had told her she would understand soon. She would have to trust him, she thought drowsily.

It was still dark when she woke again. She was still wrapped in Damon's arms, but something was different about the body that lay entwined with hers: he was aroused. Gently she shifted her position, turning on her side until she was face to face with him. She could not see his eyes, but she guessed that he was awake. Her hand snaked up around his neck and she moved her head to kiss him gently. Immediately his arms tightened about her. The gentle kiss became a long, languorous one. She felt his tongue flicker against her own and the sensation sent ripples of excitement down through her body. Damon's hands began to caress her, gently moving over her ribs and into the deep curve of her waist, then down over the swell of her hip and once again those long, sensitive fingers moved between her thighs, sliding into her and moving with tantalising slowness while an aching wave of desire was slowly building within her. She began to move restlessly on the bed, her breath coming in short gasps and still the desire was growing. She groaned, unwilling and unable to escape those teasing fingers that were rousing such exquisite feelings. Suddenly she knew the wave of desire was about to break, and at that moment Damon shifted his weight to lie above her. She lifted her hips to receive him and felt him moving within her, rousing her to a fever of excitement so that she matched him move for move and she cried out, arching her back and digging her fingers into his skin as he held her at the crest of the wave before she subsided on a sobbing, shuddering sigh.

Damon collapsed beside her and she clung to him, saying impulsively, 'Oh, thank you!'

'I take it that was better?'

'Oh, yes, I never knew—'

He laughed softly and kissed the tip of her nose. 'No, how could you?'

'Did—did you enjoy it too?' she asked shyly.

'Very much.'

'You are sure?' She frowned in the darkness. 'You spent so much time giving me pleasure, there must be more for you—'

He kissed her.

'There will be many other nights, my darling, when we will spend hours pleasuring each other. Now, though, you must go back to your own room before the servants are abroad. You must be respectable Miss Wrenn for a little longer.'

He helped her into her nightdress, then put his own garish dressing gown about her shoulders.

'You will take my banyan. I will not risk you catching a chill,' he told her.

'But if I am seen wearing this—'

'You will not be, if you go now.'

He pulled on his nightshirt and guided her back through the dressing room. She was surprised to see that the candles had not quite burned out.

'Here.' Damon found her a fresh candle and lit it from one guttering flame. He crossed to the door, opened it and looked out. 'Go now, quickly,' he whispered. As she passed him in the doorway, he stopped her and took another swift kiss. 'Goodnight, dearest Ju. You had best stay away from me in the morning, for I fear Richard will guess our secret if he only sees me look at you.'

* * *

After the warmth of Damon's arms, Juliana's bed looked cold and uninviting. She pulled the banyan around her and lay down upon the covers, taking comfort from the feel of the garish fabric, the faint muskiness that reminded her of Damon. The first grey fingers of dawn were already creeping into the room, and Juliana slept only fitfully, her mind too full to rest. It was still early when she eventually decided to get dressed and go to the schoolroom to prepare for the day's lessons. She pulled out a white muslin dress embroidered with white spring flowers about the hem and sleeves. Although the lack of colour made it suitable for a mourning dress, she had considered it too ornate for general use, but today her mood was buoyant and she wanted to wear something to reflect it. She picked up Damon's dressing gown and hugged it to her, knowing it must be returned. With no fires to light in the bedrooms, the servants would not come upstairs for some time yet. She smiled to herself—the temptation to see Damon was too great. She would take the banyan back to him. She would scratch quietly on the door, and if he was asleep she would leave it outside his room. If he was awake, however... She shivered deliciously at the thought.

It was barely light enough to see her way, but as she came out onto the gallery she could hear footsteps in the hall below as the servants made their preparations for the coming day. Juliana hung back, waiting until the hall was empty and there was no possibility of being seen, then she slipped across to the entrance to the west wing. She padded silently into the corridor and stopped as she heard the creak of a hinge. At the end of the passage a bar of early morning sunlight cut through the gloom as a door was thrown wide. It illuminated the bust of Milton, making the marble glow. Juliana watched, unable to move, as Damon stepped out of the room. He was wearing only his nightshirt, and one arm was stretched behind him, as if holding on to someone within the chamber. He looked back and said softly,

'Go back to bed, Veronique.'

Juliana whisked herself out of sight and leaned against the wall, shaking. Part of her wanted to confront Damon, but her legs would not carry her, and even as she realised this she heard the soft click of his door. For several moments she remained, motionless, her brain refusing to function. Then, in a daze she pushed herself away from the wall and forced her wayward limbs to take her along the now empty corridor. *Another moment and this was all I would have known. I should have seen nothing. I would have been happy.* The thought came to her in a detached way, rousing no emotions. At Damon's door she laid the dressing gown on the floor and walked away.

There were no tears. Juliana shut herself in her room, but would not allow herself to cry; the children would be up soon and swollen, red eyes would only invite comment and questions. She curled up on the bed and tried to think calmly, to persuade herself there was some reasonable explanation for what she had seen, but she knew there could be none. She recalled sitting in Cousin Pettigrew's kitchen with Lawrence the footman. 'Devil Collingham, pleasuring three women in one night...'

Is that how it was? Had Damon taken her to his bed last night merely because he could? Surely not, surely he loved her—but if that was so, then why had he gone to Veronique? Her hand crept to her cheek. She had no experience of this. Perhaps her innocence had left him unsatisfied—a lowering thought. She blinked away a tear—she would not cry. Desperately she sought another explanation. Sir Richard was convinced that Lady Ormiston was involved in some intrigue. If that was so, was it not possible that Damon had gone to her room to discover the truth? Juliana found that explanation no more acceptable. Having admitted that she loved Damon, she realised that she would not share him with any other woman. She *could* not share him. She pressed her clenched fist against her mouth.

'Oh, Damon, what have you done?'

The morning lesson dragged by, and if the children noticed their governess was unusually quiet they did not say so. Juliana felt as if she had split in two, and that she was some disembodied spirit, watching herself going through the routine of teaching the children their letters, correcting their mistakes. She excused herself from luncheon and afterwards set the children to drawing in their sketchbooks, when her bruised and tired mind could think of no other occupation for them. The clatter of hooves in the stable yard took her to the window and she looked out to see Damon and Lady Ormiston riding out through the gates. It was too much; the pain was too great to be borne in silence. Leaving the children to Nurse's watchful eye, Juliana made her way downstairs.

Sir Richard was strolling through the shrubbery. He stopped and turned when he heard Juliana behind him.

'Miss Wrenn, have you come to enjoy the air? I confess I thought the rain would continue all day. Damon and Lady Ormiston are taking advantage of this dry spell to go riding.'

'I know.' Juliana came up to him. 'I saw them leave. I— I wanted to talk to you, Sir Richard.'

His brows rose fractionally, but he smiled and held out his arm for her. 'Then shall we walk?'

Juliana strolled beside him, trying to find words that would not expose her inner turmoil. 'You said you thought Lady Ormiston to be in league with Mr Leeson.'

'That is correct, Miss Wrenn. I have no proof, of course, but I have my suspicions.'

'And…is Dam—is Major Collingwood helping you to discover the truth?'

'Well, yes, he said he wanted to help. That is why he is gone out with the lady now. He thinks if we set her at her ease, she will make some slip.'

Juliana closed her eyes. 'And, M-Major Collingham can be quite…ruthless, I think.' She forced herself to speak normally.

Sir Richard considered the matter. 'He is a soldier, Miss Wrenn. He was trained to be ruthless to achieve his goals. Yet to those fortunate enough to win his friendship, he can be very kind.' He looked down at her, a slight frown in his eyes. 'These are odd questions, Miss Wrenn—what is on your mind?'

Juliana looked down at the ground. If her face showed only a fraction of the anguish she felt, it would not do to let him see it.

'I—I merely wonder how far the Major will go to—to put Lady Ormiston at her ease.'

'Ah, now I understand your concerns.' He squeezed her arm. 'You need not fear that Damon is in danger of losing his heart to the lovely Veronique, Miss Wrenn. He may flatter her and flirt with her, but only until he can discover her purpose in being here.'

Greatly daring, she said, 'But they were l-lovers once, were they not?' Sir Richard hesitated. She continued, 'You may be frank with me, sir. Damon has already told me of it.'

'Well, then, yes, but it was a couple of years ago and there was never any serious intention. Good lord, Miss Wrenn, I hope you will not hold it against Damon, that he has had a mistress?'

'Heavens, no.' She forced a laugh. 'I am merely trying to understand the situation.'

Sir Richard nodded, and patted her arm. 'You need have no fear, Miss Wrenn. Trust Damon to look after everything.'

By dinner time Juliana had developed a sick headache and she sent the children down to the drawing room with Nurse to say goodnight. In the silence of the nursery wing Juliana lay on her bed, watching the summer light slowly fading from the sky outside her window. The carving on the tester above her head had disappeared into a black shadow by the time she heard the children come back upstairs.

'Can we not go in and wish Miss Wrenn goodnight?' Wilhelmina's piping voice was directly outside her door.

'Not tonight, dearie. In all likelihood Miss Wrenn is asleep by now, and we should let her rest.' Nurse's kindly tones made her smile in spite of her unhappiness. 'Come along now, and you can tell me what story you would like me to read to you tonight…'

She should get up and go to them, to make sure they were settled securely in their beds, but she felt too dull, too tired to move. She closed her eyes and tried to sleep.

'Juliana.'

There was a soft knock on the door. Juliana opened her eyes to find the room washed in blue-grey moonlight. She was curled up in a ball on the bed and did not want to get up.

'Juliana.'

Damon's voice called again from the other side of the door, more urgent this time. She remembered that her door was not locked, and she could not be sure that the Major would go away if she did not answer him. She eased herself off the bed and padded to the door to open it a little. Damon was standing outside, still dressed for dinner, but his loosened cravat suggested that it was late. The light from the candle he was holding flickered over his face, illuminating the upward curve of his lips, but not his eyes.

'So you are awake,' he murmured. 'Will you let me come in?'

'No. No, it—it is unseemly.' His frown made her add quickly, 'Go to the schoolroom, and I will join you there.'

Juliana closed the door and stood for a moment in the moonlight. She must do this. It could not be delayed. She must talk to him. She shook out her dress and made her way to the schoolroom, where the Major was lighting candles. He turned and smiled at her as she came in.

'Poor Ju, is your headache so very bad? Let me kiss it better.' Damon started towards her, but she stepped back, putting up her hands to ward him off. He stopped. 'What's this? Ju, you are shaking. Did I frighten you last night?'

'No.' She twisted her hands together. 'I returned your banyan this morning.'

He grinned. 'I know. Benns fell over it when he brought my hot water.'

She did not feel inclined to smile. 'I saw you. I s-saw you coming from Lady Ormiston's room.'

'Did you.'

'You do not deny it?'

'Deny it?' He laughed. 'No, of course not. I—'

She did not wait for him to finish. His laugh had seared through the brittle control she had placed on herself all day. A wave of anger swept over her.

'How dare you!' Her voice shook with rage. 'How dare

you sneer at me—or at her! What a fine day's work you made of it, Major Collingham. Within four-and-twenty hours you have rid yourself of a fiancée, compromised me beyond redemption and made up the rift with your ex-lover.'

His black brows snapped together. 'For God's sake, Ju, you know it is important we learn Veronique's motives for being here.'

'And did your seduction do the trick?' She threw the words at him as she paced feverishly up and down the room. She was beyond reason, wanting only to hurt him, to make him suffer as she was doing.

'I did not seduce her—I did not touch her. Listen to me.' He caught her arm. 'Listen to me, damn you!'

'Let go of me!' she cried, struggling to free her arm. 'I saw you, Damon—you were coming out of her room *dressed only in your nightshirt*!'

'I had no choice since you had my damned dressing gown!'

He released her and stepped away. 'For Heaven's sake, Ju, let me explain why—'

'There is nothing to explain!' she interrupted him. 'It is perfectly clear—she had been making eyes at you all evening, and you could not resist, could you, *Devil* Collingham.'

He gave a crack of mirthless laughter. *'My reputation, Iago, my reputation!'*

'Yes, you may joke about it,' she threw at him, shaking with fury. 'Did you laugh at me, too? Why did you take me to your bed, Damon? Because you *could*, I suppose.'

She noted with savage satisfaction how his face paled at that. His mouth tightened.

'You have a poor opinion of me, madam.'

She threw up her head. 'I have *no* opinion of you!' She

saw the anger flare in his eyes and raised her chin defiantly.
'No, that's not true,' she said slowly, deliberately. 'I hate you.'

The words hung in the air, echoing through the stillness
as they faced each other across the room, each now in a
towering rage. She saw the muscle working in his cheek and
knew his anger was barely contained.

'If I am so disgusting to you, then you will not wish to
stay here.'

'I shall have Thomas and Amy ready to leave by noon. If
you will order your carriage to take us to Blackburn, we will
trouble you no further.'

'Where will you go?'

'That is none of your concern.'

'Damnation, woman, of course it is my concern. You have
no money—or do you plan to make a living lying on your
back?'

She threw him a look of scorn. 'Alas, I do not have your
expertise in that area.'

'You would soon pick it up.'

She wanted to fly at him, to claw out those eyes that
looked at her with such fury, but she was close to tears, only
her anger kept her going. She turned on her heel and walked
away. She hurried to her room as fast as she could without
running, her spine tingling with anticipation—any moment
she expected to hear his step behind her, to feel his hand on
her shoulder, but he did not follow her.

Chapter Twenty-Four

When Juliana announced to her pupils that she would be leaving, her words were met with a stunned silence. They were in the schoolroom, with only Gwendoline, Wilhelmina and Nurse present. Juliana had already given the news to Thomas and Amy and set them to work packing their few belongings. She had forestalled their questions by saying she would explain everything later, but Gwendoline and her sister were not to be fobbed off so easily.

'By why?' cried Wilhelmina. 'I do not want you to leave.'

'My contract here was only ever a temporary one, Minna.'

'But it was until September,' said Gwendoline, 'Papa can insist you stay until then.'

Juliana hesitated, then said carefully, 'I have been offered a position I cannot afford to ignore, and—and your father has agreed to let me go.'

'Well, he had no right to do so!' declared Gwendoline, two spots of colour staining her cheeks. 'You said I could decide if you should leave us!'

'No, Gwendoline,' she replied gently. 'We agreed that if

you found me intolerable I would remove as soon as we arrived here.'

Wilhelmina ran to Juliana and clambered on to her lap while Gwendoline came more slowly. She put an arm about Juliana's neck and laid her cheek on her shoulder, saying, 'I shall miss you.'

Juliana blinked away her tears.

'And I shall miss you both, very much. And you, Nurse.'

'Oh, dearie, we have all grown so fond of you.' The old woman shook her head and wiped away a tear. 'It will seem strange without you, and what are the children going to do for their lessons?'

'Yes,' said Wilhelmina, sitting up. 'You cannot go until Papa has found somebody else to teach us.'

'I'm afraid I must, my love.' She looked round as Thomas came into the room.

'Well, I suppose you have told them,' he said, observing their miserable faces.

Amy came running in behind him and went immediately to put her arms about Wilhelmina. 'It is perfectly horrid, and I don't want to go away from here,' she said.

'I d-don't want you to go either,' muttered Minna, her lip trembling. 'You are my *bestest* friend.'

'Perhaps you can write to one another,' suggested Nurse.

Juliana said nothing. She had no intention of giving Damon her direction, wherever it might turn out to be. She could not be sure he would not come after her.

'Well, we shall see,' was all that she would say when Gwendoline pressed her.

'And it means we won't be going to the fair this afternoon,' grumbled Thomas.

Gwen looked up.

'No, and neither shall we, for Papa said we could only go if Juliana would escort us.'

Thomas turned to his sister. 'Could we not stay for one more day, Ju, please?'

She had to steel herself to withstand the four pairs of eyes fixed beseechingly upon her.

'I am afraid not, my dears. Never mind, there will be other fairs. Now, our coach is not due until twelve. We still have a little time—what would you like to do?'

'We could finish the pictures for our journal,' suggested Gwendoline.

'Oh, yes,' said Wilhelmina. 'Then we shall have something with which to remember you.'

Juliana settled the children at the big table, but they were none of them inclined to work, and had achieved very little when Giles came in, frowning.

'Juliana, I have just come from Papa. He says I am to take Gwen and Minna to the fair today because you are leaving us.'

'Oh, that is famous,' declared Juliana. 'They were disappointed to think they would have to miss it.'

'Yes, well, never mind that! I want to know why you are leaving, and why so suddenly?'

Juliana was studying Wilhelmina's drawing and did not look up. 'Goodness, such blunt questions,' she said lightly. 'I—I have received a very good offer and agreed with your papa that I will leave immediately.'

Amy looked up, about to speak, but a kick under the table from Thomas made her close her mouth again.

'Well, if it is so, I suppose you must go as soon as possible,' admitted Giles grudgingly. 'But it is very sudden.'

Juliana straightened and summoned a tiny smile. 'Sometimes that is best—I do not like long goodbyes.'

'No, of course not.' Giles looked down at his boots, then blurted out, 'I shall be sorry to see you go.'

'Thank you, Giles, but you will do very well without me, I am sure.'

He nodded, looked solemn for a few moments, then the twinkle returned to his eyes.

'There is *some* good news today. Lady Ormiston is leaving, too.'

'No!' exclaimed Gwendoline.

'Yes. She came to the study while I was with Papa and I heard her telling him that she was off to join Lord Ormiston in Scotland. She's ordered her carriage and is even now preparing to set off. Good thing, too.'

'Don't you like her?' asked Thomas.

Giles pulled a face.

'Lord, no. Silly creature. Set fire to her curtains the other night: went into her dressing room to see to her maid, who had disturbed her with her coughing, and left her candle unattended. When she saw the flames she went screaming fit to burst to m'father, when anyone but a nodcock would have made at least some attempt to put out the flames. As it was, that dour-faced maid of hers pulled down the curtains and stamped on them, so that by the time Papa got to the room there was nothing for him to do.'

Juliana froze. Was that the reason Damon had gone to her room? Why had he not told her? Why had she not listened to him?

'Where did you learn all this?' asked Gwendoline, round-eyed.

'From Papa. He was telling Sir Richard when I came upon them in the library yesterday. At first he didn't see me, until Sir Richard indicated that I had come in, and Papa stopped, then he decided to continue, saying he thought it was as well if I knew what "that damn fool woman" had been doing—his words, Nurse, not mine,' Giles added hastily as Nurse uttered a faint protest.

Juliana leaned on the back of Minna's chair, hoping her knees would not buckle beneath her. She had been mistaken, but it was too late to go back—she had said she hated him. He could never forgive that. A leaden despondency was added to her misery.

'So, I had best go and make sure the gig will be ready for us this afternoon,' Giles continued. 'Oh, and before I forget—Juliana, Papa says you are to see Brasher before you leave.'

'So you will be able to buy those ribbons after all, Gwendoline,' said Juliana with a smile, when Giles had left them.

'Yes, but there will be no one to put them in my hair for me.'

Juliana thought it wise to ignore her grumbles, and did her best to turn their interest again to their drawing.

At twelve precisely the carriage rolled up at the door. Juliana tied the strings of her bonnet under her chin and hurried the children into the hall. She stepped outside to direct the footmen, who were putting her small trunk and portmanteau into the boot, and as she came back indoors she saw Major Collingham coming down the stairs, his children beside him.

'Did you think to leave without saying goodbye?' he barked.

'I knew you would be at luncheon, and I said my goodbyes to Giles and the girls in the schoolroom.'

'But you would not eat with us. True, it is only a cold collation, since all the servants are off to the fair, but it would have set you up for your journey.'

There was accusation in his tone, and because it was not without foundation Juliana could not meet his eyes.

'Mrs Plumstead has packed up a hamper for us.'

She watched the children taking a polite leave of each other, their solemn little faces mirroring the grave looks of the adults. Wilhelmina was asking Amy if she had seen Lady Arabella, and Juliana was only just in time to stop the two girls running off in search of the doll.

'There is no time for that, Amy, I am sorry. Enough now, we must go to the coach.' She gave Amy a little push, then turned towards the Major. 'Pray give my regards to Sir Richard for me—he is out riding, I believe.'

She went to follow Giles and the children out of the door, but Damon caught her arm.

'You told the girls you have obtained another post,' he said in a low voice. 'Why did you not tell them the truth?'

She pulled herself free. 'They worship you,' she said. 'I would do nothing to change that.' She waited, her eyes fixed on the marbled floor.

Ask me to stay. Silently she begged him to speak. One word, one sign, and she would fall into his arms and admit that she had been wrong. If he loved her, surely he would not let her go. She remembered the night in Rushton Spencer when he had said he loved her—he had even threatened to take her by force rather than let her leave him. *Then* he had been desperate to keep her; now his very silence told her that his passion had died. Her resistance had been the attraction; once she had given in to him, he had lost interest in her. Stifling a sigh, Juliana turned and hurried outside, stooping to hug Gwendoline and Wilhelmina and to take Giles's hand for a moment before she stepped quickly up into the carriage. Then the door was shut and they were moving away down the drive. Amy and Thomas hung out of the window, waving furiously, but Juliana dared not look back. Tears were very close, and in an effort to drive them away she lay back against the squabs and closed her eyes.

* * *

From the doorway Damon watched the carriage bowling along the winding drive. He scarcely noticed Giles hurrying his sisters back inside to collect their cloaks, telling them that if they tarried he would be off to the fair without them. When they had gone, the silence settled about him as he watched the carriage disappear amongst the trees.

'Damnation, have I missed her?' Sir Richard was hurrying across the hall. 'Plumstead told me when I came in that Miss Wrenn was leaving, but I thought I should have time to change out of my muddy clothes.'

Damon turned back to fix his eyes again on the wooded horizon.

'You are too late, my friend. She is gone. I have lost her.' His hands balled into fists. 'I have lost her, Rick. She saw me coming out of Veronique's room after the fire and thought—'

Sir Richard put a hand on his shoulder.

'Nonsense. Miss Wrenn is a sensible young woman. Surely when you explained it all…'

'I didn't. I didn't even try to explain it. I lost my temper.' He rubbed his hand wearily across his eyes. 'I was angry that she should doubt me. I don't know what I said, something damnable… I have driven her away.'

'Well, then, go after her, man. I have never known you at a loss with a woman before.'

'This one is different.'

Sir Richard smiled. 'You say that because you care for her. Go after her, Damon.'

'If I thought there was a chance—' He broke off and shook his head. 'It is too late, my friend. I disgust her. When we said goodbye just now, she could not even look at me. She….she hates me, and with good reason.' He turned suddenly and drove the side of his fist against the doorpost. 'She thinks I tricked her. Well, perhaps it is better this way— I am over a dozen years her senior. Let her find another, younger man, one more deserving of her than I could ever be.' That thought could not be borne. He shook it off and drew himself up. 'Enough. Come, Richard, there is something to celebrate at least. Did Plumstead tell you that Veronique has also quit the house? She went off to Scotland this morning.'

'Has she, by God!' Sir Richard cocked an eyebrow. 'So soon after you refused to fall for her little seduction? Perhaps I have misjudged her—mayhap you were her only reason for coming here.'

Damon's lip curled. 'You think me that attractive, that she would follow me the length of the country to win me back?'

Sir Richard grinned. 'Actually, no, my friend! My suspicion still stands, but there is little I can do about it at this moment.'

'True.' Damon pushed himself away from the wall and linked his arm through his friend's. 'Come on into the library. Giles is taking the girls to the fair, most of the servants have already set out, so we are left to our own devices. I suggest we get damnably drunk!'

'Where are we going?'

Juliana roused herself. Amy was tugging at her sleeve. Blackthorpe and its park had long since disappeared and they were travelling through countryside she did not recognise. She took off her bonnet and tossed it aside, hoping it might ease her headache.

'To Blackburn. I shall look for work there.'

Amy looked puzzled. 'But I thought you already had a post.'

'Silly, that was only what she told everyone,' said Thomas. 'So they would not worry about us. That's correct, is it not, Ju?'

'There is no need for anyone to concern themselves over us,' she replied firmly. 'We shall do very well.'

'But you did not see Mr Brasher before you left, did you?' persisted Thomas. 'So we have no money.'

Juliana looked at their anxious faces and was determined to be cheerful. 'I have my pearls to sell, and Papa's watch. That will give us a little money until I can find work.'

'Well, if you are going to sell your pearls, you might like to take these too.' Thomas dug his hand into the pocket of his coat. 'They are only glass, but quite pretty, so you might get something for them.'

Juliana stared. There on his open palm lay a pair of exquisite diamond earrings.

Chapter Twenty-Five

'Thomas! Wh-where did you get them?'

'I ought to have given them back to Minna, I know,' he confessed, looking a little shamefaced, 'but to be honest I had forgotten all about them until now.'

'What pretty beads,' said Amy, craning her neck to see them.

'I don't think they are beads,' murmured Juliana. She looked closely at her brother. 'Tell me where you found them, Tom. The truth, now.'

He flushed. 'I didn't steal them, if that's what you think.'

Juliana managed a little smile. 'No, of course not, but I must know where they came from.'

'No, well, it was when I mended Minna's doll. Giles had gone out, so I said I would look at it. The arm had come off, you may remember, and before I could mend it I had to take off the dress. That was when I found these earrings. They must have been caught up in the material in some way.'

Juliana was thinking quickly.

'Could they—could they have been hidden *inside* the doll?' she asked.

Thomas shrugged.

'I suppose so, the body is hollow, but I did not notice where they came from, only that as I removed the dress they fell on to the workbench. I was in the workroom next to the stables at the time, and I didn't want to leave them around, so I put them into my pocket, meaning to give them to Minna when I gave her the doll, but it was getting late, and I had to hurry to repair it and get her back before Minna went to bed and—well, I forgot all about the earrings.' He looked up. 'If you like, I will put them in a letter and post them back to Blackthorpe.'

Juliana picked up the earrings and looked at them. 'I think they are rather too valuable to be sent in the post, Thomas. I think they are diamonds.'

'Diamonds!' He laughed. 'That's silly—who would give Minna such a thing? She is just a baby.'

'Perhaps they belonged to her grandmama and she hid them in the doll at Kewhurst.'

'Oh, Lady Arabella was never at Kewhurst,' piped up Amy. 'She was given to Minna in London.'

'Oh?' said Juliana. 'How do you know that, Amy?'

'She told me all about it. She and Gwendoline went with their aunt to visit the dressmaker, and one of the assistants gave Minna the doll to stop her crying.'

'A dressmaker?'

Amy nodded.

'Minna and Gwen didn't like her because she took no notice of them, and spoke to their aunt in her funny French voice.'

Juliana sat back, her face pale. 'She was French?' she said at last.

'Yes, Aunt Louisa says she is the best dressmaker in London.'

A succession of thoughts and ideas were running riot through Juliana's head. If the dressmaker was so very fashionable, it was very likely that Lady Ormiston would know her. Her thoughts raced on—Lady Ormiston had left this morning, and Wilhelmina's doll was missing...

'We must turn back!' She sat up and pulled the check string.

'Back!' the children cried out in unison and she held up a hand to stem their questions while she issued her instructions to the driver. When the carriage was moving again, she dropped the earrings into her reticule and sat back to find Thomas looking at her with anxious eyes.

'I am sorry, Ju, I did not know they were diamonds, I never thought...'

'And why should you?' She patted his knee. 'I shall give them to Sir Richard. He will know what to do with them.'

Amy clapped her hands. 'I will be able to see Minna again!'

'No, my love. You forget, Giles is taking the girls to the fair this afternoon. I shall stop only long enough to give the diamonds to Sir Richard, then we must be on our way again. But pray do not look so gloomy, my loves. Who knows, there may well be a reward for finding these jewels.'

'A reward!' said Thomas, brightening. 'Then it should be mine, since I discovered them.'

'Indeed it should,' admitted Juliana, a glimmer of humour lightening her depression. 'But perhaps you would be very good and let me borrow a little of it, just until I can establish myself, of course.'

Thomas drew himself up. 'Don't worry, I shall look after us all, since I am head of the household now.'

By the time the coachman had found a place to turn around and they were at the palings of Blackthorpe Hall, an hour had passed. Juliana called to the coachman to drive in through the woods.

'We shall save a good twenty minutes if we take the back lane rather than drive all the way round to the front gates,' she told the children. 'I am not too proud to walk in through the housekeeper's door.'

However, when the carriage had made its way up the muddy drive that led to the servants' quarters, the house was strangely quiet.

'It's the fair, miss,' said the footman as he opened the carriage door for her. 'The master always lets the servants go off at mid-day to attend the fair.'

The tone of his voice indicated that he too should have been at the fair rather than escorting a governess and her family around the countryside. Juliana suppressed her inclination to apologise.

'Pray stay here with the children,' she said. 'I shall only be a few moments and we can be on our way again.'

The outer doors at the back of the house were all locked, and she wondered if she would be obliged to go to the front door after all, but the coachman suggested she should try the side door leading in from the stable yard.

'There's a wicket gate into the yard in the wall over there, miss, and you should find a key to the side door underneath the bucket beside the doorway.' The coachman touched his hat and gave her a fatherly smile. 'It's the way here at Blackthorpe, so we don't have to wake up the porter every time we comes in late.'

Juliana found the key just as the driver had said. She had just unlocked the door when she heard the faint jangle of harness and the scraping of hooves upon gravel. She walked towards the arch and saw the back wheels of a travelling coach pulled up on the front drive. Moving cautiously forward, she could see the driver hunched in his seat, then came the sound of a loud, hacking cough from inside the coach. Juliana froze. Lady Ormiston's maid was in the carriage. That could only mean that Veronique had returned.

Juliana hurried back to the side door and quietly entered the house. There was no sound from the lower rooms. Without its servants the house seemed eerily quiet. Juliana had just reached the great hall when she heard a noise from upstairs, as if some piece of furniture had been knocked over. Her heart beating wildly, she ran swiftly up to the landing. Which way? The corridor to the main bedrooms was silent, deserted. She went back to the gallery, straining her ears to catch the slightest noise. There was the faint rumble of voices ahead of her. Following the sound, she realised it was coming from the nursery wing. Some instinct told her that she must not be heard. She crept along, moving her feet cautiously over the old boards, thankful that she remembered which ones creaked. She was halfway along the corridor when she heard a groan quickly followed by a laugh, brittle and tinkling as glass. Common sense told her to turn and run, to get help, but her feet continued to carry her forward and she could hear the voices more clearly now. They were in the schoolroom. The door stood half-open, allowing a band of strong, white light into the passage. Damon's deep tones were unmistakable and Juliana's heart clenched when she heard the lilting tones of Lady Ormiston.

'So tell me where they are, Damon.'

'I have no idea.'

'Come now, Damon. I have my pistols, you see, and I know how to use them. Would you have me kill your friend?'

'Of course not, but I tell you I haven't seen the damned stones.'

'Be sensible, *mon ami*. They were in the doll when it left London—Charles swore to me the doll was intact when he caught up with you.'

'So it was you who set him to follow us.'

Veronique's heartless laugh echoed through the quiet rooms.

'Such a simple task, to recover the doll. Those two imbeciles should have managed it in Bond Street, before you left town, but they bungled the attempt. So I sent Charles to bring it back to me. I thought he would accomplish it easily, but no, he panicked and snatched the child as well. What a pity your bullet did not kill him, Damon. He was such a fool.'

'Was?'

'You do not think I could let him live, knowing so much? He was weak, Damon. One should never deal with weak men. Now you, *mon cher*, you are not weak.'

'Neither am I a fool, madam. I can see only one way this can end.'

Juliana marvelled that Damon could sound so cool. She edged closer to the doorway, desperate to know what was going on. She peered through the crack between the door and the frame and what she saw made her feel suddenly faint. On the far side of the room Sir Richard was slumped against one wall, blood trickling from a gash on his head. Damon stood a little in front of him, as if to shield him from further attack. She could not see Veronique, but guessed from Damon's watchful look that she was standing just inside the room. Juliana moved forward a little more towards the shaft of light, then drew back quickly. Veronique was standing in the doorway, holding a slim silver pistol at her side. In that brief glance Juliana had not seen her other hand, but she had spoken of pistols, and from her stance she guessed she was levelling another one directly at Damon. His next words confirmed her fears and a cold chill ran through her.

'Perhaps before you kill me, you will tell me how those diamonds came to be in my daughter's doll?'

'It is a fashion doll, of no interest to anyone but the *modiste*. We arranged for the doll to come from Paris; it should have been foolproof, but her assistant gave the doll to one of your infants before the diamonds had been removed.'

'And without them you cannot pay for the ship that is to snatch Bonaparte from St Helena.'

'So you know of that, too,' purred Veronique. 'You are too clever, Damon. I was going to spare you, for the sake of our former friendship—'

'Even though I would not make love to you the other night?'

'I am generous, *mon cher*, I can forgive you for that. I thought I would lock you in here while I go in search of your children. Now I will have to shoot you after all.'

Juliana knew an impulse to hurl herself into the room, to shield the Major as he was shielding his friend, but it was not possible. Veronique stood between them. She looked around helplessly. She must do *something*.

'You will not touch the children, madam.' Damon spoke quickly, his tone cold as ice.

Lady Ormiston laughed harshly.

'No? And what can you do to stop me? In a few moments you will be dead, and then I shall wait on the road until the children come back from the fair. I shall make them tell me what they have done with the diamonds.'

'I tell you, they know nothing.'

'My dear sir, if you cannot tell me, what else am I to do but ask the children? You tell me the doll has not been out of their possession, so one of them must know about the stones.'

Damon's voice cut through the air like steel, quiet and deadly. 'If you touch them, I swear I will kill you!'

Juliana flinched, tensing herself for the inevitable shot, and when it did not come she knew she dare not wait any longer. She began to inch forward until she was directly behind Lady Ormiston. She was in the light now and clearly visible. She prayed that Veronique's attention would remain fixed on Damon, and that he would not give her away by so much as a glance. The lilting, taunting voice continued.

'No, no, Damon. It is *I* holding the pistol, not you. But I have tarried long enough, let us end this.'

Veronique raised her arm to take careful aim. At the same time Juliana grasped the only object within her reach. She swept the bust of Prometheus from its pedestal and raised it above her head as she stepped forward.

'You will—not—touch—my man!' she gasped as she brought the bust crashing down. Veronique had become aware of someone behind her, but even as she looked round the bust shattered against her head before she could squeeze the trigger. The weapon fell from her fingers as Veronique crumpled to the floor.

'Oh, well done, Ju.'

There was the faintest tremor in Damon's voice. He strode forward and dropped to his knees beside Veronique. Juliana leaned against the doorpost, staring in horror at the lifeless form.

'Don't worry, you haven't killed her, although you might have done so if that bust had been marble instead of alabaster, and Veronique had a less flamboyant taste in hats.'

Juliana looked at the shattered bust and the crumpled wreck of Lady Ormiston's fashionable bonnet, the ostrich feathers fluttering gently amongst the fragments of alabaster.

'I am glad I am not a murderess,' she said unsteadily. A

movement across the room caught her attention and she hurried to Sir Richard, who was beginning to stir.

'Be still, sir.' She knelt beside him. 'Do not try to rise until I have looked at that cut on your head.'

'I have a damnable headache,' he muttered.

She took out her clean handkerchief and pressed it to the wound. 'You have had a nasty blow to the head.' She looked at the red rag on the floor beside him.

'Oh—it is Minna's doll.'

'Aye,' said Sir Richard. 'I heard a noise and looked in here to see the thing lying on the floor. I bent to pick it up and as I turned something hit me.'

'She used the poker on you,' added the Major.

'Damned foolish of me to be taken unawares.' Sir Richard winced as he put his fingers to his bruised head.

'Even more foolish of me to come running in,' growled Damon. 'Veronique had hidden herself behind the door and caught us both.' He helped Sir Richard up on to a chair. 'That was just before you arrived, Ju.'

Leaving Sir Richard to hold the handkerchief to his brow, she dug her hand into her reticule. 'I wish I had been a little earlier, then you might have been prepared for her. She was looking for these, I think.' The two men stared at the diamonds winking on her palm. 'Thomas discovered them when he mended Minna's doll for her, but he thought they were glass and forgot about them.'

Damon gave a low whistle. 'The Borghese earrings, I presume, Rick?'

'Yes, by God. Well done, Miss Wrenn. With these and what the lady has let slip today we have a case, without doubt. I shall take her back to London and interrogate her further, of course, and hope we can flush out the rest of the group.'

'Amy told me Minna was given the doll when she went with Lady Varley to visit her dressmaker.'

'Madam Fleurie,' said Damon. 'That would explain Louisa's postscript on her letter that she wanted a doll returned. I didn't know what she meant and gave it no more thought.'

'Better and better.' Sir Richard grinned. He stood up, a little unsteadily, and pointed to Lady Ormiston. 'She's coming round. Damon, have you somewhere secure we can keep her until I can take her to London?'

'Aye, there's a cellar with a stout door, and nothing in it save a few boxes. She will not be able to harm herself or others from there.'

Juliana held out the diamonds to Sir Richard. 'I have done now, and had best be on my way—'

Sir Richard gripped her hand. 'Not yet, if you please, Miss Wrenn. I would be glad of your help in cleaning up this cut on my head. Foolishly I have let my man go off with the others. He has his eye on that pretty little chambermaid who comes to make up the bed and I thought it would be cruel to keep him here. Had I known this would happen, of course, I would never have consented to his going…'

She felt the corners of her mouth lifting almost reluctantly.

'There is a pump in the kitchen,' said Damon, stooping to gather Lady Ormiston into his arms. 'Perhaps Miss Wrenn would be good enough to escort you there, Rick, and clean you up a little while I see to our prisoner.'

Juliana hung back, unhappiness welling within her. Damon would not look at her, could not even bring himself to talk to her, it seemed. He would not give her an opportunity to admit she had been mistaken. She wanted to be away, to leave the house and enjoy her misery to the full. Sir Richard's grip on her hand tightened.

'Please, Miss Wrenn.'

His gentle tone worked: she could not ignore his plea for help. She nodded.

'Of course, sir. Lean on me.'

The kitchen was unnaturally tidy, the big table scrubbed and empty and all the copper and pewter dishes put away. Juliana helped Sir Richard to a chair, then went over to the sink where she began to pump water into a small bowl. Whipping a cloth from the drying rack as she came back to the table, she proceeded to clean the blood from Sir Richard's brow with gentle strokes.

'Let us hope I shall look a little less frightening when you have finished,' he remarked as she worked away.

'You look almost respectable already, sir, although there is a little blood on your cravat.' She put down her cloth. 'There, I have finished. The wound is not too deep and has stopped bleeding, so I think we need not subject you to the indignity of a bandage. Now, if you will excuse me, Sir Richard, Thomas and Amy will be wondering what has happened to me.'

'Must you go?' he asked her. 'It is very late to be setting off.'

'I know; that is why I must make haste.'

'Is your new employer expecting you? Let a servant ride over with a note, to explain.'

'No. I will not stay in this house.'

Her voice broke on the words. He gripped her hands.

'At least give me your direction. There could be a substantial reward…nay, I am sure of it—for the capture of Lady Ormiston, and for the diamonds—you must have your share. Tell me where you are going.'

Juliana closed her eyes and sank down on to a chair. Exhaustion weighed her down. She said dully, 'I will not lie to you, Sir Richard. I have nowhere to go when I leave here, which is why I must go now if I am to find decent lodging for us tonight.'

'Oh, my poor girl—' He broke off.

A hasty step sounded outside the door and the next moment Damon came in.

'Well, she is safe enough, although not too happy with her quarters.' His lip curled. 'She's not so much to be pitied. I found her maid outside in the carriage and locked her in the cellar with her mistress, along with the coachman. I promised to feed them all presently, if they behave themselves.'

Sir Richard nodded. 'Good. You should warn the servants not to go near the cellar, Damon. I wouldn't want to lose her now.' He paused, looking down at his chest. 'Dear me, I believe there is a bloodstain on my cravat, so if you will excuse me I shall go and find a fresh one.'

Juliana rose. 'And I must go, too.' She made to follow him out of the door, but Damon blocked her way.

'One moment, Miss Wrenn. You have not yet let me thank you for your services today.'

She kept her eyes lowered. 'I need no thanks, sir.'

'For saving our lives? I think you do.'

He spoke evenly, but she knew him too well to miss the hint of amusement in his voice. How dare he laugh at her, when she had been through so much? She gathered the remains of her strength.

'I would do the same for any man,' she retorted coldly. 'Please, let me go. Thomas and Amy are waiting for me outside.'

'No, they are not. I have sent them upstairs.'

She raised her head at that and gave him a scorching look. 'You had no right to do so.'

'It is far too late for you to travel today.'

'Surely, sir, that is for me to decide.'

'Not when you are using my servants.'

She eyed him resentfully, but it only seemed to increase his amusement. He put up his hands. 'You have my word that if you are still of the same mind tomorrow, my carriage shall take you wherever you wish to go.'

She considered this, and nodded. 'Very well. Then if you will excuse me, I am very tired and wish to rest.'

Still he barred her way. She clenched her jaw, determined not to lose control.

'Major Collingham,' she said carefully, 'please let me pass.'

'Not until you have explained yourself.'

'I have told you, I came back here to bring the diamonds to Sir Richard—any true Englishwoman would do as much.'

'That does not explain your behaviour in the schoolroom.'

She sighed in exasperation. 'She would have shot you both. I am very sorry if you were attached to that particular sculpture—'

'No, I had always considered that representation of Prometheus a very poor example.' He laughed. 'Quite apt, though, don't you think? The Greek myths,' he explained, observing her puzzled look. 'There's one version that says Prometheus smashed a rock against Zeus's head and Athene came out, fully formed.'

The suspicion that Damon was not quite sober entered her head. She stepped back a little.

'I fear we are straying from the point, Major.'

'Indeed we are,' he agreed cordially. 'I have no objection to you smashing the bust—it was what you said that intrigues me.'

'I don't understand.' She found herself fixed with his unrelenting gaze.

'It was your words as you came in, as glorious as any avenging goddess, and felled Veronique. Say it again for me.'

'I—I don't remember,' she said, blushing.

'Oh, I think you do.' Damon came towards her.

'I was frightened. S-surely you take no notice of what people say when they are in *extremis*?' She stepped back and found herself pressed against the panelled wall.

'Say it again.' He took another step forward.

'No!'

He placed his hands on the panelling on either side of her head, and fixed her with those dark, hawk-like eyes.

'Say it again.'

She swallowed. 'Y-you cannot bully me, Damon. I am not a r-raw recruit to be ordered about by you.'

He smiled. It was so unexpected that it caught her by surprise and her heart turned over.

'You are right. *Please* say it again.'

'I—um—'

He leaned closer. 'Go on.'

'I think I said…you shall not…Damon.'

His lips brushed her cheek. 'Say it all,' he murmured.

'I said…you shall not…'

His mouth had moved to her brow, where he dusted a featherlight kiss on the edge of her hair. 'Say it. All of it.'

He was standing so close she could feel the heat of his body. She pressed back against the wall to prevent herself leaning into him. She raised her face, inviting him to kiss her, but his mouth was just out of reach. It was difficult to breathe.

'Go on, Ju.'

'You shall not…touch…'

'Yes?'

Her eyes were level with his lips. She could not look away.

'You shall not touch…' she whispered the words, then swallowed again. He was so close, around her and above her. There was no escape. She thought wildly that she wanted none. 'You shall not touch…my man.'

There. She had said it. Now he would kiss her, surely he would kiss her! Instead he brought his hands forward to cup her face and scowled at her.

'You said just now that you would do the same for any man. Would you have said that about any man?' he demanded.

'Not—perhaps anyone,' she conceded.

His eyes narrowed. 'Richard, then—were you talking about Rick perhaps?'

With a small squeal of frustration, she reached up and pulled his dear, frowning face down to hers, giving him her answer with her lips. Only for a second did he resist her, then his hands slid over her shoulders and the next minute she was crushed against him and answering his passionate kiss with her own. Her arms slid around his neck and she clung to him. She revelled in his savage embrace, rejoiced in the feel of his hard body against hers; clearly his passion had not died. When at last he lifted his head she buried her face in his coat.

'I doubted you, Damon, I should not have done so. I am so sorry.'

He hugged her. 'You must never be sorry,' he muttered fiercely into her hair. 'I should have explained, made you believe me. We must be married, as soon as possible. I won't risk losing you again.'

She pushed away from him and looked up. 'Is—is that a proposal?'

He kissed her again. 'No, it is a command.'

'Because the children need a mother?'

He scowled at her. 'No, because I need a wife. A friend. A lover.'

A bolt of liquid fire ran through her body and she trembled. She would have looked away, but he caught her chin and forced her to meet his eyes. The glow in their granite-grey depths made her breathless.

'You know I have a damnable temper, God knows you have felt the lash of my tongue already. I will try to mend it; but I make no promises: in any event you are more than a match for me and will give me my own again if I grow too tyrannical.' He gave her a wry smile. 'Do I not have the wound on my arm to prove it?'

'Pray do not remind me of that, Damon. I never wanted to hurt you.'

'It was only a scratch, Ju, but enough to bring me to my senses.'

She smiled up at him mistily. 'For days afterwards I was afraid it would become infected and give you a fever,' she told him, her voice breaking.

He hugged her tightly. '*You* gave me a fever, Ju. I could think of nothing but you.' He looked up at the ceiling and gave a deep sigh. She waited patiently and at last he looked at her again, a touch of uncertainty in his eyes.

'I love you, Juliana. I have no great fortune to offer you, but Giles's engineer is confident the coal mine is viable and I plan to build the cotton mill—in a few years they could both be giving a good return.'

'Do not forget the reward Sir Richard spoke of,' she added shyly.

He shook his head. 'That shall be settled on Thomas and Amy. Well, Ju, will you agree to marry me, and to share my life and my fortune, such as it is?'

She lifted her hand to his cheek.

'*You* are my fortune, Damon. And my life.'

Chapter Twenty-Six

Juliana woke up to the sound of birdsong. She stretched languorously and felt Damon's sleeping form beside her. She reached out a hand and ran her fingers over the silky hairs on his naked thigh. He stirred.

'Good morning, Mrs Collingham.'

Mrs Collingham! She had been married for a whole month and still smiled when she heard that name. Damon turned and pulled her back against him, kissing her neck. He cupped her breast in his hand and she sighed with contentment.

'What shall we do today, sir?'

'Fewell's brother is bringing his plans for the new mill.'

'Have you told Giles he is coming?'

'Yes, he will be there. He is interested in machinery and has a natural gift for such things—I think he will be very useful. I am sending him to Birmingham; Sir Richard has contacts there amongst the engineers and Giles is to work with them, learn what he can.' His arms tightened slightly. 'You will come to the meeting with me, will you not? You won't find it dull work?'

'By no means.'

His fingers moved down over her body, caressing her stomach, then down to thread themselves among the soft curls at the hinge of her thigh. She caught her breath.

'It is still early.' Damon nibbled at her ear.

He was curled around her and she smiled as she felt the hardness of him pressing against her skin.

'Then I think you should be looking to maintain your reputation in the bedroom,' she murmured provocatively. '*Devil* Collingham.'

With something like a growl, he pulled her round to face him. 'You will be gaining something of a reputation yourself, madam, insatiable as you are.' He captured her mouth, her lips parted invitingly and her body moved sensuously beneath his caressing hands until the ache deep within her was too great to be denied and she rolled on top of him, taking him within her as he had taught her and revelling in the exquisite, joyful pleasure of their mutual love.

* * * * *

The Angel and
the Outlaw

KATHRYN ALBRIGHT

Dear Reader,

The idea for this story came to me on one of my visits to the Old Point Loma Lighthouse in San Diego and the nearby tide pools. Inspired by the beauty and ruggedness of the terrain, the tales of shipwrecks off the coast, the whaling station nearby and the last of the California bandits, I wondered what type of man would choose to live such an isolated life.

It seemed that a stubborn man like Stuart, who is running from the law and in need of redemption, could use a little help from a feisty woman to make peace with his past. Rachel, with her tough life in the backcountry mining camps, is not the type to shy away from a challenge.

This is my first published book, and I would love to hear from my readers. You can reach me at PO Box 606, Rockton, IL 61072, USA or contact me through my website at www. kathrynleighalbright.com.

I hope you enjoy *The Angel and the Outlaw*!

Kathryn

To my mother and father,
who taught me to go after my dreams.
Thank you for your love,
support and encouragement.

Prologue

San Francisco, California, 1870

At the sound of someone running up his ship's gang-plank, Matthew Taylor looked up from the scatter of charts on his desk.

"Matthew! Let me in! I must speak with you."

He strode to the door and stopped short at the sight before him. "Linnea!"

The light from the cabin's oil lamp exposed harsh bruises against the pale skin on her face. Blood dripped from a cracked lip. Under the dark hooded cloak, her blond hair, usually swept up in the latest fashion, hung unkempt to her shoulders.

"My God! What happened?"

"I...I killed John!" she gasped. "He was going after Hannah."

Suddenly he realized the bundle she held was her daughter. "Let me take her." He pulled the cover away, breathing a sigh of relief that Hannah was free of any sign of battering. She was shaking, just as her mother was. He laid her on his bunk and turned back to Linnea. "Tell me what happened," he said, the rage in his voice barely subdued.

Her eyes filled with tears. "I… Might I use your handkerchief?"

He handed one to her. God, he couldn't stand the tears. "Don't cry, Linnea. You know I'll help."

"Yes," she said softly. "I know."

With his fingers under her chin, he lifted her face to the light. "How long has this been going on?"

She turned away from him. "Awhile."

He poured a brace of whiskey into his mug and handed it to her. "It's all I have."

"Taylor!" John Newcomb bellowed from outside.

Linnea's eyes widened. "I thought he was dead!"

"Taylor!" John was closer now. "You holing up with my wife? You send her on out here. We've got unfinished business."

Linnea started to rise.

"No," Matthew said, and motioned for her to stay put.

She grasped his arm. "Matthew. Be careful. He's changed since you last saw him."

He stared at her, taking in the changes the past few years had wrought on her. A hundred things went through his head in that moment, none of which he could say to her as a married woman. *Why did you marry this animal? Why didn't you wait for me?* He sighed. At the least, he could protect her.

He squeezed her hand. "I'll just talk to him. I don't

want a fight, but I won't run from one, either." He reached into a desk drawer and drew out his Colt .44.

On the wharf, John Newcomb leaned heavily against the railing, his tie askew against his linen shirt. "Send my wife out, Taylor. She don't belong with you."

"You're drunk, Mr. Newcomb. Go home and sleep it off."

"I'm not leaving without my girls. Linnea! We need to talk. I…at least give me a chance to apologize."

Matthew heard the door creak behind him.

"Go away," Linnea said softly, her body half-hidden behind the door post. "We'll talk later."

"We'll talk now," John growled, and started up the gangplank, clutching his chest. "Then I'll have words with Taylor, here." Suddenly he stopped and leaned awkwardly on the ship's railing. As he straightened, he pulled a gun from his belt and aimed past Matthew.

A shot rang out.

"Mama!" Hannah screamed.

Matthew watched in horror as Linnea crumpled to her knees, a look of stunned surprise on her face.

John stormed up the gangplank, aiming his gun for a second shot at her. "I'll teach you to at shoot me."

"No!" Matthew roared. He whipped up his Colt and squeezed the trigger.

In the loud report of the gun, John Newcomb staggered, but then regained his footing. He swung his gun toward Matthew. "You can't have her, Taylor. I'll kill you both before I let that happen."

Matthew steadied his gun, aimed at Newcomb's chest and fired.

Newcomb fell forward hard, landing with a heavy thud. The wharf's gas lamp cast a yellow light over the blood saturating his shirt and dripping onto the wooden planks beneath him.

Matthew threw down his gun and hurried to Linnea. Blood trickled across her forehead. She was so still, so pale. Crouching, he gathered her in his arms, unable to breathe, afraid she was hurt or—worse—dead.

Her large gray eyes fluttered open. "I'm all right."

His heart pounded in his chest.

She raised her hand to his cheek, the worry in her eyes for him now. "Matthew, I'm all right."

He let out a long, shuddering breath. "I thought…"

"Yes. I know."

He hugged her to him, burying his face in her neck until his heartbeat slowed to normal. He couldn't bear to lose her.

After a moment she struggled up on her elbows. "Is he dead?"

Matthew followed her gaze. He walked over to the still form. Not breathing. He rolled Newcomb over to his back and felt for a pulse at his throat.

Nothing.

"What happens now?" Linnea asked, her voice shaking. "Should we contact the authorities?"

Chapter One

Southern California, 1873

Stuart Taylor crouched on a flat boulder and pulled his trap up from the harbor floor. A small brown lobster slid to the corner of the crate. He grabbed it, turning it over to make sure of its size, and then tossed it back into the water. "Come back when you've grown," he murmured. Then, placing new bait in the trap, he stood and swung the trap out as far as possible, releasing the hemp rope at the last second. The crate splashed into the brine and sank quickly beyond sight.

He looked for his other lobster trap, but it was gone—rope and all. Someone was still stealing from him. He'd warned off two boys a few days ago with a bullet into their boat. Their sudden departure had convinced him they wouldn't try again. Maybe he'd been wrong.

Great. Guess he and Hannah would be eating beans

tonight. Not the best way to celebrate a birthday. He grabbed the bucket at his feet and made his way up the narrow dirt path.

Hannah stood at the stone doorstep, anxiety filling her heart-shaped face until she caught sight of him. She wore her one good dress, the dark-chocolate-brown one he'd laid out last night. A white pinafore covered it, wrinkled in one spot now where her hands had twisted and worried the fabric. Uncanny how that trait of her mother's manifested itself in Hannah, though she'd only been three when Linnea died.

"Did you eat?"

She nodded, and with the bob of her head, he spied her tangled mass of blond hair. "Forgot something, birthday girl," he said gruffly, turning her toward the kitchen. "You can't go into town looking like something washed in by the waves."

She crossed her arms over her chest and stood stiffly while he brushed her hair then tied it in a ponytail with an old blue ribbon. The face that stared back at him grew more like her mother's every day. The dove-gray eyes shone with anticipation for the promised trip. She was lonely here. So lonely the thought of a trip into town had her flushed with excitement and up before dawn. He felt it, too—the isolation, the quiet. But it was safe.

He followed Hannah outside and boosted her onto his horse, Blanco. She fidgeted, patting the dusty animal on its withers. He grabbed the lead rope. "See that you don't wiggle right off your perch."

They took the trail that led from the tip of the windy

peninsula, four hundred feet above sea level, to the small town on the water's edge. He didn't get into town much, only when supplies ran low, but today was August 10, Hannah's birthday, and he wanted to make it special for her.

He drew closer to La Playa and his anxiety increased in measure. Surely the risk of discovery had diminished now. It had been more than three years since the accident. Hannah didn't even look the same. She had stretched up into a thin wisp of a girl who seldom stood still. Her naturally pale skin had taken on a golden glow over the long summer days.

He rubbed his smooth chin, remembering the dark beard and mustache that once covered his face. He didn't look the same either. Still, doubts niggled at his mind. Dorian wasn't stupid, and he wasn't a quitter. San Francisco might be five hundred miles away but sooner or later Dorian would find him—and if Dorian found him, so would the law. Perhaps he should think about moving on.

Halfway to town, the trail sloped steeply through a brush-studded canyon. Two small lizards scurried from under the horse's shadow and dashed into the nearby chaparral as he led Blanco around one last sandstone curve. The harbor opened up before them, deep blue and sparkling in the sunlight. Barely visible through the scruffy bushes to the south lay the whaling port. He raised his face to the wind and sniffed. "Smell that, Hannah? Just salt and sage. No whale butchered today."

Turning toward La Playa, he led Blanco past a steamer moored at the new wharf before heading up

San Antonio Street and past the Mexican Government Custom House. A few odd-shaped buildings, some built of wood and some of adobe, hugged each side of the square like ticks on the ears of a short-haired dog.

Stuart stopped at the community well and filled his canteens, all the while taking in the surrounding sounds the way a deaf man would who for one day is able to hear. Loud clanging rang out from the livery's half-opened doorway as the blacksmith forged a new tool or horseshoe. A thin, aproned woman swept the front boardwalk of the town's only mercantile.

Hannah tugged on his shirt.

"All right, all right. I'm going."

Looping the two canteens over the saddle horn, he walked back to Morley's Mercantile. Two young women stood at the opened doorway of the store, giggling and whispering behind gloved hands. He glanced up while tying the reins on the hitching rail. Both attractive, especially the blonde. He turned back to help Hannah.

"There on his forehead. Do you see it?"

He slowed in the act of setting Hannah on the ground. So he was to supply their gossip for today. He clenched his hands. He'd hate to disappoint them. Straightening, he leveled his gaze at the two.

The blonde quieted. She must be the banker's wife—or daughter. Her dress was quality through and through, right down to her matching green parasol. He hadn't seen anything so fancy since he'd left San Francisco. Her eyes judged him coolly before she whirled about with a toss of her head and entered the store.

Anger surged through him. Already he could feel people staring at him through the streaked window-panes. He couldn't care less that they talked about him. But Hannah—Hannah, he worried about. She might not talk anymore, but she could hear just fine. He'd rather take her anywhere than into the store right now.

But it was her birthday. And he'd promised this trip for weeks.

He grasped her hand and helped her jump onto the boardwalk before stepping up himself.

The other woman, the one who'd gotten an earful, remained standing in the doorway, curiosity etched in her strong face. He wouldn't call her pretty—yet the sum of her features pulled together in a pleasant way. She wore a plain yellow dress, simple and sturdy, and a straw hat that covered thick auburn hair.

He stepped close—closer than was conventional—and dragged off his seaman's cap, giving her a good view of his scar. He met her unflinching gaze full-on—challenging her to speak. She was older than he'd first thought. Fine lines splayed from the corners of her eyes and her nose was sunburned and peeling. He let his gaze wander the length of her until he arrived again at her face, and found himself slightly irritated for enjoying the trip. "By all means, believe everything you hear."

Her cheeks flamed scarlet. With an almost imperceptible nod of her head—or was it actually a raising of her chin?—she stepped aside for him to enter the building.

The scent of cloves and cinnamon intermingled with the barrel of pears in the doorway. He breathed deeply and tried to shake off the discontent he felt. This was Hannah's birthday trip, and by God he'd make it special.

The blonde stood at the counter speaking with the lanky owner of the mercantile and glancing over her shoulder at Stuart every few seconds. Terrance Morley drummed his fingers on the countertop. "Mornin', Taylor. Things quiet up your way?"

Stuart hesitated a fraction of a second and then nodded. Things were always quiet at the lighthouse. He handed Morley the list of needed supplies.

Suddenly, Hannah let go of his hand and dashed across the room. Stuart followed slowly, a sinking sensation in his stomach. He hated to put a damper on her fascination with the trinkets and products, but whatever the item might be, likely they couldn't afford it. He'd planned only to buy her six sarsaparilla candy sticks, one for each of her six years, and a new hair ribbon.

She spun around holding a new doll with shiny waves of painted black hair and red lips. She fingered the doll's pretty green dress and ruffled underthings. He knew what would come next and steeled himself against the disappointment that would transform her face. Before the accident he wouldn't have thought twice about the cost of the doll. Although not rich, he had been comfortable, and the future held such promise. But now, on a light keeper's salary, the toy cost more than he could afford.

The woman in yellow entered the store, the sun casting her shadow across the hardwood floor. Morley glanced up, started to greet her and spied Hannah holding the doll.

"Put that down!" he shouted.

Startled, Hannah jumped. The doll crashed to the floor, its china head shattering at her feet. She stared in frozen shock at the pieces.

"Now look what you've done!" Morley yelled and pointed a bony finger at the mess. He charged around the end of the counter and jabbed Hannah's shoulder. "Children have no business being in here without proper supervision. You'll pay for that, missy."

Stuart leveled his gaze. "That's enough, Morley."

Tears brimmed in Hannah's eyes. She was scared—and sorry—even though the words wouldn't come. Stuart put his hand on her shoulder. "It was an accident, Hannah."

Next to him, the blonde turned on Hannah. "You must apologize to Mr. Morley this instant, child."

"I said that's enough," Stuart said, making sure there was no mistaking the warning in his voice. "And I'll thank you to keep to your own business, ma'am."

She glared at him, obviously perceiving the double meaning of his words, then stuck her nose higher in the air and walked from the store.

Slowly Hannah stooped and picked up the fragments of china.

I should scold her, Stuart told himself, but Mr. Morley had done a strong job of that. "Hannah," he said, sharper than he intended.

She stopped her gathering and glanced up, the tears spilling onto her cheeks in earnest now. Tightness wrapped around his chest and squeezed at the sight of her misery. Linnea would have handled this differently. He gentled his tone. "Put those on the counter and wait outside."

When she had done as he asked, he stepped up to the counter. He would settle the cost of the toy, but he'd have to omit an item or two from his list. How could he salvage her birthday after this?

The woman in yellow stooped to pick up one last fragment of china and the body of the doll. She placed them next to his parcels.

"Miss Houston, you don't need to clean up," the clerk said. "You'll cut yourself."

"You frightened the girl."

Her reproachful voice held a hint of soft Midwestern twang.

"She should sweep the entire floor for her punishment," Morley said.

Stuart pressed his lips together, checking his urge to hit the man. "I'll take care of my girl. You just mind your store." He looked over his stack of supplies and removed the canned beef and fresh bread. He could hunt rabbits and quail as usual. And there was always fish. They'd make do with the tin of crackers. It would last longer than the bread, anyway. Stubbornly, he kept the six candy sticks. "Now what is my total with the doll?"

While Morley tallied the order, Stuart found himself watching the woman, surprised she had spoken in Hannah's defense—and a little suspicious, too. She strolled to the yard goods, smoothing her hand across one piece of fabric and then another.

She must have felt him staring. After a glance in his

direction she looked away, but her cheeks flushed pink. She selected two bundles of yarn and set them on the far end of the counter. The scent of honeysuckle wafted over him, feminine, inviting. How long had it been since he smelled anything other than the brine of the ocean?

"You aren't charging full price for the doll, are you Terrance?" she asked.

Mr. Morley stopped his tallying and frowned over his glasses at her.

"Part of the fault lies with you," she continued.

"That doesn't excuse the cost."

"But you startled the girl. If you'd asked her to put the doll down rather than speaking so sharply, she wouldn't have dropped it."

Morley caught Stuart's gaze. "Three dollars, Taylor."

The clerk's attitude disgusted him. The sooner Stuart got out of here, the better. He counted out the money and dropped it on the counter then picked up the box of supplies. The doll he left behind purposely. To have what was left of it would only distress Hannah.

He packed his saddlebags, and then helped Hannah onto Blanco. Despair knifed through him at the silent shaking of her shoulders. She had dressed so carefully this morning, had been so excited about this trip into town, and it had ended in a nightmare. Stuart's stomach knotted. He couldn't do anything about other people. They were cruel. Hell, life was cruel, but somehow he'd make it up to her.

A flash of yellow in the doorway caught his eye. He glanced up to see the woman watching him. He didn't

quite know what to make of her. In the end she'd been
kind, and so he tipped his cap to her.

She acknowledged him with a nod, her gaze steady.

Anxious to put the town and its people behind him,
he led Blanco home. The bustling sounds of the harbor
grated on his ears. The silence that shrouded them daily
at the lighthouse would be safe—safe for him and safe
for Hannah. No one and nothing would bother them...
nothing but the never-ending quiet.

"Your yarn, Miss Houston." Terrance Morley leaned
on the wooden counter and smiled—a smile Rachel could
easily mistake for a leer if she gave room to the thought.

"Thank you, Mr. Morley."

"It was Terrance a moment ago."

"Yes, well. It was a bit presumptuous of me."

"But you've been coming in here for over two
months now. I'd like you to use my given name."

"Oh," she said, not particularly thrilled with what
others might read into the familiarity. "I'm a little uncomfortable with that." Her position as the new schoolteacher in this small town hinged on the degree of
respectability she could maintain. At her interview with
the school board she had downplayed the last few years
she'd spent at the mining camp where coarseness and
crudeness frequently overpowered a gentler nature.
Instead, she had reframed the questions to answer them
from her earlier life when she'd helped at the one-room
schoolhouse in Wisconsin.

She picked up the yarn and turned to go, but stopped
when she saw the broken doll. The head was shattered.

No amount of gluing could repair it. Fingering the mint-green satin dress and miniature crinoline, she thought of the girl's sad face. The wrinkled, too-small dress, the small hole in one stocking below the knee, all spoke of a girl with no mother to do for her. Rachel knew what it was like to live without a mother. At least she'd been lucky to have known hers for the first fourteen years of her life. How lonely the girl must be on the peninsula with no one but her father.

Since she'd moved to town two months ago, she'd heard stories of him. How he kept to himself and was unfriendly toward the townspeople. She didn't know what to believe and most likely shouldn't listen to half of it.

Still, she'd expected someone much older to be the town's enigma—someone grizzled, with bushy brows and an irascible nature. At most, Taylor must be all of thirty years—or perhaps thirty-five—for he had the solid, filled-out look of a man. His clothes were simple, serviceable—a faded blue chambray shirt, slightly snug across the stretch of his shoulders, tucked into canvas pants, and scruffy boots that passed for comfortable on his feet. A thick wisp of dark-brown hair fell across his temple and had obscured his scar until he purposely exposed it for her.

It was a hideous scar—puckered and red. She wondered how he'd really gotten it. Amanda said he'd been struck with a red-hot fire poker when he escaped from prison. That was ridiculous, of course. The lighthouse board would never have hired a convict. Since coming to town two months ago, Rachel had heard other stories about him as well, enough to know that no one knew anything definite about him at all.

Besides, it wasn't the scar that drew her, but the intensity of his blue gaze. When he'd stopped no more than a foot from her in the doorway she'd scarcely been able to breathe.

No, he wasn't her idea of a light keeper at all.

Chapter Two

Rachel jerked open the oven door and pulled out the roast.

Finished. Except for the gravy. Lamb wasn't her favorite dish, but she couldn't very well serve rabbit or fish tonight—not with company coming.

Reverend and Emma Crouse rented two rooms to Rachel and her brother, Caleb, on the condition that they would help with odd jobs around the place. That usually meant cooking for Rachel, and tending the horse and small carriage house for Caleb. Of course, four dollars a month from Rachel's teaching salary also helped cover their rent. Reverend and Emma Crouse were in their late sixties and ready to slow down a little. Staying with such an upstanding couple had helped with her acceptance into the community. One couldn't be too careful that way, especially after the years she'd lived in the mining camp. The roughness of the camp had rubbed off on her and try as she might to put it all behind her, unfortunate things would spring out of her mouth—or show up in her actions.

She pushed a strand of damp hair from her forehead, then leaned across the small table to open the window. A cool evening breeze swirled in heavy with the scent of brine from the ocean. Looking out into the early evening, she wondered what the light keeper and his daughter would be eating tonight. The two had been in her thoughts throughout the day, popping in unexpectedly.

She hadn't liked Amanda's attitude or Terrance Morley's for that matter. Maybe what they said about the light keeper was true. Perhaps he was a criminal. But even so, the girl—Hannah, he'd called her—should not be condemned along with the father. The man obviously cared for his daughter or he wouldn't have protected her from Terrance's tirade. There must be something good in him.

The kitchen door opened and Reverend Crouse entered. It seemed the room warmed as much from the heat that emanated from him as it did from the stove. "Supper ready?"

"Nearly." Then, knowing his next question, she answered, "Mrs. Crouse is in the parlor with the guests."

"Ah. Then I'd best get out there and greet them, too. Are you doing all right in here without Emma's help?" She nearly smiled at the relief on his face at her quick nod. Then he headed to the front of the parsonage.

Suddenly the back door crashed open and her brother barreled into the kitchen along with his dog. At fifteen, Caleb was neither a boy any longer, nor yet a man. Clumsy was what he was. He was growing so fast—already four inches taller than she. He reached for a dinner roll, and she caught the bony knob of his wrist just in time.

"Not before supper. Now take Settie right back outside."

He ignored her. "She's getting close, don't you think?"

Rachel studied the large black animal. The dog's bulging abdomen swayed as she walked around the small kitchen sniffing the different aromas. "Any day now, I suspect. She is so big I don't know how she manages to move."

"Enrique said he'll take a male. He thinks it might make a good hunter."

She frowned. Caleb could use a good friend, but someone other than Enrique. Together, the two of them got into too much mischief. She turned back to her preparations. "Well, for now Settie goes outside. Wash up. The food is ready."

Behind her, she heard Caleb maneuver the dog out the back door. When he didn't come right back in, she glanced through the window. He stood in the yard talking with Enrique and another boy. The way they leaned toward each other, whispering, unsettled her. She watched a moment longer and then tried to shake off her misgivings. Time to get supper on.

She carried a platter with the roast lamb surrounded by new potatoes to the dining table. When they were all seated, Rachel sat down across from Terrance

Morley and his sister, Elizabeth. The bouquet of roses he'd brought graced the center of the table, their delicate fragrance completely overwhelmed by the odor of mutton.

"Where's Caleb?" Emma Crouse asked.

"He's just outside with a friend. He'll be in shortly," Rachel said. "Perhaps we should go ahead before the food cools."

The reverend frowned, but bowed his head to say the blessing. Then the dishes were passed around and the talk turned to local business and how New San Diego was quickly becoming a ghost town. Rachel tried, but she just couldn't follow the conversation.

"If you'll excuse me a moment," She said, standing. "I'll just see what is keeping Caleb." Rachel walked into the kitchen and peered out the window into the empty yard. A feeling of foreboding enveloped her. She'd have to have a talk with her brother about manners—a good hard talk the moment he came back. But oh, how she dreaded it. Lately her talks had met with considerable deafness on his part—or anger.

She sat back down with the others. Elizabeth leaned toward her. "How is the teaching going?"

"Well, I think. The most difficult part is getting some of the local children to show up regularly. Last Tuesday I caught several boys heading toward Old Town to watch the horse races."

"Perhaps you won't have long to worry about such things," said Emma. "You will settle down with some lucky man and start your own family. Except, of course, that would mean the town would need to hire another teacher." She laughed softly.

Rachel tensed at her words. Although none of these folks knew much about her past, she'd already spent most of her life taking care of her father and Caleb, following the whim of a man caught up in gold fever. She forced a smile and tried to keep her voice light. "Oh, I don't know. I rather like making my own way at the moment."

Terrance raised his brows. "I should think marriage, taking care of one man and raising his children would be enough to satisfy a woman."

A slow burn started inside her. "I like teaching. And I'm good at it. Don't I have a responsibility to use this gift?"

"Yes," Terrance said, frowning slightly. "Of course, for your own children."

"Ah-hem." Reverend Crouse placed his napkin carefully by his plate, signaling that supper—and this conversation—was over. She bit back her retort. "Rachel, if you're still set on riding out to the lighthouse, we'll go first thing in the morning."

Terrance paused in taking his last bite of strawberry dessert, looking from the reverend to Rachel. "Uh…if you don't mind my asking, what business do you have at the lighthouse?"

"I want to invite Mr. Taylor and his daughter to attend services," the reverend answered.

Terrance quickly covered his mouth with his napkin, subduing a snort. "Good luck, then. He's been living out there for nearly a year and this week was only the third

time I've ever seen him in the store. He's a lost cause—
his daughter, too. You shouldn't waste your time on
those two."

"Lost causes are the Lord's specialty," the reverend
said, rising to his feet. "And I'm beginning to believe
Rachel's too."

The others followed suit. Amid compliments to
Rachel and Emma for the fine dinner, they gravitated
toward the parlor to play games.

Terrance stayed behind as Rachel began to clear the
table. "Excellent meal, Rachel."

"Thank you." It had better be edible; she had been
cooking since she was fourteen. "Oh, you don't need
to help—"

A loud knocking on the front door interrupted her.

"Rachel?" Reverend Crouse called. "You'd best
come here."

She put down the dirty plates and walked into the
parlor. Sheriff Thorne stood in the entryway holding
firm to Caleb.

"Miss," he acknowledged her and then the small
group, sweeping his battered hat off belatedly. "Perhaps we'd better take this out on the porch so your
guests can carry on."

She nodded and followed him outside, feeling Terrance's presence behind her. Thorne was the town's
part-time sheriff, splitting his time between La Playa
and Old Town San Diego. She didn't know him well,
but he drew a lot of respect from the people here. "What
is going on?"

"I caught your brother with his friends, startin' a fire

down by the old hide houses. A fire this time of year could destroy the whole town."

Her brother hung his head and didn't look at her.

"This is one more mishap in a line of minor scrapes, miss. You're his guardian. I'd suggest you keep a closer eye on him."

She nodded, acknowledging the responsibility. She couldn't believe Caleb would try something so foolish on his own. It had to be the coercion of the other two boys. "Have you got anything to say?" she asked her brother.

His jaw set, he glared at her from under his red brows and shook his head.

"Then go to your room. We'll talk about this later." He shuffled past her and inside the house.

She turned back to the sheriff. "Thank you. I'll watch him more closely." She didn't know how she could, but she'd try. Every day Caleb pulled further and further away from her. She was losing him. Her one bit of family left.

Sheriff Thorne touched his hat. "Sorry to intrude upon your day."

She watched him stride down the steps and back toward the Custom House that held the small, makeshift jail.

Terrance stepped onto the porch from the doorway. "I'll help the best I can, Rachel. Boys can be tough."

A heavy sigh escaped. "He won't listen to me anymore. Not like when he was younger."

"His father should be the one looking out for him," Terrance said. "Not you."

Rachel pressed her lips together. Her father hadn't

taken much of an interest in either of them since her mother passed away. He'd just been interested in finding gold. If only Caleb had someone who could help him through this rocky stage. She certainly wasn't much help. The tighter she held on, the harder he pulled away. Plus she worried about how Caleb's actions would affect her standing in the community. The selfish thought nudged her and she felt small for thinking it. But she still worried. Teaching was her livelihood—and Caleb's too, for the time being.

Terrance cleared his throat. "About tomorrow. I… wish you would reconsider about going out to the lighthouse. It will be a long ride, and Taylor won't take you up on your offer."

"I don't shirk a challenge, Mr. Morley. The girl needs to be in school and I'm going to convince him of it."

By the look on his face, it wasn't the answer he'd wanted. "Nothing I say will dissuade you?"

"My mind is made up." She didn't add that the more students she had in school, the better job security for her, although the thought had crossed her mind a time or two since seeing the girl.

"It seems like everyone dislikes him. Are they true— the things I've heard?" But even she could hear the beginning of doubt in her voice.

"Rumors have some truth to them in most cases. Otherwise how would they start?"

She shook off the misgivings. "I'm sure I'll be safe enough with Reverend Crouse."

"Yes…well," he said, his gaze hardening slightly,

"you know how I feel about you going out there. It's a fool's errand."

He waited. Probably still hoping she'd change her mind. When she didn't say more he continued. "Thank you for supper. Until Sunday services then."

She nodded and watched him walk down the porch steps to the street. Sunday was the furthest thing from her mind.

Chapter Three

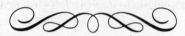

Reverend Crouse yanked sharply on Jericho's reins to avoid a large dried rut in the dirt road, yet their carriage still bumped through the edge, jostling Rachel to one side. She grabbed her seat and smiled gamely. "I hope after all this, we find them at home."

"I don't know where else they would be. Light keepers as a rule must not leave their lamps unattended."

"Well, that gives us a place to start, then," she said, thinking of her brother and how easily he slipped out of sight whenever he wanted to. "Trying to tie Caleb down and keep track of him is not easy."

Reverend Crouse chuckled. "It may seem that way now, but you're doing the right thing. Caleb will be the better for it in the long run. He's not a bad boy, he just needs direction."

"I suppose." Rachel sighed, thinking her brother more and more showed signs of being like his father. "I'm glad you had chores for him to do today."

"Terrance Morley stopped by earlier. He has things Caleb can help with at the mercantile."

She shook her head. "Caleb needs something physical. He's never been one for being cooped up inside. Often he talks about joining up with the whalers. And I'm afraid he might. That would suit him."

The reverend skirted another deep rut where rainwater had gouged out the quickest path to the sea several hundred feet below. To Rachel's left glistened the deep-blue waters of the harbor, and to her right the ocean stretched out unbroken to the horizon. Stunted light-green sagebrush and chaparral lined both sides of the road, struggling to keep a foothold in the dry ground. No homesteads broke the monotony of the single dirt road they traveled, a road that striped the ridge of the peninsula like the line down a lizard's back.

Jericho pulled the carriage up one last rise and the lighthouse came into view. The sandstone house and tower stood sharply defined against the brilliant blue of the Pacific sky. Two short chimneys straddled the peak at each end of the two-story roof, the far one emitting small burps of black smoke. The light tower rose straight up through the center of the roof's peak. She searched the black iron catwalk that circled the lamp for any sign of the inhabitants.

The reverend stopped Jericho at the picket fence that surrounded the lighthouse and enclosed a small, barren yard and the shriveled remains of a garden. "He's home, all right," he murmured, his eyes focused on the opening door.

Mr. Taylor stepped outside, his shoulders dwarfing

the size of the doorway, his mouth set in a tight scowl as he slipped his shoulder suspenders into place. He wore a cream-colored muslin shirt, open at the collar on this warm and windy day, and dark brown pants that, as his clothes yesterday, appeared serviceable.

A small thrill went through her. What was it about this man that his very presence commanded attention? Would he lump her with all the other people from town? Most likely. She sat straighter in her seat, the urge to prove him wrong infusing her with courage. She wasn't here for him, but she did need his support regarding his daughter.

"Hello. Mr. Taylor, is it?" Reverend Crouse climbed from the carriage. "I'm Reverend Crouse and this is Rachel Houston, the schoolteacher in town. We've come to invite you and your child to Sunday services."

If it were possible, the light keeper's scowl deepened further. His gaze flicked to Rachel, still seated in the carriage, and then settled back on the reverend. "Then you've wasted your trip, Pastor. I'm not on speaking terms with God."

The blunt reply surprised Rachel, but the reverend seemed unruffled. "If not for yourself," the reverend continued, "surely you want your daughter growing in the faith."

Sarcasm twisted Mr. Taylor's mouth. "I'm certain the good people of La Playa want nothing to do with her or me. You must have heard about what happened at the mercantile." This time his stormy gaze settled on Rachel.

She swallowed hard, unable to look away, and felt her heartbeat quicken.

"An unfortunate incident, to be sure," said the reverend as he swept off his black-brimmed hat. "You'll find Hannah is treated better in church."

Taylor turned back to Reverend Crouse, and Rachel took the moment to descend from the carriage and approach the two men. "That has not been my past experience."

Reverend Crouse's silver brows knitted together. "We are not a group of perfect people. Everyone is welcome in God's house."

Mr. Taylor didn't answer, but his eyes hardened to blue slate. He folded his arms across his chest. "Look, Pastor, I mean no offense, but it's best if you just leave. It's too bad you had to ride all the way out here just to hear me say no, but no it is."

The reverend shrugged his shoulders and gave a brief smile. "There is always that chance in my line of work. However, my job is to sow the seeds. Only God can make them grow."

He seemed on the verge of continuing in the same vein, but then pulled back. "Very well. I won't press you further. Remember, though, the invitation stands in the event you change your mind."

"Good day, Pastor."

"One more thing," the reverend continued, smoothly filling in the awkward quiet. "We are planning to hold the annual community picnic here in a few weeks. You weren't here last year, so I wanted to forewarn you."

Taylor pressed his lips together. "Thanks for the warning."

Concern softened Reverend Crouse's eyes. "You're welcome to attend, of course."

Mr. Taylor nodded his acknowledgment.

"Come, Rachel." The reverend started back to the carriage along the hard dirt path.

When she didn't move, Mr. Taylor's steely gaze fastened on her. She swallowed hard. He made it difficult to breathe, let alone speak. It seemed he really hated their intrusion into his life. "I...I brought something for Hannah."

Conscious of being watched, she walked to the carriage boot, and withdrew her present. She'd wrapped it in a large scrap of brown cloth to protect it from the dust on the trip. Perhaps Mr. Taylor would be angry about the gift. Perhaps it would remind him about the incident in the mercantile and he'd refuse it. She hadn't thought of that when wrapping it, and now that made her nervous. But when she turned back to him, she caught a glimpse of his daughter peeking around the door frame. Curiosity and shyness warred on the young girl's face, and Rachel's confidence grew. This wasn't about Mr. Taylor. It was about the girl.

Returning to stand in front of him, she unwrapped the cloth to reveal a papier-mâché doll. Pupilless glass eyes stared up at the light keeper from under painted brown hair. The doll was not new—spidery, hairline cracks ran along the chest and shoulders—but Rachel hoped Mr. Taylor would let Hannah have it. She drew back the cloth further to reveal the green satin gown that had dressed the doll at the mercantile. "The dress fit perfectly. I thought Hannah might give my doll a good home."

Mr. Taylor's brows drew together. "We don't want your charity."

"That's good, because I'm the least charitable person I know," she said, her anger surfacing. "You've already paid for the dress. Sarah sits in a box under my bed day in and day out. She needs a little girl to play with again."

"I'm sure there are plenty of girls at your school. What about them?"

Frustration knotted within her. "I want Hannah to have Sarah."

He continued to watch her silently.

She was not going to back down!

"Do you bribe all children this way?"

He would think such a thing! She struggled to keep her voice low so that Hannah would not hear her anger. "You, sir, are being ridiculously suspicious of a simple kindness. This is not a bribe. And I do not appreciate your rudeness over a simple gift!"

"Perhaps I've had a little experience with Greeks bearing gifts," he said. But he turned to stare at his daughter in the open doorway. Hannah's heart-shaped face was filled with anxious hope. Tangles of blond hair fell over her thin shoulders and onto the same brown dress she'd worn at the mercantile. Timidly, Hannah inched down the stone walk to stand behind her father.

Rachel glanced up at Mr. Taylor but his closed expression told her nothing. A shiver stole through her as she watched him. He was a formidable man, standing a full head taller than her, and she was not a small woman. Yet, he hadn't actually refused the gift. She squatted to the child's level and then held out the doll. "This is Sarah. She was my doll when I was little. I brought her for you."

Hannah glanced up at her father and then slowly reached for the doll, her eyes filled with wonder. She pressed Sarah against her in a hug.

Rachel smiled and let out the breath she'd been holding.

She rose and met his gaze, determined to ignore his surliness. "I know you said church is out of the question. Would you consider school? Hannah is old enough to be in the first or second grade by now."

His look of incredulity gave her his answer even before he spoke. "Absolutely not."

"Mr. Taylor, you can't keep her isolated out here. She'll never learn that there are decent people in this world. She'll always expect the worst."

Anger flashed in his eyes. "Hannah. Go back inside." He held up a hand, forbidding Rachel to speak again until Hannah had done as she was told. When his daughter was at a distance that she could not hear him, he turned to Rachel. "You were there. You saw how they treated her! They talked as though she couldn't hear."

Rachel remembered all too well the lack of empathy in the mercantile. She was still upset at her friend, Amanda. "It bothered me, too," she admitted. "They just need to get to know her. If you were to bring her to school, I would take extra care with her. You must know that this constant isolation is not good for her."

Her words hung suspended in the air between them.

His eyes narrowed, but he seemed to consider her suggestion for the space of an instant. "Prove it. You tutor her."

Startled, she met his gaze. "Tutor her? But that's not what I meant!"

He waited, watching her closely.

The thought took hold. Could she do it? She had so little teaching experience, and Hannah was not an ordinary student. Did she have what it would take to help her? She swallowed hard, intrigued with the idea.

She met his gaze. Was that hope in his eyes beneath the hardness? Perhaps he was reaching out. In his own way, he was asking for help and she suspected he was a man who seldom asked for anything. He confused her—and he fascinated her.

But how could she agree to his offer? If the school board got wind of any arrangement, she'd lose her job for sure. They wouldn't see it as her teaching Hannah. They'd see it as an unmarried woman visiting an unmarried man—without an escort. It could jeopardize her employment at the school.

"I…I'm sorry, but I haven't the time," she said, her excuse sounding weak, even to her ears. "As I said, bring her to school. I'll see she's looked after and not hurt by the others."

He shook his head. "Why should I trust you any more than the others?"

"I guess you have no reason to. It's just tha—"

"Just forget I asked. I'll teach Hannah what she needs to know."

"You must understand, Mr. Taylor—"

He shut her out. "The reverend is waiting. You better leave now."

She felt her chance slipping away. "Mr. Taylor. I really do want what's best for Hannah."

"You've made your point, Miss Houston. Apparently, we're at a standoff. I won't change my mind." He walked past her and then headed to the carriage where Reverend Crouse waited.

Well that didn't go as planned, she thought. Disheartened, she followed him and let him help her up onto the burgundy-cushioned seat. Her fingers tingled where he steadied her with his callused hand. Unsettled, she busied herself adjusting her skirt about her knees even as she felt him continuing to study her. Then her curiosity got the better of her. "The other day at the mercantile…"

He nodded curtly, listening though she sensed he was impatient for her to leave.

"What did you mean when you said I should believe everything I hear?"

"Why don't you ask that friend of yours? She seemed to know it all."

"I prefer to know the truth."

He just stared at her.

She refused to be baited—handsome or not—and plunged on. "Amanda said you killed your wife."

Beside her, Reverend Crouse inhaled sharply and grabbed the reins. "Rachel! That's quite enough. I believe we have just overstayed our welcome."

Stubbornly she notched up her chin. "If one can call this a welcome at all." She wasn't about to back down. Mr. Taylor had dared her. "She said you escaped from prison."

The light keeper leveled his gaze at her and she felt a twinge of remorse.

"Isn't there something in the Bible about gossip, Reverend?" he asked. Suddenly, with the flat of his hand, he struck Jericho's rump. The horse bolted.

"Oh!" Rachel grabbed her hat with one hand and the edge of her seat with the other, holding on tight as the carriage careened away from the yard.

Reverend Crouse struggled with the reins for control and finally maneuvered Jericho into a jerky canter down the dirt road. They neared the rise and Rachel glanced back, fervently hoping Mr. Taylor's palm stung like the bite of a ruler against bare skin. To her keen disappointment, he snapped an obviously fine-feeling hand to his brow in a mocking salute.

Chapter Four

Stuart descended the circular stairway after checking the lamp. It should be good until dawn when he would extinguish it. He sat at the parlor table. Through the window in front of him, he could see the beam from the light above sweep across the peninsula and then out across the moon-dappled water. The strong smell of ocean and sage permeated the room. Opening his logbook, he wrote:

September 16, 1873
11:45 p.m. Mild wind from the northwest. Clear night.
Visitors—Reverend Crouse. Rachel Houston.

He straightened in his chair, stretching his back as he considered how much he should write about the visit. *Invitation to church?* No. It was no one's business but his own. And the less he mentioned about Hannah, the better.

He swiped his hand across his face. Lord, he was

tired. Hannah had been moody and difficult about everything until Miss Houston had come and given her that doll. Then she had disappeared into her room to play.

Miss Houston. Now there was an interesting woman. Outspoken to be sure, but then, words meant only so much. Actions told a lot more about the character of a person—man or woman. And she had character to spare. She sure didn't back down. First, at the mercantile when she stood up to Terrance and then today, when he was her problem.

His head started to nod and he jerked. What the heck were people saying about him in town? He wanted to keep a quiet existence here, not have people talking about him. He'd had little experience with such things before moving here, finding it easier to hide out in more populated areas. He was getting a fast introduction to small-town nosiness.

His head nodded. The pen fell from his hand. He lowered his head to the desk and closed his eyes. *Just for a minute….*

Stuart pushed open the heavy oak door to the captain's cabin. A soft light from the whale-oil lantern illuminated the nooks and crannies of the small room, spilling a rich golden hue on the wooden beams overhead. Linnea sat at the end of his bunk and leaned over a makeshift bed, singing in a low chant to her daughter.

"Linnea?" he whispered.

She placed her finger against her lips. "Hush. She's

nearly asleep." She smiled at him briefly, then continued her song. The dark bruising along her chin had healed to a yellow color but the shadows beneath her eyes confirmed his worry that this voyage had not healed her spirit. She wasn't sleeping. But she hadn't complained. She never complained anymore.

A thrill rippled through him at the scene in the small cabin. Three-year-old Hannah lay curled on her side, a white cotton nightgown covering her chubby limbs and a matching sleeping bonnet taming her fine blond wisps of hair. Wet spiked lashes quieted against pale cheeks. So there had been another battle of wills about bedtime. He smiled to himself.

Assured that all was well, he returned to the deck. The last pink rays of sunlight sparkled across the water as he barked out orders to adjust the sails and take full account of the northern winds. On the ship's port side the purple outline of California's southern coast rose above the sea, the hazy mountains familiar sentinels on his journey to San Pedro.

Linnea came to his side, pulling her shawl tighter around her for warmth. The breeze whipped golden tendrils of her hair across her neck and cheeks.

"She's asleep now."

He nodded his acknowledgment.

"Do you think John's family will come after us?"

"Yes," he said quietly.

"My father, too?"

"Especially your father. We left a mess in San Francisco. They will want to set it right."

"By condemning you."

He kept silent a moment, looking at but not seeing the water. "I killed him. John's family will want revenge, or payment in some way. So will the law."

"Oh, Matthew. I'm sorry to have dragged you into this. I just didn't know where to turn."

Stuart pulled her close, his arm around her shoulder. "You did the right thing. Never doubt that." He felt the rise and fall of her shoulders as she took a deep breath.

"Yet there is one more favor I must ask of you."

He waited.

"Promise me you'll take care of Hannah if anything happens to me."

"Lin—"

"No. I mean it. I've thought about this a lot. We don't know what will happen. John's family and my father have the law on their side. They have all the resources. Our running away looks like we planned John's death. They'll think we are lovers. John accused me of that so many times—I think to rationalize his own lack of fidelity."

"He didn't deserve you."

Her chin trembled. "I should have waited for you, Matthew. I was weak and lonely at that school. I ruined everything."

He squeezed her arm. "We're together now. And don't worry about Hannah. I'll stand by both of you." He looked over the water, subconsciously noting the increase in whitecaps while he tried to figure out what they should do after delivering the cargo to San Pedro. The voyage had given him time, but a reckoning was swiftly catching up.

First Shipmate Saunders approached with a worried

look on his face. "Captain, I don't like the looks o' that horizon." He raised his thick wiry brows toward the stern of the vessel indicating billowing clouds in the distance. A line of dark gray in their belly foretold of the rain within.

"I see it," Stuart said grimly. "If it heads this way we won't be able to use the stars tonight to guide us. We may have a swift race to port. Make sure the crew is prepared."

"Aye, sir." Saunders hesitated.

"What is it?"

"Touhy stands watch tonight."

Stuart considered the level of experience of the younger man. "Have him wake me if the wind changes course."

"Aye, sir. Can't help thinkin' one of Mr. Lansing's steamers would have been a better choice for this trip."

"Only our ten-year friendship makes it possible for you to say that, Saunders," Stuart said with a sternness he knew his first shipmate would see right through. "The *Maiden* is old, but fit. Rather like you," he teased lightly. "And she's mine, not Dorian's. That makes all the difference on this particular voyage."

With a salute—and a wink—Saunders left.

That night Stuart awoke from his makeshift pallet on the floor. He sensed a change, a creaking of the ship as though forced on a new course. In the bed, Linnea slept fitfully, her soft breath puffing against the sheets. He rose and dressed quickly.

Above deck the light breeze of the evening before had transformed into a bitter gale. Stuart searched the black skies for any sign of lightness, anything to mark his bearings. The darkness was so thick he could only guess at the horizon, where sky dissolved into ocean without a trace. It would be time for the third watch— Touhy should be in charge. Why hadn't the man woken him?

He grabbed the rail to steady himself and walked aft. When he neared the binnacle that housed the compass, a flash of lightning illuminated the sky. In that instant he recognized the familiar peaks of Santa Catalina Island rising not five hundred yards off the port bow. In the few moments the wind had grabbed control of their ship it had blown them far south of their plotted course.

"Bear away before the wind!" he shouted above the gale. Shipmen raced to obey his commands. "One thirty-five on a broad reach! Touhy! Get Saunders! Then take position in the stern!"

The *Frisco Maiden* surged ahead, her bow lifting high in the inky water, running on the forefront of the storm. Suddenly, sheets of rain plastered his shirt to his skin, chilling him to the bone. The storm had overtaken them. He glanced astern and his heart turned to ice at the sight of the monstrous waves forming. The vessel began to pitch and yaw, a toothpick in the violent, churning waters. Mast and foremast alike, weighed down with wet sails, creaked and groaned, protesting the strain as though alive.

No storm that Stuart had ever seen possessed such fury. Linnea! Hannah! He had to make them safe. Should the ship not clear the island— He refused to think of what might happen. He clung to the thick wooden railing along the gangway and made his way toward his cabin. Sailors ran before him, jumping to the bark of his commands.

Another bright, jagged flash of lightning coursed through the rain. The craggy islands stood behind them now. A wave crashed over the stern adding to the deck's slickness as though layering it with whale oil. At the boom he joined his men pulling on the rigging to lower the foresail. If only he could get a few sails down before the next gigantic wave overtook them.

A deafening crack pounded his ears.

He looked up and found the main topmast hanging at right angle to the lower main mast. The eerie blue-white glow of Saint Elmo's fire raced the length of the yardarms and danced along the top of the two standing masts. The light wavered and then disappeared against the backdrop of black.

Suddenly a swell, which had to have measured as large as the island itself, lifted the *Frisco Maiden* high into the air, high enough that Stuart could see the end of the storm front approaching from the north. For one brief, suspended moment he thought he saw a beacon of light shining from the mainland. It had to be his imagination. No lighthouse beam was that powerful. Then the swell curled over, crashing in upon itself and swallowed the ship.

Stuart clung to the railing with all his might. Frigid seawater swirled over him, alternately pushing and then pulling him. The salt stung his eyes, blinding him.

When he could drag a deep breath of air into his

lungs, he straightened and took note of his surroundings as best he could in the dark. The ship listed to its side and he knew without being told that she was taking on water. How could he order his men into the small lifeboats in such a wild sea? But if they remained on the schooner, there would be no hope for them at all.

"Lower the lifeboats!"

The words rasped out of his throat, raw from the constant abuse of the storm and brine. Single-minded now, he made his way grasping at rigging and railing until he entered his cabin.

"Linnea!"

A mewling sound came from the bunk. He groped his way there, touching upon Linnea's ankle. She sat huddled on the far side of the bed.

"Are you all right? Is Hannah?"

"She's here, Stuart. I have her." Seawater soaked the bed and the two shivered in their wet nightgowns.

"The *Maiden*'s taking on water," he said, hugging them to him. "I must get you to the lifeboat."

Lightning flashed outside, illuminating a small portion of the cabin through its only porthole. He could see the terror in both their eyes, see the white-knuckled death grip with which Linnea held to her bedpost anchor.

There was no time to waste. Stuart peeled her hand loose and immediately she grasped his arm, surprising him with her strength. He snatched Hannah to him and together they made their way above deck.

One boat full of crewmen already tested the turbulent ocean. Panic mixed with relief marked the faces of the fourteen men. They veered away from the *Frisco Maiden,* rowing with a vengeance to get clear of the larger ship. Waves washed over them, tangling kelp and sea grass around their bodies, fashioning them into grotesque monsters rising from the deep.

The ocean churned and heaved, playing with the *Frisco Maiden* and mocking her tenacious grasp on life. Stuart helped the remaining crewmen and Saunders make ready the second lifeboat. When they had all settled into the boat along with Linnea and Hannah, he hesitated.

"Come on, Cap'n!" Saunders yelled. "She'll go under any minute. Save yourself. No need for heroics!"

"Are all the men accounted for?"

"Yes, sir."

Stuart glanced about the deck one last time, then climbed over the railing and down the rope ladder to the lifeboat. Sheet lightning flared in the sky, this time farther to the south.

"We're caught up!" Saunders yelled from the bow.

Stuart looked down into Linnea's frightened eyes.

"I cannot do this by meself!" Saunders's gravelly voice competed with the crashing of waves. "Give a hand!"

Stuart squeezed Linnea's hand. "Hold tight to the side. I must help Saunders or we'll be dragged under with the ship."

His words seemed to penetrate her fear, for he felt a loosening of her grip. Quickly he moved her hand to the side of the lifeboat. He looked briefly at Hannah, and then crawled toward Saunders in the bow.

Kelp, seaweed and a plank of wood had tangled about the *Maiden*'s ladder. There was no hope in untangling the floating mass. He would have to cut them loose.

"Hold my legs!" he shouted at Saunders and grabbed the large knife he carried in his belt. He inched forward until more than half his body hung over the bow and then sawed at the thick hemp rope. In short time the rope gave way and they were free. Winded, he inched back into the boat and sprawled on the seat to catch his breath.

A swell rose fifteen feet above the lifeboat like a vengeful Poseidon rising from the deep. Stuart watched in horror as the swell broke at its apex and crashed down on them. The turbulence battered him, pushing saltwater into his eyes and filling his mouth. He gripped anything he could hold on to, climbing over his crew, trying to reach Linnea. When the water calmed enough to see again, surprisingly the boat still floated right side up.

But Linnea and Hannah were gone.

"Cap'n, don't do it!"

He heard Saunders yell, felt hands reach for him, but there was no time to wait.

He dived in.

Groping frantically through the water, he searched for Linnea and Hannah. The waves shoved him about like a plaything. Kelp tangled around his legs, pulling at him, binding him.

Something drifted across his face—seaweed? More kelp? He struggled closer. In vain he tried to see through

the murky waters. Then something bumped against
him. He reached—and his hands closed on cloth.
Hannah! He pulled her close, and suddenly Linnea was
there, too, grasping his forearm with both hands.

Renewed strength flowed through him. He kicked
hard for the surface, struggling with the weight of the
two. His lungs burned with the need for air.

Lightning flashed above him. The surface was so
close, so close. His legs muscles tightened into knots. He
forced himself to keep kicking, straining. He had to
breathe, had to reach the surface. Then Linnea's hold
loosened and he felt her hands slide down his arm. He
tried to grasp her, but her fingers slipped through his. He
reached again—and his hand closed on nothing but water.

Stuart woke with a start, disoriented, his body coated
in sweat. He stared at the logbook on the desk, seeing
it without knowing where he was, what it meant. He
struggled to get his bearings. His heart pounded, yet
quiet surrounded him. Through the window flashed a
beam from the lamp, the circular pattern somehow
familiar and settling. He buried his face in his hands.

The dream had come again.

He drew in a deep breath to steady his heartbeat, then
closed the logbook and rose from his seat. It had been
months since he'd dreamed of it—almost a year. He
longed for the night it would leave him for good, and
yet he feared it, too. The dream was his punishment for
not protecting the woman he loved. Yet, in the dream
he could still feel her touch and hear her voice.

He climbed the stairs to Hannah's room and leaned

against the door frame, studying her. At least he'd never forget Linnea's face. Hannah was her mirror image. She slept on, her new doll crushed beside her.

That doll.

The events of yesterday rushed back into his thoughts. He'd been rude to Reverend Crouse and Miss Houston. But he wouldn't apologize for his blunt words nor would he place his trust in a God who allowed an innocent woman like Linnea to drown. Still, he did feel a twinge of remorse. Hannah surely liked that doll.

Back in his bedroom he poured cool water into his bowl, then splashed it on his face. His hand strayed to the raised quarter-inch-wide slash that started just over his right brow and extended into his hairline. The angry red mark never let him forget it was his fault Linnea had died…his fault Hannah no longer talked or laughed.

Odd, when he thought over the previous day, how the vision of Miss Houston formed in his mind sharper than that of Linnea. She was nothing like Linnea, who had been soft and biddable. Miss Houston seemed all strong angles and had a decidedly sharper tongue. She certainly hadn't been cowed by him—not with that parting question about prison time. Still, her urging to start Hannah in school nagged at him. Linnea would have insisted on private tutors long before now.

He'd said he could teach Hannah himself, but he wasn't sure he could. He knew all about shipping, about commanding a schooner or steamer and bartering the best price for goods. That wouldn't do Hannah any good. Was he selfish in wanting her to stay here with him? She needed to learn of life beyond the peninsula—

but at what cost? All he wanted to do was protect her. His gut twisted. He'd done a damn poor job of that so far.

He could throttle Miss Houston for stirring up the ashes, for bringing back the nightmare. And that doll! He knew better than to accept it. Why had he? Now his conscience would prick him every time Hannah played with it—and he would think of *her*.

Chapter Five

San Francisco

Dorian Lansing hurriedly mounted the steps of his mansion on Nob Hill, his walking cane tapping a rapid-fire cadence across the smooth-tiled entrance.

"Rose! Rose! Confound it, Whitlow, take these." He shoved his cloak and top hat at the butler. "Where is that woman!"

"In the dayroom, sir…. Dr. Garrett is with her."

Dorian dropped his cane in the wrought-iron rack by the door and headed down the hall. His wife lounged with her feet on the couch, still dressed in her pearl-colored morning robe. At least she'd allowed Mattie to draw her hair back with a pink ribbon today in deference to the doctor's visit.

Dr. Garrett stood as Dorian entered the room. The heavy drapes remained closed against the light of day. No air stirred.

"You're home early, dear," Rose said in her birdlike voice. He detected a slight trembling of her hands.

"May I have a word with you, Mr. Lansing?" Dr. Garrett subtly nodded his head toward the hall.

"Certainly. I'll be right back, Rose." He followed the doctor to the hallway.

"How is she today, Doctor?"

"Thinner, paler."

He'd thought so, too, but to hear his fears out loud made them so much more real. "What else can we do? We've tried everything."

"This is not so much an illness of the body as it is an illness of the spirit. You must find something that captures her interest. She needs a reason to continue living."

Dorian thanked the man and dismissed him. A reason for living! Of all the nerve. Apparently taking care of her husband and household wasn't enough of a reason! Disgruntled, he strode into the dayroom, crossed the parquet floor to a southern window and drew back the heavy burgundy drapes.

"Please...leave that closed." Rose struggled to sit taller. "What did the doctor say?"

He left the drapes as they were and began plumping the pillows at her back, avoiding her gaze. "Nothing new. You're doing just fine."

She caught his hand and motioned for him to sit. She didn't ask why he was early today. He knew better than to hope for a show of interest from her. It had been years since he'd seen any spark in her eyes. He dragged a straight-back chair near and sat. This was his last hope.

"I have information regarding Linnea."

The muscles in her neck worked convulsively as she swallowed. After Rose's panic attack a year ago, the doctor had said not to bring up the accident or the past, but to wait for her to mention it first. So far, she never had.

By God, he'd had enough. Enough! He was not the type to sit around and take this situation a moment longer. He was through with waiting. "I heard from Miss Forester's School for Young Ladies. The headmistress there confirmed my suspicions. She knew John Newcomb well."

"That means…"

The plaintive plea in her voice knifed through him, and he turned from her, unable to bear seeing her hurt more. "Yes. John married our daughter to get his hands on her inheritance. He used her just as we suspected." Dorian kept quiet about the mistress. Such information was not for a genteel lady's ears.

"Oh, Dory."

The reproachful tone set him off. "She should have known better!" His voice quaked with anger. "How could she have been so gullible as to let a man like that into her life? She was a Lansing, for God's sake. Why didn't she listen to me?"

Rose dropped her gaze and turned from him.

"I know what you're going to say, Rose. But I was angry. And frustrated."

"And you turned her away when she finally did come to us for help," she said dully.

"She had to learn to live with her choices. Make the best of it." He took his wife's frail hand. "Well, no matter now. She is gone and we cannot change the past.

But for certain, the child, our granddaughter, belongs with us."

"Matthew is still involved, isn't he? That's why he hasn't come back."

Dorian stiffened at hearing that name and chose to ignore her question. He'd kept the part about the murder from his wife. She'd suffered enough. But he knew Matthew was involved, whether the rumors of adultery were true or not, it was his gun found on the docks. He'd probably pulled the trigger. "I've decided to hire another detective. Randolph has given me a name."

A flash of fear crossed Rose's face.

"I know we had little luck with the first one. I'm willing to try again. More important, are you?"

Her shaking grew worse, but when she looked up at him, her gaze was resolute. "Yes. Do try. It's time we were a family again." She drew a breath and added, "Even…even Matthew."

Dorian felt a sickening lurch in his gut and hardened his heart at her words. "I don't want to hear that man's name spoken in this house or have you forgotten that?"

Rose visibly shrank in front of him. "No. I've not forgotten. But Linnea ran to Matthew. And he took her in. He loved her—as a brother would and…and possibly more."

"Confound it!" He beat his fist on the arm of the couch. "The girl belongs with us. He isn't her father." The hate boiled up inside, choking him.

"But the things you said—"

"He as good as killed Linnea. Matthew murdered our daughter."

Rose shrank away from him and lay back against her cushions. "Oh, Dory. Do what you must. I want nothing more than to find Hannah. She belongs here. This is her birthright. Bring her home any way you can."

Dorian took her hands in his. "If there is a way on earth to find her, I will. And when I do, Matthew will have no choice but to hand her over to me." The vengeance in his voice surprised even him. Slowly he loosened his grip. "I'll take care of everything."

Chapter Six

The strong September sun had finally burned away the fog that hovered each morning over the peninsula. Rachel lifted her face to its warmth for a moment and then glanced behind her. Two wagons and five carriages loaded with churchgoers and food snaked their way to the point like an army of determined ants.

She sat in the bed of the wagon, one arm resting on a picnic hamper, the other holding tight to the wooden side. She had spent all of yesterday baking. Her mouth watered at the thought of the pies nestled between the slow-baked beans and cold chicken.

"So, how much longer do I have to put up with this prison sentence?" Caleb asked from his sprawled position beside her. "Haven't I been okay for the past couple weeks?"

"The sheriff said at least two months," Rachel answered. "You're lucky he didn't put you in jail for starting that fire."

Caleb scowled. "No one cares about those hide houses anyway. One less wouldn't hurt anything."

"But they aren't your property!" she said, exasperated with his attitude. "Besides, you could have torched the entire town. It was irresponsible."

He clamped his hands over his ears to shut out her voice and glared at her. After a few minutes he looked up at Reverend Crouse. "Is the light keeper coming to our picnic, Reverend?"

Rachel tensed. It had been three weeks since her visit with Mr. Taylor and three weeks spent pondering the man. Impulsively, she'd even ordered a book on sign language from back east, just in case it could help the young girl.

"He's welcome, as is anyone," Reverend Crouse answered her brother. "After all, this is a *community* picnic."

"It's not a good idea," Caleb said.

Reverend Crouse glanced over his shoulder. "Why do you say that?"

"'Cause he shot at those fisherman a while back. He's not right in the head. Living out here has made him crazy. Enrique said—" Caleb stopped at the amused look in Reverend Crouse's eyes.

"Don't believe everything you hear. Rumors have a way of growing and changing over time."

"I still say you shoulda had the picnic somewhere else."

They crested the last brush-covered rise and saw the lighthouse. When they neared, Mr. Taylor stepped through the open front door, his jaw set tight. Resentment radiated from him, thick and strong.

"Look at him." Heaviness lodged in the pit of Rachel's stomach. "He doesn't want us here."

"Whether he does or not is of no concern. This is government property. The town has had a picnic here for the past seven years." He stopped Jericho at the gate. "In any case, I'll ask if he and his daughter would like to join us."

Rachel couldn't hear what was said between Reverend Crouse and Mr. Taylor but watched while Hannah inched up to her father and tucked her hand in his. She looked once in Rachel's direction. A moment later she slipped back into the darkness of the house. Mr. Taylor soon followed his daughter and firmly shut the door.

The reverend climbed back into the wagon. "We're welcome to enjoy the view but he prefers not to join us." He clucked at Jericho, urging the horse on, and then waved at the others to follow.

"What of Hannah? She might like the games later," Rachel asked.

"He'll keep the girl with him."

Rachel didn't understand the ambivalence she felt. She'd worn her favorite navy-blue skirt and white blouse, trying to appear tailored like the perfect teacher in order to impress them. And she'd packed enough food in the hope that Hannah and even Mr. Taylor would join them. But now, learning they wouldn't, a wave of relief washed over her. Perhaps she could relax now and simply enjoy the day.

A hundred feet farther, Reverend Crouse pulled the wagon to a stop on a stretch of level ground. Rachel spread out their large quilt with the faded star design between two small sagebrushes. The wind swirled and caught the edges of the makeshift tablecloth whipping it about. "Caleb! Help me, please!"

Amanda Furst caught a corner as Caleb caught the other.

"Didn't want you sailing off," Amanda said.

Rachel glanced up from anchoring her corner with a rock. Amanda, as always, looked prim and proper in her brown satin dress. "Why, thank you."

Amanda nodded toward the lighthouse. "He won't join us?"

"Mr. Taylor was invited, along with his daughter," Rachel answered. "He said no."

"Well, at least he has some common sense." Amanda stood and twirled her parasol over one shoulder. "He would make us all uncomfortable. He treated me abominably in the mercantile."

"He was just looking out for his daughter. And we *were* gossiping."

Amanda raised her chin. "I don't gossip. I was telling the truth."

Why Rachel should feel the least bit protective of Mr. Taylor, she couldn't fathom, but she thought a change in topic was warranted to keep the peace. "I see your brother is here," she said, nodding toward where a few men were setting up tables.

Amanda wrinkled her nose. "Trying to get on Mother's good side. He's up to something."

"I hope he stays clear of my brother." Sam was well-known as the town terror. A few years older than Caleb, he had harassed her brother more than once when she and Caleb had first arrived at La Playa.

Amanda nodded. "Me, too. I suppose Mr. Morley will be sitting with you?"

Rachel stopped pulling things from the basket and looked up. "I'm not sure. He has relatives visiting from San Diego. I imagine they're talking business."

"Oh." Amanda blushed. "Well...that's nice. I, ah, better get back to help Mother." She spun around and returned to where her family was setting out food.

Rachel sat back on her heels. Amanda was interested in Terrance! Before the thought registered any further, a flash of white from the lighthouse drew her eye.

Hannah stood on the catwalk, her chin on the railing, watching the people below. Rachel started to wave a greeting, but then lowered her hand when Mr. Taylor appeared behind the girl and placed his hands on her shoulders. Without turning, Hannah reached up and grasped one of his hands. Such a small gesture, full of trust and innocence. And with it Rachel's heart softened considerably toward the light keeper.

As if he felt her watching, Mr. Taylor's gaze caught hers...and held. Something tenuous reached out to her. Almost without realizing it, she rose to her feet, her gaze still locked on his. The wind picked up the ribbons on her bonnet and tickled her cheek, but she barely noticed. His eyes held hers as though he tried to read her thoughts, see into her soul. Before she could muddle through the strange sensation, he pulled Hannah back from the walkway and disappeared from sight.

Rachel let out the breath she had been holding and turned back to setting out the tin plates and napkins. Her cheeks flamed with heat as she tried to concentrate on the dishes, but could only see his face before her. Even her breasts tingled with awareness of him.

Caleb lugged over another basket and dumped it awkwardly in the middle of the quilt.

"My pies!" She reached out and righted the hamper, glad to have a diversion from her thoughts of the light keeper. She held up a squashed cherry pie in her hand. "To think it made the trip all the way here, and then to end up as flat as a sand dollar."

"Where's the problem, Rach? I'll eat it, anyway."

She lowered the pie, placing a cloth napkin beneath to protect the faded quilt. "No matter, I guess," she said grudgingly. "It will still taste the same. Besides, we have the apple pie, and there will be ice cream later. Just try to be more careful." Caleb was getting clumsier every week. Lately he reminded her more of a disjointed rag doll, all elbows and knees, than a flesh-and-blood boy.

Across the quilt from her, Reverend Crouse rose awkwardly, pressing on his knee with one hand. Skirts and coats rustled as those assembled stood for the blessing. Once he was finished, everyone gathered around the tables piled with food to fill their plates.

At Rachel's makeshift table, the chicken pieces disappeared quickly. Rolls with butter and then molasses cookies followed. Caleb sectioned off a large piece of mashed cherry pie and ate it with boyish gusto. Rachel had just put her tin plate back in the basket when Terrance strolled up.

"Hello, Rachel."

He towered over her, pulling on one end of his

drooping mustache. He nodded to the reverend, Emma and Caleb in turn, and then his gaze locked on her to the exclusion of the others. What was it that Amanda found appealing about him?

"Ready for that walk?"

She glanced over at the other picnickers. They were finishing their meals. "What about starting the children's games?"

With a wave of her hand, Emma Crouse intervened. "Oh, go on now, you two. I still remember a game or two. And Caleb can help me."

Terrance pulled Rachel to her feet. "It's settled, then." He offered his arm.

He led her along the perimeter of the peninsula. From this high position, she could see a steamer leaving the harbor. Two ships headed toward San Diego, their white sails taut against the wind as they navigated the deepest part of the channel.

A burst of laughter and giggles came from behind her. Rachel looked back toward the picnickers. Emma and Elizabeth organized the boys and girls for the three-legged races, handing out long strips of cloth to bind legs together.

"I should get back and help," Rachel said, starting to release Terrance's arm. She glanced again at the children and Elizabeth. Where was Caleb?

Terrance patted her hand back into place. "Those children get you all week. They can do without you for a few more minutes."

Reluctantly, she allowed herself to be led toward the ocean side of the point. Here the ground dropped steeply down hundreds of feet. Sagebrush and scruffy vegetation covered the higher ground, but in two areas, the wind had bitten into the high land, carving naked sandstone cliffs. Far below, the waves beat against their base. "Is that a beach down there?"

"A small one. You can't see much from here."

She searched for something to say. "How are your cousins from San Diego enjoying their stay?" she asked.

"They're hoping to see a whale or two while here. So far there haven't been any."

"I'm not sure it's the season for them," she said, trying to remember what a Portuguese whaler had recently told her in town.

Terrance stopped walking and faced her. "Rachel, ah, I don't quite know how to say this."

She glanced up at him. "Just say what's on your mind. I don't bite."

He offered a weak smile. "You know that I sit on the school board."

"Yes."

"Well, the others have asked me to inquire into your qualifications."

Suddenly concerned, she met his gaze. "But they've already done that—when they interviewed me. They don't think I'm doing a good job?"

"No, it's not that."

He ran a hand through his straight hair, and she noticed a pink tinge to his usually pale face.

"Will you be taking the teacher examination this year?"

"I plan to—after studying more. Probably in early spring."

"Oh…well, then. That should appease them," he said, but he wasn't looking her in the eye.

She tried to remain calm, but her insides were in turmoil. She needed this work. "Would they hire someone else? Someone with a certificate in place of me?"

He hesitated in answering at first. "I'll be honest."

"I would prefer it," she said, her alarm growing.

"A few of the board are talking about it."

"Terrance, they hired me knowing I didn't have that piece of paper. And I promised to work toward it. Surely they can give me a little more time. At my interview they said they understood my experience in Wisconsin was as valuable as that certificate."

He stepped close, and this time he did meet her eyes. "I'll talk to them. I, for one, want to keep you happy. If that means teaching for a year or two, so be it."

"Thank you." Her smile trembled a little. "You know my schooling has been haphazard. There are gaps in it because my father moved us around so much. But I'll study and be ready for the test in the spring. You can count on me."

"I know. And I'm sorry to worry you."

"I need this job, Terrance. Caleb and I—we both do."

He nodded his acknowledgment just as a chorus of lively shouts rose behind them. "Maybe we should join in the games now."

She smiled slightly. After all, this was a picnic and she intended to have a good time. "Let's join in the race. I promise I won't trip you."

He raised a brow. "Think we'll make a good team?"

"Of course," she said quickly, then realized as he continued to watch her that he wasn't talking about the race at all. She swallowed hard. Did her job depend on her relationship with Terrance?

They neared the lighthouse, and she glanced once more at the empty catwalk. She had to talk with Mr. Taylor before she left today. Just once more—to encourage him to send Hannah to school. It was best for the girl, and it wouldn't hurt her own job security to have another steady student.

Suddenly a series of loud pops exploded through the air. Someone cried out, and people began running to the cliff's edge. A woman screamed.

Rachel scanned the cluster of people for Caleb. She found him crouched at the edge beside Sam Furst. Her heart pounded in her chest as she picked up her skirt and raced toward them. What had happened?

Murmurs rose from the group. "It's little Benjamin! Somebody get a rope."

Several men rushed past her, heading for their wagons.

The crowd moved back to allow Reverend Crouse in. Rachel peered over the edge, and then covered her mouth to stifle her cry.

Thirty feet below, seven-year-old Benjamin Alter clung to a small outcropping of sandstone and brush, his stomach flush against the side of the cliff. Blood trickled from a large scrape across his forehead. Hundreds of feet below him, the ground fell away to the foaming ocean and jagged rocks. The boy looked up at them with terrified eyes.

"Hang on, now," Reverend Crouse said. "We're getting a rope."

Rachel's heart pounded in her chest. Ben could lose his grip on the ledge at any minute. She met the reverend's worried gaze. "Surely Mr. Taylor has rope."

Before the words were out of her mouth, the light keeper appeared at her side, a thick coil of rope slung over his shoulder, his manner so commanding that everyone backed away to give him room.

"Help! I can't hold on!" Benjamin yelled.

Caleb grabbed the rope from Mr. Taylor's hands and began tying it around his waist.

Rachel gasped. "Caleb! No!"

"It's my fault he fell," her brother mumbled. "It's my place to get him."

Stuart watched as the boy fumbled with the thick rope at his waist. It was a poor attempt at a knot and one he knew from experience would prove unsafe. Stuart could handle the rope and the climb. He'd climbed among the rigging of schooners being tossed and pitched about by the sea for years. He snapped the rope from the boy's hand. "Step back."

Tying an efficient knot at his own waist, he looked directly at Miss Houston. "Keep Hannah from the edge."

At her wide-eyed nod, he handed the other end of the rope to Terrance Morley, wondering for a moment if he could trust him. But then another man, and then another gripped the rope, their faces set with determination.

Stuart lay down on his abdomen and lowered himself over the cliff's edge. His last look at the handful of onlookers centered on one person—Rachel. Her eyes had clouded with worry. Likely for the boy; surely not for him.

"Don't look up," he yelled down to the boy below. "The loose sand will get into your eyes. And don't move. Let me take hold of you."

Pebbles and loose dirt shot out from beneath his boots as he scrambled down the steep wall of sandstone. All at once his feet met air rather than the cliff and he swung around, smashing his shoulder against the gritty wall. Finally he slid even with the boy.

"Just a minute more and I'll have you. Don't let go yet."

The boy gasped as he struggled to hold on while Stuart wrapped the extra length of rope tightly around the boy's waist and tied a lighterman's hitch. To his credit, the boy remained still as instructed rather than panicking and grabbing hold of Stuart too soon.

"What's your name?" Stuart asked gently.

"B-Benjamin."

The boy couldn't be much older than Hannah.

"Onto my shoulders now," Stuart commanded. "Slide over to my back."

"I can't."

His plaintive voice tugged at Stuart's heart. "Sure you can."

"I'm scared."

"The rope will hold you."

"My hands—they're s-stuck."

Stuart glanced at Benjamin's white-knuckled grip on the ledge and a small tuft of weeds. How had the boy managed to hang on this long?

"Okay. Just do the best you can. I won't let you fall."

Benjamin's eyes filled with unshed tears. Stuart could almost see the boy's mind working, trying to bolster his courage.

"I'll count to three and you grab my neck."

A small nod.

"One…two…three!"

Stuart leaned toward the boy, snaking his arm around Benjamin's waist and hauling him close. He struggled to keep his grip on the rope while the boy locked his legs around Stuart's hips. Frantically, Benjamin grabbed Stuart's shirt then scrambled up and wrapped his arms around Stuart's neck. He could feel the thudding of the boy's heart against his back.

He breathed a sigh of relief. "Good job. You ready now?" He felt Benjamin's nod rub against his back. Looking up, he yelled, "Haul us up!"

The men pulled on the rope, a rhythm building as they heaved against the weight. Stuart braced his feet against the cliff to steady the swinging. Sweat beaded on his forehead. Above, Stuart could see the first man's arm muscles bulging with the effort to draw him up.

Finally he and the boy came flush with the ground at the top of the cliff. Strong hands reached out to grip Benjamin and pull him from Stuart's neck. More men reached down to help Stuart over the edge. He crawled a few feet then sprawled onto his back and gasped for air.

People crowded around congratulating the men who'd held the rope. A few nodded to him by way of thanks, but most seemed a little unsure what to make of him. He rose slowly to his feet.

An elderly couple stopped before him. The old woman dabbed tears from her eyes while she thanked him profusely for saving her grandson.

Stuart nodded once. "Bring him to the house to wash out those scrapes," he said gruffly. Then he began gathering up his rope, ignoring the sting of his rope-burned palms.

"Are you all right?"

Miss Houston's soft Midwestern voice came from behind him, the concern in it catching him off guard. He slung the coil of rope over his shoulder and turned to her. His heart did a quick thud. She surely had fetching green eyes—the kind a man could drown in. And they seemed to hold as much worry as her voice.

"I'm fine."

"Hannah stayed at the lighthouse."

"Good."

She seemed to want to say something more, but Morley and Caleb stepped up. Not anxious to speak with anyone else, Stuart started toward the house. He could feel the eyes of the entire assemblage staring at his back as he walked away.

By the time he'd cleaned himself in the kitchen, someone was rapping on the door. He opened it to Miss Houston and Benjamin, aware his pulse had kicked up a notch again and tried to ignore it. She held out something covered with cloth.

"For you…for helping Benjamin."

"No need." He grabbed a kitchen towel that was

slung over the back of a chair and wiped the water from his neck. "Come in and wash out his scrapes. There's warm water on the stove."

She pursed her lips at his refusal of the gift but still ushered the boy inside. Looking about quickly, she placed the cloth-covered item on the kitchen table. "I wanted to repay you in some way—to thank you. I hope you like apple." She pulled the edge of cloth aside to reveal a pie.

He hesitated, not wanting to take something more from her. First the doll, now this, but it sure looked delicious. With his simple cooking, he and Hannah would never have something so fine. He nodded his acceptance. "Hannah will like it."

She checked the temperature of the water in the pan on the stove, pulled Benjamin's sleeves up to his elbows and slowly submerged his scraped, bloody hands. The boy winced and jerked his hands back at first, but then allowed her to wash them with soap.

She was gentle with the boy, Stuart noticed. Didn't rush him, but let him go at his own pace. He liked that about her. Suddenly he realized she was addressing him.

"Have you given any more thought to bringing Hannah to school? She needs to have a few friends her own age." She wet a nearby washcloth and dabbed at the cut on Benjamin's forehead.

How could she ask again? "Did you see what caused Benjamin to fall, Miss Houston?"

She looked up, surprised. "No. I just heard his scream, and then everybody yelling as they ran toward the cliff. Did you?"

"He was near the edge when two older kids set off the firecrackers right beside him. He jumped at the noise and lost his footing. I don't know if those older boys were being stupid, or whether they were being mean, probably a mixture of both, but I don't want them near Hannah. It's the innocent ones that get hurt. Hannah and I don't want anything to do with those others." He moved closer, breathing in her scent, lowering his voice. "But you can repay me, you know. You tutor Hannah."

She drew a sharp breath, and color rose in her cheeks as she bent to dry Benjamin's cuts with a towel. She was thinking about the proposal all right. He waited—and was perturbed at how much he wanted her to say yes.

She shook her head. "I really can't. It…it wouldn't be proper."

He pulled back. "Hannah's had more hurt in her six years than anyone should have in a lifetime. Propriety be damned."

"Mr. Taylor!" She slid her gaze to Benjamin in warning.

Obviously his cussing hadn't endeared him to her, but it hadn't shocked her, either.

"My coming here wouldn't change anything. She still needs friends, needs school, the socialization. You're not helping her by secluding her out here."

Well, he'd tried. He wouldn't beg. "Thank you for the pie." He started for the circular stairs. "You can see yourself out when you're done."

That night Rachel tossed and turned in bed, pulling the thick covers over her head one moment, then

kicking them off the next. Benjamin's narrow escape
from death played over and over in her mind. Caleb had
said it was his fault Benjamin fell. She could only
assume he'd been the one to set off the firecrackers.
What was he thinking? And where had Sam run off to?
She hadn't seen him again.

Yet, it was the look in Mr. Taylor's eyes just before
he had taken the rope from her brother that haunted her.
She knew instinctively he would never have let Caleb
go over the cliff even though he'd seen him set off the
firecrackers. For all the rumors that followed Mr.
Taylor, there was something in him quite noble.

When he had opened the door to her, a queer
feeling had skittered through her. Water drops splattered his neck and shirt. He'd wet combed his wavy
hair and for the first time she could clearly see the
jagged scar on his forehead. His clean-shaven face
was so different from the bearded, mustached style of
most men she knew, but she found his strong chin and
the straight line of his nose agreeable—actually more
than agreeable.

On the way home, she had spoken to Reverend
Crouse about the tutoring. "Absolutely not!" he'd said.
"The people of this town wouldn't stand for it.
Remember what happened to Martha Carter. The same
could happen to you. Besides, Caleb needs a firm hand
and where would that leave him?"

The previous teacher, Martha Carter, was seen taking
a meal alone with a married man. The school board
found out about it and fired her. It had happened more
than two years ago, but people still spoke of it. Rachel

had to be careful. Decent paying jobs were hard to come by for a woman, and Caleb depended on her.

She tugged her cotton wrapper about her and silently climbed the narrow stairway to her brother's attic bedroom. Caleb lay sprawled in bed in his nightshirt, the covers twisted beneath him. A damp breeze blew off the ocean and through the small open window above his head.

Rachel walked over to the glass, intending to shut the window. Instead she looked out. No one traveled on the blue moonlit ribbon of dirt that headed out of town. Everything was quiet. Beyond the town, the revolving beam from the lighthouse kept up its never-ending course. The light sparkled off the surface of the water and slashed across the cloudy sky above La Playa.

What exactly did light keepers do? Was Mr. Taylor asleep while the light rotated around and around? Or did he keep watch, looking for ships in trouble? And if he was awake all night, then how could he teach Hannah during the day? He had to sleep sometime. Just the thought of him tousled and sleepy made her pulse quicken.

I mustn't think such thoughts, she scolded herself mentally, blaming it on her time in the mining camp. She'd seen things there that most women were not confronted with until married. A man would rise from his cot and shuffle outside his tent to relieve himself in the brush in the early light of dawn. Most were not appealing in their half-awake, grumpy state, and she stayed clear of them. But Joseph had been a surprise. When she'd skirted the edge of camp to draw wash water from the river, he'd come upon her. And he'd been charming.

She shook her head to rid herself of the images. It hurt now, to think of them. She'd made the mistake of believing Joseph. Of believing in him. She'd never make that mistake again.

Her thoughts turned back to the light keeper. She could help his daughter. She was almost sure of it. Inside, the desire to work with the girl started to burn. Each time the beam sliced overhead, Rachel felt a piece of herself rip away. Each flash of light was as though Mr. Taylor asked anew for help, and each time she turned her back, torn between obeying the unwritten rules of society and following her heart.

Again the beam pulsed through the sky. Until now the light had always comforted her, always made her feel safe. But now…now it reminded her of Mr. Taylor, and all she felt was a sense of restlessness. He'd gone after little Benjamin for no other reason than because it was the right thing to do.

She could do no less.

Chapter Seven

Stuart planted his feet firmly on the black iron catwalk that surrounded the lantern, whipped a faded red rag from the waist of his pants and dried the portion of glass he had just washed. He moved the short ladder around to the next large pane and began again. Soapy water sloshed over the glass and dribbled down his arm to his chest, mixing with his sweat. Finally he tired of his shirt sticking to his skin like paste and peeled it off, slinging it over the railing.

Sometimes, with the wind buffeting him, he could close his eyes and almost believe he walked the deck of the *Frisco Maiden.* He could even trick himself into believing he felt the roll of wooden planks under his feet as the schooner cut through the ocean swells, could hear Hannah playing and Linnea gently reprimanding her.

Linnea—how it hurt to think of her. What would she think of the way things had turned out? Her daughter a mute, and hidden away from the world. Why hadn't the sea taken him instead? His chest ached at the thought, but no longer did the hurt rage inside as it once had. Now there was only emptiness.

Taking a breather, he stopped working and looked about the peninsula. White clouds scudded across the sky high over the ocean. A steamer maneuvered through the narrow inlet to San Diego. Far below him on the lighthouse steps, Hannah silently drew stick pictures in the dirt.

Unbidden, the image of Rachel Houston shot through his mind. Miss Houston wasn't as sweet-tempered as Linnea, but there was something about her. Something honest and…sturdy. He chuckled unexpectedly, surprising even himself. What woman would want to be known as "sturdy"? None of the Nob Hill society he'd known.

The sun beat against his shoulders and back as he slowly rounded the base of the window, washing and drying, washing and drying. The mundane action worked like a balm, and his edginess eased. The cool ocean breeze swirled over him. He began washing the last large pane and felt the beginning tingle of a burn across the back of his neck and shoulders.

He picked up his bucket of supplies and shirt, then inched through the small doorway, on his way double-checking the lamp's wick and reflectors. Trimmed, polished—good. They were ready for their work later tonight. On the first landing, he shoved his bucket in the supply closet, then headed down to the kitchen. He rinsed his face and neck over the water bowl, grabbed a nearby towel and started drying when the unfamiliar sound of voices floated into the room from outside.

Straightening, he joined Hannah at the open door and slowly lowered his towel.

Rachel Houston, wearing a pale-blue dress and carrying a familiar straw bonnet, climbed down from her carriage seat. She seemed nervous. She fingered her hat, every once in a while tucking a stray strand of auburn hair back toward the knot of hair at her neck. But her green eyes were resolute as she headed toward him.

Behind her the same boy he'd seen at the cliff's edge jumped from the carriage with a thud. Stuart acknowledged him with a curt nod, which was returned with a scowl, then waited for Miss Houston to speak. He didn't suppose she had come so far for her pie tin.

"Mr. Taylor, I…" She twisted the hat brim between her hands, her gaze glued to his chest while a blush started up her cheeks.

Suddenly realizing he was bare from the waist up, he tossed down the towel and shrugged into his work shirt. He glanced up from buttoning the last button. "I wasn't expecting visitors. What is it you want?"

She blinked and drew a breath, moving her gaze to his. "Mr. Taylor. I have decided to tutor Hannah."

Had a cannonball dropped at his feet, he wouldn't have been more surprised. He stared at her in stunned silence.

She swallowed hard. "That is, if you haven't found anyone else. I would like to try."

He still couldn't accept her words. They were too good to be true, so he searched for a reason to discredit them. "What about your job at the school? How can you manage both?"

"I'll only be able to tutor Hannah on my days off—and probably not every one of those as it is. I do have other obligations."

"I don't see how that would be enough to do her any good."

Her chin notched up. "It is better than nothing at all. And it is all I can offer." She murmured a few words to the boy who began to gather the horse's reins.

For a second Stuart hesitated, wavering. "Wait. I haven't found anyone else." At this point, there was no one else he trusted—including her. He hoped he wasn't making a terrible mistake.

The quiet pressed in as they both stood there and measured each other. He liked the way she held firm to her position, even though she was uncomfortable.

"You may as well know from the start that I am not a qualified instructor. I haven't passed any teaching exam, although I am studying for my certificate. The school in La Playa is small and I was the convenient choice for the job. I will be taking my exam in the spring."

"You'll do," he said, recalling the way Hannah seemed drawn to her and her gentleness with young Benjamin after his fall. "What changed your mind?"

"We owe you a tremendous debt, Mr. Taylor. Benjamin is very special to all of us in La Playa."

He watched her face, finding nothing in her eyes of dishonesty. Could it be she really did want to teach Hannah? "I don't want your gratitude. I said before I am willing to pay you."

She took another deep breath. "I won't deny that the

extra income enticed me, too. However, there is something more if a bargain is to be struck."

He waited.

"Your job will be to teach my brother about your work here. Caleb needs—" she glanced over her shoulder, and then lowered her voice "—a man's perspective."

Another surprise. "Where's the boy's father?"

She pressed her lips together and then answered. "Unavailable."

He studied the boy's profile, knew it was the same boy who'd set off the firecracker. Did he really want a troublemaker around Hannah? The resemblance between Caleb and Miss Houston was obvious, yet there was something more. "You seem familiar."

The boy blanched, but he shook his head hard.

Miss Houston cleared her throat. "I'll also expect fifty cents a session."

He pushed aside his suspicions about Caleb and turned to her. Bartering was not her forte—her face was too easily read. "Sounds a bit high for someone with so little experience."

"It is your call, Mr. Taylor. But I won't do it for nothing. And it is a long way for me to travel each time. I…as I said, I have obligations to meet."

He wondered what those might be but had to admire her for sticking to her words. After a moment he held out his hand. Miss Houston took it. His hand tingled at her touch. Suddenly he was acutely aware of his rough palm against her smooth skin. He shook her hand once, firmly. "Done. We'll give it a few weeks, see how things go."

A smile broke out, transforming her face from pleasant to beautiful. She had one dimple—on her left cheek. He pulled his gaze from it back to her eyes as she spoke. "Fair enough. Look, I didn't mean to interrupt your work. But since I am here, and it is such a long ride, I'd like to stay awhile to get to know your daughter."

"Suit yourself. Hannah. Show Miss Houston around." He gave Hannah a nod by way of encouragement. "Go ahead."

Hannah took her teacher's outstretched hand and walked with her up the narrow flagstones to the house. Caleb followed at a slow shuffle. Only when they disappeared inside did Stuart turn and head for the shed.

Fifteen minutes passed and then a half hour. Stuart worked soap into Blanco's saddle, rubbing the leather in a circular pattern. He wondered what the three of them were up to. They didn't have any books, any paper or supplies. What could they possibly be doing?

He walked to the shed door and looked out. No one. He sat down and rubbed a few more circles of saddle soap into Blanco's saddle. His hand stilled. By Jupiter, Hannah was his responsibility. With a frustrated growl, he jumped up and strode toward the house.

Just as he reached for the handle the door swung open.

He backed up a step and shoved his hands in his pockets. "You are going?"

Miss Houston shook her head as she tied on her hat. "In a minute. Hannah seems to want to show me something."

He followed as they walked toward the cliff to a place where the ocean spread all the way to the horizon. In the never-ending wind Miss Houston's yellow bonnet ribbons danced across her face and her skirt wrapped around her ankles. He took a second look. She had quite trim ankles.

Caleb inched toward the edge.

Stuart yanked him back. "What in blazes are you trying to do? Tempt fate? I'm not climbing down there again, so stay clear."

Caleb jerked from his grasp and gave him a dark look.

"I mean it," he repeated. "Stay clear of the edge."

The boy's chin jutted out and Stuart again noted the family resemblance with Miss Houston. "Don't treat me like a kid."

Stuart snorted. "Actions say it all."

Caleb eyed him coolly. "I'm just here 'cause my sister is making me come. Says she needs a chaperone. So you watch yourself and keep your hands to yourself."

Stuart stared right back at Caleb. The cocky kid. "She should have a chaperone, especially with Vasquez still running loose in these parts."

The boy's chest deflated an inch at the mention of the Mexican bandit, and then his eyes narrowed. "You, ah, don't happen to know him, do ya?"

Stuart let him worry a good half minute and then shook his head. "No, but it doesn't hurt to be cautious. Your sister shouldn't come here alone. Neither of you should."

"Humph," Caleb mumbled. The prospect of being a chaperone obviously didn't thrill him. After a moment he nodded toward the surf. "Any good fishin' spots down there?"

Stuart pointed farther north. "Off that large flat rock."

"Is there a way down?"

"A trail." After a brief pause he added, "If you live long enough I'll show it to you."

Caleb shrugged his shoulders, the sullen look back on his face.

Suddenly Hannah tugged on Miss Houston's hand and pointed out to sea.

"What is it?" Rachel asked.

Stuart put a hand on Hannah's shoulder and concentrated on the blue-green waters. "I don't see anything." Then he did. Dark shadows moving just beneath the surface. "Porpoises," he breathed.

"Oh! Look! One is jumping!" Miss Houston cried out.

Two more shadows emerged behind the first. Before long another surfaced and jumped.

Her green eyes twinkled. "Caleb, just look at them!"

Her delight pulled at Stuart. He studied her face, entranced. She wore her emotions the way she did her hat. What was it going to be like to have a woman around again? He pushed back the sudden guilt that rose in his chest. A teacher for Hannah was all he wanted. Nothing more. She would be a good influence. Surely Linnea would have agreed with his choice.

Miss Houston knelt by Hannah and pointed out the flat-topped Table Mountain across the border in Mexico. She counted the porpoises when they came up for air, the mist spouting from their blowholes. Strands of dark burnished hair floated free from under her bonnet and mixed with the blond wisps of Hannah's. Both faces were alight with the magic of their find.

In another place, another time, it would have been Linnea beside Hannah. It should have been Linnea now, but for his fumbling rescue attempt. Irritated for allowing himself to remember again, he spun on his heel and headed toward the lighthouse.

It was late. Color had washed from the facades of the town buildings until all looked drab and gray. Rachel urged Jericho down the street toward the parsonage.

Reverend Crouse stood at the back door of the house. He spoke to a short, oriental man with a basket of fish slung over his shoulder. When he saw Rachel and Caleb, he waved the fisherman on, then joined them at the small carriage house. He grabbed Jericho's bridle while Caleb climbed down from the high seat. "Kind of late."

She swallowed hard, feeling Caleb's gaze on her. "Yes. The time got away from me."

Reverend Crouse stared at her for an interminable length of time, during which she clumsily wrapped the reins around the brake lever for storage. "Mind the hour from now on," he said, frowning. "It's getting dark earlier and you shouldn't be out after nightfall."

"I'll be more careful. I'll get supper started."

"Good. Caleb? See to Jericho. Make sure he has plenty of water before you come in."

"Yes, sir." Caleb's shoulders hunched forward, and the mutinous look in his eyes warned Rachel not to get in his way as he rounded the carriage to unhitch the horse. He hadn't wanted to go with her in the first place. She just hoped he'd adjust to her plan and not give it away.

"Rachel—" Reverend Crouse paused. "Mr. Morley is here. He's waiting in the front parlor."

Now what could he want? She didn't need an inquisition from him. Her stomach was in knots as it was.

As she hurried by, the reverend touched her shoulder. "He's a good man," he said gently.

She slanted a look at him.

"Our small congregation thinks highly of the entire Morley family."

She nodded her acknowledgment. "I know you mean well, but I don't care a fig what the rest of the congregation thinks in this matter."

"That'd be your father speaking words right out of your mouth."

"Just because my fath—"

"I know, I know. Your father had his faults just as I have mine. I'm just saying don't be too hasty to dismiss Terrance. I hate to see you all alone in your old age, that's all."

"Caleb is with me."

"That's not the same. Besides, he'll grow up and move on. Then where will you be, Rachel?"

"Right here I hope. After following my father all around the state of California, it seems to me the best thing about Terrance is the fact that he'll probably stay put in one place to run his store."

She ignored the reverend's raised brows and hurried into the house, stopping in the kitchen just long enough to remove her hat and smooth her hair before she walked through to the parlor.

Terrance sat rigidly on the sofa drumming his fingers on the padded arm. She had to admit he looked pleasant enough in his work suit—minus the apron. He jumped to his feet when he saw her. "Hello, Rachel. A package came for you at the store. Thought I'd take the opportunity to deliver it personally." He held out a brown-paper-wrapped box.

She took it and checked the return address. A thrill of excitement started in the pit of her stomach. "Thank you."

"Aren't you going to open it?"

"Not now." She couldn't bear to wait to open the package, but wait she would. It wasn't for Terrance's eyes. "I have to start supper."

"Don't you want to make sure it's what you ordered? I noticed it came all the way from San Francisco."

She was certain what it was. She'd asked Elizabeth to order it more than five weeks ago under strictest confidence. "Later. I'll look at it later."

"Well, I'd better get home then." He paused at the door. "I heard that the light keeper asked you to tutor his daughter."

She swallowed hard. He couldn't know—not in one day, could he? He must have been talking with Reverend Crouse.

He took her hands and held them together, his

fingers as cool as the coins in his store's money box. "I'm surprised the man had the gall to ask you. You are much too busy trying to get the school here off the ground. Did he even consider the cost to your reputation?"

"He's just interested in helping his daughter. I doubt he gave any thought to social etiquette. He's been isolated so long, he probably isn't aware of such things."

Terrance grunted.

"You don't like him much, do you?"

"I don't trust him. Besides, the girl is beyond help."

A burn of indignation started inside her. "She just needs a little guidance."

"Guidance?" His eyes were cynical beneath dark raised brows. "Look, Rachel, you can't go out of your way for someone like her. Mrs. Greensboro or Mrs. Attenberry would do just as well as her teacher. They are both older, widowed."

"And set in their ways. Hannah couldn't relate to them."

In the light of the gas lamp, exasperation showed plainly on his face. "Why are you so interested in this girl? Are you sure your interest doesn't have more to do with Taylor than his daughter?"

Heat raced up her cheeks. "Of course not!" But the words stuck in her throat. The light keeper fascinated her—more than she cared to admit. Even the thought of him had her heart racing faster. But her job was to tutor Hannah, and she wouldn't lose track of that.

Terrance studied her a moment, then glanced once more at the package before stepping outside. "All right.

The school board is meeting tonight and wanted me to find out the date of your teacher's examination."

"In late February. I'll have to travel to Los Angeles."

"I'll let them know. Studying for that will keep you busy. I'll be happy to take you to the stagecoach when the time comes."

She couldn't hold back a small smile. Terrance had unwittingly given her an excuse to be unavailable for the next few months. "I would appreciate that. Thank you."

"Well, I guess this is good night, then."

She closed the door behind him, worried about his dark expression. He couldn't possibly know anything about her visit to the lighthouse today, could he? She couldn't get cold feet—not when she had barely begun.

She flew to her bedroom with the package, shut the door and tore off the brown wrapper. Embossed in black on the front cover were the words: "American Sign Language: From the American Institution for the Deaf and Dumb." She flipped several pages, excitement mounting as she glanced through the book. Hannah could do this!

The back door slammed shut and heavy footsteps sounded in the kitchen. Quickly Rachel shoved the package into a drawer. She squared her shoulders and walked into the kitchen to begin the evening meal.

Chapter Eight

"Hannah! Covering your ears will not help you learn."

They sat in the parlor, Hannah on a stool and Rachel on the tapestry-covered chair near the fire. The coal fire had dwindled to nothing more than an occasional puff of smoke from the hearth. The simple rhymes and ink drawings on the page in front of Hannah had captivated her until Rachel tried to explain the alphabet. Then Hannah slumped in her chair and pressed her hands over her ears.

Rachel sighed. "Perhaps we've done enough for one day. Let's go outside. I should check on Caleb."

On the lighthouse steps, Rachel paused. The wind blew constantly, but over the sound of the wind, she heard a barrage of questions coming from her brother. She found him near the shed with Mr. Taylor. They hunkered over a battered lobster crate, twining wire around and through the slats.

"You ever got your hand caught in one of their

claws?" Caleb asked as he pulled the end of the wire tight. "Did it let go on its own? How'd you get it off?"

Mr. Taylor used pliers to wrap more wire around Caleb's piece and crimp it off. Methodically he tested the strength of the wire and wood around the crate before answering. "I chopped off the claw."

"Oh. Right." Caleb quieted after that.

Rachel stifled a smile and followed Hannah to the lookout bluff. Before turning her attention once more to her teaching, she glanced back at her brother. He had begun his questions again. She cupped her hands to her mouth ready to call to him when Mr. Taylor looked up. At the subtle shake of his head she paused, then lowered her hands.

He certainly was patient with Caleb. She recalled Terrance's irritation whenever her brother had a question. And she'd never seen Terrance without his suit, and with a sheen of sweat on his brow like Mr. Taylor wore now. Reluctantly she turned away and followed Hannah.

Hannah led her to a sandstone hollow, protected from the worst of the wind and warmed by the concentrated afternoon rays of the sun. A footpath in front of them switchbacked down the steep hill until it disappeared far below. Seagulls careened at eye level along the edge of the point floating on the updraft.

Rachel leaned back against the gritty sandstone wall and patted the ground beside her. "I could fall asleep here, it is that comfortable and warm." She fussed with her hair, which the wind had teased from its knot while she mulled over how to broach the subject of signing with Hannah.

"How about drawing a picture for me in the dirt? Anything you like."

Hannah plopped down.

When she ignored her suggestion, Rachel roused herself and picked up a nearby stick. She began drawing a picture. "I used to live far away from here in a place where I could actually smell the earth. Can you even imagine that, Hannah? The dirt was so rich it was nearly black. A person could grow anything they wanted. Here it smells of the sea and sage, and the dirt isn't dirt at all but sand. It is a wonder that anything grows."

She sighed and concentrated on her drawing of a whale. "There, now. I've started it. You finish."

Beside her, Hannah leaned forward, and with her finger fixed the fluke and added a water spout.

"Much better. It did need something more." She leaned back against the wall. "Hannah? How are we going to talk to each other? I want to know what you're thinking—when you understand something, or more often when you don't. Any ideas?"

She watched the parade of thoughts crossing Hannah's face.

"What about talking by using our hands?"

Hannah raised one brow.

Rachel wasn't worried. She had memorized a few choice words, just to get started. "For example, how does this look for a whale?" She held her first three fingers out on her right hand and curved them in front of her left forearm, which she held across her chest. She moved her fingers slowly up and then down. "Can you see the whale going through the waves? You give it a try now. This could be fun. Our own language that no one else knows."

The idea of a secret language worked. Hannah sat up straight and began mimicking Rachel's motions. Rachel did the hand sign for *father,* then *shell,* then *horse.* Hannah copied her movements, repeating them until she got them just right.

After twenty minutes Rachel rose, dusting off the back of her skirt. "That's enough for today. We'll learn more next time."

Stubbornly Hannah crossed her arms over her chest.

It didn't take a teaching certificate to understand this particular look. "Let's go back to the house and I'll give you a few things to work on until my next visit."

Hannah wouldn't budge.

Finally exasperated, Rachel admitted, "I don't know any more words! You should learn the *right* signs—not just made-up ones."

Suspicion entered Hannah's gray eyes.

Rachel sighed. She wanted Hannah to trust her. "It isn't exactly a secret language. Come with me. I'll show you what I mean."

She strode to the carriage boot with Hannah right behind her, grabbed the signing book and placed it in the girl's hands.

"There are others who cannot speak, Hannah. Like you. Children and adults. This is how they talk to each other and their families."

Slowly Hannah flipped through the pages. Slower and slower she studied the drawings. Totally engrossed in the book, she walked to the stone steps of the lighthouse, sat and balanced the book in her lap. Rachel followed quietly.

Behind his daughter, Mr. Taylor appeared in the doorway, wiping his hands on an oily towel. He looked over Hannah's shoulder at the book and his eyes hardened to blue crystal. Reaching down, he pulled the book from her lap and studied the title. His lips pressed together in a grim line. "Hannah. Go inside and set the table for supper," he said in a voice that discouraged any opposition.

Hannah jumped up and ran inside. Rachel suddenly had the uncomfortable thought that her employer might not approve of her methods. He shoved the book at her. "You need to discuss things like this with me first, before wasting Hannah's and your time. She doesn't need this. She'll speak again."

Dismayed, Rachel took the book.

"Understand—I don't want her treated differently. She is no different from any of your other students. Use the methods you use at school. Not this." He strode toward the shed before she could think to reply.

Hannah had made progress today. Real progress. Couldn't he see his stubbornness would hurt her? This was too important to dismiss so quickly. She followed him into the shed and found him putting away the tools he and Caleb had been using. "Mr. Taylor, we need to finish our discussion."

He looked up, his eyebrows raised. "We weren't having a discussion."

"Well, I have a few things to say."

"You don't seem to understand. There is nothing to

discuss. I explained how things would be done and that's that."

She drew in a deep breath and said a prayer that she wouldn't lose her job on the first real day of teaching. "No, it's not."

"She's under my care and I determine what she should learn. You simply teach it."

"I see. I simply teach it." She struggled to keep her voice low. She wanted to polish that righteous expression right off his face. "And just how do I manage that when I can't tell what she's thinking?"

"That's a problem, isn't it?" Stuart calmly resumed organizing his tools. "Hannah and I seem to do all right. I know you'll work it out."

Her temper snapped. "How can you be so close-minded? You're stopping me even before I've started. She must learn to communicate in some way. With this, we meet her in the middle. It's her only alternative. Writing she simply does not comprehend yet."

Slowly he put the hammer he held onto the workbench. His voice took on an edge of steel. "It's your job to teach her to comprehend it."

"Then you must support me in how I go about it."

She stared at him across the small room. She would not back down.

He pointed to the book. "Rachel, you can't be serious. No one else understands this kind of talk. She'll look like a fool."

His use of her given name jolted her. She liked the sound of it in his deep baritone voice. For a moment she lost track of the point she was trying to make. "Not to me. And not to you either if you learn the words. Are you more worried you will look the fool? Is that what you're afraid of?"

He scowled and she pressed home her point.

"She could teach you. That would help her learn, too. Then you could actually have a conversation with her. Don't you wonder what goes on in her head? What she's thinking?" She persisted in spite of the doubts she had of her own ability to teach Hannah all the words. What if she couldn't do it? Still, she needed his support, for Hannah to have any chance at all. There had to be some way to make him understand. "It would make her feel important."

He walked up to her and stood towering over her. Even though she knew it was a tactic to press home his authority, she still took an involuntary step backward.

"Enough," he said. "That is my answer. I won't pursue this further and I won't change my mind. The hand signs stop now."

How could she have ever thought he would understand? The camaraderie she had witnessed earlier when he worked with Caleb obviously didn't extend to her. "I don't know why I expected you to be different. You're just like any other man, blinded to any thoughts but your own." Trembling with fury, she continued. "Why don't you ask her what she wants? She'd tell you, but of course you wouldn't understand her anyway."

His jaw dropped open at her tirade and then clamped shut. She'd lose this job for sure now. Whirling about, she marched through the door.

She walked until she could go no farther, to the very

tip of the peninsula, struggling to calm her chaotic thoughts. She'd made a proper fool of herself. Her cheeks burned with the thought. Of course an adult shouldn't ask a child what they should learn. What was she thinking to say such a thing? She was grasping at wisps of thoughts—anything to make her point.

In front of her the ground dropped away sharply to the sea. Picking up a rock, she threw it over the edge, watching it bounce and ricochet off the angles of the cliff. She felt like that rock right now.

As it disappeared from sight a chill blew through her. That could have been Benjamin! The thought stopped her anger cold. She backed away from the edge and took a deep breath, remembering the picnic and the screams of a brave little boy. It would have been impossible for Caleb to save Benjamin. He would have died in the attempt had Mr. Taylor not insisted upon climbing down himself. She owed him a debt of gratitude even though he didn't want to accept it.

What was she doing arguing with him? Her purpose here was to teach. Perhaps that was why he upset her so. The signing had been her only plan and without it she didn't know what to do. Maybe she couldn't help Hannah at all. The thought scared her.

She turned back to the lighthouse and stopped. Mr. Taylor watched her from the doorway. She took a deep breath. He'd soon learn she could be stubborn—as stubborn as him, if need be. And she would figure something out, some way to reach Hannah. This entire argument was just a challenge to her to be more creative, that's all.

She marched up the lighthouse steps. "Hannah and Caleb are too quiet."

Their hands grabbed the brass door handle at the same time. His skin burned against hers for a moment before she snatched her hand away, unable to hide the turmoil he caused in her.

"We'll sort this out, Miss Houston," he said quietly.

He stood so close she could feel his breath on her neck. She glanced up into his blue eyes and saw the concern there. All she could comprehend was that he had not called her Rachel, and for some reason that hurt.

He yanked open the wooden door, standing aside for her to enter.

"Rach! Come look at this!" Caleb called from the parlor. A rectangular slash of orange sunlight fell upon him and Hannah kneeling before a small opened trunk.

"We need to start home," she said, acutely aware of the man behind her. His presence seemed to fill the room.

Caleb tossed something small across the space to her.

She caught it and turned it over. "What's this?" A wood carving. She ran her fingers over the smooth grain, taking a moment to gather her senses before turning to Mr. Taylor. With effort, she kept her voice light. "So, is this what light keepers do on long winter nights?"

He seemed wary of her mood. "The boat, many years ago. When I was Caleb's age."

"And this?" She picked up another carving. "The whale?"

"Last year."

"You had a bit of trouble with the tail?"

"It's not broken." He opened his mouth to say more, but stopped and turned to Caleb. "You heard your sister. Time to go."

Caleb slipped something into his pocket and closed the trunk. Rachel was about to ask him what he had in his hand when he pointed to the top of the trunk and asked, "This you, Mr. Taylor?"

Rachel leaned closer. The initials "M.S.T." had been burned into the wooden lid just above the words: "Lansing Enterprises."

"I'll tell you what," Mr. Taylor said. "You keep your secrets and I'll keep mine."

Chapter Nine

Stuart found a level spot on the large flat boulder and sat, motioning for Caleb to do the same. He'd wanted to escape the lighthouse and the lesson. Fishing was the perfect answer. Rachel gave her best as a teacher, and Hannah seemed happy to learn anything—anything with the exception of the alphabet. After three weeks of struggling, Stuart didn't know who was more frustrated—Rachel or Hannah.

Beside him, Caleb pulled an extra length of string from his pocket and cut the frayed end with an old knife that Stuart recognized as one of his. Caleb added more string to his line, deftly tying a fisherman's knot.

Stuart held up the string. "You know something of fishing." He didn't miss the flash of pride that Caleb quickly covered up. "You can swim, right?"

Caleb nodded.

"That's good," he said, looking down at the swells that crawled up the rock, then crashed back into themselves seven feet below them. The swells continued toward shore on either side of the rock, growing into white foaming cliffs that raced onto the beach behind Stuart.

He placed the can of bait between them on the dark-gray rock. They baited and then threw in their lines. A comfortable silence fell between them as the sun warmed their shoulders.

Stuart wondered how the teaching session was going. To Rachel's credit, she'd played by the rules—his rules. He hadn't expected such stubbornness the first time they'd talked. Now he knew better. His only experience with women had been his mother, Linnea and her mother, Rose. They'd been sweet and yielding to the men in their lives. He chuckled to himself. Nothing like Rachel.

He glanced sideways at Caleb. "I think this is preferable to being in the way while your sister tutors."

Caleb grinned. "You mean safer, don't you? I don't know what you did to make her mad, but you better watch your back."

"She doesn't have to like me. She just has to do right with Hannah." He started to say more but Caleb's line went taut.

"Think I got one!"

"Careful." Stuart stood, ready to lend a hand if need be. "Slow and easy."

Caleb worked the fish, allowing it a little line and then reeling it in with a steady hand. He landed the fish at his feet. "A sand bass!"

Stuart grabbed the line above the squirming, flopping fish, took it firmly by the gills and removed the hook from its mouth. He walked over to a shallow natural pool in the rock and slipped the bass down into it. "That'll make a nice supper for you."

"If I can get Rach to fix it. She hates fish."

"I could teach you, I guess." In answer to Caleb's questioning look he added, "To clean it and cook it up."

"Ah, I know how to do all that."

"Good. Then you don't need to bother your sister with it."

"Are you crazy? Why should I do it when she is supposed to? It's her job. I'm not doing woman's work."

He settled back on the rock and threw his line. "You eat the fish don't you? Then you can clean and cook them just as easy as she can."

"Why do it when she will if I just wait her out?"

Stuart bit back a smile that threatened. He couldn't fault Caleb's logic, but he also couldn't abide laziness. "Guess you do need watching, just like the sheriff said."

"Now wait one minute!"

"Your actions give you away. You figure it out."

At sixteen, Stuart had been by all counts a man. Dorian had seen to it he had not had one moment of idle time, making him work as a hand on one of his merchant ships. Perhaps that's why he enjoyed the odd friendship with Caleb, the endless questions—so many that he wondered if Caleb got much of a chance to voice his opinions around home. He had finally realized why the boy seemed so familiar. The red hair should have alerted him sooner. Caleb had been the one to steal his lobster.

"So who is this Enrique you run with? The one with the boat."

Caleb shrugged.

"A friend?"

"He's okay."

Silence followed, but a red line crept up Caleb's neck.

"How long have you known?" Caleb asked in a low voice.

"Awhile."

The boy's shoulders slumped. "You gonna tell my sister?"

Stuart shook his head. "No, but I want my trap back."

Caleb nodded. "It was a dare." Suddenly he sat up straight. "I can't believe you took a shot at us! What'd ya do that for? You scared the pee right out of me."

Stuart struggled to keep from smiling. "You're lucky I wasn't feeling meaner."

Caleb's eyes narrowed. "You wouldn't have hurt us."

"No. I just wanted to scare you off. The shots worked. I've never seen anyone row as hard as you and that friend of yours."

He pointed across the water to a long boat riding the swells. "Whalers. I'm surprised they got one so early in the season. Didn't expect to see any migrating for another two or three weeks."

The vessel drew nearer, hauling the carcass of a gray whale about forty feet long. Barnacles covered patches of the skin and blood clotted at the blowhole.

"Town will stink for days now," Caleb said, his nose wrinkling.

They stayed until they each had two fish, then

Stuart stood and gathered his things. "We better head back. I want to see how the tutoring is going and you've got fish to clean."

At the top of the trail, Stuart handed off his pole to Caleb with instructions to put them away and get started cleaning the fish behind the shed. He walked to the house, mentally bracing himself for another battle of wills with Miss Houston regarding Hannah. He had to commend her perseverance though. And thankfully, she hadn't resorted to tears to get her way.

The scene in the kitchen brought him up short.

Hannah, a towel tied around her waist, stirred a large bowl of dough at the table. The determined look on her face amused him—and made him proud. Rachel chopped squares of chocolate into smaller bits and added them to the stiff dough. When he stepped into the room, she stopped with the knife in midair. Brushing wisps of burnished hair off her face with the back of her hand, she dared him with her look to remark about her teaching method this time.

But it was the smell he couldn't get enough of. He hadn't had cookies since he was a boy. He couldn't breathe deep enough to take in the wonderful aroma of them baking. He felt almost foolish, standing there, simply breathing.

Rachel glanced at her brother, who'd entered behind Stuart.

"Any luck?"

Caleb nodded. "I need a bowl to put the cleaned fish in. Hey! Cookies! Any for us?"

"Over there." She motioned with a wooden spoon.

"Wash your hands first, though. I don't want them smelling like fish. We baked sugar cookies first. These are taking a little longer. Hannah measured the ingredients just fine but mixing them has slowed her down."

Rachel held up her cookbook and tapped the recipe with the spoon. "In case you don't approve," she directed the remark to Stuart, "I'll have you know Hannah read all of the amounts correctly after the first few tries."

Stuart acknowledged the jab by raising his brows. He knew when to keep quiet. Besides—this is more what he had in mind in the way of teaching—much more. This was practical. Something Hannah could always use. "I doubt you were able to find all you needed in my cupboard. What do I owe you?"

"Nothing. I'll take some of the cookies home for us." She stopped dropping spoonfuls of dough onto the baking sheet. "You didn't have much in your cupboard. Is there anything I can bring from town to save you a trip? Perhaps some fruit?"

"No. You are doing enough." He walked over to Hannah and lightly squeezed her arm. "I didn't know making cookies required such muscles."

Hannah crinkled her eyes with delight, but Rachel looked at him as if she couldn't believe he had actually teased. Guess he had been gruff with her, but it was best to keep his distance.

"Can I have a taste?" Caleb asked, leaning over Hannah's shoulder and hooking a finger of stiff dough.

"May I…" Rachel corrected. "Now out of here." She looked pointedly at Stuart. "Both of you."

He wasn't about to let her have the upper hand. "You have flour on your nose, Miss Houston."

"Oh." Her hand flew to her face, patting more flour in the same place and making her sneeze.

He stifled a grin. "Here. I'll do it." He grabbed a towel from the table and gently wiped the flour off the side of her nose and cheek. Her skin had darkened to a golden sun-kissed tan since her first visit to the peninsula, and she still had those cute freckles across the bridge of her nose that reminded him of a schoolgirl. "How old are you, Miss Houston? All of sixteen?"

Suddenly he became aware of how she watched him. Acutely aware. Her gaze lighted on his face, his scar, his mouth and everywhere her gaze touched, he tingled. She didn't breathe. Her lips parted.

And his heart stopped.

Slowly he drew the towel away and studied her face, the soft rounded line of her chin, her straight nose. Her green eyes sparkled with life. The urge to kiss her slammed into him. Her lips looked so soft, so yielding. He took a deep breath.

Watch yourself, Taylor. You don't deserve someone like her. You don't deserve anyone at all.

"Finish those before you head home," he said. "We'd just burn what was left." He tossed the towel at her. "Oh…and next time you come? Wear a hat. You're getting freckles."

Chapter Ten

San Francisco, November 1873

Dorian Lansing's ornate carriage pulled by two large black horses jostled toward the pier. On the dock, sailors unloaded wares from the large cutters and steamers. A sweaty beggar, carrying the stench of the streets, brushed past the carriage. Dorian remained aloof, ignoring the curious stares of the common people and his fellow merchants alike.

His wife sat beside him, a scented handkerchief daintily pressed to her nose. He seldom brought her here to his place of business. Ever since the accident the ships and the commotion unnerved her. However, information had finally arrived—news of their granddaughter, and Rose had wanted to come with him. Dorian rapped his black cane on the carriage's ceiling when they neared his ship, the *Rose.*

"Here, Johnson."

The coach lurched to a stop and the driver jumped down and placed a stepping stool at the door. Dorian assisted his wife out and tucked her hand in the crook of his arm. He tightened his grip on his cane. This place festered with ruffians but he would keep her safe.

They walked up the ship's gangplank to the deck where his captain waited, stiff and formal. "Greetings, sir, ma'am. You'll find everything in order."

"Productive voyage, I trust?"

"Yes, sir. As usual."

"Well done."

He had few worries where Captain Ross was concerned. The man had been in his employ for seventeen years and had faithfully seen to his duty. A shame he hadn't been captain of the *Frisco Maiden* on her last voyage. Dorian had no doubt the man would have salvaged the vessel, not to mention Dorian's own daughter and granddaughter. Matthew had sailed often with Captain Ross, but experience and wisdom are not one and the same, and Matthew had lacked in the latter. "Where is Mr. Pittman?"

"My quarters, sir."

Dorian nodded, dismissing the captain to his duties, and led his wife to the quarters on the foredeck. He tapped firmly on the oak door with his cane. The door opened and a short mouse of a man peered out through thick glasses.

"Ah! Mr. Lansing. I thought I might see you upon docking."

He looked over to scrutinize Rose and then back to his boss.

"Mr. Pittman, this is my wife, Mrs. Lansing. We received your telegraph and have come to hear news of our granddaughter." He led Rose past the short man and into the cabin.

"I've learned a few interesting facts. Won't you have a seat?" He indicated a chair at the desk for Mrs. Lansing, then waited for her to settle.

Mr. Pittman hunched over the captain's desk and shuffled through some papers in the pretense of busily reading them. Dorian would have none of it. He rapped his cane twice on the floorboards. "What news, man? We've waited long enough," he said briskly, coming to stand beside his wife. "Out with it, Mr. Pittman."

"Your granddaughter, Hannah Taylor…oh yes, she still goes by that name…rather uncreative of her, ahem, alleged father, don't you think?" Pittman removed his spectacles and made a show of wiping a smudge from the lens with a cloth. When finished, he replaced them on his nose, curling the wires over his large ears. "Well, a doctor in Los Angeles admitted to seeing her about eight months ago."

"Was she ill?" Rose perched on the edge of her chair.

A patronizing smile crossed the detective's face. "Just a little matter of a sore throat. However, I did find it strange the doctor was a specialist—the only one of his kind on the west coast."

Rose gasped, paling. "Oh my. Something must be dreadfully wrong."

Dorian squeezed her thin shoulder. "It will be all right, dear. We're getting closer." He looked over at Mr.

Pittman, narrowing his brows in warning. "He must have had her address?"

"Yes." Mr. Pittman cleared his throat. "But it turned out to be a dead end. The address was counterfeit—made-up."

"Matthew is no doubt still worried about his part in Newcomb's death. He'll never be safe with that on his record."

"It would appear so. He is being cautious. I must say I'm surprised he would stay along the coast. One would think he'd head inland. But then maybe he is trying to second-guess us."

"Matthew could not survive away from the sea," Rose said quietly, gazing out the port window.

Pittman glanced at her irritably. "Another avenue of thought would be that he heard I was nearby and asking questions."

"So, where do you propose we go from here?" Dorian said.

"I am much closer. Believe me. It won't take long. I just need a little more…ah, capital to continue."

Dorian had the fleeting suspicion that he'd chosen the wrong man for the task. Perhaps he should have hired from the Pinkerton Agency as he'd first been inclined rather than listen to his brother-in-law. He'd give Pittman one more month. By that time the detective had better have more information than this. To wait all this time and only realize disturbing news simply would not do.

Pittman removed his glasses again and took the cloth from his back pocket to clean them. "People are moving in and out of the area constantly now with the land speculation. It's not easy."

"I see." Dorian remained quiet, methodically going over the scant information.

"I have my associates positioned, with two keeping watch of that man, Saunders. Any information about the location of Hannah or Matthew Taylor will be forwarded to me."

Rose shifted in her seat, leaning forward. "Surely there is more you can do than that. How can we just sit back and wait?" She clutched her handkerchief to her breast.

"Dear." Dorian leaned over his wife. "You're getting overwrought. This is the first news we've heard in over a year. We can be patient awhile longer." He looked up to find Mr. Pittman watching the exchange closely.

"I'll find her, Mr. Lansing. I'm just sorry you waited so long to obtain my services."

"I had other concerns at the time, which I'll not go into now." He helped Rose stand. "I'm taking my wife home. She's had enough of a shock. Then I'll be back to settle accounts."

"Yes, sir." The man peered through his glasses at Rose.

"Open the door, Mr. Pittman."

"Yes, sir." He jumped to obey.

Chapter Eleven

Hannah crumpled her work paper and threw her pencil across the room. Dodging Rachel's arms, she raced up the stairs to her room.

Hands on hips, Rachel heaved a sigh as the girl disappeared. Hannah wasn't the only one frustrated. She'd like to throw a thing or two herself. She marched to the table and gathered her teaching supplies.

"This is crazy," she muttered, slamming the books into a stack. "I can't do it. No one could do it under these circumstances."

"Trouble?" Stuart asked from the doorway.

She jumped, startled. How long had he been standing there? "Mr. Taylor. You expect the impossible. I'm just not getting through to her." Even to her own ears, she sounded a bit hysterical.

"You can't expect too much too soon. Isn't that what you told me?"

"But I expect something—some glimmer of understanding in those intelligent eyes of hers."

"She did fine with arithmetic and the cooking."

"But not spelling, not words." Mortified at the whine in her voice, she struggled to take hold of her emotions. "Please, please, reconsider your decision about the signing."

Stuart's eyes hardened. "That subject is closed."

"Then maybe this teacher has had it." Her chest tightened with defeat. She had to look away from the troubled expression on his face. He expected too much, wanted too much from her.

"You don't mean that. You are not a quitter."

She didn't trust herself to answer him, afraid she'd burst into tears and make a complete fool of herself. Right now she felt like a quitter. She couldn't teach—at least not someone as complicated as Hannah. What had ever given her the notion that she could? She threw her cloak over her shoulders, preparing to head back to town.

Mr. Taylor stepped closer. "You're giving up? Leaving?"

"People leave," she said in low voice, thinking of her father and Joseph.

"You've been at this for five weeks and I know it hasn't been easy. What you and Hannah need is a holiday."

She stared at him. He'd never shown one ounce of caring about her feelings. Surely his concern was only for his daughter. If Rachel quit, he'd have to find another tutor.

"Let's go down to the water. I need to work on my boat. We'll take a picnic."

The offer sounded stiff on his lips, so stiff Rachel had

to turn away from him to the cupboard to hide the smile that suddenly threatened.

"What do you say?" he persisted.

He wasn't used to asking for anything, she realized, inanely flattered that he'd felt compelled to stop her. Her resolve to leave ebbed. "All right. I'll pack a few things. *You* can deal with Hannah."

Fifteen minutes later, she stepped from the lighthouse and tugged her cloak about her shoulders. On the footpath, scruffy brush snagged her skirt and loose gravel made the going slippery. Enviously she noted Stuart's canvas pants and loose muslin shirt that offered him freer movement. Even his cap stayed on better in the wind than her hood. With his toolbox in his right hand, he shifted the weight of the rolled quilt under his left arm, making her sharply aware of the long line of his powerful back, and headed down the path ahead of her.

As though he could read her thoughts, he stopped suddenly and turned, waiting for her to catch up to him. Then without a word, he started down the path again, this time at a slower pace.

Two hundred feet ahead, Caleb and Hannah raced on the narrow strip of beach, their footprints dotting the wet sand. They skirted the ocean-smoothed boulders and jagged rocks that jutted out into the water, stopping every few feet to dig for the sand crabs that washed up on the beach. Caleb yelled triumphantly when he caught the first one, showed it to Hannah, then with a quick overhand arc tossed it back into the surf.

Rachel turned her attention back to the end of the trail, watching Stuart jump effortlessly down the three-foot drop-off to the sandy beach. Her descent would be anything but graceful in her full skirt. She handed him the picnic basket and had crouched down when the warm press of his fingers against her sides surprised her.

A tingling awareness shot through her.

He set her firmly on the sand, then started up the beach. Was it just the tug and pull of her own emotions that she felt? Ever since the day she'd baked cookies with Hannah he had confused her. One minute he'd be almost friendly, then the next as distant as the ships on the horizon, which was an attitude she could barely tolerate. She preferred even his grouchy moments to being ignored. Picking up the basket again, she hurried after him, trying to match his long stride.

"I'll check on the boat first," he said without looking back.

The gritty sand quickly worked its way into her shoes and stockings, slowing her down. The sides of her feet were rubbed raw in less than fifty steps.

Turning to wait for her, Stuart frowned. "Take off your shoes."

Her cheeks warmed. "It's not proper. What kind of example would I set for Hannah if I did that?"

"You're ruining them. Besides, I expect a healthy dose of common sense to go along with Hannah's education."

"But," she said, weakly, and then sighed. Why argue? He was right.

She motioned Stuart to turn his back, then sat down

on a nearby boulder and removed her shoes and stockings. When she glanced up and caught him spying, she stood abruptly, letting her dress rustle into place.

He ignored her discomfort and stared at her feet. Then slowly his gaze moved up the length of her to her face, leaving behind a trail of tingles. "It has been a long time since I walked barefoot with a beautiful girl."

Her mouth dropped open.

He picked up her shoes and handed them to her, pausing a moment before turning and heading up the beach.

She dug her toes into the sand, trying to concentrate on the grainy feeling against her skin rather than the rapid thudding of her heart.

Beautiful?

Bemused, she followed at a slower pace.

A short way farther, he ducked inside a tarp-covered lean-to. Curious, Rachel peeked inside. The faint odor of fresh paint stung her nostrils. A neat array of coiled ropes and equipment lay in the bed of the ten-foot whitewashed dory.

The boat seemed small to Rachel. "This is what you go out in?"

He reached for a piece of sandpaper. "She's fit. Rescued enough stranded fisherman in her day to prove her worth."

She'd avoided thinking about the dangerous part of his job. How could he risk his life when Hannah depended totally on him? Why didn't he take a safer job? Rachel didn't understand him, and that made her more curious than ever. She wouldn't pry. Their friendship—if that's what it was—was too fresh, too new. But she'd find out eventually. Of that she was sure.

He bent to his work using exacting, swift strokes of the sandpaper. He tested an area for smoothness, then, dissatisfied, returned to sanding, moving into a rhythm—back and forth, back and forth. The muslin shirt pulled across his broad shoulders, and she thought how strong and able he was. How pleasant it might feel to have him sliding his hands over her instead of the boat. As soon as the thought registered, she felt her cheeks flush.

Before long the furrows of tension in his brow disappeared, and a sheen of sweat glossed his forehead. He paused and removed his cap, wiping his brow with his forearm.

She broke her stare. "I'll...go and lay out the quilt." She ducked through the tarp's open flap, breathing easier once out in the fresh air.

She busied herself spreading the quilt and anchoring it with the picnic basket. The early-morning overcast had burned off, and the sun warmed the beach. She removed her cloak and tossed it on the quilt, and then she walked to the water's edge where Hannah and Caleb played.

A short while later, Stuart joined her.

"The boat?"

"I finished what I came to do. She'll need another coat of paint but that's work for another day."

Rachel felt him staring and because it made her feel odd to be studied so closely, she turned her attention to the surf pounding against the rocks. "This was a good idea."

"You are a good teacher—an excellent one. Don't be discouraged."

His words warmed her. "I might not be discouraged at all if you'd let me try the signing." But she knew he wouldn't and kept her voice light, cajoling.

He shook his head. "Let it alone, Rachel. You never give up, do you?"

She smiled sweetly. "Not when I'm right. I'm just trying to use that common sense that you so want Hannah to learn."

"You can't wear me down," he warned.

"I know." She turned to meet his gaze, serious now. "I wouldn't think much of a man who didn't hold to his convictions. As much as you oppose my position, I still respect yours and the fact that you feel strongly about it."

A slow smile spread across his tanned face. "Good. Then we'll get along."

Rachel's heart beat faster. The twinkle in his eyes was entirely too interesting. *Common sense,* she told herself. This was a business relationship, nothing more. "It strikes me that you are always taking care of things—Hannah, the boat, the light." And her. Today she'd been ready to quit teaching, feeling like a failure. He'd known somehow that she needed a break, needed to step back.

"The light?" He shrugged his shoulders. "That's my job. The boat? It helps me do my job."

"And Hannah…"

"Hannah. Well…Hannah is my responsibility."

"Ouch! I'm glad she isn't close enough to hear that,"

Rachel said. What a strange way to think of his daughter. But the love was there in the way he treated her. "What happened with her, Stuart? How did she lose her voice? Or—" she paused as the thought occurred to her "—has she never been able to speak?"

He picked up a smooth stone and skimmed it over the water.

She watched it arc two, three, four times before dropping underneath the surface. "Well? Are you stalling?"

He let out a huff of breath, avoiding her gaze.

"Perhaps it would help me to know. In order to teach her better."

A slight smile played about his mouth. "I doubt that. I guess you're entitled though. You've put a lot of effort into her lessons. And as much as it may have pained you, you have followed my wishes."

"Which has been the hardest part of all," she teased.

He started walking slowly along the shore and she kept pace with him. Suddenly he stopped and faced her. "Let there be a bargain. I'll tell you about Hannah, but then you have to tell me something about you."

She pursed her lips.

"Ah, I see. Turnabout is fair play, Miss Houston."

She scowled. He was almost charming. Had she misread the awkwardness at the lighthouse? "But my life is ever so boring."

"We'll see about that," he said, cocking his head. "I won't say a word until you agree."

"This sounds suspiciously like blackmail."

He smirked. "You're the one who mentioned there

were rumors about me. I wouldn't want to disappoint you."

"Well, so far, Mr. Taylor, you have been anything but disappointing. Exasperating, yes. Disappointing, no."

He smiled, and it transformed his face.

She thought his chest puffed out a little, too. "You go first, then."

He nodded, his mood changing swiftly to serious. "When Hannah was three, her mother drowned in a ship accident at sea. Hannah hasn't spoken since."

Rachel had heard of such things…of being so traumatized that blindness or deafness occurred without a physical reason for it. "Has she seen a doctor?"

"I took her to a specialist up the coast."

"And…?" she prodded. "What did he say?"

"He said that she'll speak again. Someday."

His words didn't exactly answer Rachel's question, and she suspected there was much more to the story, but the fact that he'd trusted her with this much would do for now.

"Your turn now." Stuart skimmed another stone over the water. "Obviously by your accent you are not from here."

"La Playa is filled with strange accents—Spanish, Portuguese, Chinese. Compared to those, a Midwest one isn't too exotic."

"True enough, but yours is pleasant. Go on."

"Remember, it's quite boring," she warned.

"I doubt that."

She groaned, but was warmed by the fact that he was interested. "When I was fourteen my mother died from the influenza and my father came west. Caleb and I followed him from camp to camp looking for gold. We moved here in '70 when he heard that gold had been discovered in the back country."

Stuart nodded. "I remember hearing of that."

"After a few years, he was ready to move again, but I had had enough. I was tired of the dirt and fleas and roughness of the tent cities. I wanted a real home, with a roof over my head that didn't leak. I heard La Playa was looking for a schoolteacher, so I applied for the position and then came to stay with Reverend Crouse and his wife."

"That's it?"

She buried a shell deep into the soft sand with her toe. "Pretty much."

"You're what—twenty-three at most? In all these tent cities there were no suitors? No one special?"

Her cheeks flushed. How could he fluster her so easily? She couldn't tell him about Joseph. Joseph who'd captured her heart and then nearly destroyed it when he'd left. "I'm a few years beyond that," she admitted. "You must be unaware of the power of gold. Once a man gets caught up in it, it takes hold of him and won't let go. Nothing is as important as chasing the next rumor of gold—not even a woman."

He scrutinized her. "So you came here."

She took a deep breath. "I'd rather be on my own, taking care of myself, than saddled to a man who would always put me second in his life behind gold."

Stuart looked at her strangely, and for a moment she thought her words had revealed more than she'd meant to.

"Papa promised he'd be back, but we haven't seen him since." When she looked up, the anger on Stuart's face surprised her. She couldn't understand what had upset him, so she hurried to explain. "We're doing just fine. I have a good job teaching. We're all right."

"But a man should take care of his family—not run off and leave them to their own fate."

"A nice thought, but hardly reality. People leave." Joseph had left her. Her voice lowered to barely a whisper above the roar of the waves. "Everyone leaves."

His brows knitted together as he frowned. "You don't really believe that, do you?"

"I have to. Caleb depends on me, at least for now, but one day he'll be gone too. More and more he talks of trying his hand at whaling. I can't afford to believe anything else." She didn't add that it would hurt too much to hope that someone would come along, someone who would care so much that he'd put her and her welfare before his ambition or dreams.

Stuart strolled along the beach, waiting when she stopped to examine a seashell. "What about Morley?"

"Terrance?" She looked into his blue eyes.

"The mercantile owner. You were with him at the picnic."

So he'd noticed that much and remembered. "He's just a friend."

"But he wants to be more."

She thought so, too, but wasn't ready to admit to it. She pulled her gaze from his and started walking again. "Enough about me. You know far more than I do about you."

He flashed a grin. "An employer's prerogative."

"Rach!" Caleb splashed through the shallows toward her. "Take a look at this!" He held a sand dollar in his palm.

She jumped back from the water spray, but was grateful for the distraction. "It's huge! Where did you find it?"

She followed her brother around a large boulder. Hannah crouched there next to a wet rocky crevice. She placed a shell in Rachel's hand. The shell moved!

"Oh!" Rachel nearly dropped it.

Stuart caught her hand in his, steadying her, and turned the shell over. "It won't hurt you. See? Just a hermit crab."

Rachel stilled, more aware of Stuart's warm touch than the tickling trail of the creature. "It just startled me." She dropped the crab back into the pool and found five more shells trundling along the sides of the rock. She squatted down and touched an unusual-looking sea flower that clung to the rock beneath the water's surface. The tentacle-like petals grasped onto her finger. "Oh!" Quickly, she pulled back.

"Sea anemone," Caleb said. "They always do that."

She frowned at Caleb, who grinned back at her.

"Now, that is a surprise," Stuart said with a bemused look. "I didn't take you for the skittish type."

"She doesn't like creepy-crawly things," Caleb said. "But she tries not to show it."

"Good idea not to let people know. They could use it against you," Stuart whispered into her ear. "Especially your brother."

"Exactly," she mumbled, her eyes shooting play

daggers at Caleb. "It doesn't help to pass along a silly fear to Hannah." She enjoyed watching the creatures in the tide pool—as long as they stayed there. "This must be where Hannah finds the things for the treasure box in her room."

"Too many if you ask me," Stuart said.

She rose to her feet. "It's a good way to keep memories."

"Memories," he murmured. "More a curse than anything."

She thought of her mother and father. The good and the bad. Of Hannah, now voiceless since the death of her mother. "Yes…they can be. But they make us who we are, whether we want them to or not."

Stuart's gaze met hers, but he didn't say anything more.

She followed him, picking her way over the rocks back to the beach. Once there she brushed the sand from her hands and looked around. To the south the large flat fishing rock walled her in and to the east and north, the cliffs. She pointed partway up the sandstone. "I can't believe that's the waterline."

"High tide."

"It changes so drastically. Where we are standing is underwater then."

A half smile moved across his face. "The pull of the moon is an amazing thing. The flood current—" he caught her questioning look "—high tide, comes in here fast. When it does, there is no place to reach the trail."

He stooped, choosing a stone, and in one fluid move, skimmed it across the shallow surf.

She watched, fascinated, as he repeated the motion. Strange though it would be to the people of La Playa, she liked talking with him. The sound of his deep voice rumbling on about tides and currents mesmerized her until she really didn't hear what he was saying, just enjoyed the sound.

The wind swirled within the sandstone cavern creating a haunting moan. She shivered and rubbed her arms, wishing for her cloak that she'd left behind on the quilt. "Funny how cold it gets as soon as we're out of the sun."

He glanced down at her arms encased in cotton sleeves. Light flashed through his eyes.

She shivered again. This time, not from the cold.

Slowly, as though he couldn't quite help himself, he reached out and rubbed her upper arms. Heat from his hands burned through the material to her skin. The fact that only an hour ago at the boat she'd dreamed of his touch shot through her mind.

"Rachel…" His voice rasped softly. She heard desire banked in it. He tightened his grip.

Her heart hammered in her chest. "My teacher's position doesn't cover this sort of thing."

"Oh, I'm sure there's a rule against it." His eyes were the bluest thing in creation, hooded now, pulling her in.

Common sense, she told herself. Use common sense. "Yes…I…" Yet she wanted his touch. It shook her to realize how much she suddenly yearned for it. But if she were to let him closer, he'd end up leaving her eventually. It was better not to let that happen, better to keep focused on her work. She took a deep breath and stepped from his grasp.

He stared at her a moment, then dropped his hands to his sides before shoving them in his pockets. "Let's go back with the others. You'll warm up faster in the sun."

She swallowed hard and watched him start back around the fishing rock, feeling the cold once again seep through her skin.

He glanced back once, stopped and faced her. "There's more to your story, Rachel. A lot more."

As he turned to leave, she raised her chin. "I could say the same about you, Mr. Taylor."

Chapter Twelve

Stuart climbed the circular stairs, his supplies for the lamp in one hand. At the top, he set the bucket on the plank flooring and unrolled his linen apron, following the lighthouse board instructions in rote manner, barely thinking of the actions he had done so many times over the past year.

In the distance the church bell rang out, calling those that would go to Sunday worship. There wouldn't be many, for most of the area's inhabitants were Portuguese or Mexican. They would go to the Catholic church in Old San Diego. Rachel would be sitting quietly. Caleb, on the other hand, would be fidgeting, anxious for the service to be over.

Thoughts of Rachel haunted him more and more lately. He looked forward to her visits, but when she arrived, he did his best to keep his distance, yet still found reasons to brush up against her or hold her as she climbed into and out of her carriage. Innocent yearnings—and yet not quite innocent.

The thought troubled him. He didn't want to like her.

And that situation at the beach...well, that was another thing entirely. Loneliness on his part perhaps, maybe lust. His monkish existence was getting to him. Having Rachel so near, and so beautiful, had undone him for a moment. He would have to be more careful from now on. She deserved better than him. She deserved someone with a future.

He blocked the faint tolling of the bell from his mind and continued his work. For him, Sunday was not a day of rest. It was just like any other day filled with the same monotonous yet necessary chores. He trimmed the wick to the required length and shape, remembering the precise shape the flame had to have upon burning, and then polished the carbon off the reflectors. The endless repetition of caring for the lamp was tedious.

He looked out to sea. A steamer headed toward the harbor, still far enough away that any persons on deck were indiscernible. The wind was mild, the water calm. He missed the ocean. He could say that now, although it hadn't always been that way. For the first two years after Linnea died, he'd hated it. Now he wondered if he would ever be able to go back.

When he finished with his chores he stored his equipment in the small storage space at the bottom of the inside ladder that led to the catwalk. He peeked in on Hannah. She sat in her bedroom, her back to the door, playing with the doll Rachel had given her. Dust motes circled around her head in the bright morning sunlight that streamed through the window.

She sat so still he grew curious. He stepped closer,

wondering that she could concentrate so hard and not hear him. Suddenly she flipped her hands about in a coordinated dance, and then tried to make the doll copy her. Suspicious now, he moved closer. A book lay open in her lap. A book with pictures and symbols.

"Hannah! What are you doing?" He strode to the bed and snatched the book from her.

Her eyes widened with fear. She should worry—she had disobeyed him.

"You may not do the hand signs!" He paced the length of the room, his anger growing with each step. "I can't believe Miss Houston left this for you. She knows how I feel about it."

Book in hand, he stomped down the stairs and paced the length of the gravel walk. He could wring Rachel's neck! How dare she encourage this in Hannah? He'd been sure that finally they were of the same accord on things—that trust was developing. Well, she'd see just how serious he was. They'd have this out once and for all.

He sat on the outside steps. Behind him, Hannah's footsteps sounded on the stairs, and then he felt the brush of her arm as she sat beside him. He hardened himself against the sight of tears on her wet spiky lashes.

"Go to your room."

She wouldn't look at him, instead she pointed to herself, and then crossed her arms over her chest.

"You are not allowed to use that. Dr. Jarvis said it was just a matter of time before you started talking again. Now go back upstairs."

Her chin quivered, but she didn't leave. She shoved the book he held toward him and repeated her motions.

"Hannah. It's for your own good. You will speak again one day. You just need time."

Determination sparked in her clear gray eyes. Stubborn determination.

Stuart swallowed. "I will punish you if I see you talking with your hands."

He hated being stern with her and cringed at the sound of his voice. Rachel had done this. Had driven this wedge into his relationship with Hannah—and she would pay for it.

Hannah pushed the book at him again, harder this time.

"All right," he said irritably. "I'll look this once." He flipped through the pages searching for the arms-crossed-over-the-chest picture. Finally, on one dog-eared page, he found it:

"I love you."

His heart jolted as he stared at the page. He drew in a deep, shuddering breath. Had he been such a fool? The book slipped from him, and he buried his face in his hands, trying to think beyond the lump in his throat. Hannah had never told him before. When she could talk, aboard the ship, she'd been too afraid of him, afraid of all men—a legacy left from her father.

He felt a tug on his sleeve.

Slowly he straightened. The words surged from deep inside him, rusty and awkward. "I...I love you too, Hannah."

She burrowed into his arms. For the first time since the accident, he felt a measure of peace.

* * *

Rachel and Caleb had been unable to come for more than a week. He wondered what had kept her away as he walked toward her now. The days were getting shorter and perhaps that left little time for her to tend to her other obligations in town. Well, once he had his say, she might have plenty of time. Suddenly he wasn't so anxious to put the coming confrontation behind him.

She stood by her carriage, hands splayed on hips. The brown skirt and cream-colored blouse made her look very "teacherly" as did the furrow between her brows. "What's wrong?"

He glanced toward the shed, checking for Hannah and Caleb.

Rachel's eyes narrowed. "They can't hear you."

Watching her, he couldn't believe she'd left the book on purpose. And yet what other explanation could there be? He couldn't let go of the notion that she'd gone behind his back to get her way. The thought had even robbed him of sleep. "I found the book."

"Book?" she said, a bewildered expression on her face.

"The signing book. Did you think I wouldn't find it eventually?" The anger that he'd pushed down inside forced its way up and flooded his voice. Even Jericho snorted and pranced sideways.

"Well," Rachel recovered quickly. "Good. I've been looking for it."

"Hannah has been practicing the gestures."

Amazement crossed Rachel's face, irritating him further. "Don't look so pleased."

She scowled. "What exactly are you accusing me of? I didn't leave the book with her."

"Then how did it end up here?"

Caleb rounded the side of the lighthouse with Hannah and glanced uneasily from Stuart to his sister. "What's going on? What's all the shouting about?"

Stuart ignored him. "My word has to mean something. And I specifically instructed you not to teach the signing." He swatted at the tug on his arm. "Hannah, stop pulling at my sleeve."

The instant she had his attention, Hannah started signing, her hands dancing in short jerky movements.

Stuart let out an exasperated grunt and turned to Rachel. "You are the expert. What is she saying?"

"I…I don't know. Hannah, slow down. Remember, I haven't learned all the words."

Hannah repeated her motions. When no one could understand, she dropped in a heap to the dirt. In her frustration, she began tearing out the sparse tufts of grass and throwing them angrily at the ground.

Rachel stared helplessly at Stuart.

He felt more than a twinge of guilt. All he'd been striving for was the truth. He hesitated. Maybe that wasn't the important thing here. Maybe the way Hannah had obtained the book didn't really matter— not anymore. What mattered was how he handled it from here on out.

"All right, Hannah. This seems to be very important to you. Get the book."

He ignored Rachel's quick glance of surprise at his words. Hannah's hands stilled, full of grass. Slowly she raised her head. Uncertainty filled her eyes. After all his bellowing about rules, she must think she hadn't heard right.

"I'll get it. Where is it?" Caleb asked.

"Kitchen table," Stuart said, his gaze still locked on Hannah.

Caleb dashed up the dirt path to the lighthouse. When he returned to the group, Stuart opened the book. "Now go ahead. But slowly this time."

From her seat in the dirt, Hannah ever so slowly began making one word at a time with her hands. Her fingers trembled, and once, she had to start over, but that determined look he'd come to know so well stole over her face and remained.

He flipped through the book, searching for the pictures of her motions. "I've got that. Next." He felt Rachel watching him closely throughout the exchange and kept waiting for the words "I told you so" to slip from her lips.

When Hannah finished, he closed the book with a thud and helped her up from the ground. "Thank you for being honest."

He let out his breath slowly and then looked at Rachel. "Apparently Hannah took the book from your carriage. I...I apologize for assuming it was you."

Rachel raised her brows but remained silent.

"About the signing..." He took a deep breath. "I want it to continue."

She looked dubious. "You're sure?"

"At this point, I'm not sure of anything." *Except you,* he wanted to say as he studied her upturned face. *I'm beginning to be very sure of how I feel about you.* But saying the words would only complicate his life. He couldn't offer her a future. He didn't have one.

Chapter Thirteen

Something changed over the next weeks between the four of them. Quickly, Hannah learned to connect the images in the book—the word, the picture and the hand motion. Now that they were aware of her thoughts, she became so much more a part of them. Stuart wondered why he'd ever fought against the idea of sign language. Any argument he had used now sounded hollow against the rush of joy he felt at knowing Hannah's thoughts.

Stuart watched Hannah at the water's edge, her tin bucket in hand, searching for shells. Caleb joined her, kicking up water and making her squeal. Behind him, Rachel called out, "Stuart, this looks like a good place."

That was another thing that had changed. Rachel no longer called him Mr. Taylor. He liked the way his name sounded on her lips.

With a snap of his wrists, he spread out the quilt, and before long Rachel and then Hannah joined him. Hannah rinsed the shells off in the bucket of water and laid them out to dry while Rachel set out the food. Whistling sharply, Stuart caught Caleb's attention and motioned him over to eat. Seagulls, drawn by the hope of an easy meal, scattered as he ran up.

"With any luck," Stuart said, winking at Hannah, "we'll see our whale today." He finished his apple and stretched back on the quilt, propping himself up with his elbows. He forced himself to concentrate on the swells rising and then crashing down, although the urge to study Rachel was more appealing. The ocean was safer.

"Haven't most of them passed by?" Rachel asked, popping a grape into her mouth.

He shook his head. "There's a special one Hannah and I watch for. Should be heading south any day now."

She eyed him skeptically. "Right. And how do you know it's the same whale?"

"What? Don't you believe me?" he said teasingly.

"No. I don't think I do." But the dimple gave her away. "You will have to prove it to me."

As he studied her full lips, he decided proving it the way he'd like might be dangerous. "A torn fluke. Someone harpooned her or perhaps a shark bit her. Whatever the case, she got away. We first saw her last March when she migrated north. She had a calf with her."

His answer seemed to satisfy her, then her eyes widened. "A torn fluke...like the carving you made?"

He smiled, pleased and a little surprised that she remembered. More than ten weeks had passed since that first day of tutoring.

Hannah finished her lunch, tugged on his hand and pointed to the tidal pools.

"You go on." He tweaked her nose and waited for her to take off. Caleb quickly followed.

Stuart glanced at Rachel—and then couldn't look away. If she'd just quit enjoying those grapes he might be able to think clearly. He studied her profile as she watched Hannah and Caleb dash toward the water.

"Here." She held out a cluster of grapes for him.

He shook his head. It wasn't food he was after. "Thank you for all your help with Hannah."

"I've enjoyed it, although a few moments have been challenging."

"I'd like to make those up to you." He inched closer to her. Dangerous or not, he wanted a taste of her. He reached out and tucked a loose strand of hair behind her ear.

The teasing smile on her lips slowly disappeared as she realized his intent. Her green eyes grew large.

"Come here, Rachel."

"This is not wise," she whispered, but she didn't pull back.

"Probably not." He hooked his hand behind her neck and pulled her to him. "But I think we both know it's time. Come here."

He met her lips tenderly, softly. Slowly he let go of her neck and she stayed there, her mouth moving under his, answering his need.

"Stuart…" she breathed into his mouth.

Gently he pressed for more, using his tongue to tickle the seam of her lips. They parted and tentatively she touched her tongue to his. A bolt of desire coursed through him.

She gasped and pulled back, staring at him as the color heightened on her cheeks. A moment passed before she finally spoke, her voice shaky. "I believe that more than made up for any rough moments with your daughter."

"That made up for a lot of things, but not everything." He leaned in for another kiss. There was a rushing sound in his ears that had nothing to do with the nearby waves crashing to shore. Then he felt her hand splay against his chest and hold him away.

"No. Stuart." A look of distress passed over her face as the pressure on his chest increased. "Why…why don't you tell me about your scar?"

"My scar?" What was she talking about? He couldn't get his mind off the kiss.

"Yes! How did it happen?" she said sharply. "Now, mind you, I expect a fascinating tale. There are so many rumors in town. Like the one about the mountain lion that attacked you. Then there's the one where you were shot fleeing from prison."

He still reeled from the kiss and wanted another one, but obviously she wasn't ready. She was babbling in her nervousness and that wasn't like her at all.

He raked his hand through his hair, wondering whether to be amused that so many stories were circulating about him or upset that his existence hadn't gone as unnoticed as he'd hoped.

"Although I have to wonder," she continued, "if you did have a criminal record, how you managed to get the job of light keeper."

She was talking so fast. Her words tumbling over each other. She was nervous, he realized. Of him.

"A friend helped me get this job. Man named Saunders."

"And the scar?"

"I got it when I was swimming. The stern of a lifeboat rammed into me." He shrugged. "Not that exciting."

"You really need to embellish that story if you expect it to entertain as well as the rumors." But there was a twinkle in her eyes again, and her breathing was back to normal as she wrapped her arms about her knees, smoothing her skirt.

"I never set out to be the one everyone talks about," he said under his breath, angry at the thought. "And I'd never hurt you, Rachel."

"I know that," she said softly. "I…I was just scared. That's all. Of myself."

That makes two of us.

He nodded slowly. "I see."

Rachel sat up straight. "Wait a minute. You said lifeboat—not just boat." Her gaze narrowed. "This happened during the storm, didn't it?"

"You aren't going to let this go, are you?" He'd learned that much about her stubbornness. Yet if she knew the worst about him, she'd want nothing to do with him. He couldn't let that happen.

"My schooner was to land at San Pedro—that's the port for the Pueblo de Los Angeles. Normally good weather, like this today, comes with the northwest wind. Southeasters bring the bad weather where heavy black clouds roll in." He swallowed hard, remembering. "But it was neither. It was freakish—coming out of the north-east, with the strangest sky I'd ever seen. It pushed us farther south. The ocean had a force all its own. We started taking on water and had to man the lifeboats. I went forward to help Saunders, my senior officer, cut the boat loose from some debris. Before I could get back to my seat, a wave swept Linnea and Hannah overboard."

"Oh, Stuart." Her teasing mood had evaporated.

He didn't want her pity. "I dove in. Amazingly I caught hold of them both. I kicked for the surface, but couldn't get any closer. Linnea must have known I was struggling—trying to save both her and Hannah. I wasn't going to let go of either of them. But then she let go. Linnea simply let go."

He waited for the bitterness and self-hate to come as it did after his dreams, but it didn't come. He just felt numb. "Ironic, isn't it? I must have rescued at least ten people since manning the light tower, yet I couldn't save Linnea."

"It sounds as though it wasn't your choice."

"Oh, I had a choice, all right" he said bitterly. "Let Hannah drown while I tried once more to find her mother, or take Hannah to the surface."

She stared at him through eyes clear and steady. "That's no choice at all. You did the only thing you could have done."

He wanted to believe her, but there was that small voice inside him that said if only he'd tried harder, if only he'd been stronger. "Linnea had a slight build, but she was strong. She had a fierce hold while sitting in the lifeboat. Why didn't she hold on like that just a little while longer?"

"So Linnea made the choice for you. Since she knew you did not have the strength to save both her and her daughter."

The thought had crossed his mind before. He'd been afraid to believe it.

Rachel scanned the horizon. "That was three years ago, Stuart. How long do you plan to punish yourself?" she turned back to face him. "Don't you see? You've proven yourself by the way you've honored Linnea's memory. You've done a good job with Hannah. It's time to let it go, to forgive yourself. I'm sure Linnea would want that."

He stood and walked away a few paces. He couldn't accept this absolution she offered. She still didn't know the half of it—not about the murder, or the fact that Hannah wasn't even his child. "You don't understand. It was my ship. My responsibility. I've known the sea all my life, known the pull of the tides like they were inside me. Linnea should have been safe. It was my fault she died." *A man takes care of his own.*

While Caleb handled the reins on the bumpy ride back to town, Rachel sat next to him and contemplated what she had learned that day. The scar on Stuart's forehead was nothing compared to the scar on his heart. That one hadn't healed—might never heal. The rumors in town were wrong. He wasn't a fugitive from justice, he was a fugitive from himself. He couldn't forgive himself for Linnea's death.

In his unguarded moments, Rachel had caught a

glimpse of what he must have been like before he lost his wife. It scared her how desperately she wanted him to be like that again.

She buried her face in her hands as the thought came to her. She loved him! *Oh, Lord help her, she loved him.*

Chapter Fourteen

A brisk November breeze bit into Stuart's face while he looped Blanco's reins over the hitching rail in front of the mercantile and helped Hannah down. He took her hand and stepped onto the boardwalk, his gaze drawn across the square to the parsonage where Rachel lived. He felt a sudden tug on his hand and glanced down at Hannah. A question burned in her eyes.

"No. I'm sure they are busy. Besides, it will be dark soon." Her shoulders slumped and he almost smiled at the sluggish gait she assumed. He felt the same way. He couldn't block Rachel from his mind. Constantly he wondered what she was doing. An unfamiliar twinge of jealousy shot through him as he thought of her visiting with friends and neighbors, going on about her daily life here in town—especially her relationship with Morley.

How he wished he didn't have to deal with that man today. But his was the only mercantile between here and Old San Diego. He had no choice.

Two large barrels full of apples propped open the double doors to the shop. A tall woman in a dark dress stood behind the counter, her back to him as she reached for a jar of peppermint sticks on the highest shelf. She could just touch the jar, pushing it away from her when she probed for it.

"I'll get that for you," Stuart said.

At his voice, the woman spun around, a relieved look on her face. "Thank you. I would not bother you, but the step stool broke this morning."

"No trouble, ma'am." He walked around the end of the counter, took the jar from the shelf and handed it to her. Her cool fingers touched his a second longer than necessary. Still, she drew back and her eyes widened when she caught sight of his scar.

"Elizabeth!" Terrance strode through the doorway from the back storeroom. A scowl darkened his face when he saw Stuart.

Elizabeth jumped back at his voice, and Stuart noticed her resemblance in mannerism and height to the clerk, but where Terrance's brown eyes were suspicious and beady, hers held a friendly warmth. "Is there something I can help you with today, sir?"

"A few supplies for the lighthouse. I'll need a receipt to give to the board." He drew a folded piece of paper from his pocket and handed it to her.

"What lovely printing," Elizabeth said, her gaze moving from him to Hannah. "Here, dear." She handed Hannah a peppermint stick. "Because your father was so nice to help me." Looking back at Stuart she said, "I'll get these things directly."

Stuart relaxed slightly. He squeezed Hannah's hand and began to look about the store.

"Please don't handle the items unless you plan to purchase them," Terrance said. "And keep hold of that girl of yours."

Coldness washed through Stuart as Terrance stepped closer. Stuart met his stare with a measuring one of his own.

"You had mail this week." Terrance retrieved an envelope from his desk and slapped it on the counter. "We'll be getting mail drops more often now that the U.S. Army is moving to Ballast Point."

Stuart had seen the soldiers at the whaling station. "What of the Johnson Company?"

"They have to leave. Just as well, I guess. The whales are hunted out."

Outside, hard footsteps fell on the boardwalk as somebody ran by the front of the store, stopped and tripped back to the doorway.

"Caleb," Elizabeth called, shaking her finger at him. "You better get home. Your sister was here not fifteen minutes ago looking for you."

The boy ignored Elizabeth's warning. Instead he walked over to Hannah, hunkered down and tugged on the white ribbon sash from her navy blue dress. "Hey! Where's the dance?"

Hannah smiled, dropped Stuart's hand and signed something to Caleb.

"Whoa! You can't be ahead of me on your sand dollar collection. I don't believe you."

Hannah nodded, pure superiority shining from her face.

"Well, maybe…" He scratched his head as though perturbed. "I have a surprise at my house. Want to come?" He glanced at Stuart for permission.

At the thought of seeing Rachel, hope pulsed unexpectedly through Stuart. He turned to Elizabeth—her finger rested halfway down the piece of paper—then nodded to Caleb. "I'll collect her when I'm finished here."

"Come on, Hannah. I'm late. Bye, Miss Morley." Caleb raised a hand in farewell to Elizabeth who had stopped to watch the exchange. He tore out of the shop and dashed down the street with Hannah in tow.

A stunned look crossed Elizabeth's face. "My! I don't remember ever seeing Caleb so…so… He actually teased your daughter!"

Terrance walked up to the counter in front of Stuart. "You and Caleb seem to know each other quite well. Funny, I don't remember you speaking with him much at the picnic."

Stuart matched Terrance's hard stare but didn't enlighten him. What Caleb and he did with their time wasn't Morley's business.

"Hurry up, Elizabeth." Terrance tossed the words over his shoulder. "I'm sure he needs to get home before dark. You aren't supposed to leave the lighthouse, are you? There's a rule to that effect."

The challenge in Terrance's words was unmistakable.

Stuart turned away from the taunting. Elizabeth

hastened to fetch his supplies, her movements nervous and flighty. Terrance had her jumping to his every mood. How could Rachel think for a minute she would be happy with this man? He could barely stand the thought of him treating her as he did his sister.

Stuart strode to the far side of the room. A slow burn built inside at the way the man manipulated people. Terrance wouldn't have lasted long on one of Dorian's ships. He'd have been food for the sharks. Stuart glanced down at the letter in his hands. The writing was familiar. It was not signed, but he knew it was from Saunders: "Had a visitor yesterday. Lots of questions. He's still looking. Best to take note. S."

Saunders could easily talk a man into a comatose state, but when it came to writing, his letters were short—and few and far between at that. Stuart let out a long breath. Dorian was still searching for Hannah—and him.

When would that man give up? Had the time come for him and Hannah to move on? Stuart could think of only one reason to stay—Rachel.

"What's that your girl does with her hands?" Terrance said, pulling Stuart back to his surroundings.

Hadn't Rachel told him? He thought for sure she would have.

Elizabeth cleared her throat. "Anything else, Mr. Taylor?"

At the shake of his head, she pushed the slatted box of supplies toward his side of the counter. He paid quickly and, under the skeptical eye of Morley, carried the box to his horse. One by one he settled the apples and other items into his saddlebags, distributing the weight evenly. He started back into the store to return the box, but stopped short at the sound of heated voices coming from inside.

Elizabeth's voice rose. "All I have to say is that you had better watch yourself. If Rachel is meeting with that child as you suspect, she's also seeing him. You'd better make up your mind between her and Amanda."

"She wouldn't do that to me. Not Rachel. She has more class than that."

"Open your eyes. She's a woman. And a very independent one."

Stuart dropped the box by the doorway and strode to his horse. Hadn't Rachel mentioned her work to anyone? If Terrance and his sister were suspicious of her comings and goings, did the whole town wonder? Why had she kept it a secret? But he knew the answer to that—she'd lose her job without a doubt. The school board wouldn't stand for her visiting a single man and his girl.

Maybe he'd been wrong to ask her to tutor.

He glanced back at the lighted mercantile, watching Elizabeth's silhouette as she pulled the blinds. He'd lived for so long without a thought for anyone but himself and Hannah that he'd conveniently continued that way after Rachel and Caleb started coming to the lighthouse. He hadn't given any thought to the complications it might add to Rachel's life—the gossip, the speculation.

Until now....

People could be cruel. Just look at the way they'd treated Hannah. Why did he think they'd be any nicer to Rachel? They would circle like sharks the minute they sensed blood.

The mercantile door closed with a bang, shattering Stuart's thoughts. The store's lamps were out. Terrance locked the door and followed his sister down the board-walk, their footsteps echoing loudly until the sound died away into the stillness of twilight. That weasel Terrance didn't deserve Rachel.

But then…neither did he.

The strong aroma of bean soup filtered out into the night air as he led Blanco toward the parsonage. He heard voices coming from the back of the house. He tied Blanco's reins to a large saltbush and walked into the backyard.

A big black dog poked her nose out of the carriage house doorway and watched him. Behind her a small chorus of whining and yipping started up. The sound of whispers came from the shadowed building. A moment later Caleb emerged with Hannah at his side. Both of them carried a whimpering bit of black fluff. Hannah grinned at Stuart.

"Be careful of the pup's teeth, Hannah," Rachel warned from behind him. "They're sharp, like little cactus needles."

He spun around. She stood on the back house steps, wiping her hands on her apron. The way her sleeves were rolled up, he must have caught her in the middle of cooking supper. She looked hot, disheveled and beauti-ful. The urge to kiss her swept over him like a tidal wave.

Behind her Reverend Crouse cleared his throat. Rachel stiffened at the sound. And in that moment

Stuart realized she hadn't said a word to anyone about her trips to the lighthouse.

He nodded, shoving his hands into his pockets. "Miss Houston...Pastor. Cute pups. How many?"

"Eight in the litter." Her voice sounded strained. She wasn't very good at deception. She had better pray the pastor stayed behind her where he couldn't see her face. "These are the last two."

"How old?"

"Over three months now."

He crouched down next to Hannah and patted the pup on its rump. "Which one do you like best?"

She held up a black puppy marked with white on its chest and paws.

"My favorite also," Rachel said, her voice steadier. She stepped down to the ground. "We may keep that one."

"I think she wants the pup for herself, Rach," Caleb said. "She hasn't let go of it."

"Well, that's up to your father, Hannah. It might be hard to watch after both you and a puppy."

Hannah turned hopeful eyes on him. And he sighed. A puppy would be more work.

"Caleb," Reverend Crouse said. "The Women's Circle is meeting in one hour. Get on over to the church and sweep the meeting room before we sit down to eat."

Caleb grimaced, but unloaded the puppy he held. "See you later." He loped across the yard and disappeared into the church's side door.

"You are welcome to join us for supper, Mr. Taylor," said Reverend Crouse.

Stuart would be willing to sit across the table from this man and listen to his preaching if it meant he could be with Rachel a little longer. Of course Hannah would love to stay, but he was afraid he might let something slip out about their trips to the lighthouse. It was obvious Rachel hadn't told the reverend anything.

Stuart took the puppy from his daughter's arms. "No, thanks. I need to get back to the lighthouse. It'll be dark soon."

Shaking his head, Reverend Crouse went inside. A whiff of cooking beans escaped as the door opened and closed.

"He doesn't know." Stuart nodded after the man.

In the lantern light pouring from the kitchen window, Rachel's cheeks flamed scarlet. "I asked him after the picnic. He didn't want me to tutor. He said the people here would fire me. They wouldn't want me teaching their children."

"He's right." He glanced down at the puppy in Hannah's arms. He was stalling, he knew. He didn't want things to change, but he couldn't have Rachel hurt. And after reading Saunders's note, he needed to think about moving on soon. The tutoring would have to stop. "Listen, if you don't have a home for this pup, we'll take him." At his side, Hannah beamed up at him. Perhaps it would help her get through the next few months without Rachel.

"I'll get you a sack for the ride." Rachel disappeared into the house and then came back with an empty flour sack. "He'll be coated with flour dust by the time you get home," she said as she handed it to him.

"No matter." Stuart put the puppy into the sack and tied a knot in the end, then looped it over his saddle horn. "Just for the ride home, little mite. Can't have you falling off and getting hurt." A miniature sneeze erupted from inside the bag.

He lifted Hannah onto Blanco then climbed on behind her. At last he faced Rachel. "Look," he said reluctantly, "I appreciate all you've done with Hannah, but it is time to reconsider this arrangement."

Her gaze flashed to his. "You don't mean that."

He blocked out the hurt in her plea, the ache in his chest. Caring for her only made it more important he do this. He had to take the responsibility to do the right thing. "You shouldn't come anymore, Rachel."

"But—"

He stopped her with a hard stare. "Don't come anymore."

With a slight tilt to his seat he urged Blanco from the yard. Out on the street he couldn't keep himself from looking back once. She stood, a lone black figure silhouetted against the shadow of the house.

Stuart whipped the rope around the bar and pulled it taut, then tied a half hitch to secure the dory in place. The wind had kicked up during the night, and the surf, higher than usual, had pounded against the lean-to, undermining one of the support beams. Days would pass before he could get to town for the supplies to fix it. Besides, he wanted to avoid town.

A bittersweet ache started in the pit of his belly... again. Like a knife already planted there, twisting, always twisting. This was crazy! He had no right to even think of her, let alone want her. How many times had he told himself over the past month that he didn't deserve her?

He spun on his heel and walked down the beach calling for Hannah. He found her searching through the tidal pools, the pup dancing around her heels.

"What have you found now?"

She held up a sand dollar and signed that she was saving it for Rachel.

"Rachel isn't coming anymore, Hannah. You know that."

She signed something more.

"Slow down. I can't read that fast," he said, impatient with her for bringing up the name he was trying so hard to forget. Then, angry at himself for being grouchy, he sat down on a rock to pay closer attention.

She signed again, slower this time.

He dragged his hand through his hair. "No, you didn't do anything wrong. She had to stop the lessons because—" He stopped abruptly. How could he explain things like social rules to a girl who knew nothing of people?

He gazed down the long expanse of beach. How would he stand the silence?

Funny how a man could look strong on the outside, yet on the inside feel so incredibly weary. A deep ache settled in his chest. He had tried not to care. All those he cared for he eventually hurt.

A man takes care of his own. Dorian had ingrained that truth in him from the moment he'd first signed on his ship. He'd believed those words—he still did. Yet he'd failed with Linnea. He couldn't risk failing with Rachel, too.

Hannah climbed on the rock and sat quietly beside him, in tune with the glum wanderings of his mind. He wrapped an arm around her, squeezing her close, and watched the sun start into the sea.

Chapter Fifteen

Stuart dumped a scoop of oats into the feeding bucket and stifled a yawn. He wasn't getting enough sleep. At least not enough good sleep. The minute his eyes closed he had visions of Rachel. Rachel leaning over Hannah as she studied. Rachel walking along the beach as the breeze made her bonnet ribbons dance. Green eyes. Always those green eyes. He gripped the edge of his workbench, letting the rough wood punish his palms. God he missed her. She had worked her way into his life and now his heart. Had it only been ten days since he last saw her? It seemed like an age. Yet there was no way he could see her again. It had to be over.

The sound of horse hooves against packed dirt caught his ear. He strode to the shed's door and stopped. Caleb had pulled Jericho up to the picket fence and stopped the carriage. Hannah bounded down the lighthouse steps, making a beeline for Rachel. Wide awake now, Stuart walked up and with his body, blocked

Rachel's climb from the carriage. "Turn around now and head back."

Her stormy look held a warning. "I'm going to explain and you are going to listen."

Hannah tugged at his sleeve, a hopeful expression on her upturned face. He wavered. A little. "All right. Five minutes." He reached up and helped Rachel from the carriage.

"Caleb?" Rachel called over her shoulder.

Her brother looped the reins about the brake handle. "I'll watch her. Come here, Hannah." Jumping down, he stepped to the back of the carriage and lifted a crate from the boot.

The lobster trap.

The anger Stuart had felt just a moment before released into the wind with his exhale. They'd come a long way—he and Caleb—since that morning he'd stolen the trap. Caleb waited, and when Stuart nodded his acknowledgment, set the trap down.

Without a word Stuart picked up the crate and took it to the shed. He didn't trust himself with Rachel right now. He wanted to hold her, to shake some sense into her. She should leave immediately.

He knew she had followed him when her shadow blocked the light from the doorway. He turned on her, irritated at her stubbornness, frustrated because to see her had started that ache in his chest he knew wouldn't stop. He strode toward her and pulled her from the door into the shadowed interior of the shed. "What will be your excuse today?"

The shocked look on her face quickly turned to

defiance. "Well, that's a fine hello. I'll think of someth—"

He stopped her words with a kiss, crushing her firm body to him until he could feel the length of her against him. Her hat fell off as he forced her back, her mouth stiff against his lips. It only added to his frustration. He didn't want to hurt her, but she hurt him just by being here. He was tired of playing the saint.

A shooting pain erupted in his foot as she stomped down hard. With a growl he pushed her away, watching her stumble back a step before he grabbed her arm to help her catch her balance.

Her chin went up. "Stop it, Stuart. Don't you dare kiss me in anger." Her voice trembled with suppressed emotion, and her cheeks flushed pink.

He swiped the back of his hand across his lips. "I suppose I deserved that. But dammit, Rachel, you shouldn't be here. People in town are noticing."

"It's none of their business." Her eyes glistened with unshed tears.

He dragged in a brace of air and slowly let it out, willing his heart to stop racing. "You're right about that. But whether you like it or not, your reputation is important. It's important to me. If I'd given any thought to the situation I'd have stopped the tutoring before it started. I wasn't thinking right when I first agreed to it."

She straightened her shoulders. "It wasn't all about Hannah, Stuart, as much as you may think that. I needed someone to take an interest in Caleb. He was running with the wrong group in town. His so-called friends had just set fire to one of the hide houses. They could have torched the whole town. Then at the picnic he lit that firecracker and caused Benjamin to fall. Things were out of hand. I needed help. I explained that when we first agreed to the tutoring."

"Fair enough. We both helped each other. It was a good arrangement. But it stops now." Didn't she realize he had needs? That having her so near did crazy things to him?

She crouched down to pick up her hat from the dirt floor.

"Hannah and I are thinking about moving on, anyway."

Rachel slowed as she stood, her knuckles white on the hat's brim. "You're leaving?"

He hated the plaintive question. She would think it was just one more person walking out on her, but he couldn't tell her the truth. It was better that she didn't learn he was hiding out from a murder and that Hannah wasn't his. He couldn't bear the look in her eyes if she ever discovered that. "Something's come up. And with the tutoring finished, now is a good time."

"Oh." Slowly she turned toward the door.

"I'd like to say I'm sorry about the kiss, but I'm not." He wanted much more than to kiss her. Much more.

She wouldn't look at him. "I...I'd like to spend some time with Hannah, then. And Caleb hoped to go fishing with you one more time."

He saw through her to the hurt she felt inside. He wanted to kiss it away. Wanted to hold her. He stepped forward. "Rach..." And then thought better of it. "All right. I'll take him fishing. Then we'll say our goodbyes."

Fishing turned out to be nonproductive in spite of the old tale that fish bite best before a storm. The clouds overhead had thickened into a dark-gray mass and the wind had kicked up to a mild gale that had the portent to get much worse.

Stuart started to reel in his line. "This weather is turning bad. We'd better give this up for today."

Caleb pointed out to sea. "Look at that. What are they doing out in this?"

Stuart squinted. A white sail. "I don't know. Not too smart, though. It's beyond choppy."

He stood, and the first large drops of rain splattered against his face. He made his way across the rock, finding it slippery as the rain started pelting down.

Suddenly Caleb yelled, "The boat has gone over!"

Stuart whirled around and spotted the white overturned hull of the boat, the keel listing in the growing swells. Three men clung to the boat.

"We'll need the dory," Stuart said.

They dropped their fishing gear and raced toward the lean-to. On the sand the boat was awkward and heavy. Stuart was glad to have Caleb's help maneuvering it around and into the water. By the time they made it through the waves, they were both soaked to the skin.

The wind whipped rain into their faces while they rowed out to sea. The sky had darkened to iron-metal gray, making it difficult to see the vessel between the swells. Determination filled Caleb's features, and he matched Stuart's rowing, stroke for stroke. A flash of pride surged through Stuart. The past two months had wrought a definite change in the boy.

Stuart pulled hard at the oars, straining against the battering waves. "Bear to port."

Caleb raised his brows.

"Left! Head left!"

They were thirty feet from the overturned vessel when one of the men pushed himself off and swam madly for them.

"No!" Stuart shouted. Visions of Linnea sinking in the water choked his mind. "Hang on! We'll get closer!" He hurled a coil of rope toward the struggling man. It unwound in the fierce wind and fell short of its goal.

"Samuel!" Caleb yelled.

The young man's blond head disappeared once beneath a swell, then resurfaced, panic slashed across his face.

"I'll get him," Caleb yelled and started to place his oars in the bed of the boat.

"No!" Stuart shouted. "He's tangled in the kelp. Bring the dory alongside."

Five hard strokes and they came abreast of Samuel. Fear was etched deep into the sharp angles of his face. He flailed his arms, trying to move closer to the boat. Caleb leaned over the dory's side, his stomach pressed against the hard ridge of wood, and stretched out his hands.

Samuel clamped on with a death grip.

"Hang on!" Caleb ground out through clenched teeth, pulling against the heavier weight. He slid toward the water. Stuart sprang forward and anchored Caleb's feet. For an instant Sam furrowed through a rising swell, dragging a heavy line of kelp around his legs. Then he lost his grip and slipped under the surface.

Stuart yanked Caleb back into the boat, relieved he hadn't followed Sam into the water. He searched for a trace of the boy. A field of amber kelp twisted just beneath surface, thick and tangled.

"We gotta do something!" Caleb cried. Desperation filled his face. He looked wildly about the floor of the dory. Suddenly he pulled his knife from his pocket.

Stuart lunged forward. "No! Caleb!"

But Caleb dove into the frigid water and Stuart's fingers closed on empty air.

Stuart looked at the men hanging from the sailboat hull and knew his eyes mirrored the dread that filled theirs. If he jumped in after Caleb like his gut instinct told him to do, those men would pay with their lives if he didn't return. So he stayed where he was, gripping the edge of the dory, ready to drag Caleb aboard the second he surfaced.

A full minute passed with no sign of either boy. Then Sam broke the water's surface and dragged in a lungful of air. Stuart lunged toward him, grabbed his shirt and then hoisted under his arms while the boy inched his leg over the side of the dory and fell into the boat, coughing and spitting out saltwater.

Seconds later Caleb surfaced.

"Thank God!" Stuart breathed and tugged the boy into the boat.

Caleb shivered violently.

Stuart grabbed Caleb by the collar and shook him. "You're lucky you didn't just go to meet your Maker. Don't you ever pull a stunt like that again!" He locked his arm about Caleb's neck and hugged him tight.

The sailboat floated thirty feet away now. Swells rose in a contrary rhythm between the two crafts, propelling them apart. At one point the gap between the two boats closed enough that Caleb, with a loud grunt, heaved the rope. One man caught the end but there was no place for him to tie it to the boat. He nodded to his companion. "You go, John."

The heavy man clung to the keel of the sailboat and refused to budge.

"Let go," Stuart yelled. "Make your way over."

"I can't! Me arms are bloody numb. I'll sink like a stone if I let go."

Stuart cupped his hands about his mouth. "You don't have a choice. You have to do it."

"I can't, I tell you. There's got to be another way."

Caleb leaned toward Stuart, a question in his eyes. "I could jump in again."

"No!" Stuart roared. "Help me on the rope. We'll get closer."

Together they pulled, straining against the swells, hand over hand, until the dory came alongside the sailboat. Stuart's fingers were nerveless from the cold. How had the men managed to hang on for so long?

John floundered like a big fish, struggling to climb into the dory. Stuart and Caleb grabbed each of his arms and heaved up. With a final, awkward kick, John landed in the bottom of the boat.

"You next, Russ!" Sam yelled through chattering teeth.

Russ gripped the rope with both hands and let Caleb and Stuart pull him across the water and into the dory.

The three sailors lay sprawled across the floor of the boat, shivering and wet, but alive.

Stuart took up his oars and with Caleb's help turned the dory toward the beach. Soon the boat surged ahead and he had the chance to consider his "catch." Russ appeared to be in his fifties and John somewhat younger, perhaps thirty-five. Sam, the youngest, stared at Caleb with a closed expression. By the cut of his clothes, Stuart pegged him for a "Sunday" fisherman.

A thought blindsided him. They were from La Playa—at least Sam was—which meant they knew Rachel. A sinking sensation filled him and he searched for another choice rather than to take them to the lighthouse. His gaze lighted on John—wet, cold, and exhausted—and he had his answer. There *was* no better choice.

Rachel pulled the cotton curtain aside and peered through the rain-streaked window. Something was wrong—terribly wrong. Otherwise Stuart and Caleb would have been back rather than out in this foul weather. She brushed her fingertips over her bruised lips, remembering the embrace. Remembering how her body had wanted to respond, although she refused to give in. Never had she seen Stuart so angry.

And he was leaving.

She turned and paced the length of the small kitchen. Where could he be? Why hadn't he returned by now? She checked the coffeepot for the umpteenth time to make sure the coffee hadn't boiled away, just as Hannah dashed from the kitchen table to the door. But instead of shutting the door after looking outside, she swung it wide with a bang.

Rachel followed her to the door to find not only Caleb and Stuart, but three other men soaked to the skin.

"Their boat capsized just off the rock," Stuart said.

He had a scrape along his right cheek, red and raw, but not bleeding. She glanced quickly over Caleb. Although he was wet and shivering, otherwise he looked unharmed. "Is everyone all right?"

A heavy, bearded man stepped forward and nodded. "Thanks to Caleb and Mr. Taylor, miss. Just soaked through to the bones."

She recognized the boy at the rear of the group. "Samuel?"

He nodded. "It's me under all this water."

"Your family will be relieved to know you're well."

Stuart caught her attention. "Would you make coffee while I find towels and blankets?"

"Of course. Please, all of you come in by the fire and dry off." She grabbed a chair from the kitchen and carried it into the parlor to set it close before the small brick fireplace. She'd kept the fire going, finding it cheery on this stormy afternoon, but now she tossed on extra coal for added warmth.

When she turned and dusted off her hands, she caught the men watching her. She could feel the precise moment their looks turned to speculation about why she was here. Warmth flooded her cheeks and she fled to the kitchen, wanting to evaporate on the spot. Since disappearing into the cracks in the limestone wall wasn't an option, she busied herself making strong coffee and trying to erase the embarrassment from her mind.

Upstairs, Stuart called for Hannah to gather towels and blankets. Before a cricket would have had time to warm up his legs, Hannah returned, loaded down with comforters, and shyly passed them out to the shivering group.

When Stuart didn't return immediately, Rachel wondered what he was doing, but then through the window she saw the lamp's beam of light sweep across the low cloud cover. The sight did little to comfort her jumpy nerves. It was getting dark. She should be on her way home.

She didn't want to go back into the parlor and face the questioning stares of the men. She wanted to slip out with Caleb and pretend none of this had happened. But the coffee was ready, they were cold, and hiding in the kitchen wasn't helping anybody. She stepped over to the stove and filled each mug. Footsteps sounded on the circular stairs and at their sound relief grew in her— relief that she wouldn't have to face the men alone. She placed the mugs on a tray and looked up as Stuart appeared.

He had changed from his wet clothes into dry pants and was fastening the last button on his shirt when he stopped at the bottom of the stairs. "You know your way around this kitchen like it was yours."

"Unfortunately, I believe the men noticed that too. Stuart—what should we tell them?"

He rubbed his forehead, his eyes clouding with concern. "Nothing. We'll say nothing." He sighed. "We didn't count on this. Come on. We'll go in together."

The men sat in front of the fireplace rubbing their hands before the heat. Each murmured thanks and told her his name when he took his mug of steaming coffee but still she felt the questions behind their politeness. They sipped the coffee and soon looked more revived from their ordeal.

"So—" Stuart said, sitting Hannah on his knee. "How did it happen?"

John shifted in his seat. "Samuel, you might as well tell it. I expect he'll be makin' a report."

Stuart nodded, but Sam didn't say anything.

"It's a bit embarrassin' y' see," John explained. "We were fishing the kelp beds. Got an early start this mornin'. Expected the weather to clear off like it usually does by ten or so. The bloody storm took us by surprise." He glanced at Rachel. "Excuse my language, miss."

Sam looked up from his place on the floor. "We did catch two good-size yellowtail. Guess that don't matter now. We figured we had time to catch one more fish. Then the wind came up and we laughed about having a race to the harbor. We hoisted the sail and right away a gust slammed into the sheet and tipped the boat way over. Russ lost his balance and fell into me and I grabbed on to John. The next thing I knew we all were in the water and the boat was upside down."

John slapped his knee. "Young Sam here wanted to swim for shore! Only thing that stopped him was he knew the rest of us couldn't make it. At least not me. My whole body was numb."

"You were right to stay with the boat," Stuart said.

"How'd you find us?"

"We were fishing off the large rock, just getting ready to leave when Caleb spotted you."

Samuel met Caleb's gaze. "Thanks for jumping in after me. Guess what I did was pretty dumb."

The men glanced at each other.

"After all," Sam continued, "all I ever done since you moved here was get you in trouble."

Caleb shrugged. "I've always been a pretty good swimmer."

Rachel gasped, looking from one boy to the next. "You didn't go in, Caleb! Tell me you didn't!"

"I'm all right, Rach."

His words did not reassure her. "How would I live with myself? Never, never do such a thing again!"

"He won't have another chance." Finality filled Stuart's voice. He slid Hannah from his knee. "When you get to town," he said to Caleb, "let Sam's folks know about the accident. Have them send a wagon back."

"That sounds fine," John said. "My brother will want to reward you, anyway."

Rachel started. It was embarrassing enough these men knew she was here. But the whole town—what if everyone found out? How could she face them? She met Stuart's gaze and knew he was thinking the same thoughts.

"No reward," he said quickly.

"But you're a hero! Both of you!" Samuel sputtered.

"I was doing my job."

John shrugged his shoulders. "Have it your way, then. What about you Caleb? We'd still be out there if it weren't for you. You're the one who spotted us and dove in after Sam."

All eyes turned to Caleb. His face turned pink in the firelight as he basked in John's praise, but he shook his head. "No reward."

Rachel could have kissed him.

"All right. I doubt you'll ever see us out there for a second chance."

Murmurs of agreement filled the room.

"Is there any hope of saving the sailboat?" Samuel asked.

Stuart shook his head. "I'll keep an eye out for it, but most likely it will be smashed on the rocks by morning."

Rachel glanced out the window. Rain pelted steadily against the glass and the sky was a deep pewter color. The ride home would be a slow, wet one. She stood and gathered the mugs. "I'll just be a minute."

She hurried from the room, feeling their stares marking her back. In the kitchen, she set the cups into the large wash pan on the stove, then poured steaming water from the kettle over the few dishes. She was suddenly acutely aware she could never return here, never work with Hannah again, never see Stuart again. Her eyes stung.

"Not much light left," Stuart said from the doorway, "but enough to get you home if you leave the dishes and start now." Hannah stood at his side, clinging to his arm.

Her hands stilled in the wash water. "It's over, isn't it?"

He dragged a hand through his hair. "You're a big

girl, Rachel. I think you had an idea when you started coming here that a day like today was inevitable. I don't want you in any more trouble on my account."

When had seeing him become as important to her as breathing?

She dried her hands and held open her arms to Hannah. Crouching down, she hugged the girl tightly. Tears blurred her vision, but she kept her smile in place. "You must keep practicing your letters so you can write to me."

Hannah nodded.

"Check on Sarah," Stuart said quietly, nodding his head toward the stairs. "I'll be up soon."

After Hannah left, Rachel turned back to Stuart. "The other night at my house, you were right to tell me not to come. I understood the consequences. But Stuart, given the chance, I'd do it all again. I have no regrets."

He placed his hands firmly on her shoulders. The heat from his palms burned into her skin, familiar now, reassuring. "We haven't done anything wrong, Rachel. Don't let them tell you that you have."

She looked into his blue eyes. How could she never come back? Never see him again? Her chest ached at the thought. With trembling fingers, she brushed the familiar wisp of hair off his brow, and then just as slowly traced the bruise forming around the gash on his cheek. *So many scars.*

His gaze locked on hers. "Rachel…don't."

A shiver raced through her. He pulled her against his chest and she breathed in the scent of rain on his skin. His heartbeat pounded in her ear, and she thought he must have stopped breathing because surely she had.

"I gave you fair warning," he murmured. With strong fingers he tilted her head back and slowly lowered his mouth to hers. Tenderly he deepened the kiss until he seemed to draw out her very soul. If not for holding him about his neck, she'd have fallen.

"Rachel," he whispered, his warm breath caressing her ear. "I'm sorry if I've hurt you."

Beneath her hands, the muscles in his shoulders rippled. He kissed her once more, softly this time. This kiss said goodbye. Slowly he pulled away.

"Stuart, I—"

He pressed his fingertips to her mouth. "Don't. Just go."

She stood there, shaken, while he spun around and headed for the stairs. With a trembling hand she brushed her fingertips across her lips. "I'm not sorry. Not for any of it," she whispered. He paused at her words but did not look back, then continued up the stairs two at a time.

She stepped outside, barely noticing the stinging wind on her cheeks, and closed the door behind her.

Chapter Sixteen

The final notes of "God of Our Fathers" rang out over the small congregation. Rachel sighed with relief. Only the closing hymn to get through while everyone filed out of the church.

She glanced up from the piano and met Terrance's gaze in the third pew. Her stomach rolled into a knot. Again. Throughout the service he'd watched her, a suspicious stare on his face. He couldn't know about her part in the boat rescue, could he? Her cheeks heated with the thought. She looked out over the congregation. Sam and his family were conspicuously absent.

Reverend Crouse said the benediction, and she stretched out her fingers and forced herself to begin the final hymn. When the last person had left the building to join those visiting on the street, Terrance strode toward her.

"A little rusty today," he said, raising one eyebrow. "Two mistakes."

She closed the hymnal with a thud. "I'd better practice this week."

"Thought you were out at the Hummels' on Friday." His eyes sharpened on her hers. "I rode out there to deliver their new water pump. Didn't see you."

A moment of panic seized her. She wouldn't lie, but what could she say? "The weather turned so ugly that I decided to return early."

He watched her face closely. Her heart pounding, she put the hymnal back on the small music shelf.

"Are you still coming for dinner today?"

She had completely forgotten their plans!

Terrance's smile appeared strained. "You know, your face is transparent at times. I'll be by for you at one o'clock. Don't forget."

When he left, Rachel slumped on the bench and stared at the piano keys. Terrance had been toying with her. He knew something.

By Wednesday Rachel felt a little calmer. It appeared no one was wise to her recent excursions and life could go on as though her time with Stuart and Hannah hadn't existed. The thought was both comforting and disturbing. In her heart she'd never forget it.

How could something that felt so right be so wrong?

She cleaned up the remnants of breakfast from the table and dumped the scraps into a bowl for Settie. Today would be her day for getting on with her life. After school, her first stop would be the mercantile to mail her application for the teacher's certification test.

Someone banged on the front door. Before she could

reach it, Terrance burst in, his face twisted with anger. In one hand he held the keys to his store and in the other, the *San Diego Herald*.

"Rachel!" Fury filled his voice when he caught sight of her.

Apprehension stilled her. "What is it?"

"That's what I'd like to know. I was just opening the store when I saw this." He shook the newspaper. "What were you and Caleb doing at the lighthouse?"

"Let me see, Terrance," she said, striving to remain calm.

He shoved the newspaper at her. A front-page story lauding Stuart and Caleb's heroic rescue paraded before her eyes.

"Oh, no," she murmured and sank to a chair. The newspaper! This was much worse than she could have imagined. Now the entire town would know.

"What is going on?" Terrance demanded.

Certain phrases stood out more sharply than others. Phrases such as: "The coffee served by Miss Rachel Houston did much to revive the spirits of the soggy fishermen before they took their leave." She leaned over and covered her face with her hands.

Terrance finally sat in the chair opposite her. "Don't even think about coming up with a lie."

"Terrance—"

His usually pale complexion had turned a mottled pink. "I don't know what kind of game you are playing but I won't have it played on me! You've been out to that lighthouse more than just once. That girl is learning her letters and hand signals. Admit it! All these weeks you've been spending time with that dumb girl and her father."

The attack on Hannah helped Rachel stiffen her spine. "She is not dumb!"

Terrance jabbed at the paper. "What were you doing out there? He's the same man who shot at Enrique! You know he's not stable."

"They were just warning shots. And Enrique deserved a scare. He stole from Mr. Taylor's lobster traps, as a regular occurrence, I might add."

Terrance paced back and forth. "It's different when you see him in town. He wouldn't dare raise a hand to you here, but out there he is on his own land. You would have no protection from him."

"He's not dangerous. You are blowing this all out of proportion, Terrance."

"Do you admit you've been out there more than once?"

"You're doing an excellent job of putting two and two together." Anger built inside her. She didn't deserve his outrage. He didn't have any say over her. "I have my reasons for doing what I did and they are good ones. You don't own me."

Terrance stepped back at her words. "Does Reverend Crouse know?" he asked.

"No. Not yet at least. Not until he reads this." She slapped the newspaper down on the tea wagon between them. "Terrance, all I've done is help Hannah. Is that such a terrible thing?"

"How long has this been going on, Rachel?"

She sighed, noticing how he'd ignored her question. "Since the picnic."

"The picnic! That was over three months ago!"

"I felt I—the church—owed the man something after he saved Benjamin."

"What else has he demanded in payment?"

"Nothing!" Rachel cried, shocked at what he suggested. "And he didn't demand the tutoring. All he cares about is his daughter and her happiness. Trust me on this, Terrance."

"Trust you! How? Why?"

"I've done nothing wrong."

He looked at her down his long nose. "Prove it, then. Prove to me he hasn't taught you a thing or two while you've been teaching his child."

He grabbed her arms and pulled her toward him. She struggled, suddenly frightened of this new Terrance.

He stared hard at her a moment and then shoved her away. "I guess you haven't learned much."

She trembled. "You need to leave, Terrance. I'll see you after you've calmed down."

"If I thought he had touched you, I would…" He sighed and didn't continue.

But he left more than enough room for her to worry. The way he said the words scared her—so quietly, so very calmly.

"I know we weren't officially courting, Rachel, but I thought we had an understanding."

She tried to gather her thoughts. "There have been no words of commitment between you and me. Just friendship. Until now."

He snorted. "My sister was right. I put you on a

pedestal. The daughter of a gold panner. What a fool."
He squared his shoulders. "There will be talk at the
township meeting tomorrow night. Are you still planning to take the teacher's examination?"

"Yes, of course."

"The school board members may not want you
teaching their children."

Stunned, she stuttered, "No…they wouldn't go that
far." Would they?

"This affects everything." He waved the newspaper in
the air. "I've lived here all my life. I know these people."

"Terrance. Caleb was with me."

"Every time?"

She nodded. "Yes."

"I'll mention that in my report. I don't know that it
will help much."

"Thank you." Her intentions had only been for good.
How had they become so distorted?

"Rachel Houston!" The kitchen door slammed shut.
Reverend Crouse stomped down the hall and into the
parlor, followed quickly by his wife. He ignored
Terrance and slapped another copy of the newspaper
into her lap. "Explain yourself!"

"I…uh…"

"Have you been at the lighthouse?"

She nodded, miserable. "I've been tutoring Hannah."

The reverend suddenly noticed Terrance. "I hope you
realize this has been without my knowledge, Mr. Morley."

Terrance nodded. "We've discussed it. The article
disrupted an otherwise peaceful morning."

Terrance looked at her as though she were a misguided child. "I believe Rachel when she says that nothing happened, but there are people that won't."

Emma Crouse nodded. "Mabel and Phyllis Olsen came to see me this morning. They wanted answers. This is only the beginning." She bustled over to sit next to Rachel on the settee. "Are you all right, dear? Has he done anything to hurt you?"

Rachel shook her head. "No. He has acted the gentleman on each occasion." She refused to tell them about the one time when he kissed her in anger.

"Well, then it will all work out. You'll see." Emma hugged her firmly.

Reverend Crouse picked up his copy of the paper. "You'll have to bear the consequences of your actions. They may not be pleasant."

"I wasn't naive about my choice in this. If it causes any repercussions on your ministry—well, that I hadn't counted on."

He sighed and patted her hand awkwardly. "It won't matter there. Emma and I have had to handle many situations over the years."

Terrance squared his shoulders. "It's earlier than we anticipated, but perhaps this would be the opportune time to announce our engagement. A solid front would help ward off the gossips."

Startled, Rachel looked up at Terrance. "You're serious," she said, amazed at the turn in conversation.

He nodded.

"But why?" After seeing what lay beneath his surface, she was sure he wasn't for her. Besides, her heart was already taken, whether Stuart wanted it or not.

The reverend looked just as surprised as she felt, but recovered quickly, a smile growing on his face. "Yes. Yes! Splendid idea."

"No." She stood, and repeated firmly, "No."

Terrance frowned. "You've made a mess of things, Rachel. It's up to you to fix them. Besides, marrying me will take the pressure off. You can help in the mercantile and you won't need to worry about teaching anymore. You won't even have to bother with the examination."

Terrance took her hands in his, his voice smooth and gentle—so gentle she could almost forget the bruising pressure of his fingers on her shoulders just moments before. "This is where we were heading—you and I. We'll just shorten the usual waiting time. People won't dare talk about my fiancée if they want to do business with me."

"I...I'm not sure I..."

"Trust me in this. You'll find it's the sensible thing to do. You've let your heart rule, rather than your head. Unfortunately, that is a hazard of being a woman."

She stiffened.

"Don't misunderstand me," he said quickly. "Your soft heart will be an asset when dealing with me and with the children we'll have one day. I'll balance it as the one expected to discipline and keep you all in line."

A sickening sensation built in her stomach. He was serious! After all she'd been through with her father—living in a tent with the dust and the flies, trying to make dinner out of hard tack and gruel, following him from stream to stream in search of gold—she wasn't about to give up her independence over something like this, no matter what happened to her reputation. She pulled her hands from his. "This is a noble gesture, Terrance, but the truth is…I don't love you."

Chapter Seventeen

"I don't care what you say," Amanda Furst declared and hung the last crocheted ornament on the pine tree. "A Christmas without snow is not Christmas at all."

Amanda, Elizabeth and Rachel were putting the finishing touches on the decorations for the community party that evening. The meeting room in the Mexican Custom House was just the right size for the gathering. They had pushed the chairs to the walls to make room for dancing to the mariachi band and hung large bows on each of the wall sconces to perk up the plain room. The pine tree filled one corner and the podium another.

From her perch on the ladder, Elizabeth fastened a sprig of mistletoe to the front doorway and exchanged a smile with Amanda. Rachel wondered at their sudden friendship. Elizabeth had never been one to put up with Amanda before, but ever since the newspaper article came out three weeks ago, they'd begun doing things together...and excluding Rachel. They only helped with the party preparations today because they had promised weeks ago.

Rachel steadied the ladder as Elizabeth climbed down, and then they moved it to the center of the room to hang the piñata, a festively painted pottery jar filled with candy and dried fruit.

"Are the games ready?" Elizabeth asked after securing the rope that would be used to raise and lower the piñata. It was the first question she'd directed at Rachel all afternoon.

Rachel nodded.

"Then I guess we are done," she said, wiping her hands on her apron. "I need to get back to help at the store."

Amanda shrugged into her cloak and flipped her blond hair over her fox fur collar. "Sorry I can't stay and help clean up the mess. I'll walk over with you, Liz."

Rachel watched them go, hurt by their uncharacteristic coolness, then began picking up the trail of colored ribbons and cut paper snowflakes. She adjusted the poinsettia arrangement on the table for the fourth time, wishing the party tonight was already over. She didn't want to face the stares and whispered speculations, but Reverend and Emma Crouse depended on her help. Emma had told her she must act as if everything was fine, that she'd done nothing wrong. The same way she'd been acting for the past three weeks. When were people going to recognize the truth for what it was and let things get back to normal?

The cleanup didn't take long, and soon Rachel left, walking to the parsonage while the sun set and sent its last splash of orange-pink rays spreading across the harbor.

That evening she dressed carefully—a cream-colored, full-skirted dress with a deep-blue sash. She had sown tiny seed pearls in two rows along the modest neckline. It had been tedious work, but she found that it soothed her. Since she was no longer tutoring, she'd had time to take out Caleb's pants at the cuffs and even help Emma with some of her mending. Bolstering her courage to face those at the party, she threw her cloak over her shoulders and headed out the door.

Rachel took a place next to Emma and helped serve the cider punch as people arrived. Terrance showed up with Amanda on his arm and Elizabeth at his side. They stood across the room as the children recited passages from the Book of Matthew. Benjamin played the angel bearing tidings of great joy. When the door opened and a gust of damp air blew through the room, he faltered in his speaking lines. A stranger strode in, noticed the Christmas play in progress and pulled back against the wall to watch.

After the short play Reverend Crouse addressed the group and then everyone sang a round of their favorite carols while Rachel accompanied on the piano. She tried to steel herself against the stares of several people, telling herself it was curiosity on their part—not true ill thoughts about her.

Caleb started off the games. He blindfolded little Maria and spun her around, then pointed her toward the piñata, handing her the end of a sawed-off broomstick.

Everyone stepped back. Maria swung while Terrance pulled on the rope, raising and lowering the pottery jar.

Nine children took their turns before the tenth one broke the jar. Squeals of delight filled the air as candies and fruit rained down upon them. The children scattered over the floor, grabbing handfuls of sweets. Hannah would have fun with this game. The sudden onset of tears made Rachel squeeze her eyes shut. Oh, would she ever get over this?

The evening wore on and everyone had their fill of cider and fruitcake and candies. For the last game before the dancing, Rachel had fashioned a large spider out of wire and hung it from the ceiling. Ribbons of every color crisscrossed and wound about the room, acting as the spider's web.

She lined up the children and handed each of them a piece of ribbon. "Your Christmas present is at the end of the ribbon that matches your swatch."

She found herself grinning while the children followed the ribbons down from the spider and worked through the maze of colors to find their presents. It was all such a tangled mess of fun for the little ones. Before long, small hands clutched paper dolls, whirligigs and Jacob's ladders. She looked up to see Terrance staring at her from across the room.

Behind her, Amanda whispered loudly, "You obviously have been leading Terrance on. You haven't been honest with him. He still thinks there is a chance between you two. Someone should set him straight."

Her attack hurt and Rachel turned to face her. "You, for instance?" When Amanda didn't say anything, she added, "I bet you are happy to have Samuel back in one piece."

Amanda looked at her flatly. "Yes. Yes, I am. Too bad it made things more difficult for you." At her side, Elizabeth said nothing before turning away with Amanda.

Rachel clenched her hands at her side. Why had she ever considered Amanda her friend? Her words hurt, but even more was the way others had followed her lead. Amanda was the prettiest, richest girl on the peninsula. If she led a vendetta against Rachel, Rachel would have a difficult time keeping her teaching job at the school.

Emma Crouse stepped up. "Give them time, dear. They'll see."

Rachel drew in a shaky breath. "They're so spiteful."

"Yes. They are."

She sighed and forced a small smile as Pastor Crouse joined them and then suddenly kissed his wife on her cheek.

"You are in a dangerous area, dear, standing under that weed. I may have to steal another kiss."

Emma Crouse looked up to find the mistletoe above her. A blush painted her crinkled cheeks. "Stanley! Behave!"

Rachel relaxed slightly. She'd made it through the worst of the evening. Only a little longer and she could slip away gracefully.

People began to cluster in the center of the room as the four men in the mariachi band started warming up. A stranger, a short man with brown hair and spectacles, started toward them.

"Pastor Crouse?"

"Yes," the reverend said, turning. "What can I do for you?"

"Name is Pittman. Sorry to interrupt the festivities. My timing is not always the best."

"What can I do for you, Mr. Pittman?"

"I was looking for the owner of the mercantile. It was closed up tight when I went by just now."

"Mr. Morley?"

"Yes. That's right. Is he here?"

Reverend Crouse called across the room to Caleb. "Run outside and get Terrance for me. He's talking with Luis Rose and Thomas Whaley."

Caleb gave a quick nod and hurried out the door.

"I'm interested in information concerning Matthew and Hannah Taylor. Do you know of them?"

Rachel's heart skipped a beat.

"Are you a friend of the Taylors'?" the reverend asked.

"Oh, no. I'm here on official business."

She stepped forward. "There is no Matthew Taylor."

The man turned his attention to her for the first time, and a chill went up her back. "Perhaps he goes by Stuart, then. They are one and the same."

Terrance appeared at her side. "I'm Terrance Morley. You wanted to speak with me?" His eyes seemed brighter than normal as he glanced from Mr. Pittman to Rachel.

"He's asking after the Taylors," she said.

Mr. Pittman unfolded a newspaper he had tucked under his arm and pointed to the rescue article. "I believe you sent this to me, Mr. Morley?" At Terrance's brief nod, he continued, "I'm Detective Pittman. Matthew Taylor stole property from Lansing Enterprises three years ago. There is a reward out for information on his whereabouts."

Stunned, Rachel could only exclaim, "No...there must be some mistake!"

"Oh, I'm quite sure I have the facts straight. Mr. Lansing has hired me to find Taylor and arrest him."

Then the rumors had been right? Stuart had been a criminal all along? She looked at Caleb's face and saw that his doubt mirrored her own. Had they both been naive in trusting the man? A weight settled in the pit of her stomach. "He wouldn't do anything illegal. He's not like that."

Terrance made a sound of disgust. "Rachel—you don't know the man. It's quite odd Taylor showed up here just after this property was stolen."

"Oh there's more to it than stolen property," Mr. Pittman said. "Much more. Taylor is also wanted for kidnapping and murder."

The room grew quiet as everyone turned their attention on Detective Pittman and Rachel.

"What?" Her voice trembled. "That can't be true. I won't believe it."

"Well, that's convenient for Taylor," Terrance said snidely.

It had to be a mistake. Stuart had said his wife drowned. She rubbed her temple. She had to think, had to reason it all out. How had Terrance known to contact this detective? "Who is this Lansing?"

"You should know," Terrance said. "Does Lansing Shipping mean anything to you?"

Her eyes widened. The mercantile frequently got cargo with that imprint on the crates.

Caleb snorted. "And here I thought Taylor was so perfect. Even took that lobster trap back to him. He shouldn't be pointing any fingers!"

Caleb! Don't think so of him. Not after all he has done for you. But Rachel couldn't voice her thoughts. She didn't know who to believe.

"Where could I find him now?" Mr. Pittman asked, looking from Terrance to Rachel.

She took a step backward, shaking her head. She wouldn't tell. She wouldn't be the one to hurt Stuart or Hannah.

"He lives at the lighthouse, about six miles from here," Terrance interjected smoothly. He sighed when he saw her frown. "Rachel, Mr. Pittman here could ask any number of people in town and would get the same response. It's silly to keep it from him."

"Hmm. Rather dark to head out now. And I want to alert the sheriff before confronting the man." Mr. Pittman removed his glasses and wiped the lens with his handkerchief, looking down his nose at those assembled. "I'll wait until morning and get a fresh start. The hotel here appears to have rooms available."

"I'll walk with you, just give me one moment." Terrance took Rachel aside. "Are you going to be all right?"

No, she wanted to scream. *I'll never be all right again.* She tried to ignore Detective Pittman's penetrating stare, and focused on Terrance's face. "How did you learn he was wanted?"

"The last shipment from Lansing held a flyer that asked for information on him. I simply sent the news article."

Any small hope she might have had inside deflated with his words. That article again. She'd give anything to turn back the clock and relive that day differently—except that if she and Caleb had not gone out to the lighthouse, Sam and his friends would surely have drowned.

Terrance placed his hands on her shoulders, forcing her to look up at him. "It had to happen sooner or later. Aren't you glad you are no longer involved with that family? The scandal now will be much worse."

"It's Hannah I'm worried about." But that was a lie. She was worried about Stuart too. "How could you let this happen, Terrance? How could you send for this detective?"

"I could because I care about you. It is too bad Taylor will drag his daughter down with him—if she even is his daughter. But I won't have him dragging you down too. Given time you'll realize I'm right."

Rachel couldn't stay here any longer and listen. She glanced about at the couples pairing off for the dancing and noticed Amanda watching her closely. The room started to swirl as the band began a lively tune. She didn't know if it was the dancers moving or whether it was the sudden wave of dizziness that overcame her, but everything began closing in on her.

She shook loose from Terrance's grip and grabbed her cloak from its peg near the door. "It's late." She looked once more at the paper-strewn room and then at Reverend Crouse. "I'm sorry. I just cannot stay. I…I'll clean up tomorrow."

The reverend frowned. "You are not to go out to that lighthouse," he said, the warning clear in his voice.

Her head pounded with thoughts of Stuart and murder and drowning, and still she knew that the lighthouse was the only place she wanted to be. "Of course not."

"I have your word you'll go straight home?" His eyes bored into hers and she hesitated a moment too long. "Rachel. It's not safe. There are coyotes about. Besides, Taylor could use you as a hostage."

She turned her full attention on him. "How would I see? There's no moon."

"Good. Then Caleb and I will pack up. We'll see you at the house."

She threw her cloak about her shoulders and left, passing through the stares and curious looks of the rest of the townspeople who stood on the fringes of the dance floor.

Her thoughts were in chaos as she hurried the short distance down the dirt street. Something had to be done! Not for a moment was she worried about Stuart using her as a hostage. Reverend Crouse's warnings fell on deaf ears. But to go to Stuart, to go to the lighthouse now would seal her fate. She would be stripped of her teaching position for sure. And she and Caleb would have to move.

She had just turned the doorknob on the parsonage when her toe stubbed against something. The plain

brown-paper-wrapped object was slightly larger than
Reverend Crouse's Bible. She picked it up, surprised at
its heaviness.

Large uneven letters sprawled across the top of the
package spelled out Merry Christmas. A tingling sensation started deep within her. She recognized the
writing. Hannah. She tore away the paper, revealing a
beautiful cherrywood box.

Quickly, she glanced about the yard and street,
hoping to see Stuart. There was no sign of anyone. She
stepped into the parsonage and lit the gas lamp on the
tea trolley, and then sat down on the brocade chair,
stroking the smooth wood and running her fingers over
the simple design of the box. She unhinged the brass
latch and opened the lid.

Inside, a handful of sea shells lined the bottom, along
with two large sand dollars and a shiny new pocket
knife. Tucked in a corner sat the whale Stuart had
carved. Her breath hitched, her emotions spinning. An
envelope with her name printed in achingly familiar
childlike letters rested among the treasures. Her hands
shook as she reached for it. She tore the wax seal and
removed a note written in a man's strong script.

Oh, Stuart. Her heart squeezed in her chest.

"Better than fish, right?" it said.

She smiled. He had remembered she didn't like fish.
The words blurred as tears filled her eyes.

"The pocket knife is for Caleb. Warn him that it's
sharper than the one he 'borrowed.'"

Another smile.

This is a small "thanks" to you and Caleb. Hannah learns new words every day and tugs at my arm constantly so that I will watch her and learn them, too. The shells are from her for Caleb. She wants you to have the sand dollars.

I started making this box after one of your first visits to the lighthouse. Hannah said you once told her you never had your own treasure box. Fill it full, Rachel.
Stuart

She crushed the note to her breast, drawing in an unsteady breath. Closing her eyes, a mental image of him swam before her, the strong angle of his chin, the crystal blue of his eyes. How she missed him—his strength, his teasing, even his stubbornness. He once told her he didn't believe in saving things, yet he had made this for her.

She stroked the smooth edge of the wood, running her fingers from one corner to the other, caressing the grain and thinking all the while of Stuart's strong hands sanding each side. She reached inside for Hannah's small collection of sand dollars and shells, picking them up in turn, knowing Hannah had chosen each one carefully.

He had to be warned. That's all there was to it. She wasn't afraid of him or the dark. And the coyotes were fat off the never-ending supply of rabbits. They wouldn't bother her. Rising, she carried the box upstairs to her room and placed it inside her bureau drawer.

In the kitchen she left a note for the Crouses:

"Don't worry about me. I'm all right. I had to do this."

She fastened the toggles on her cloak at her neck and hurried out to the carriage house to saddle Jericho.

Chapter Eighteen

Stuart leaned over the bed and checked Hannah's forehead. Thank God, no fever. Her eyelids closed and he snuggled the blankets around her. "Sweet dreams, short stuff. You'll feel better tomorrow." He ruffled her hair, then headed up the curved stairway.

Darkness came early with the short December days and lengthened his job of tending the lamp. The fog had closed in early this evening, too, before they'd returned from town. The lamp had already burned steadily for five hours.

Someone hammered on the door. The sound startled him, and he nearly dropped the lid to the oil filter. His heart pounded. It wouldn't be visitors at this hour. Was a ship in trouble? He headed downstairs and cracked the door.

"Rachel!"

He flung the door wide. She was pale and shivering and her blue cloak was damp from the heavy fog. Strands of her auburn hair had come loose from her bun and lay plastered to her skin. She looked wonderful—

better than great. He struggled against the strong urge to crush her to him.

She swept past him and into the parlor to stand near the fire as she fidgeted with the collar of her cloak, undoing the toggle. He glanced out the door once more before closing it, looking for Caleb. "You are alone?"

She nodded. "I have to speak with you. It's urgent. Where's Hannah?"

He helped her with her cloak, surprised to see her dressed in a fancy party dress, but then, everyone had been gone when he dropped by the parsonage earlier to leave the box. "She's in bed with a cold. Nothing serious," he added when she glanced up the stairwell. Her eyes held a certain fearfulness he hadn't seen before. A knot formed in his gut. Something was terribly wrong. "You came all the way out here in the dark? Not an easy thing to do. What has happened?"

"There is a detective in town. He came to our Christmas party this evening looking for a Matthew Taylor. He said that's you."

A chill coursed through him. *Dorian.* "Did he say why he wanted me?"

"For kidnapping, theft and murder."

"Is he on his way here now?"

When he didn't immediately deny the charges, her eyes opened wide.

"No. He'll be here, or the sheriff will, in the morning. Stuart, what have you done?"

He would have done anything to take that stunned look from her face, except lie. He crossed the room and stirred the ashes in the fire, trying to still his chaotic thoughts. Her news, her nearness, played havoc with his concentration. He had to figure out what to do next.

"You're shivering," he said, wishing she'd relax. He opened the trunk at the foot of the stairs and removed a large quilt. As he draped it over her shoulders, he allowed himself the agony of letting his fingers linger for a moment on her smooth skin. She let out a shaky breath and gathered the quilt closer.

"Stuart," she repeated. "What have you done?"

He felt the trap tighten as worry filled her voice. His options? He could run like before. Gather Hannah and be gone within the hour. He met Rachel's eyes and took a deep breath. "So the law has finally caught up with me," he said, his words sounding harsh and callous, even to his ears. "I've done all those things."

She slumped into the nearest chair and covered her face with her hands. "Oh, my God."

He walked to the small window to stare out at the night. He didn't want to see the moment she started hating him—or worse—started fearing him. The smart thing to do would be to escape before the sheriff arrested him. He could pack a few belongings and leave with Hannah before dawn. Maybe take her up the coast to Saunders's place. Dorian had set the hounds on him once before and he'd managed to evade the detectives. He had no doubt that he could do it again. Leaving might be harder on Hannah, though. The lighthouse was her home now. She would have to leave behind things that mattered to her—friends, toys. How many times had he told her not to collect things? They'd only tie her down, make her miserable when it was time to leave.

And now they had tied him, as well. He turned to see Rachel watching him silently, waiting for him to explain. The thought of leaving her hurt beyond all else. Looking back, he could see there were times he could have stopped her visits—should have stopped her visits. He remembered the moment in the kitchen when she had looked upon him, not as Hannah's father or as the light keeper, but as a man. He should have stopped the tutoring then. Instead he had chosen to ignore the warning. He'd been too caught up in how good it felt to be cared for. Didn't she realize she was the one who could stop him?

It seemed as though an eternity passed before he heard her speak. "I don't believe you."

He stared at her.

"I don't believe you. You must have had good reason if you were forced to take such actions. You wouldn't knowingly commit murder. Everything you have done since I met you makes a lie of your admission— rescuing Benjamin, caring for Hannah, refusing to continue the tutoring for fear of my reputation. Everything you do tells me what kind of man you are. There must be a mistake. They want the wrong man."

Her perception of him was so slanted. He wasn't this knight she had somehow painted in her mind. "You've heard the rumors. Your faith in me is misplaced."

Her stubborn reply came quickly from her lips and thundered through the stillness of the room. "No. It's not."

A weary sigh escaped him. This was crazy. He should see her home—at least to the edge of town— then come back and pack.

Her eyes glistened with unshed tears. "What have you done that was so awful? Why can't you tell me? I think I deserve your honesty."

She was right. He was being a beast—and would be more of one once she found he'd run. He'd leave her just like the other men in her life who should have stayed, confirming to her that no one cared enough to think of her, to look out for her. He walked up and placed his hands on her shoulders, softening his voice. "Don't cry, Rachel. I made this mess. I'm only sorry I've dragged you into it."

She wiped furiously at her eyes and stood to face him. "I wanted so badly for you to deny it."

Slowly he raised his hand to the curve of her cheek. "You came here to warn me, and I thank you. But you've taken too many risks for me."

She trembled. "What will become of Hannah if the sheriff takes you away?"

He didn't plan to let that happen. "Don't worry," he murmured and moved closer. "I'll think of something." Gently he tilted her face toward his, searching her eyes.

"Stu…"

He bent down. He needed her, needed this. "No more words Rachel. No words." And he took her mouth, salty in tears, tenderly with his.

Her heart hammered in her chest as he deepened the kiss. He claimed her with his mouth, pulling her gently toward him, setting in motion something she could no longer deny. In her heart she didn't believe his guilt—couldn't believe it. She trembled at his closeness, the possessive strength of his hand on the small of her back as he drew her against him and wrapped his arms around her.

She closed her eyes, melting against him like butter on warm bread, every muscle dissolving until she was sure she'd end up a puddle on the floor if not for his strong embrace. His mouth burned hot against her cold lips. This was what she wanted, and yet…something wasn't right.

He slipped his hand within the folds of her quilt, to the curve of her waist.

She tensed. And everything jolted into place. She wasn't some brainless young schoolgirl to let her body shut out the warning in her mind. She pushed away from him. "The truth," she said, her voice unsteady at first, then stronger. "I want the truth. Tell me about the murder, the kidnapping—all of it."

He stared at her for a full moment. "All right, we'll talk. But you must promise me that when I'm done you'll head back to town."

"I promise."

He turned away, distancing himself. "I didn't kill Linnea if that's what you're thinking."

She stilled at his words.

"I didn't kill her. I told you how that happened."

"The storm at sea. You tried to rescue her…." she prompted.

"I tried—and failed. I couldn't help them both. Together, they were too much for me. The sea was so rough."

It wasn't making sense to her. "But that isn't murder!

You made the only decision you could have. Hannah was the weaker of the two. You had to take the chance that Linnea could help herself. Besides, you said she let go. *She* let go. But you did all you could. And as for the ship—that's not even theft. It was an accident. The cargo—" She stopped, suddenly realizing that she wasn't letting him get a word in. "I'm sorry. Please go on."

"The *Frisco Maiden* had seen better days, but she was mine. Saunders and I had taken her up and down the coast many times. When she went down, a large amount of Lansing's goods sank with her."

"But that loss couldn't be helped."

"You don't understand the influence Lansing has. Dorian has been searching for me for years. I thought perhaps he had given up, at least I hoped he had. I should have known better." A bitter laugh erupted from deep in his throat.

"Is that why you use the name Stuart instead of Matthew?"

He shook his head. "The men on my ship knew me as Stuart but Dorian always insisted on calling me Matthew."

"Always? I don't understand."

"He took me on as a cabin boy when I was ten. My parents were acquaintances of his. Not quite upper crust, but respectable. Linnea was always around when we were in port, and she and I became good friends. When she was eighteen, Dorian sent her up the coast to a finishing school. I guess he was afraid we were getting too serious."

"You weren't good enough for her?" she repeated.

Stuart shook his head. "While she was in that fancy finishing school, she ran off and married a man against her father's wishes. Although her husband had plenty of money, I think he hoped for a part of her wealth, but Dorian wouldn't acknowledge him or Linnea. When Hannah came along, Linnea's husband started to drink more. He was an ugly drunk and took out his ill humor on his family. Linnea was frightened and took Hannah to Dorian hoping to find safety. But he turned her away."

Stuart had been staring at the fire as he talked. Now he looked at her. "Funny. Dorian always drilled into me that a man takes care of his own. Yet when Linnea needed him, he refused her. I could never forgive him for that. Neither could she."

He turned back to the fire. "Then one night Linnea showed up at my ship. She was covered with scrapes and bleeding. Her husband had beaten her and then slapped Hannah across the room. Linnea grabbed a gun and shot him. She thought she had killed him and, scared out of her mind, she came to me for help. But she had only wounded him. He followed her to my ship and pointed the gun at her. And so I killed him. I killed the bastard."

Her mind swirled with all he'd told her. "Were there any witnesses? It's not exactly self-defense, but you were protecting Linnea. Surely that would make sense to any judge."

"Not when it was her husband. He had rights over her that I did not. And he had money. Within hours the rumors were flying around San Francisco, rumors saying her husband had been in a jealous rage because I had seduced Linnea. His family was well connected. They didn't care about the truth—they just wanted revenge for the death of their son. Before the authorities could put me in jail, I weighed anchor and left with Linnea and Hannah. And then the storm happened. Perhaps it was God's retribution, but if so, I should have been the one to drown, not Linnea."

Something still didn't sound right to Rachel. "Why would Dorian charge you with stealing his cargo when the storm caused the accident?"

"He's not interested in the cargo I lost. He accepts losses as a part of his business. That's not the reason he has hunted me down these past three years. He doesn't care about catching me."

"Then why?"

"What he wants is another daughter to replace the one he lost." He met her gaze. "He wants Hannah."

"Hannah!" Her mind reeled with the sudden realization that Hannah was not Stuart's daughter, in fact had never been his daughter. Stuart would never let go of Hannah. But then, Hannah wasn't really his child.

"I promised Linnea I'd watch out for her daughter. I won't go back on my word."

"But Dorian is her grandfather. He has rights too."

Stuart scowled. "He gave them up when he turned Linnea away."

How could one man have so much power that he would use it to destroy another's life? In the end it would hurt Hannah more than anyone. She had lost her mother so violently and now she would face the very real possibility of losing the only man she knew as father too. Agitated, Rachel paced the length of the room and back.

"Stuart. You must leave. Take Hannah and go."

His voice took on a deadly calm. "That was my intention at first. Now, I've changed my mind."

She waited.

"I'm not running."

Her stomach seemed to drop low inside her. "But you said yourself he'll take her! There is time before morning to get away. You can't let him win."

"If I leave here, he's already won."

She stared at him. "What do you mean?"

"I mean that Hannah and I will be looking over our shoulders the rest of our lives. We'll never have peace. I was willing to accept that type of existence before, but no longer. I won't go back to that kind of life."

"None of that will matter if you are in jail and Hannah is with him. I won't—I can't—have the two people I care most about pried apart like some…some clam! You belong together."

The corners of his mouth tilted up in a grim smile. "If I don't face him, I'll never be free."

"You stubborn, stubborn man!" Frustration swept through her even as she understood his reasons for making a stand. She walked to the window and stared out at the mist-ridden blackness.

He was behind her in a second. "Rachel," he murmured, the word muffled into her hair. A shiver coursed through her. "You of all people must understand why I do this. It may be that Hannah will be better off with her grandfather. Dorian has the resources, the doctors and the money to give her the best of help. I know I made that promise to Linnea to keep Hannah and care for her. I've tried to honor it the best I could. But it…it could be I'm hurting her more by holding on."

She turned to face him. "You're wrong. You love her as only a father can. He has no right to Hannah. He turned them away! His own daughter!"

"Shh," he said gently, and gathered her close again, caressing the slope of her shoulder, the curve of her neck. "You've done enough by warning me. I'll consider everything you've said." He smiled grimly. "You do realize that you are an accomplice now?"

"Is that supposed to worry me? It is of no consequence considering what you are going through."

"Perhaps Hannah and I should be gone come morning after all."

She swallowed hard. Morning would come so soon. Too soon. And with it the sheriff or Mr. Pittman. She thought of the note she'd left for the Crouses. She was implicated whether Stuart escaped or whether he stayed put. Either way, she would likely lose her teaching position if she hadn't already. She dragged in a deep breath. This would be her last time alone with Stuart. Nothing mattered but that they were together. She spoke softly into his shirt. "Hold me, Stuart. Please hold me."

His hand stilled on her back.

Slowly she looked up into his eyes. Astonishment showed on his face—and desire.

"Rachel…do you understand what you ask? I can't

just hold you. I...I want you too badly. And I can't promise you any type of a future with me." He looked away, his voice low. "I'd be no better than the other man who left you."

"No. That's not true" she said, thinking how different the two men were. "Joseph had the choice to stay and wouldn't. You don't have that. Tomorrow you'll either be behind bars or gone. I can't change that." She cupped his cheek, pulling his gaze back to hers. "I may lack experience in these matters, Stuart. I...I have never lain with a man. But I am not naive. I know what I'm asking you. I understand the consequences. Even so, I would have this night."

The words were barely off her lips when his mouth slammed into hers. He crushed her to him, deepening the kiss. She opened her mouth to his tongue, and fire exploded through her blood, setting all her nerves' on end.

He slipped her dress off her shoulders and trailed kisses down her neck, his breath warm against her cool skin. Shivers raced down her body to her core. She would have melted into the floor had he not held her tight against him. He pulled away and she drew in a shaky breath. "Come with me," he murmured, holding out his hand.

Although her legs felt weak, she followed him.

"Wait here," he instructed at the base of the stairs. In the kitchen he lit a tallow candle, then came back to grasp her hand. His eyes glittered with desire in the light of the flame.

Slowly, holding the candle in front of him, he

climbed the circular stairs. He led her into his bedroom and closed the door, then crossed to his nightstand to set the candle down. "I want you, Rachel. I've wanted you for so long." He turned to face her. "But if you tell me to stop, I will."

She shook her head. She had never been more certain. "I won't change my mind. There will be no regrets come morning. And whatever happens after…"

She let the words trail off as she stepped toward him and slowly unbuttoned his shirt. She could feel his gaze on her face as each button gave way and his shirt finally fell to the floor. Sliding her hands over his warm chest, she felt the strong, steady beat of his heart, heard his sharp intake of breath. She leaned closer and kissed the dark-brown hair sprinkled between his nipples. She raised her face to look at him, and then his mouth was on hers.

His lips slanted across hers, sucking first her lower lip and then her upper one. He teased her with his tongue, flicking across the fullness of her lips and then plunged inside, claiming her. Gone was any thought of the outside world. She wanted only this moment, only this intensity that Stuart could give her. With his hands splayed against the bedroom door, he pressed her back against the wood, his warm body heavy against her.

She arched against him, wanting him closer yet, her breath coming faster and deeper. She pulled his face down so that she could kiss him as thoroughly as he had her, and saw his scar. Tenderly she kissed the puckered skin and then trailed kisses down along the firm line of his jaw, delighting in the roughness of his day-old whiskers and the safety she felt within the circle of his arms.

He picked her up in one fluid motion and strode to the bed. Settling her on his lap, he rained kisses down her throat and across her chest, pushing her damp hair over her shoulder. Her bodice gave way under his fingers and suddenly she was in her chemise, his mouth hot against the cotton material, nuzzling through to her breast. Her nipple responded, puckering in the warm dampness. Her heart hammered as she untied the small bow at the gathered neckline and loosened the material farther.

He slipped his hand beneath the cotton and grasped her breast, molding its softness with his fingers. His breath caught, and he leaned forward to kiss her again. She trembled, moaning into his mouth as waves of desire raced from her breast down through her center. The exquisite torture she felt while he placed light kisses on her neck had her squirming to offer him more flesh. When he finally arrived to suckle at her breast she spread her fingers through his thick dark hair, and let her head fall back in complete surrender.

He moaned and shifted, moving to catch her other nipple between his lips and give it equal attention. Against her buttocks she felt the firm rise of his body and pressed against him, reveling in the sensations that pulsed through her core.

She drew the chemise over her head, before him naked and trembling—although not from the cold.

"You're so beautiful," he said, his voice hoarse. "In the candlelight—you glow."

Pleasure suffused her. She couldn't take her eyes from him either—his dark hair tousled from her fingers, the seductive shadows and valleys of the muscles across his chest and shoulders, the strong line of his jaw. In the flickering candlelight his skin shone a pale gold.

He moved her from his lap and then removed his pants. She caught just a glimpse of him before he pulled her into his bed. A thrill rushed through her. She snuggled against him and caressed the width of his back and down his arms, enjoying the feel of his firm muscles, the exquisite pleasure of her skin molding to his, thigh to thigh, breast to chest.

He groaned, and with the sound a feeling of power came over her. "Oh, Stuart," she sighed into his ear and kissed the soft lobe. "I want your touch as much as you want me—probably more."

"That's impossible," he murmured, rising on one elbow and pushing a strand of her hair away from her cheek. Looking directly into her eyes, he moved her beneath him, grinding his firmness against her pelvis. She gasped as pleasure exploded through her body, her eyelids drifting closed to block out everything but the sensation. Her skin tingled as he smoothed his hand along her torso, down her hips, between her thighs.

She moaned and arched up against his fingers, opening her legs farther, longing for his entry. Wanting him. "I…I need you," she whispered against his neck.

"Shh. I know." He met her gaze. "You're so beautiful, Rachel. So damn beautiful." He took her mouth once again with his, moved on top of her and then thrust himself into her body, stifling her sudden outcry with his kiss. She clung to him, barely breathing as he paused, letting the sensual feelings race over them both. Then the sweet rhythm of his body pushing into hers, deeper and deeper, carried her away until she lost all thought and could only feel and respond in kind.

Time slipped away and her world became his world. A small, candlelit room that shut out the cold and wind and dark. He was her refuge, her warmth, her desire. She strained against him, asking for more with her body, wanting him closer, deeper inside. The sensation built until her body bucked and she gripped him tight as wave after wave of feeling overwhelmed her.

"You're mine now," he gasped and shuddered into her with such force, it took her over the edge of all feeling. Then he collapsed on her, breathing hard, his energy spent as he wrapped his arms around her.

She felt his heart beating against hers, the rhythm slowing, and drew comfort from him. She wanted this to last forever, this feeling of safety and caring and contentment. Knowing it wouldn't brought the sting of tears to her eyes.

He rose up on his elbows over her, then leaned down and kissed the wetness, his lips tender. "I'll remember this moment forever," he murmured against her ear.

And then he held her, as she'd asked.

Stuart lay awake as the gray light of dawn seeped through the window, wondering how things would play out today of all days. Rachel snuggled deeper into his arms, her backside flush against him. He chuckled into her hair and kissed the nape of her neck. She had given him such a gift last night.

The thundering report of a harpoon gun echoed loudly through the small room, the sound shaking the small window.

Rachel tensed and her eyes flew open.

"The Johnson Company—after a whale. Probably their last one." He smoothed back the tendrils of hair on her forehead as he felt her relax back into his pillow. He sighed. "And my notice to get moving." Turning away from her, he climbed reluctantly from the bed.

"Not yet, Stuart. Come back."

He smiled, but continued to pull on his pants and chambray shirt. "You make it hard to leave the bed, but I need to put out the light."

She groaned into the pillow and then stretched languorously. The wool cover slipped, revealing a soft breast.

His breath caught at the sight. She was beautiful, lying there, her dark-auburn hair spread over the pillow. He swallowed hard, wanting nothing more than to lose himself in her again. Instead he stepped away from the bed.

"Hannah will be up soon. I doubt your being here would upset her, but the sheriff might react differently."

She squeezed her eyes shut. "The sheriff! Oh, Stuart. You should have left…you should have gone," she moaned. "Perhaps there is still time?"

He shook his head. "It's time to face the consequences. That became clear last night."

She sighed, meeting his gaze. "Everything will change now."

He understood. Everything had changed. He left the room to begin his duties with the light.

Downstairs she was making coffee when he came into the room and walked up to wrap his arms around her waist. The party dress from last night was wrinkled, her hair was loose, and she had a well-satisfied look about her. She couldn't look more stunning. He breathed deeply against her hair. "Did you find the box?"

"It's beautiful. Thank you." She poured some coffee into a mug and turned around, handing it to him. "Tell Hannah thank you."

"You can tell her yourself. She is stirring." He took a sip. "Much better than mine."

She poured herself a cup. "I do have one question about all you said last night."

He smiled. "Only one?"

She returned his smile and elbowed him. "How did you get the job here? Surely the lighthouse board hired you without knowing your past."

"Someone owed Saunders a favor."

"You and this Saunders must be very close."

Stuart put down his mug. "We go way back. I'm fortunate to call him a friend."

"I suppose you can call me a friend too," Rachel said, a teasing light coming into her eyes.

"We passed that point long ago. And last night… well, last night proved it." He pulled her to his chest and kissed her thoroughly. She returned his kiss with matching ardor, until he knew the moment her legs gave way and she began to sink. He pulled her up, reluctantly moving to kiss her cheeks, her face and her neck. He breathed her scent, then whispered in her ear,

"Rachel, we have to stop or Hannah will find both of us on the floor."

She stumbled back from him and dragged in a deep breath. "You're right, of course."

He nearly grabbed her to him again, she looked so beautiful and disheveled, her eyes misty. He searched his mind for something to keep his mind off her lips and his hands off her body. "I saw the article in the paper. Caleb brought it out. How bad has it been for you in town?"

She didn't speak for a moment. "I'm handling it. Mrs. Crouse says it will blow over."

"You're a strong woman."

"I don't feel very strong. At least not right now." Her voice trembled. "The school board has suspended me from teaching."

"Oh, Rachel. I'm sorry." He sure had messed up her life along with his. What would happen over the next week or month? Would she come to hate him? He'd deserve it if she did.

She drew in a shaky breath. "Well, at least now they have a valid reason to keep me from influencing their children."

He frowned. "What happened last night was wonderful—not wrong. It could never be wrong." He took her by the shoulders and looked deep into her eyes. "You are worth staying for. Believe that."

Her gaze skittered away. "I don't have much experience with people staying, Stuart. You know that."

He wanted to punch the men who'd done that to her—made her feel as though she were unworthy. They were the ones who'd been wrong...and selfish. He touched her chin, turning her to face him. "I wish I could promise you I'd be here tomorrow. But I can't."

"I know." The words were barely a whisper.

"No regrets, remember?"

"No regrets."

A loud pounding vibrated the lighthouse door.

Chapter Nineteen

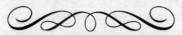

Stuart waited a moment, giving Rachel time to collect herself. Then he opened the door to Sheriff Thorne and Terrance. As one, the two men looked from Stuart's face, past him, to see Rachel.

"I see there is no need to explain why I'm here," Sheriff Thorne said.

Terrance's eyes narrowed suspiciously on her face. In the harsh morning light, Stuart saw distinctly when Morley noticed her heightened color, the puffiness in her lips. With an enraged snarl, Terrance sprung forward and rammed his fist into Stuart's face.

Pain exploded in his nose and cheek. Stuart staggered back, blood spurting from his nose and coating his lips.

Rachel raced across the room toward him, but stopped abruptly when he straightened and put out a warning hand to her to stay out of the way.

"Maybe I deserved that," he said in a low controlled voice. "But I won't take it. Not from you, Morley."

"You deserve much worse!" Terrance hauled back his fist, preparing to strike again.

"No!" Rachel screamed. *"Stop!"*

Terrance struck down.

Stuart blocked with his arm, at the same time plowing his fist into Terrance's gut. With a loud whoosh, air exploded from Terrance's lungs and he landed in a heap on the floor.

"That'll be enough from both of you," Sheriff Thorne said, pushing them apart, his hand on his gun.

Stuart staggered back a step and then regained his balance. He straightened slowly, keeping one eye on Terrance and the other on the sheriff and his gun. The metallic taste of blood tinged his mouth.

Terrance caught his breath, propped himself up on his elbow and glared from Stuart to Rachel, but it seemed the fight was out of him. His eyes narrowed on Rachel and a look of disgust crossed his face.

Stuart would have done anything to knock that look off his face. With a growl he started toward him, grabbed his collar and hauled him to his feet.

"Hold on!" the sheriff barked, and swung Stuart around, jabbing the gun into his ribs. Blood splattered from Stuart's nose over Terrance.

"Don't move, Taylor. Git me a rag, Miss Houston."

The alarm in Rachel's eyes stopped him from jerking out of the sheriff's grip and tearing Terrance apart. He quieted as she grabbed a cloth from the cabinet. The sheriff whipped it out of her hand and threw it at Stuart.

"Take care of your nose. You're gushing everywhere." He turned back to Rachel. "Mrs. Crouse put a package for you in my saddlebag. You are to open it now."

She nodded as if in a daze and stepped outside.

The sheriff turned to Stuart. "You know why I'm here. No dancin' around the cow as they say. Collect your things, Taylor. The logbook too. And get the girl ready."

"Where's this detective?"

"He's waiting at the jail. Didn't want to dirty his hands if you put up a fight."

"That's noble of him," Stuart said, sarcasm ripe in his voice.

"Humph," the sheriff huffed.

"I don't plan to give you any trouble, Sheriff. Only if Morley gives me more grief." He turned and headed up the stairs. Hannah had heard the commotion, and he found her sitting in bed, the quilt covers up to her nose, her gray eyes big.

"It's okay, Hannah. Get dressed. We're going into town." He gathered her few clothes and bundled them together. While she dressed herself, he went into his bedroom and got his few things together.

When he returned downstairs with Hannah, Rachel had changed from her party dress into the yellow everyday dress he'd seen before. Her hair was still down, tousled over her shoulders. She looked pale, shaken.

"Mrs. Crouse's package," she said, indicating her dress. "I tied up the puppy and gave him food and water. Caleb can come out later to keep an eye on things."

Silently he nodded his thanks.

Thorne watched him closely. "Saw your name in the newspaper. Quite a hero, you and Caleb."

"Neither one of us wanted that story in the paper, Sheriff. I think you can figure out why."

Thorne nodded. "It hasn't gone easy for Miss Houston. When the townsfolk found out she came out here so much, they suspended her from her teaching position."

"She told me."

"It was just until the school board's next meeting," Terrance said. "But now…"

Stuart met his gaze. "I hired Miss Houston to tutor my daughter. Nothing more."

"That doesn't change the fact that she raced out here last night to warn you and then stayed," Terrance said stonily. "Although, maybe we should thank her. She probably kept you from running when you had the chance."

Stuart glanced at Rachel. She was so still that he knew she believed what Terrance had said.

"Yes," Sheriff Thorne said. "I've been thinking about that myself. Why didn't you run, Taylor?"

Stuart shrugged. He wasn't about to go into something that personal with these two. "I have my reasons, Sheriff. But I guess I should get a lawyer, or at least wait until Dorian arrives and I have a better idea where things stand."

"That may be best. A few things just don't add up here and I'd like to get to the bones of it. Officially I am arresting you for kidnapping and possible murder." Thorne stood and then glanced at Hannah. "You got any kin around that could watch the girl?"

"No."

"Mrs. Baier might take her in at the boarding house."

He scratched his temple. "What about Miss Houston? Seein' as how she's been tutoring the girl…"

"Rachel could lose her job permanently. No, she's done enough for us as it is."

Terrance shook his head with disgust. "Interesting how you seem to care so much now that it won't help. Her reputation is ruined."

It was all he could do to keep from beating Morley to a pulp. "Her reputation is only ruined if you or Sheriff Thorne mention her being here last night. I'm sure the Crouses won't. The school board doesn't have to know."

Terrance snorted. "In a town this size? The whole thing will be impossible to keep quiet."

He hated to ask, but he'd do it for Rachel if it would help. "If you really care about her, why don't you bring her into town in another hour, rather than have her ride in with the Sheriff and me?"

Stony silence met his request.

Rachel stepped forward. "At this point, town gossip is the least of my worries, Stuart. But perhaps it would be easier for Hannah to ride with me. And I do want her to stay with me at the parsonage."

He stared at her a long time before answering. It was what he wanted. Hannah would be frightened in a strange place all alone. And he couldn't bear the thought of either one of them watching him ride into town and being jailed. "All right."

"What about the light?" Thorne asked.

"You'll have to contact the lighthouse board when we get to town. Caleb knows how to manage the light if you'll trust him."

"He's kind of young," said Thorne, rubbing his chin. "But all right. Let's go. You coming, Morley?"

Again Terrance met Stuart's gaze. "I'll start back with Miss Houston and the girl in half an hour."

Hannah ran to Stuart then and threw her arms around him. He crouched down on one knee in order to hug her back. She clung hard, locking her fingers together behind his neck. Stuart squeezed his eyes shut to keep the sudden moisture in check. It wouldn't do to show any signs of weakness—not in front of Rachel. And this was probably the last time he'd see Hannah. The thought staggered him. How could he live with himself?

"Time to go," Thorne said again and tried to pull Hannah away, but she held on tighter. "Taylor..." Warning crept into his voice.

"All right, Sheriff. Hannah, stay with Rachel for now." He talked softly, reassuring her, all the while prying her fingers away one at a time. Tears rolled down her soft cheeks, making his chest ache. This is how he'd remember her.

He pressed her hand into Rachel's and squeezed. Then, standing, he looked at Rachel hard, memorizing the way she looked—her hair down about her shoulders, wavy and curled slightly at the ends, her lips puffy from their last kiss, her green eyes luminous. He said firmly, "Don't come to the jail."

Then he turned and stepped outside with Sheriff Thorne. They walked to the shed and he saddled Blanco under Thorne's vigilant gun. When he was settled on the horse, Thorne reached into his pocket and pulled out handcuffs.

Stuart swallowed hard. This was it.

He steadied his gaze on the sheriff. "I won't run, you know. I would have been gone by now if that's how I wanted to handle this."

"I figured that. But I don't plan on making any mistakes. And who's to know if you should change your mind about coming peacefully once we get closer to town? Here. Put your hands out."

Stuart hesitated. There would be no chance of turning back after this. He took a deep breath and held out his arms.

Chapter Twenty

Ping!

Rachel glanced out the kitchen window to see Caleb practicing in the backyard with his pellet gun. The frequent clatter of a tin can falling from the fence proved how good a shot he had become since Sam gave him the gun as a gift. The last of Settie's puppies darted under his feet and dashed about the yard in a circle, yipping and barking at the noisy cans.

She turned back to the table and finished quartering the potatoes for supper, her thoughts scattered, sometimes worried, sometimes angry but always on Stuart. The stubborn, mule-headed man! He was so close—just around the square—and she wanted to go to him. She had struggled for the past three days over doing just that.

The church door slammed, and Reverend Crouse crossed the lawn. He stopped and watched Caleb knock down two more cans. "It will be dark before long. You should leave for the lighthouse. Make yourself ready."

"Yes sir." Caleb followed Reverend Crouse into the kitchen.

"I have a satchel for you," Rachel said, motioning to the cloth bag on the table. "Enough for two days, at least. You should be able to find more in the pantry there."

"Thanks, sis."

"Are you managing out there?"

"Sure. It's quiet, but that's okay. Sam's coming out to visit tomorrow. We might do a little fishing—from the rock."

Reverend Crouse handed Caleb a box of matches. "It is a man's job you are doing. Hopefully, the board will find a replacement soon."

"I know how to work the light," Caleb said, throwing a frustrated glance at them both. "I've seen Mr. Taylor do it before."

Reverend Crouse smiled. "I don't doubt that you do. I am worried that you will be called upon to do more rescuing if a ship comes to trouble."

Rachel hugged her brother. "Be careful, Caleb."

He grinned and settled his hat on his head. Nodding to them both, he ducked out the kitchen door and headed for the carriage house where Stuart's horse was now kept.

Rachel turned back to the table and began slicing the carrots for the stew. Her brother was looking forward to proving himself. He viewed this as a challenge. She wouldn't have thought him capable of handling the responsibility six months ago, but a lot had happened since the picnic and Benjamin's fall. Caleb had grown up quite a bit and she— Well, she had fallen in love.

"Oh!" Stinging pain radiated through her hand. Blood dripped from the cut on her finger. She dropped the knife, sending it clattering across the floor and grabbed her apron to apply pressure to the cut.

"What happened?" Emma asked, coming through the kitchen door and looking from her husband to Rachel. "Dear, are you all right?"

"Yes," Rachel murmured, hunching her shoulders. Emma stepped closer and reached for her injured hand.

Rachel jerked away, but couldn't keep her eyes from filling with tears.

Emma took one look at Rachel's face and shooed her husband from the room. "Supper will be a while yet. I'll help." She pulled out a chair for Rachel, pushed her into it and then began cutting the celery for the pot. "Now, you sit there and tell me all that's bothering you, Rachel."

"I said I'm fine."

"Well, I'll believe that when there is a smile on your face, but not now."

Emma had always been kind, but in light of all the snubbing Rachel had endured, it meant so much now. She rewrapped her finger with her apron and squeezed until it went numb, wishing she could do the same to her heart. "Everything is such a mess," she said, and felt hot tears spill over.

Emma pulled out her handkerchief and dabbed at Rachel's face. "I've been around a bit longer than you. Perhaps I can help you muddle through some of your mess."

* * *

Early that evening Terrance surprised her with a visit.

"We need to talk," he said, standing in the parlor, holding Rachel's cloak open for her. "Let's take a walk."

Since returning from the lighthouse she had stayed inside, going out only for necessities. "I don't know, Terrance. The way things have been it's not a good idea."

Terrance's smile turned impatient. "I've had time to calm down, to think through a few things and I believe I deserve a chance to have my say."

Still she hesitated.

"I want to discuss the things those on the school board are saying."

Reluctantly Rachel tugged her cloak about her neck and hooked the toggles. Terrance's mood worried her and she wasn't sure she wanted to hear what he had to say. After all, he had been the one to relay information to that detective. He'd had a hand in Stuart's arrest.

Purposely she started off in the direction away from the jail. They walked around the Custom House, down Talbot Street toward the livery. Lanterns glowed in several of the houses and she saw one figure watching through an open window. A dog barked from a darkened porch as they passed, and one impudent skunk slowly walked across the road in front of them. At the schoolhouse, Terrance stopped her. He'd been quiet, unusual for him.

"Still wishing you could teach?"

She nodded.

"I know you don't want to hear this, but you need to be realistic now."

"What do you mean?"

He met her eyes. "Do you think people here would want you teaching their children now that they know what has happened?"

"And what exactly has happened?"

"You know what I mean. Most of the town has heard one version or another of your exploits."

"My exploits!" A sarcastic laugh escaped before she could clamp her mouth shut tight. "What are they saying?"

"It isn't funny," Terrance said. "I don't like what they're saying about you, whether you care or not."

"I do care. It's just that there is nothing I can do about it. Nothing I say will change their minds. It is the mob mentality."

He grasped her hand, tucked it in the crook of his arm and patted it. "In a week Taylor and Hannah will both be gone. And you are the one who will still be here fending off the rumors."

"A sadder but wiser girl, is that it?"

They walked on in uneasy silence, his words troubling her. They retraced their steps past the church and the parsonage, until they finally came to the jail. Terrance's grip on her hand tightened as they strolled by the darkened windows. Each step echoed loudly on the wooden boardwalk. Her spine stiffened. She refused to look, refused to wonder whether Stuart saw her.

At the edge of town near the new wharf, Terrance stopped and looked across the harbor. A few isolated lights twinkled in the distance, ten miles away in New San Diego. Water slapped against the rocks at her feet.

Terrance faced her and sighed. "I've been angry. Very angry. I needed a few days to sort through things."

"And have you?"

"Enough to know that I want to make things work between us."

Rachel pulled back. This was the last thing she expected to hear from him. "Terrance. There is no 'us.'"

"I'm not a fool. I know you don't feel the same way about me. I just thought I could help you through some of this. Maybe still take you into San Diego for your teaching exam."

She studied his long face, his mud-colored eyes that watched her so closely. "You'd do that for me? After all that has happened?"

"You should have something to think about. Something to take your mind off Taylor. It's time to get on with your life."

His thoughtfulness confused her after the way he'd acted at the lighthouse. "I never thanked you for accompanying me home the other morning."

"That's easily remedied."

She looked up and suddenly he was kissing her, his lips hard against hers, his oiled mustache brushing her cheeks. When he pressed his entire length against her she broke away, shaking. "Stop, Terrance."

His voice came low and angry. "You were happy enough to take Taylor's kisses. Mine aren't good enough for you?"

The hair on the back of her neck prickled, and the first inklings of fear crept into her. She stepped back. "I want to go home now." When he didn't move, she forced a calm she didn't feel and said firmly, "I mean it, Terrance. Take me home."

"Not until I get a proper kiss from you." He grabbed her shoulders and pulled her toward him.

She struggled, trying to loosen his grip, but he was too strong for her. He crushed his mouth against hers and forced her lips apart, invading her with his tongue.

Suddenly he released her. "Daughter of a gold panner," he said with derision. "You could have been so much more."

She stumbled back and wiped her bruised mouth. "Never touch me again, Mr. Morley. Never." Then she turned and strode toward the parsonage.

He'd seen enough—the kiss, the embrace. Stuart turned away from the jail's window, the sight of Rachel and Terrance too much to bear. He gripped the black iron bars tighter, in his mind reliving the satisfied smirk Terrance had tossed in his direction when he walked by with Rachel on his arm. Stuart wanted to strangle him. It twisted his gut to see another man with her.

Especially Terrance.

With a growl he turned from the window and paced the length of his cell, and for the hundredth time he questioned if he had done the right thing in staying.

He'd heard and seen plenty his first few days in jail.

Amanda Furst visited the mercantile daily, mostly to flirt with Terrance, her high-pitched giggle drifting across the street and grating on Stuart's nerves. Samuel had come to visit once along with his parents. They had offered him a reward for saving Sam's life—money he could use to purchase the services of a lawyer.

He welcomed the day that Dorian would arrive and put an end to this purgatory. Anything was better than what he suffered now.

If only…

He clamped down on the thought. No point in dwelling on what couldn't be. He plopped down on the cot and glanced at the window. Rachel had already paid dearly. And it was his fault…his fault! He smashed his fist into the thin pillow.

Chapter Twenty-One

Four days later, the sky spit rain from leaden clouds as a team of dapple-gray horses pulled a private coach to a stop in front of the small jail. Stuart rose from his cot and peered through the iron bars of the window that faced the street. A tall, thin man stepped down to the dusty street and paused to glance about the town. In his hand he grasped the ivory-handled cane he carried with him at all times—more for a display of power than for any need of assistance to walk.

The old ambivalence resurfaced while Stuart watched. He could well imagine the man's musings, probably comparing the haphazard array of wooden slapped-up buildings against the solid structures of San Francisco. Most likely anger built as he assessed the kind of place his granddaughter had lived in for the past year, and found everything wanting.

The years had changed him. The gray fox eyes seemed just as bright, just as startling as they once had, but the silver hair combed straight back from his forehead had thinned, with white scalp showing through at the temple. He still held himself straight and rigid, like he had when he walked the deck of his own ship and was used to having everyone obey his slightest command. He adjusted his coat more comfortably over his narrow shoulders, settled his stovepipe hat on his head and strode into the jail.

Stuart moved to watch the sheriff and Dorian through the small barred opening. Thorne studied the stranger from underneath the low brim of his Stetson. He leaned back in his chair and chewed on a stalk of winter grass. Stuart had witnessed a couple of his run-ins over the past week and wondered now who would have the upper hand. The outcome would make an interesting wager if he were a betting man, but either way he was bound to end up the loser in this game.

Dorian tapped his cane against the floorboards, two sharp staccato beats that sent dust flying and commanded the sheriff's attention. He removed his tall hat with a flourish and tucked it against his waistcoat. "Good day. I understand you are holding a prisoner for me?"

"Well now, that depends on who you are," Sheriff Thorne said.

"Dorian Lansing, merchant and sole proprietor of Lansing Enterprises of San Francisco. I was informed by telegraph that you had arrested Matthew Taylor. I came at my earliest opportunity. He is here, is he not?"

"He's here all right. I'll need some identification before you can see him. Also, you'll have to remove any weapons or firearms. You can understand that, I'm sure."

"Of course. And might I know your name for my records?"

Stuart leaned against the bars, watching. Dorian was always primed for a power struggle. The sheriff drew in a long, slow breath and leaned forward on his seat, hands on his knees, belly protruding over his wide leather belt.

"It's Thorne—Randolph Thorne. T-h-o-r-n-e. Got that?"

Dorian's steel-gray eyes didn't blink but drew into slits as he looked over the sheriff. "Thank you, Sheriff Thorne. Here are my papers."

He withdrew a small packet of papers from his waistcoat pocket and dropped them on the desk. Thorne looked them over for a full minute before standing and offering them back to Dorian.

"Seem to be in order. Ah…about the firearms."

Dorian unbuttoned his coat and withdrew a derringer from an inside pocket. He placed it carefully on the desk.

"Follow me."

The sheriff took the key ring from its hook and proceeded to the door separating the two rooms. Stuart met his gaze through the small window, tight-lipped and grim, a man doing his duty but not wholly agreeing with the lay of things.

Stuart backed up to his cot and took a deep breath.

The door banged open.

"Visitor for you, Taylor," the sheriff called out.

Dorian walked slowly to the door of the cell, a hard expression on his cosmopolitan face, his cane tapping out a determined third beat to his polished boots. He stopped directly in front of Stuart and studied him through the bars—first his face, then his coarse cotton shirt and Levi's, down to his worn boots and then back to his face.

Stuart couldn't read a thing in the man's gaze. He knew better than to try. So he just stood there, letting the man who had once been like a father to him look his fill, remembering that this man had turned his back on his only daughter in her time of need.

"So," Dorian said at last in a gravelly voice. "I have finally tracked you down."

Stuart remained silent…waiting.

"How long has it been?"

"Three years."

"I doubt I would have found you now had it not been for the newspaper article. Of course, the mercantile owner helped quite a bit, too. I'll have to stop by to thank him personally."

That newspaper article again! It had hurt Rachel and now it had come back to haunt him. Who'd have thought rescuing three men in a boat would be the bait to ruin his life?

"I was happy enough to know where you had stolen my granddaughter off to."

Stuart's hold on his temper slipped. "You turned your back on her and her mother."

"You and I both know that is not the case. I was trying to make my daughter see the error of her ways. The choices she made were her downfall."

"Twist it any way you like. You're still wrong."

"Well, now we come to it," Dorian said.

Fear rose like bile in Stuart's throat. If Dorian challenged Stuart's right to Hannah, he would win.

Dorian sighed and spoke to him as though to a child. "Hannah is not your flesh and blood. She's my daughter's child but not yours. You have no right to her."

"My right comes by way of Linnea." He'd failed Linnea before, he wouldn't let this go without a fight. "She wanted me to raise Hannah. Not you. It was the last thing she asked of me."

"Well, things have changed considerably since that time. Hannah will be the sole surviving heir of Lansing Enterprises. She needs to be brought up properly, according to her station."

"So that's why you manufactured the kidnapping charge."

"Along with the loss of the cargo. It proved a convenient way to cast a net to pull you in. The murder charge—well that will be settled in court. You did a deep disservice to me when you ran off that night. And, I might add, Rose has never been the same since. Under the circumstances, there is little to commend you as a merchant—or a father."

Stuart glared at the man before him. "I learned from the best."

Dorian looked shaken for a moment, for once unsure of how to proceed. He sank down on the bench along the wall and sighed.

"You are not going to win this time, Matthew," he said in a low voice, his hands clenched together on the knob of his cane. "You took my only daughter from me. You will not have my granddaughter, too."

"Linnea asked me to raise Hannah."

"You turned her head!" Dorian cried out in his gravelly voice. "You used her vulnerability. All you ever wanted was her money, her position. Now look what's become of her. She has the ocean as her grave!"

Stuart rushed to the bars and gripped them tightly. "Never again put me in the same class as the brute she married," he ground out through clenched teeth. "Understand this once and for all. I never cared about her money—your money. That should be evident enough. I have nothing now. Just a lowly job as light keeper. But what I have is mine. And Hannah is *mine!*"

Dorian's eyes narrowed as he said icily. "I may be getting older, but I am no fool."

"What would you know about the feelings we had for each other? Did you ever try to understand your daughter?"

"Don't talk to me about Linnea. If you both had been honest with me none of this would be happening now."

"Is that what this is all about? Honesty? You're angry Linnea ran to me when you refused to help her? I should think you'd thank me! Or are you just irritated she didn't come crawling to you a second time? You always liked being the one with total control."

Dorian had twisted their relationship into something ugly, and Stuart wouldn't have it. He'd had feelings for Linnea from the start—but when she had gone off and married another man he'd come to accept it. He released his grip and turned away from the man who had at one time meant everything to him. "Believe what you will. You've chosen the way you want to see things so that you can justify taking Hannah from me."

"A daughter for a daughter, Matthew."

Stuart stared at Dorian but remained silent.

The small room filled with the oppressive silence of two strong wills, fighting for the thing they considered most dear, one in control, one in despair. After a while, Dorian rose to his feet.

"Where is she?" he said in a low voice.

Stuart wouldn't answer.

"So be it," Dorian said. "You'll be tried in San Francisco in two weeks."

"How convenient. A place where you can line the pockets of the lawyers and judge. The charges?"

"Kidnapping, theft and the murder of John Newcomb." He strode out of the room, slamming the door on his way.

As Dorian tapped by the window and climbed into the coach, Stuart pushed his face against the cold iron bars. "You may take Hannah, thinking in some crooked way that it's justified for the life of your daughter, but you'll be wrong. I pity you, Dorian. Do you hear me? You're a sad, old man."

Chapter Twenty-Two

Rachel removed the towel covering a large earthenware bowl and leaned over to see how much the dough had risen. The afternoon sun slanted through the kitchen window, refusing to give off much warmth this time of year, but it had done its job with the dough. Hannah sat on a high stool watching the proceedings with interest, every so often turning to Emma, who sat beside her, trying to learn the finger alphabet.

A sharp double knock came at the front door.

Emma rose. "I'll answer it."

Voices came from the other room as Rachel continued working the dough. Emma returned with a sad look on her face. "He's here."

Rachel's heart dropped to her stomach. Dorian. She glanced at Hannah and tried to smile before following Emma into the parlor.

A tall, wiry stranger, stylishly dressed beyond anything she'd seen in La Playa, sat in the wingback chair. He cradled his hat in his lap and turned the rim—

whether out of boredom or a case of nerves, Rachel wasn't sure. When she approached, he stood.

"I'm Hannah Taylor's grandfather, Dorian Lansing, and I've come to take her home with me."

Even though she'd expected it, Rachel still wasn't ready for the blow.

"She is living with you, is she not?" Dorian's gaze darted to Mrs. Crouse for confirmation.

"She's here," Rachel answered. "May I see some form of identification?"

"Certainly." Dorian withdrew a packet of papers from his pocket. "This is the second time I've had to verify my identity. That sheriff of yours doesn't leave anything to chance."

"Yes," Rachel said dryly. "We're lucky to have him. I take it you've been to see Mr. Taylor, then."

"Yes. He is aware that I am here for Hannah. These papers assign me authority to take Hannah back to San Francisco."

Rachel looked over the papers and handed them back with a sigh. She had known this time would come, thought she was prepared, but now her heart lodged in her throat and she wanted nothing more than for this cultured stranger to turn around and walk back out the front door.

"We have become rather attached to Hannah in the past week," Emma said, her experience as a pastor's wife coming to the fore as she graciously motioned for Dorian to enter. "She is a good child. Won't you come in?"

"I'll fetch Hannah." Rachel turned and walked slowly

into the kitchen. A smudge of flour slashed across one of Hannah's cheeks, and dashes of the white powder dusted the table and circled the girl's feet. Rachel untied the oversize apron and hugged her. "There is someone here to see you," she said, carefully keeping her voice light. She smoothed Hannah's hair and brushed the flour from her cheek. "Someone from long ago who knew you when you were a baby. Your grandfather, Dorian Lansing."

Hannah's eyes widened with delight. Her first reaction would depend largely on how Rachel handled this herself, so Rachel held her hand reassuringly and led her into the parlor.

Dorian sat down suddenly when they entered the parlor, his stern expression dissolving into one of shock. He stared from under thin black brows at his granddaughter's face. His fingers trembled on the ivory handle of his cane. "She looks like her mother," he said huskily, his face softening. "Come here, child."

Hannah released Rachel's hand and approached him slowly. Rachel could tell she did not remember the man, but she could also see that Hannah was not fearful of him. When she stood, respectfully quiet before Dorian, he suddenly smiled.

"Do you know who I am?"

Hannah glanced at Rachel as if asking permission to answer. Rachel smiled reassuringly. Hannah turned back to the old man and nodded her head.

"I am your mother's father, dear. Your grandfather."

A puzzled frown met his words at the mention of Hannah's mother.

"Have you nothing to say of that, child?"

He waited, expecting an answer. Finally Hannah brought her hands in front of her and signed, "Hello, Grandfather."

Dorian looked to Rachel. "What is this? A game?"

Again Hannah signed, "Hello."

Dorian caught her hands in his large grasp to still them. "Dear. I don't know this game you play. You will have to teach me on our way to San Francisco."

At that, Hannah's eyes grew wary.

"Yes. We are going on a trip. It is time you saw your grandmother Rose. She misses you terribly, just as I have. She will be surprised to see how you resemble your mother. She has been sad a long time, but I'm sure seeing you will cheer her up."

Hannah pulled away from Dorian's grasp and began signing in earnest, her small, slender fingers flying in front of his face.

Dorian's brows drew together in a frown. "Would someone please tell me what is going on here?" he said, impatience creeping into his voice. "I don't have time for these silly games."

The tone stopped Hannah's fingers, and she backed away, an uncertain look on her face.

"You just might want to learn these silly games," Rachel said steadily. She sat in the chair at right angles to Dorian, took a deep breath and smiled at Hannah. Above all, she didn't want the child frightened. "Slow down, Hannah. Start again."

Her fingers slowed, and Rachel caught the idea of what Hannah said.

"She wants to know where San Francisco is,"

Rachel interpreted for Dorian. "And how far it is from here."

Dorian sat back. "She cannot speak?"

"No, not since the accident at sea."

Dorian peered at Hannah for a moment. "Has she been to a doctor? Is there something wrong with her throat?"

"The doctor said her muteness was due to shock, not an injury to the vocal cords. She may regain the use of speech in time or the cords may atrophy and she will never speak."

"Only one doctor? Didn't Matthew get another opinion?"

"He respected this doctor and did not feel the need to go to another to hear the same thing."

"Or have the funds to see to her welfare," Dorian said angrily. He clasped Hannah's hands to his chest, making the girl flinch. "We'll just see about that! I'll have the best doctors this side of the Rockies see her. And if they cannot help her, then I'll take her to Boston myself."

"You would take her that far away?" Rachel asked, a catch in her throat.

"If I have to."

This was all moving too fast. Stuart would never get to see Hannah if Dorian had his way. Surely there could be some compromise.

Hannah began her finger ballet again, this time earnestly watching Rachel's face. When Rachel realized the message, she hesitated at first, and then translated for Dorian. "She wants to know if her father will be coming to San Francisco also."

A frown passed over Dorian's face. "He'll be there, but he can't come with us."

Hannah's fingers flew to their own rhythm again.

"Oh. I don't think so Hannah." Rachel shook her head.

"What?" Dorian sat forward. "What did she just ask?"

Rachel's cheeks warmed. "She asked if I would be going with her."

Dorian's gaze narrowed on her. "Why would she ask that?"

Her breath hitched at the question. She didn't want to reveal anything to this man that he might use against Stuart. "I've been tutoring Hannah for some time now and we've become good friends. My brother and I rode out to the lighthouse to work with her."

Dorian's sharp eyes narrowed as he listened to Rachel. Could he read behind her words? It certainly felt like it. Heat rose in her cheeks. He pulled once at his gray handlebar mustache, reminding her fleetingly of Terrance.

"I appreciate the care you have given Hannah." He rose from the chair and walked to the door. "I'll stay the night at the Horton Grand Hotel in San Diego. I have some shipping business to conclude there. At noon tomorrow, I'll return to fetch Hannah. Please see that her things are packed and ready to go. I'll, ah, have a small donation for the church for the care that you've given her." He nodded to Emma and started for the door.

"Wait! Sir!" Rachel cried out suddenly as a thought came to her.

Dorian stopped in the process of settling his hat on his head. "Yes?"

"You will let Hannah say goodbye to her fa— I mean, Stuart."

Dorian's lips pressed together in displeasure as he looked from Rachel to Hannah. That Hannah understood what was happening was all too evident by the terrified expression on her face.

"He's watched over her for three years," Rachel said, knowing that had Dorian known where Stuart was, those three years would not have happened.

A muscle worked in Dorian's jaw. "I'll let her say goodbye." The door closed with a soft thud as he left.

They stared at each other in silence—Emma, Hannah and Rachel. Large tears welled up in Hannah's eyes.

Rachel rose to her feet, keeping a protective arm around Hannah's shoulders. "How can he separate the two of them?"

"He can—and it looks like he will," said Emma. "I'm sure he feels that what he does is for the best. After all, he is her grandfather."

"But by bringing charges against Stuart?" Rachel's voice trembled with anger.

Emma eyed her sternly. "Think before you say such things in front of Hannah."

Rachel drew in two deep, shaky breaths, then let them out slowly.

"Some good has come of all this, Rachel. We have to believe things will be better for Hannah now. She'll get the best of care. She'll want for nothing."

Chapter Twenty-Three

Stuart watched without interest as a brown beetle scuttled along the base of the wall toward the bowl of oatmeal mush Sheriff Thorne had placed in his cell that morning. The cereal remained untouched, cold and congealed. A knot the size of a masthead bend had tightened his stomach beyond the point of digestion ever since Dorian had arrived in town yesterday.

Dorian. So changed now since Linnea's death. He tried to conjure up Linnea's image, but found he could no longer recall the distinct lines of her face. When he thought he had them, they shifted in his mind until all he could see was Rachel.

The sound of a carriage pulling to a stop in front of the jail stopped his ruminations. He stood and looked through the window to see Dorian alight, then turn and assist Rachel and Hannah from the transport. Hannah was dressed in traveling clothes, topped with a deep burgundy wool cape and stylish hat to match that must have been purchased by Dorian. She clasped Rachel's hand tightly. Rachel gave Hannah a reassuring smile before walking with her into the building. His heart ached at the sight of them both together—most likely it would be his last.

Sheriff Thorne opened the door and ushered the small group into the room. They remained quiet, unwilling to begin the course that would eventually separate all of them. Even Dorian hung back.

"I...ah...thought you might like a moment alone with the girl," Sheriff Thorne said as he moved to the cell bars and fiddled with the keys to open the lock.

"Just a moment," Dorian suddenly said. "I'd like to talk to Matthew."

The sheriff paused and then nodded.

Rachel raised her brows at Stuart, but clasped Hannah's hand again and said, "We'll just wait in the other room."

Dorian's gaze followed them until the door closed, and then he turned to face Stuart. "I've had the opportunity to learn a few things since speaking with you yesterday."

Stuart remained silent. The man could have his say. It would change little between them.

"I found out that Rachel is more than just a teacher to Hannah, that she has worked miracles with the girl. Truthfully, I am amazed that a stranger would take such an interest in a mute child."

"Rachel has more compassion than most. She told me once that she felt compelled to help Hannah."

"Yes," Dorian said. "I find her quite charming, when I can get past her fierce loyalty to you."

Stuart met his gaze without flinching.

"I heard what she did."

Stuart raised his eyebrows.

"Though I must say people are closemouthed in this small town. The owner of the mercantile was more than willing to give out information. Why Miss Houston cares for you, I cannot fathom, but you've always had a way with the ladies. In any case, she must not realize the whole story." He twisted his hand upon the ivory head of his cane. "Quite noble of you to honor Linnea's memory that way. I thank you for that."

"I loved her."

Under Stuart's steady gaze, it was Dorian who first looked aside. The older man sighed, sat on the bench by the wall and stared through the bars.

"I'm not doing this just for myself, Matthew, just to be cruel. Rose needs that girl. She hasn't been the same since you took Linnea from her. Linnea was the joy of my wife's life and she doesn't know how to let her go. Now Hannah will be that joy. Rose will become whole again."

"I'm sorry, Dorian," Stuart said honestly. He remembered Rose's fragility. "Rose was always good to me."

Nonplussed for a moment Dorian sputtered, "Yes… well." He drew himself up from the seat and cleared his throat. "I came here with the intention of offering you a way out. Against my better judgment, but in respect to the associate you once were to me, I extend it now."

Stuart silently gazed at Dorian, afraid to hope. Whatever his proposal, it would probably cost him dearly.

Dorian cleared his throat. "My bargain is this. You

may have your freedom. I'll drop all charges against you. You will be free to pursue your relationship with your lovely Rachel."

"What do you get out of this?"

"In return, you must give Hannah over to me willingly so that in the future there will be no more battles between us. It will simplify things for me, keeping this out of court, avoiding lawyers."

"What about the murder charge?"

"Like you said. I can call up a few favors and have that taken care of. Although the newspapers pushed the idea that you and Linnea were having an affair and that John had the right to come after you with a gun, I believe you were acting in Linnea's defense. Besides, Rose will not be able to withstand a court battle. She still has a soft spot in her heart for you."

Stuart grasped the bars tightly. "And so you wish me to choose between Rachel and Hannah? Between honoring my vow to Linnea or dishonoring her memory? What kind of choice is that?"

The man's eyebrows rose as he answered smoothly. "A good one, I should think. At least you will have one of them—and your freedom, too."

"You are asking me to break my promise to Linnea. I could never do that."

Dorian sighed and twisted the cane once more, slowly. "I thought that might be the way of it. Although, I had hoped you would come to your senses." He walked to the door. "Say your goodbyes."

The door swung open, and Rachel, Hannah and the sheriff entered. The sheriff fumbled with the key set, finally producing the one that fit the cell lock and opened the door.

"I don't guess you're any danger to these people if I let you see them without bars separating you," Sheriff Thorne said, meeting Stuart's eyes.

"Thank you," Stuart said, understanding the unspoken words and the measure of trust the sheriff granted him.

Hannah burst into the small cell, her face crumpling into tears, her fingers flying as she signed over and over, "Don't make me go. I love you, Daddy."

Stuart lifted her in his arms and hugged her to him, eyes closed, breathing deeply of her soapy scent. He held her tight, unwilling to have this last goodbye end.

Dorian cleared his throat from across the room.

Stuart slowly put Hannah down, but still she clung to him, gripping him fiercely about the waist.

"I must make my ship by this evening. We'll go out with the morning tide," Dorian said. He extended his hand and tapped his cane impatiently on the wooden floor. "Hannah, it's time to leave."

"Give me a minute, won't you?" Stuart glared at him.

Sheriff Thorne stepped forward. "Enough, Taylor."

"Don't you see? He's taking everything! Everything!" Stuart said through gritted teeth. He knelt down at Hannah's level and hugged her once more quickly. "Mind your grandmother Rose. She is a good woman." He looked up at Dorian, unable to keep the anger from his eyes, and then looked back at Hannah. "Write when you can. I'll answer your letters. Rose will give you my address."

Hannah signed, "I want to stay with you."

Stuart shook his head, his heart heavy in his chest. "Your grandparents will take good care of you."

Hannah signed something emphatically and stamped her foot. With that, Dorian gripped Hannah's hand firmly and pulled her tripping toward the door. She struggled against his iron grasp.

"You're hurting her!" Stuart yelled and rushed to the open cell door. Before he could reach Hannah, the sheriff slammed shut the bars. Stuart moved to the window as Dorian dragged Hannah into the carriage and spoke to the driver. Then Dorian turned back and entered the jail.

"Don't ever give her false hope like that. She will not receive any letters."

"It's your call, isn't it? It's always been your call." He grasped the iron bars and jerked them in impotent rage. How much more must he endure?

Dorian nodded smartly to the sheriff, whirled on his heel and walked out of the building.

Rachel leaned against the bars that separated them. Tears glistened in her eyes. "We are going to the light-house to gather Hannah's things and the puppy. Is there anything I can bring back for you?"

He thought about the few items in the house he could call his. "There's a leather satchel under my bed that has a few papers."

"That's it?"

"I never did keep much, remember?" But he was thinking of Linnea, Hannah and Rachel—not things.

"Yes. I remember," she answered softly and turned to leave.

He moved to the window to watch her climb into the carriage. More than anything, he wanted to call her back. How could he stand going on without her? Life without her—without Hannah—would be meaningless. But asking her to stay wouldn't change anything. In the end, it would hurt her more. When he boarded that coach bound for San Francisco and his monkey court, the best thing he could do for Rachel would be to be out of her life for good.

Chapter Twenty-Four

Hannah couldn't believe the tall old man sitting next to her had taken her away from her father. She hated him. He wanted her to teach him some of the hand words but she never would. Not ever. They were special words, just for Father and Rachel and Caleb. She slumped lower in the seat, hoping to get so small that he couldn't see her.

She had heard him say that they would go to his house and it would be a long trip. She always wanted to go on a trip. But not far away, not without her father or Rachel.

She looked out the window of the carriage. They were nearing the lighthouse. Rachel had said she must say goodbye to her house today. She would bring everything with her—her mother's special blanket and the toys in her room, her treasure box of seashells. Grandfather had said he would buy her all new toys once they reached his house. But she didn't want new toys.

The carriage stopped and her grandfather stepped out, turning to help her jump down to the ground. She waited as he placed his funny tall hat on his head and tapped his cane once on the dirt. "Gather your things quickly, my dear," he said. "We need to make haste in order to get to the ship before sundown."

She hated it when he called her dear. She wasn't his dear. She did not even like him—him and his big nose with hair in it. She slowed down, trying to tug her hand from his. She couldn't go on a ship. Didn't he know that? People died on ships! Mother died on one. Her heart started racing in her chest. She tugged harder to free her hand.

Grandfather let go and turned to help Rachel down from the carriage. Hannah raced up to the house and flung open the door looking for Caleb. Where was he? Up the stairs she ran, peeking in each room and cubbyhole until she reached the ladder to the catwalk. She raced back downstairs, past Grandfather and Rachel and out to the shed. Tugging at the heavy door, she finally opened it wide enough to squeeze through. Caleb wasn't there and neither was her puppy. Her heart beat even faster.

"Perhaps they've gone down to the beach, Hannah," said Rachel from the doorway. "I saw some tracks."

Grandfather frowned. "Will they be back soon?"

"I don't know. But Caleb will want to say goodbye to Hannah."

"The climb back up is too steep for me. Leave Hannah here and you go. Be quick about it."

Hannah saw Rachel nod and walk from the shed. She ran after her. She didn't want to be alone with the strange man. His stick came up and blocked her path.

"You and I shall go upstairs and collect your things, young lady."

* * *

"Matthew!" Dorian bellowed. "You manipulated this, didn't you?"

Stuart looked up to see Dorian stride into the sheriff's office and smack his cane on the desk. He walked straight to the door and pulled on the handle. The door was secure. He brandished his cane like a cudgel, waving it erratically. "Sheriff, open this door immediately!"

Thorne ambled over to Dorian. "What's the problem? And what the heck are you doing back here?"

"That's none of your business!" Dorian's voice rose a notch in volume.

"Well, I don't know that you are in a state of mind to see the fellow on the other side of that door."

Stuart gripped the bars of his cell. He'd never seen Dorian so angry—so furiously angry. The man was known for his cool head and unemotional handling of problems.

"What's happened? Is Hannah all right?" Stuart called through the door.

"I'm sure you know better than me," Dorian sputtered. "Now, Sheriff, *open this door!*"

"I'll take your gun again," Sheriff Thorne said calmly.

Dorian dug in his coat pocket and then tossed the derringer to the sheriff.

Thorne unlocked the door, swinging it wide.

"She's gone and well you know it," Dorian said, waving his cane again as he entered the cell room. "You planned this! Anything to see me look a fool."

"Hannah's gone?" Stuart gripped the bars tighter as fear took hold of him. "Where? Dorian. Where?"

"At the lighthouse. She rushed after Rachel, down to the beach to look for Caleb. Well, Caleb came back but not Hannah or Rachel. He never saw them."

Stuart's heart nearly stopped.

Dorian pointed a bony finger at Stuart. "You put the idea into her head. Don't even think about trying to deny it."

Stuart shook his head. "Have you searched everywhere?"

"Caleb went down to look on the beach. It was too steep of a climb for me. I came back here to make sure they hadn't returned here."

Panic knifed through Stuart. "Let me out! Let me find them!"

"Oh, you'd like that, wouldn't you? Do you truly think I could be so gullible?" The ghost of a sickly smile played about his thin lips. "Come, Matthew, you know me better than that."

"She's probably terrified. How could you let her get away from you?" Stuart demanded, his anger matching Dorian's. "She's just a little girl."

"Considering that you planned the whole thing, to her possible detriment I might add, I'm sure you know where she is right now. Safe and cozy."

"You fool! Can't I make you understand that I had nothing to do with this?"

Dorian shook his head. "I'll never believe you, Matthew. This would be the easiest way for you to obtain what you want."

Stuart felt numb inside. With an edge of steel to his voice, he said, "I would never put Hannah at that kind of risk. I would do anything to protect her—even to go so far as handing her over to you."

"Which you did. Remember that. She is mine now."

Stuart shook his head. "You couldn't even protect her for a few hours and yet you blame me for being unable to save Linnea during one of the worst storms at sea in twenty-five years." He pushed his head against the bars and closed his eyes in frustration. There had to be some way to make Dorian see reason. Hannah's life depended on it. "Dorian, please. Let me help. I have to know she is safe. I'll go crazy in here not knowing, not doing something."

For the first time, doubt rose in Dorian's eyes. He stepped backward and sat heavily on the bench along the wall.

Stuart tried to shake the bars. "It will be dark within the hour. We've got to move now!"

Dorian looked vacantly at the sheriff who watched from the doorway and then back at Stuart. "I'll never find her. Not if she doesn't want to be found. And she can move a lot faster than me."

"Your best bet was to get Caleb to help with the search. Hannah trusts him. But I'm your next choice. And I know the area even better."

Dorian sat still as if he hadn't heard.

"You're wasting time you don't have. She may be in trouble. For all we know, she could be hurt and unable to call for help."

Slowly Dorian lifted his gaze to meet Stuart's. "If she would come at the sound of their voices, how much more she would come if you called for her," he said, resignation clearing the furrow between his brows.

Stuart stilled. His heart pounded in his chest as he waited, hoping, yet afraid to hope.

The sheriff stepped closer. "What is it exactly you are saying, Mr. Lansing?"

Dorian paused, staring at Stuart, then said with a sharp edge to his voice, "What I'm saying is, may I have this man released in order to locate my granddaughter?"

"Are you dropping the charges?" the sheriff asked.

Dorian looked sharply at Stuart. "I can't do that. The authorities are waiting in San Francisco to question him regarding a suspicious death. When Hannah is found, she comes with me. The charges stand."

"Well, looks like you're stuck between the bark and the tree, Mr. Taylor. But I expect you to be cooperative," Sheriff Thorne said. "Otherwise, you'll be right back in here and we'll search for the girl without you. Understood?"

Stuart set his jaw. He didn't have a choice. Making sure Hannah and Rachel were safe was all that mattered. He nodded his agreement.

Thorne retrieved the keys from the hook on the wall and unlocked the cell door. "I'll be keeping an eye on you, Taylor."

When Stuart stepped out and came face-to-face with Dorian, he paused, battling with himself to keep from ramming his fist into the man's face.

Dorian kept his eyes on Stuart, acknowledging Stuart's anger. "My carriage is outside."

Chapter Twenty-Five

The sun sank below the horizon, yet its last rays still managed to cast an orange glow over the water and the cliffs. The steady roar of the ocean waves muted everything. Rachel rubbed her throat. She'd called for Caleb until she was hoarse. She'd checked the boat tie-down. Everything looked in order, but Hannah was nowhere to be found.

Down the beach a flutter of yellow among a sandy bed of kelp caught her eye.

Hannah's hair ribbon? Edging closer to the spot, she noticed small footprints in the sand. Then a wave rushed to shore and obliterated the evidence, pushing the strangle of kelp farther up the beach.

Rachel ran down the beach, a premonition building inside.

A puppy barked. It sounded far away. So far that Rachel couldn't be sure she heard it at all.

She picked up her pace and then stopped suddenly, staring in apprehension at the waves licking her feet.

The tide was coming in! Panic rose swift and sharp within her.

Ahead, she heard again a puppy's high-pitched whine blend in with the sounds of the sea.

"Caleb!" she called again. She sloshed through the surf, around the large rock that jutted out into the ocean where they'd hunted at the tidal pools so many months before. The water churned and spit froth as if it were angry, now covering the boulders and rocks that provided a haven for sea creatures. She gave up any hope of keeping her skirt dry as the surf battered her at hip level.

Once to the other side of the rock, she realized that the beach was gone. No one was there—not even a puppy. Had she been wrong to come here? Had she only imagined the puppy's whining? Then she spied the small opening in the cliff wall.

The cavern!

She ducked through the narrow opening, stumbling at the dip in the sandy floor, and then straightened inside a small alcove. Water swirled around her knees here, but a few more steps and she reached dry sand. Although, she knew it wouldn't be dry for long. The last rays of the setting sun made the cavern walls glow orange.

In the dim light, Hannah crouched in a niche, the puppy playfully out of reach in front of her.

"Hannah!" Rachel could barely believe her own eyes.

Hannah spun around. Her dress was dirty and wrinkled, her hair tangled and stringy, but otherwise she looked fine.

Then Rachel noticed that her cheeks were wet with tears.

Rachel ran to her and enveloped her, shivering, into her arms. The puppy dashed up and yipped at them, and then danced just beyond their reach.

"Having trouble catching him?" She wiped Hannah's face. "I'll help."

They approached the animal from opposite sides. Yet, over and over the pup dashed between their outstretched hands. Rachel quickly became frustrated.

"This isn't working, Hannah. And we have to go. The tide is getting too high to wait any longer."

She peeled off her cloak. The next time the puppy made its wild dash, Rachel threw the cloak as though she was casting for fish. The heavy wool material landed on the puppy, stopping it just long enough for Rachel to grab it and bundle it up.

"Let's get to your house before the ti—" Her voice faltered as she glanced at the narrow opening. The surf rushed in and it was way over Hannah's head. They had to get out—now.

She met and held Hannah's gaze, then purposely squatted and released the puppy. Hannah started to run past her to capture the pet, but Rachel grabbed her shoulders and forced her to meet her gaze.

"If there is time, I'll come back for the puppy, but right now you are the most important thing. You must get out of here. The pup will be scared, but she'll be all right." Rachel hoped she spoke the truth.

Hannah's eyes widened in fright. She tried to sign something, her finger ballet frantic and disjointed.

Finally Rachel made out the word *drown*. Was Hannah thinking about her mother? Remembering? "Come here, honey." Rachel caught her to her, intending only to pick her up, but the embrace for reassurance ended in a fierce hug. She took a deep breath and looked into worried eyes. "Grab on to me. Tight."

Hannah flung her arms around Rachel's neck. "Now, don't let go for anything."

The water pounded against her, twisting and tugging her heavy skirt, trying to knock her down. The ground was uneven, and where the floor of the cave dipped, the water rose to her waist.

At the entrance, the force of the surf increased, buffeting them about, the icy spray drenching them both. The water plastered her hair to her face, blinding her to the small amount of graying twilight. The ocean roared about them, swirling and crashing. A wave thundered over them and forced them under. They surfaced, sputtering and spitting the saltwater from their mouths.

Frantically Rachel tried to regain her footing. A person could be washed out to sea. She'd heard it said that even strong sailors were no match for the tides if the ocean had a mind to take them. She struggled to keep Hannah's head above water while the girl clung to her side and the water pulled at her skirt and legs. Stuart had already lost one he loved to the sea. Rachel refused to let the sea have another.

Suddenly her feet found the uneven sandy bottom. She braced herself for an instant, unsure of her footing, when another wave crashed through the small inlet and shoved them back into the cavern.

"The water's too strong," she said in gasps. *And cold.* Her lips must be blue, they were so numb.

In the last of the dim light, the distinct features of Hannah's face faded into a blur of grayness. Rachel clung to her, shivering and listening to the roar of each wave barreling toward them, wondering if this would be the wave, larger than the rest, that would cover them.

"It's almost too dark to see anything," Sheriff Thorne said as they approached the lighthouse. "Even the lanterns aren't much help. We ought to start in the morning."

"No!" thundered Stuart and Dorian simultaneously.

"I won't stop," said Stuart. "Not for a minute."

The sheriff took off his Stetson and wiped his brow. "Look, Taylor. They could be anywhere."

"I'm not quitting!" Stuart growled. "I know this peninsula better than either of you."

The beam from the lighthouse flashed over them for the first time that night. Caleb was in the tower.

Stuart grabbed a lantern and rope from the shed, and then searched the area for signs of Hannah. He found the tracks of her small-size brogans heading toward the beach trail. "Don't expect me back for several hours. Sheriff, you're welcome to follow if you think I'll escape." He headed down the trail at a run, the sheriff somewhere behind him.

Skidding and sliding, he raced as though the devil chased him, apprehension building. Ignoring the switchbacks and the trail, he raced straight down, grabbing at sage and brush for balance. Often he had nothing to steady himself but the dirt, where broken shells bloodied his hands. He dropped the glowing lantern at the last bit of even ground and then slid the last ten feet to the bottom at such a speed that he couldn't stop and splashed into the ocean. He gasped as the icy water closed around his waist. The tide was on its way in. Soon there'd be no safe place along this part of the beach.

He waded farther into the water, pushing through with a sense of vengeance. Waves crashed into him, determined to thrust him against the jagged cliff formations. He slipped once and scraped up against the sandstone, then braced himself and pushed steadily onward, ignoring the sting of the saltwater in his eyes and on the raw scrapes of his hands.

There was only one place they could be if they were still on the beach. Otherwise they would have made it to higher ground and back to the lighthouse by now.

The cave.

The large fishing rock loomed dark and forbidding before him. It jutted out into the water just far enough to make going around difficult, and with its sides too sheer to climb from this position. If...*if*...he made it around without drowning himself, he wasn't sure he could make it back. But he had to know that Rachel and Hannah were not trapped on the other side. He had to...

Stumbling over rocks and boulders in his path, Stuart fought as the water pushed and pulled him relentlessly. In some small recess of his brain he noted the temperature was frigid and the feeling in his fingers had gone beyond numb. They were not responding like they should.

Finally he rounded the large rock that partially hid the inlet to the small cave. It was too dark to see the cave now, but he knew well enough it was there—somewhere ahead of him.

"Rachel!" he called over the roar of the waves. "Rachel!"

"I'm here!"

His heart lodged in his throat. He'd found her. The current pulled against him, trying to drag him out to sea. He struggled and pushed ahead. Then a wave found his back and the force of the water hurtled him toward the narrowed inlet. At least, he hoped that was where he was heading since he couldn't see much. Suddenly his face scraped against the gritty sand floor. He pushed up and struggled to stand, the water just above his waist.

The sound was different here. The roar of the ocean muffled.

He was inside the cave.

Breathing heavily, he wiped the water off his face. He could barely discern someone's shape just ahead of him. He started toward the figure when small hands gripped his arm.

"My God!" He felt the straggly hair on the head before him. "Hannah!" He whisked her into his arms and hugged her, rubbing her hair, her face, her shoulders. "Are you all right?"

In the crook between his cheek and shoulder, he felt her nod, then shiver. Relief washed through him. "Rachel?"

"I'm fine." Her voice came from a few feet away, trembling. "We tried to get out but the water was too strong." Slowly the curve of her shoulders became visible. A swift need to touch her overwhelmed him. He had to reassure himself that she, too, was all right, that she was real. He reached for her, drawing her firmly against his wet chest. She melted against him, sliding her arm around his waist.

"Thank God you're here, Stuart."

He crushed his lips to hers, drawing what warmth he could from her lips, and in turn trying to infuse her with a portion of his strength. Perhaps God had had a hand in this.

"How did you know where to look for us?" Her teeth chattered from the cold.

"Gut instinct." He pulled her close again, unwilling to let her go. "We have to get out of here."

"But…are you free now?"

"Not exactly."

He could barely see the outline of the cave opening. A few stars twinkled in the night sky just beyond it. As he judged his options, a cold fist closed over his heart while the awful truth dawned.

"What is it?" Rachel asked.

The irony of the situation seeped through him, forcing a single bitter laugh. It wasn't enough that he'd lost Linnea and been haunted by her face in his dreams ever since. No—now he must face nearly the same thing again.

"Stuart?" Rachel's voice was rich with concern.

He ran his hand through his hair, pushing the wet

strands back from his forehead, his fingers skimming the edges of the scar—remembering.

"It's not the same," Rachel said. "Not the same situation at all."

He stilled.

"You told me Linnea pushed Hannah at you. If anyone was going to be saved she wanted it to be Hannah. She made the choice."

"You weren't there. You don't know." He hadn't meant to growl out the words, but his frustration doubled by the second. After living with his choice, he didn't need Rachel arguing the point with him. "I can only take one of you at a time—not both."

"But—"

"The surf is too strong," he lashed out at her. "I can't take you both."

He sensed her still beside him. "Then there is no choice at all."

He wished he could see her face better, but it was too dark. Her face had always told him what she thought. "I won't go until I'm sure you understand. I must take Hannah first. I can't leave her in here."

"Of course you can't. She's frightened enough as it is. I'll just wait for you."

Her calm reply almost undid him. He had asked so much of her, and still she seemed to trust him. He brushed his fingers down her soft cheek and felt her chin tremble. "I'll be back as soon as Hannah is on high ground," he murmured.

"I know."

He took a deep breath, then turned to Hannah.

"We're going for a swim, short stuff," he said with a confidence he did not feel. "This may be a little wild, so whatever happens don't let go of me. And I won't let go of you."

She grasped his neck as he waded back into the water. The urge to look back once at Rachel was strong, but he resisted, refusing to have another memory etched in his mind that might stay with him forever. *I'll just wait for you,* she'd said. He'd be back, he vowed silently.

He made his way toward the opening until the water came to his chest. Together, he and Hannah braced as the first wave thundered toward them. He shouted in her ear, and at the last minute, rather than fight the current, they ducked under the water, allowing the wave to churn violently above their heads. When they resurfaced, Hannah coughed and spit water, and they could see the stars overhead.

They were out of the cave.

He let the outgoing water carry them until he sensed they were heading beyond the rock and then he struggled to get out of its grasp. He forced his way through the surf, rounding the jagged rock, and then let an incoming wave carry them toward the cliff. Three more waves propelled them farther. Holding Hannah's hand firmly in his, Stuart and she finally arrived at the base of the trail, both out of breath, but both very much safe.

"Now, Hannah. I want you to crawl up the trail and wait for me by the lantern. I'm going back for Rachel."

She nodded, shivering, and he hugged her tight.

"If…" He hated to say it. He took a deep breath. "If

I don't come back, you must climb up the trail to the lighthouse. Caleb is there. Do you understand?"

Again she nodded, and he hugged her tight. "I love you, short stuff."

A brave smile worked its way past the shivers.

He turned back into the surf.

When he entered the small cavern again, he could no longer see—not even an outline. And the water was up to his thighs on the highest ground. "Rachel?"

A puppy whined.

"Rachel?"

"I'm all right, Stuart. I'm here."

"Ready?"

"Can you manage the pup, too?"

He hesitated.

"I could tie him up with a strip of my petticoat."

He thought for a moment. "Keep hold of the dog." He reached his hand around her waist and drew her close, flattening her against him. "The skirt will have to go. It will drag you down." With that, he unbuttoned the waistband and pushed the skirt down below the water. "Step out."

When she'd done so, he grabbed the hem of her petticoat and ripped a strip of cloth, then tied it around the dog's middle.

"Ready?"

"Yes," she said breathlessly.

His mouth found hers in the dark. He tightened his arms around her and kissed her thoroughly. Her lips were smooth and immeasurably giving. "I love you, Rachel Houston."

"I know, Stuart." She smiled against his mouth, and he felt her shiver.

"Don't let go."

"Never."

The tide rose with every minute they delayed. He took her hand and they waded toward the sound of waves crashing against the cliff. He gripped her hand tighter. "Now!"

They surged forward with the water as it receded from the cave. Another, larger wave battered them, tugging at them, trying to separate them. Stuart held on tight. He would not lose Rachel. Not this way. He strained to see in the inky blackness. If only he could see the waves coming, he'd be able to anticipate and dive under them.

Another wave washed over their heads. He came up choking and sputtering, pulling Rachel up, up, to where she could get air. He heard her gasp beside him.

Then they were out in the starlight. He felt for the sheer face of the fishing rock. The water was over his head, now, but as long as he stayed near the rock, they would make it.

They endured the brutal crash of the water over them once more, and though his fingers were raw from gripping the jagged edge, he still managed to shield Rachel from much of the force of the wave.

Finally they were around the rock and headed toward the cliff and the trail.

They came to the spot that Stuart had left Hannah, and Stuart sat down, hands on his knees, and dragged in several deep breaths. Rachel, next to him, did the same. A shiver racked her body.

"We have to get warm," he said gruffly, looking around for Hannah, realizing suddenly that a second lantern glowed nearby. Hannah stood in its glow, next to the sheriff.

"I'll help the girl," Sheriff Thorne said, lifting his lantern to take a good look at each of them. "And I'll hang on to that pup, too."

Stuart handed him the end of cloth that secured the dog. A hot fire sounded better than anything right now. He reached for Rachel, and she grasped his hand.

On the trek to the lighthouse, he never let go.

Chapter Twenty-Six

When they entered the lighthouse, Dorian looked up from his seat in front of the small fire. He looked ten years older.

"You found her. Thank God. Caleb, bring some blankets."

Caleb looked to Stuart.

"In the chest at the foot of the stairs." Stuart walked over to the fire and shoveled more coal pellets into it.

Dorian wrapped Hannah in the first quilt. He sat in the rocker by the fire and pulled her onto his lap.

Stuart watched them for a moment, surprised that Hannah had allowed herself to be held by Dorian, but even more surprised at Dorian's demeanor. Gone was the commanding authoritarian, replaced by a gentle man whose only concern was Hannah's well-being.

"Her trunk is in the kitchen," Rachel said. "I'll get some dry clothes."

Stuart followed her into the room. "Thank you for being there," he said, tugging the blanket closer around her shoulders. She looked so bedraggled, that he gave up any pretense and, using the blanket, pulled her against him. He kissed her gently. "Thank God you're safe," he murmured against her lips. "I love you, Rachel."

"I never thought to hear you say those words," she said softly, "and now you said them twice in one evening."

"I should have told you long ago."

A small smile tilted her lips. "What will happen now? Will you have to go back to jail?"

"I don't know. Dorian holds the cards."

They stood embracing, cold and shivering, both reluctant to let go.

Sheriff Thorne cleared his throat by the doorway. "I realize you're creating your own heat there, but I think the two of you better get by the fire or you'll both catch cold."

Caleb watched from behind the sheriff. Stuart suppressed a smile as he felt Rachel stiffen slightly when she noticed him.

"Would you put on some water for tea, Caleb? And might I borrow some dry clothes?" Rachel asked in a high voice. At his nod, she moved out of Stuart's arms and headed up the stairs. She paused on the bottom step as the sheriff spoke.

"I'll be heading back to town just as soon as everyone's warmed up, Miss Houston."

She looked at Stuart, but her answer was for the sheriff. "I'll be ready."

Stuart found a nightgown for Hannah in the trunk.

Hannah was in such an exhausted state that she only grumbled slightly as he changed her into the dry gown, then she snuggled back onto her grandfather. He took a seat by the fire with Dorian, noting that the sheriff had pulled in a chair from the kitchen to join them. "So," he said after a long silence, "where do we go from here?"

Dorian sighed. "This whole business doesn't sit well with me." He brushed a wisp of hair off Hannah's cheek.

Gone was the strong, strident voice, the confidence that Stuart had come to expect from Dorian. There was a hesitation totally foreign to his usual manners.

"I've had a lot of time to think, along with my worrying about Hannah's safety, while you were trying to find her. I...I don't feel right having things end this way. I've come to some conclusions about you...about me and Rose. At one time I thought replacing the daughter we lost with our granddaughter would make things right again."

Stuart wondered where this would lead, afraid to let himself hope.

"I was wrong."

Dorian stared at the fire through watery eyes. "It has been hard on all of us to lose Linnea."

Stuart stopped breathing. Had Dorian just said "us"? As in, including him?

"She was my world. But now, to nearly lose Hannah..." His voice trailed off for a moment. "Well, I place the blame entirely on my own shoulders."

Stuart had never seen Dorian so shattered.

"These past few years have changed all of us, but at one time you were as near to a son as could be to me. I don't think you've changed all that much." He grimaced. "Maybe I'm the one who changed—or didn't change when I should have."

He shifted in the rocker to look at Stuart. "You may be unaware that the banker, Mr. Furst, was prepared to cover the cost of my missing cargo along with any legal fees you incurred. He said you refused any reward for saving his son."

Stuart nodded carefully, afraid to break the course of Dorian's thoughts.

"Guess you've made a few powerful friends of your own. Well, the Fursts can keep their money. That isn't what this was about and you and I both know it. The lost cargo was just a means to finding you—a means to an end. And that end isn't anything I anticipated."

He stopped rocking and looked down. Hannah was fast asleep in his arms.

"I'll put her to bed, sir," Caleb said. At the older man's nod, Caleb gathered Hannah up and took her up the stairs. Stuart listened as the boy's footsteps sounded overhead in Hannah's bedroom.

Dorian met Stuart's gaze. "The enquiry into the death of Linnea's husband will just be a formality. I'll bear witness to the fact that he abused her and she was frightened for her life and the life of their daughter. Linnea killed him, Stuart. Not you, as much as you may have believed that. The doctor's autopsy showed it was the bullet from her gun—the gun I'd given her on her twentieth birthday—that lodged in his spleen. It took him a while to die and so he followed her straight to you."

Dazed at this new information, Stuart murmured, "But I shot him…."

"Your bullets struck his hip and shoulder. They made him fall, too weak from loss of blood to get back up."

A huge weight lifted from Stuart's shoulders. "All this time, I thought I'd killed him."

Dorian smiled sadly. "I taught my daughter to protect herself. She certainly did."

Stuart tried to take in all that Dorian had said. After so many years of believing he'd murdered John Newcomb, to learn the truth took a bit of reckoning.

"Because of Newcomb's notoriety, the newspapers had a field day, sensationalizing your link to Linnea. And I chose to believe them over you."

"I loved your daughter, sir."

"I know that now. And I know you would have done everything in your power to save her that night at sea."

"I tried. I wanted the sea to take me, not her."

"Yes, I understand that now. I've been foolish. And stubborn." Dorian stood and walked the few steps to lean his hand against the fireplace mantel and stared into the fire. "You really were the better man for her, Matthew. If only things had worked out differently."

Stuart swallowed hard. To have Dorian admit so much left him stunned. Slowly his thoughts returned to the present, and his promise to Linnea. "So where does that leave us, Dorian? Do you still plan to take Hannah to San Francisco?"

The quiet that followed his question was deafening. Only the crackling of the fire could be heard.

Dorian turned to face him. "Yes, I do."

Stuart dropped his head into his hands. He'd hoped—he didn't know what he'd hoped. There was no way, having found Hannah, Dorian would let her go again. He tried to focus on what Dorian was saying.

"And you need to come back, too. You must clear up this business of Newcomb. Perhaps while there, we can have Hannah see a specialist regarding her voice."

"What about Hannah's father's relatives? Will they cause any trouble?"

"I guess we'll face that if it comes. We'll face it together."

Emotion overcame Stuart. This was not the man he'd left three years ago. Strange to have their paths bring them back full circle.

"You are welcome in our home. Rose has asked for you a number of times over the past year. It would do her heart good to see you."

"Thank you, Dorian." He could barely get the words out.

"Pack your things while you're upstairs."

Stuart stood, for the first time noticing that Rachel had come back dressed in Caleb's old trousers. She listened from the doorway, an unreadable expression on her face.

He was going to leave her. Rachel leaned against the door frame for support. She had hoped, with all that had gone between them this night, that he would be able to stay. That he would want to stay.

He grabbed her hand and pulled her into the kitchen. "I have to do this, Rachel. This is my chance."

She nodded but couldn't meet his gaze.

"I've got to clear my name. You understand that, don't you?"

She was numb inside. That's all she understood. "You don't need to explain anything to me."

"Yes, I do. I know you don't want me to leave. If I don't go to San Francisco and take care of this, I'll always wonder if someone is out there looking for me— Linnea's husband's family or a trigger-happy bounty hunter."

Her heart was being cut in two. She could feel the chasm, the pain in her chest. In that moment she could almost hate him. Almost but not quite. Because try as she might to feel nothing, she still loved him. On some small level deep inside, she did know why he had to leave.

"I really do understand, Stuart. Now go upstairs and take care of your things. I'm sure Mr. Lansing will want to leave as quickly as possible."

He took hold of her shoulders, forcing her to turn toward him, acknowledge him. "Please look at me, Rachel."

Slowly her eyes met his.

"I don't know how this will turn out. I can't promise you anything. I have to take one day at a time."

"Believe me, I don't expect anything," she said bitterly.

He shook her gently. "I'm not just one more person leaving you," he said earnestly.

Her chin notched up. "No. You are two more people leaving. But you know something? It's okay. I've got a lot to do over the next few months—the teaching examination, getting my job back. You don't figure into any of that."

He frowned and stepped back, lowering his hands.

She knew she was pushing him away, but he didn't realize how he was hurting her. "You better go get your things together, Stuart. Daylight will come soon enough and I imagine Mr. Lansing will want to leave on the morning tide as he has planned."

He nodded slowly. "Rachel—"

"I…I don't know if I will make it to the dock in the morning. Give my love to Hannah and tell her to write."

"She'll write, and so will I." He started toward her.

"Stuart, please," she suddenly begged, her voice breaking. "Don't make this any harder for me." She turned away from him, blindly swiping at the tears in her eyes. Stepping into the parlor, she spied the one she needed. "Sheriff? Could you take me home now?"

"From the look on your face, I'd say you missed the sea," Dorian said, his gaze more than a little sly. "At least from this vantage point."

"Some," Stuart admitted, enjoying the roll of the steamer's deck beneath his feet. "More than I realized."

He circled his arm around Hannah's shoulders. Having him with her had lessened her fear of the ship, and Stuart found that daylight also eased her fears. He looked from her blond head down into the kelp beds that floated beside the ship. Linnea's vision no longer haunted him, nor the guilt he had carried for so long. Although he couldn't be sure how he would fare until the court hearing was over, for the first time in years he felt free.

"I'm not sure I approve of my granddaughter learning some of the words my crew members use," Dorian said. "She will certainly raise her grandmother's eyebrows if Rose catches on to her hand signals."

Stuart chuckled. "Rose will just have to take her for what she is."

"It could become her goal in life to smooth the rough edges you've given the girl."

"Hannah will handle it." Besides, after hearing of Rose's declining condition, he suspected seeing Hannah would do Rose's heart good. Truth be told, he missed her, too. To see her again would be good for him.

A spark of light on the peninsula caught his eye. Although it was early morning, the lantern at the lighthouse flashed once, twice, three times. Beside him, Hannah stood on her toes and pointed to the light, and then waved wildly.

"Caleb?" Dorian asked.

Stuart nodded.

"Goodbye and good journey," Dorian translated the light's familiar message to sailors. "It would seem you have made a few loyal friends here."

"A few," he murmured, his thoughts on Rachel. He had looked for her on the docks this morning, but she hadn't come to see them off. Just as she'd said. Already she was pushing him away.

He had to do this. He wished he could make her

understand. If he was to ever have a future with her, he had to do this. He only hoped Dorian was right and all charges would be dropped after the investigation.

Chapter Twenty-Seven

One Month Later

Rachel hurried across the street toward the mercantile. Her monthly had come this morning, and with it the cramping. Perhaps the store had a powder to ease the discomfort. She'd half hoped she might be carrying Stuart's baby. How wonderful it would have been to have a small part of him. But the practical part of her knew it would be catastrophic. She would never be able to support a child on her own. She stepped inside.

"Rachel?" Elizabeth called out. "A letter came for you this morning. I was going to run it over to you on my lunch break, but since you're here, let me see if I can find it. Ah, here it is." Elizabeth walked around the end of the counter and handed the envelope to her.

She tore apart the waxed seal, imprinted with a bold M.S.T. and scanned the letter.

Miss Rachel Houston:

Hannah and I arrived safely in San Francisco. It was something to see the look on Rose's face when she first saw her granddaughter. I don't think I ever told you, but Hannah is the image of Linnea.

Additional charges from Newcomb's family have postponed the court date. They are making things more difficult. I'm expecting no leniency from the judge. The jail here is adequate—but I miss Thornton's philosophical discussions—especially since I may be here a long time.

I hope the town there has come to their senses and let you resume teaching their children. They're fools if they don't. Wish things had turned out differently between you and me. Wish a lot of things.

Matthew Stuart Taylor

Rachel's hand shook as she read the message again. Her eyes burned with tears. It didn't sound like he expected to be freed.

A rustling sound from behind made her turn quickly to the spools of thread. The colors swam before her eyes. Numbly, she picked up a spool of blue. She thought she'd toughened up. In the weeks since Stuart had gone, she'd tried hard to put the past behind her and get on with her life.

"Excuse me, Rachel?" Elizabeth said.

"Yes," she answered, unable to look Elizabeth in the eye, her thoughts still focused on Stuart.

"Is it from the Mr. Taylor?"

She nodded numbly.

"How is Hannah? Is she adjusting to San Francisco?"

Rachel blew out a shaky sigh. "He didn't say much, but it sounds like she is."

"Are you all right?"

She nodded quickly, but a sob slipped past her lips. She clasped her hand over her mouth. Her one-time friend hadn't initiated a conversation with her in over two months, and now she picked a fine time to show concern—when Rachel was ready to blubber like a fool. Desperately she struggled to take hold of her emotions.

"You must miss them terribly," Elizabeth said carefully.

Rachel raised her gaze but was unable to focus for the water in her eyes. "They are doing well. That's enough." Of course it wasn't, but she wasn't going to say more to Elizabeth. Some things were too dear to talk about, especially to someone who had shunned her. She squared her shoulders and folded the note, placing it in her reticule. Her actions couldn't have announced more clearly that she was preparing to leave. But Elizabeth seemed oblivious to her signals, or else refused to acknowledge them.

"I hear you passed the teaching exam."

Rachel stopped en route to the door. If Elizabeth, who didn't even have children in the school, was going to give her difficulty about wanting to teach, she'd better think again.

"So even after all that has happened you still want to teach?"

She braced herself, prepared to endure yet another snide comment. "Yes. If I can convince the school board to give me the chance. If not, I'll look elsewhere."

Elizabeth held out a handkerchief. "Then I hope you get your chance."

Caught off guard, Rachel looked at Elizabeth in confusion. When all she saw in the woman's face was honest concern, she slowly relaxed her stance and took the cloth. "Thank you."

Elizabeth smiled tentatively. "You have a gift for teaching. You did wonders with Hannah. You loved them both, didn't you?"

Startled again by the woman's perception, Rachel asked, "It's that obvious?"

"You look that miserable."

Rachel let out a sigh, thinking of Stuart. "But I don't have any regrets, Elizabeth. I'd do it all over again in a heartbeat."

Elizabeth nodded slowly, understanding in her face. "I know."

And Rachel suddenly realized that she did. "How did you learn of the certificate?"

"Terrance mentioned when it arrived in the mail. I, ah, suppose you heard that he's courting Amanda now."

"I heard. They are suited for each other."

Elizabeth's brown eyes took on a mischievous glint. "Oh, Rachel! How can you say that? I cannot imagine her as my sister-in-law. After an hour we are like two pieces of sandpaper."

A smile, the first real one in a long time, tugged at Rachel's lips.

"That's better," Elizabeth said. "Now, what can I help you find?"

Rachel looked blankly at the spool of blue thread in her hand, and then slowly placed it back on the rack. "Shoes," she said, this time with determination. "I need them for my interview with the school board."

Elizabeth tapped her finger against her cheek, deep in thought for a moment. "Then I have a suggestion. Let's go into New San Diego and see the display at Marston's store. We'll see what type of competition Terrance and I are up against to try to bring more business here and we can see the latest in spring fashion."

Rachel found herself smiling at Elizabeth's enthusiasm. And if the town council approved Rachel's position—then she would be able to get on with her life.

She would be a good teacher, she vowed to herself. She would gain the town's respect again. She drew the drawstring tight on her bag, thinking of the letter within. And she would never trust her heart to another man. Obviously, any further pining on her part for what could have been was futile. Stuart had left for good. He wasn't coming back. Ever.

Chapter Twenty-Eight

April 1874

Stuart strode up the main street of La Playa with Hannah tugging relentlessly at his hand, urging him to go faster. His ship had steamed into port just this morning and he'd quickly delegated the duties of unloading Dorian's wares to his first mate. With that task underway, he made his way directly to the parsonage, his thoughts on one auburn-haired woman.

Reverend Crouse answered Stuart's knock. "Taylor! And Hannah too! A surprise indeed!"

"Come in," Emma Crouse said, peering from behind her husband.

Hannah didn't hold back when it came to someone she considered a friend. She rushed in and threw her arms around the woman. A look of delight crossed Emma's face. "It's good to see you again, Hannah. Just look at you! All dressed up like a little sailor."

Stuart removed his hat and tucked it under his arm. "I'm in town for just a few days."

Reverend Crouse eyed Stuart's gold-buttoned frock coat. "So you've gone back to the sea?"

"Yes, sir." He looked about the parlor, expecting Rachel to walk in.

"Well, I hope you'll feel welcome to drop in when you are docked here in La Playa."

Startled at the reverend's warm greeting, Stuart met his gaze. "Thank you. I appreciate that."

Emma Crouse stood up from hugging Hannah. "Would you like to come in for some tea?"

He shook his head. "Thank you, but no. I'd like a word with Rachel—Miss Houston."

"She isn't at here just now," Reverend Crouse answered.

Disappointment set in swiftly. Stuart was ready to turn the town upside down to find her. "Where is she?"

"She won't be home until late afternoon."

Hannah's expression changed from one of excitement to downcast, and the buoyant spirit that had accompanied Stuart the entire voyage faded away. "I see. Then, with your permission, I'll call back later this evening."

"Oh, Stanley, quit drawing this out," Emma said, pinching her husband playfully on his arm.

Reverend Crouse rubbed his chin and studied them both with twinkling eyes. "Rachel would sure hate to miss seeing the two of you. Perhaps you can interrupt her for a moment. She's teaching at the school."

"Teaching?"

"Has been for two months now."

"Then the school board didn't fire her after all?"

Reverend Crouse smiled. "She held her own against those rascals. Convinced them their children would be the losers if they let her go."

Pride for Rachel overwhelmed Stuart. "That's great! And she was right. They're the ones who would have been sorry."

"Now, you make sure and stop back here before you leave port," said Emma. "And bring Hannah."

"Thank you." Stuart backed off the porch. "I'll make sure to stop in and see Caleb later."

"You do that."

He headed up the street with Hannah. Teaching again! A fierce pride swelled in his chest. She hadn't let the town beat her down. What an amazing woman. But then, he'd known that she had grit the minute she refused to back down when she'd wanted to teach Hannah sign language. How many times had they argued over that?

And now she was teaching again...that changed everything! He had thought to swoop in and rescue her from this town of shortsighted fools, but now what? She had made them see things her way—had proved she was worth hiring back.

He would be a complication.

He reached the schoolyard, all his senses on edge. Two dark-haired boys, nine or ten years of age, stood in the shade of the schoolhouse and stared at Hannah, then turned and raced through the open doorway. Bees buzzed around the large gray-green saltbushes to each side of the door.

Rachel's voice drifted out to them. Although her words were muffled, her soft twang enveloped Stuart. He quickened his pace up the walk and stopped within the doorway.

Bedlam greeted him. Children ran about the classroom, jumping from bench to bench. But he didn't care. There was only one person he wanted to see. Where the hell was she?

Suddenly, a paper bird sailed across the air to hit…a very female derriere. The woman picked up the paper from the floor and straightened, stretching out her lower back.

Rachel.

Flushed, disheveled—beautiful. And happy.

"I think you have that aircraft down now, Percy. Why don't you try a different—"

She caught sight of him at the door and froze.

A chalk mark slashed across her jaw. Her dark-auburn hair was knotted messily high on the back of her head with a pencil stabbed into the thick mass, reminding him of all the times her hair had come undone by the wind on the peninsula.

His heart lurched in his chest. She was so beautiful, so full of life. She filled the room with it. He wanted to smile but couldn't. She looked so happy. Would she want him?

He'd rehearsed his lines on the voyage south and now he couldn't think of a thing to say that would be right. At his side, Hannah tugged his sleeve. When he didn't budge, she gave him a puzzled looked, let go of him and ran to Rachel.

Rachel squatted and opened her arms, enclosing Hannah in a warm embrace. A powerful yearning overtook Stuart. A yearning to hold Rachel like that, to feel her against him. She rose and waited.

She wasn't smiling. And she hadn't made a move to come closer. Maybe he'd been away too long. Maybe things had changed more than he thought. He glanced quickly at her left hand. No ring. He exhaled in relief.

Then he realized he was the one to take those last few steps. Even though he'd come five hundred miles for her, he'd also left her in the first place. Just like her father. It was up to him to come back.

All the way.

"Hello, Rachel." He stepped toward her. He should say more, but nothing came to mind. All he could think about was that he was here with her—finally here. And she was standing too far away.

Then it came to him. The one thing she'd driven him crazy with, the one thing they'd argued about. He took a deep breath. "Hannah's going to start school."

Rachel glanced down at the top of Hannah's head. Her gaze came back to his and he saw tears. She sniffed and wiped at her eyes. "Well, it's about time. She never even wrote. One might think she didn't know how."

He swallowed, thinking of the countless letters he'd written and then torn up before sending her. The children were listening with wide eyes—and ears. "I'm back working with shipping. A free man now," he said, stepping closer, breathing in the honeysuckle scent of her. How he'd missed that. "The courts have cleared me."

"That's wonderful, Stuart. You have everything you want now—Hannah, your freedom."

At one time that would have been enough. He'd learned otherwise. He touched her chin, cupped her cheek with his hand. "No, I don't. Not nearly enough. I don't have you."

Her gaze slammed into his. At her side, Hannah's face split into a huge grin. More than a few of the children craned their heads to see around others.

Let them listen. This was too important to worry about what tales they would carry home to their parents. "I'm starting over and I want you by my side. Where we live doesn't matter—here or in San Francisco. You can choose."

She didn't answer. Why didn't she answer? He saw his future fading beyond his reach. "I'm not leaving, Rachel. Do you hear me? I'll never leave again."

"Stuart."

"I love you, Rachel. You know I love you."

She stood still, her gaze on his. Slowly she raised her arms to cross her chest, signing the words back to him.

His heart soared. "Let me hear you say them."

She stepped close and cupped a warm hand over his mouth.

His heart thudded faster in his chest.

She tilted her face up. In her eyes shone a love he'd waited a lifetime to see. "I love you, too, and my answer is yes."

He kissed her palm, then brushed away her hand. He had to kiss her—taste her chin, her cheeks, her mouth. He leaned toward her.

Her eyes widened as she realized his intent. "The children, Stuart..."

A devilish smile worked its way up his face. "This is school, Miss Houston. Let's show them how it's done."

He scooped her off her feet and into his arms, twirling her around in a circle. She let out a breathless shriek of delight. Then, stopping, he lowered his lips to hers...and claimed her and his future in one deep, heart-stirring kiss.

* * * * *

Welcome to Cedar Cove –
a small town with a big heart!

When family court judge Olivia Lockheart causes a scandal by denying a couple's divorce, the whole town starts talking about it.

Meanwhile, her daughter Justine must decide if she should stop waiting for love and accept a marriage of convenience.

And Olivia's best friend, Grace, wonders if her own husband is having an affair.

In Cedar Cove, nothing stays secret for long.

Available 20th February 2009

www.mirabooks.co.uk

It's 1953, Coronation Year and everybody is celebrating…

Everybody except Scarlett Smith. After losing her mum and her home, she and her father are adrift in Southend. Scarlett's only happiness is her innocent romance with Tom.

When Tom leaves to do national service, Scarlett discovers the Saturday night dance hall. There she forgets her troubles with a rock 'n' roll band singer – with disastrous consequences…

Available 20th March 2009

www.mirabooks.co.uk

Regency
High-Society Affairs

*Rakes and rogues in the ballrooms – and the
bedrooms – of Regency England!*

6th March 2009
A Hasty Betrothal by Dorothy Elbury &
A Scandalous Marriage by Mary Brendan

3rd April 2009
Desire My Love by Miranda Jarrett &
The Rake and the Rebel by Mary Brendan

1st May 2009
Sparhawk's Lady by Miranda Jarrett &
The Earl's Intended Wife by Louise Allen

5th June 2009
Lord Calthorpe's Promise by Sylvia Andrew &
The Society Catch by Louise Allen

8 VOLUMES IN ALL TO COLLECT!

www.millsandboon.co.uk — M&B

An unlikely passion!

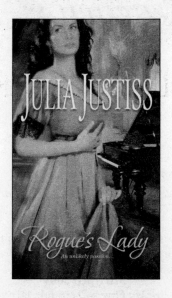

With his estate in ruins, rakishly charming and
handsome William Taverner's only hope
is to wed an heiress.

Penniless Allegra Antinori hopes marriage to an
honourable gentleman will secure her future.

They know they should part. But can an
incurable rogue and a notorious lady resist the
passion of a lifetime?

Available 20th March 2009

MILLS & BOON
Historical

On sale 3rd April 2009

Regency

THE DISGRACEFUL MR RAVENHURST
by Louise Allen

Theo Ravenhurst hardly believes his luck after meeting dowdy cousin Elinor, whose family connections could be extremely useful! Convinced her drab exterior disguises a passionate nature, Theo gives her the adventure she's been yearning for – and discovers Elinor has talents beyond his wildest imagination…

Regency

THE DUKE'S CINDERELLA BRIDE
by Carole Mortimer

The Duke of Stourbridge thought Miss Jane Smith a servant girl, so when she is wrongly turned out of her home for inappropriate behaviour after their encounter, the Duke takes her in as his ward! Jane knows she mustn't fall for his devastating charm. A marriage would be forbidden – especially if he were to discover her shameful secret…

Immerse yourself in the glitter of Regency times and follow the lives and romantic escapades of Stephanie Laurens' Lester family

15th February 2008

21st March 2008

16th May 2008

20th June 2008

www.mirabooks.co.uk

The *Regency*

LORDS & LADIES
COLLECTION

More Glittering Regency Love Affairs

Volume 17 – 4th January 2008
One Night with a Rake by Louise Allen
The Dutiful Rake by Elizabeth Rolls

Volume 18 – 1st February 2008
A Matter of Honour by Anne Herries
The Chivalrous Rake by Elizabeth Rolls

Volume 19 – 7th March 2008
Tavern Wench by Anne Ashley
The Incomparable Countess by Mary Nichols

Volume 20 – 4th April 2008
Prudence by Elizabeth Bailey
Lady Lavinia's Match by Mary Nichols

Volume 21 – 2nd May 2008
The Rebellious Bride by Francesca Shaw
The Duke's Mistress by Ann Elizabeth Cree

Volume 22 – 6th June 2008
Carnival of Love by Helen Dickson
The Viscount's Bride by Ann Elizabeth Cree

Volume 23 – 4th July 2008
One Night of Scandal & *The Rake's Mistress*
by Nicola Cornick

The *Regency*

LORDS & LADIES
COLLECTION

More Glittering Regency Love Affairs

Volume 24 – 1st August 2008
The Reluctant Marchioness by Anne Ashley
Nell by Elizabeth Bailey

Volume 25 – 5th September 2008
Kitty by Elizabeth Bailey
Major Chancellor's Mission by Paula Marshall

Volume 26 – 3rd October 2008
Lord Hadleigh's Rebellion by Paula Marshall
The Sweet Cheat by Meg Alexander

Volume 27 – 7th November 2008
Lady Sarah's Son by Gayle Wilson
Wedding Night Revenge by Mary Brendan

Volume 28 – 5th December 2008
Rake's Reward by Joanna Maitland
The Unknown Wife by Mary Brendan

Volume 29 – 2nd January 2009
Miss Verey's Proposal by Nicola Cornick
The Rebellious Débutante by Meg Alexander

Volume 30 – 6th February 2009
Dear Deceiver by Mary Nichols
The Matchmaker's Marriage by Meg Alexander

M&B